Body of Work

E. L. Wilk

H&E WILK
PRESS

All characters in this novel are fictional, and any likeness to any real persons is coincidental, with the exception of the late Allen Tyler Jr.

ISBN:979-8-9930768-2-9

**Published by H & E Wilk Press
West Palm Beach, Florida
USA**

A very special thank you to my late husband and best friend in this life and hopefully the next, Harvey Wilk.

Table of Contents

Terrible People Do Terrible Things

CHAPTER ONE — GHOULING AROUND

IAN

Ian decides there's no turning back! The thought terrifies and embarrasses him more than he's willing to admit, but he's made up his mind; he's going through with this no matter what because he's finally faced the reality that loneliness is no longer an option for him.

He walks into the bathroom to splash cold water on his face. He inspects himself in the brightly lit mirror and realizes his beard is overgrown and his dirty blond hair badly needs a trim. That's when he decides not to take a selfie because he is dissatisfied with his appearance. Also, he has no tan and is seriously thinking about finding a new barber to cut his hair. Then he takes a closer look at himself, noticing tiny lines forming around the corners of his light brown eyes and between his eyebrows. Feeling irritated, he scowls and turns off the light as he leaves.

He heads back to his laptop, which he left on his bed, and mumbles to himself, "Just do it." He reaches for the plug to make sure it's charging while working on a lengthy application.

He raises his voice and says, "Alexa, play the best of the Zombies."

Alexa replies, "Here is some music by the Zombies." The music starts playing, and the first song is "She's Not There."

He types in the web address and sighs while he waits for it to load, still in disbelief that he's actually going through with this madness. He sits in the dark room, with his back against the wall, as Bumble's bright golden company logo suddenly lights up his face.

He tries to remember everything his friend told him to do, but as he navigates the fill-in-the-blanks, his brain freezes. It's all about lady power, he reminds himself, and during their conversation, his buddy shared that this was how he met his wife.

What will my **Move Makers** be, he asks himself? He scrolls to my profile section; at least these parts are easy, he assures himself: Age - 34; Marital status - single and never married; Offspring - he hesitates, then answers, no kids, and one dog. He gets cold feet again, can't think of what to write, and then decides to go back to my **Move Makers** later.

The following heading is **Two Truths and a Lie**. He reads aloud, shaking his head in disappointment, "What a stupid way to start a relationship," he complains to his dog Scout, a beagle he rescued from a medical testing lab.

They've been inseparable since he adopted the dog six years ago. Scout is vying for Ian's attention and rolls over on the bed, hoping for a belly rub that doesn't come.

Ian writes his answer to the section, smirking at it while rubbing Scout's belly. He reads it back to the dog: "I'm looking to meet the person of my dreams (like that's ever happening), get married, and have kids someday."

Trying to decide which one is the lie will make the girls online go nuts, he gloats. He skips back to my **Move Makers** and writes in for the answer that he has no issue dating someone with kids. He hops over to **Drinking Habits** and replies that he only drinks at social events, such as weddings and birthday parties. Smoking is a never, and I won't date a smoker unless it's pot! **Religion**, hmmm, I'm going to check off all the above. He laughs, then reflects and decides he would date someone of any religion, though he would prefer someone who believes in God.

Feeling a bit more relaxed after completing most of the written part of the application, he scrolls to the age limits. That's when "Time of the Season" by The Zombies starts playing. Hmmm, he ponders.

Then, he clicks his mouse on 21 to 45, hesitates, and shakes his head as he changes it to 24 to 42.

He then clicks on the **About Me** link and adds his Spotify, Snapchat, X, and Instagram links. Right after that, he goes back to check if his Facebook link is also listed, and when it isn't, he types it in.

Travel distance. He raises his hands to stretch and asks Scout for his opinion, then responds on his behalf, "Great answer, buddy. Eighteen miles max it is!"

Sex. Well, that's a broad question, and he clicks the link to see where it takes him. Would I date a person who is trans? he asks himself. Probably not. Then it asks what I am looking for. He smirks and thinks, I'll know it when I see it. Then he wonders, what the hell do I write for an icebreaker? And he finally decides he hasn't got a clue.

He contemplates the next question. I really don't want to talk about my work at first. People, especially women, get very uncomfortable when they find out I'm an organ transporter for A.O.R.A., which stands for American Organ Recovery Alliance. They'll say something like, "Dude, you mean like dead people?"

And I reply, "Not really, it's organ parts from cadavers."

And they say, "Oh... that sounds ghoulish."

And I say, "Well, it saves lives." That's when I realize we're already done before we've even started. I already dislike the idea of moving forward with this, and I haven't even signed up yet. Why bother, he reflects, throwing his hands up in defeat, just as the song "Tell Her No" begins to play.

Scout whines, and Ian glances at the dog's big, brown, sad eyes and asks, "You need to take a leak, little buddy?" The dog hops down to the floor, tail wagging enthusiastically.

Ian asks, "Alexa, what's the temperature outside?"

"It's 27 degrees Fahrenheit, and tonight's low will be 19 degrees."

"Thank you, Alexa."

"My pleasure, just doing my job, Ian," Alexa replies courteously.

Ian pulls a thick sweater over his head, then puts a coat on top of Scout's sweater and tugs his paws through its holes. "Let's make this quick," he instructs as he reaches down to put on the dog's leash.

Ten minutes later, they return, and Ian is so cold that he leaves his thick sweater on and makes himself a cup of hot herbal tea in the microwave. He pulls Scout's coat off and warms the pads of the dog's paws with his hands. Scout leans in and kisses him on the face. "It's only November, buddy. You sure you don't want to pack up and move to Florida?"

Ian returns to the online Bumble app and groans in disbelief that he still has a while left before he's finished. He rubs his aching forehead as he remembers that he almost forgot to upload the six photos his friend told him were the most important. He looks at the pictures taken of himself while they were running around the reservoir and recalls that it was a good time.

After reviewing the past couple of years' worth of photos, Ian narrows it down to a top ten. His first choice is of himself with Scout licking his face, and the second is at the beach a few years back, showing off his physique. A few photos in the gym with him benching an incredible amount of weight (hoping to attract his audience), and the last one he picks is of him and his dog visiting his grandmother at the nursing home. Girls should find that one irresistible, he guesses.

After completing the upload, Ian has no more patience for the tedious Bumble application and wants it to be over. However, instead of finalizing the transaction, the prompt leads him to more questions: Do you want to upgrade to Bumble Premium?

Ian declines the offer, and another window opens. How about a 7-day trial to Bumble Boost? Curiously, he clicks on the offer, and it's $16.99 a month after the free trial, but it includes some nice added features, such as showcasing his photo and giving him more time to reply to a match. He rubs his tired eyes and decides to pass on the upgrade. I don't need this, he reassures himself, and I'll have plenty of responses without boosting it.

Confident that he's done a good job and is close to finishing, he takes a hit of marijuana and straightens his sore, bent-over back. When he presses Enter, a prompt appears asking, **Do you want to verify your identity?** He presses yes and waits. Then the next prompt asks, **Would you like to be taken to a third party to evaluate your application and see your ELO score?**

What the hell, an ELO what? I'm not looking for a chess partner; I'm just looking for a date. Frustrated by the delay, he decides to hit the decline button, and he finally gets confirmation that his application is complete.

Ian pulls Scout close as he says, "Alexa, goodnight," and most everything in his condo turns off on that command, including the kitchen lights, the TV in the living room, and The Zombies' music playing in the background.

CHAPTER TWO — Gift Horse

Olivia

Before the rooster crows, Olivia is already downstairs making a pot of freshly ground French-pressed coffee for William and herself. She steams raw cow's milk in a small pot on the gas stove over a flame, then sets it aside to top off the hot coffee while humming a song. She sits at the kitchen counter, taking in the coffee's rich and inviting aroma, and takes a break.

She looks around the pleasant kitchen and recognizes the thoughtfulness in its design. William's ancestors built this part of the house by hand, a little later than the rest of the house, which was begun in the mid-1850s, and it's clear that every detail was carefully considered.

She glances outside at the oversized thermometer perched on the sill of the kitchen window. It's only nineteen degrees Fahrenheit. She shivers at the thought of doing her chores outdoors and worries about Buttercup, her Appaloosa horse, asleep in the old, drafty barn.

William walks in and smiles. He enjoys a mug of coffee prepared just the way he likes it, with two sugars and frothy, whole, hot milk on top. As he takes a seat next to Olivia at the kitchen counter, he bites into some warm, buttered toast.

With enthusiasm, she says, "Wasn't last night just wonderful!"

William gulps his coffee and stays silent.

"What did you think of the marinated lamb chops?" she inquires.

"Nice."

"How about the Bordeaux I paired with them?"

"Did we finish the bottle?" he replies.

She glances at the empty bottle on the counter and nods.

"Then we both must have liked it," he gruffly confirms.

"For me, one of the nicest parts about last night was that I got both kids to bed by seven, and we finally got to relax." She wonders what he would think of her if he only knew she gave the twins Benadryl to knock them out.

William appears concerned when he asks, "Are you sure they're feeling all right, Olie?"

"I checked on them right after you know…" she blushes.

William stares at her with concern. "What's going on, Olie? I wasn't born yesterday."

She is offended by his questioning of her. She defends herself, "Nothing is going on, William, but can you keep an eye on the kids this afternoon during their nap, so I can run and get my roots touched up at John's Salon in Newton Center?"

William considers her response and senses there's more to it. She wouldn't go to that much trouble just so that he'd watch the kids for a couple of hours. "Olie, out with it?" He looks into her blue eyes and repeats, "Come on - out with it! You didn't whip up an elaborate dinner and seduce me last night so that you could get your roots touched up. I've known you long enough to know when you're up to something."

She clenches her jaw and tears well up in her eyes before she replies, "When did it become a felony for me to be nice to you and for us to have enough time for sex?"

He laughs as he says, "Well, it wasn't my birthday yesterday; there are no scratches or dents on our truck, so that leaves one last possibility."

She grins, "Well, I'm not pregnant."

William hates it when she plays these games. He needs to start repairing the tractor and finish all his chores to keep up with his farm work. "Out with it, Olie. What is it that you want?"

"Ok, I give up because you know how to read me like a novel." She avoids eye contact with him by staring at her coffee grounds as she mutters, "I want another horse."

He doesn't hesitate before firmly replying, "No!"

"But it will help me launch my riding school."

"Nope, not a chance!" he states firmly as he finishes his coffee and walks his mug and dish to the kitchen sink. "We're going into winter, the cost of feed is sky-high, plus you barely take care of Buttercup as it is, and I said, N. O. - no!"

"Fine!"

"Fine, what?" he demands.

"We're not buying…" she stretches out the word as if she's mid-thought, "…another horse." He reaches over to her to give her a peck on her cheek and abruptly leaves to start his work.

After she cleans up the kitchen, Olivia peeks in on the twins, Charlotte and Henry. They're snoring softly and cuddled together to keep warm, so cute, she thinks to herself.

Then she descends the steep staircase, her hand trailing along the antique, bespoke carved banister. She glances into the glass eyes of the hawk mounted and perched on the pedestal at the bottom of the stairs, then up at the glass-eyed elk with antlers mounted on the wall, and hopes William never takes up taxidermy like his ancestors.

She strokes the velvety, well-worn finish of the banister again as she reflects on how much love and time went into making their home. Then her mind jumps to Buttercup freezing in her stall, and she grabs her coat and gloves before heading out.

#

It's difficult to see inside the stable because everything is buttoned up to block the wind, and the sun has barely risen over the hill in the east. As Olivia's eyes adjust to the darkness, she hears Buttercup furiously kicking the stall gate.

"Whoa, girl." Olivia opens the gate and gently strokes Buttercup as she removes her blanket, saying, "Good girl," to soothe her. She continues to pet her long neck and feeds her a carrot. Olivia places her bridle and lead over her head, then pulls her out of the stall, drapes her saddle over her back, and tightens the straps. "Let's have our breakfast outside today." Olivia fills Buttercup's trough with oats and grains and removes her bit so she can eat. When Olivia walks back with a bucket of fresh, warmed water, she notices something odd about her horse: her tail is held higher than usual and twitching.

"Well, golly, Miss Molly. I think you may be in full-blown estrus," she says to her horse as she gently rubs her velvety soft muzzle. "I bet you'd love some more carrots this morning." At that moment, a light bulb goes on in Olivia's brain. "Let's take a stroll over to Jameson Farm down the road and say hello to the old troll."

Olivia replaces Buttercup's bit, then she mounts her and heads over to where William is working on the tractor's carburetor.

He asks, "What's up, Olie?"

"I was getting Buttercup warmed up, and I forgot that I told Hattie I'd help her with something this morning."

She can tell from William's expression that he doesn't believe her explanation because Hattie and Olivia are like oil and water. They never mix.

She asks him, "Can you listen for Charlie and Henry until I get back?" She hands him the baby monitor.

Not taking his eye off the old carburetor he's cleaning, he replies, "Sure."

Olivia trots over to Jameson Farm and spots Hattie in the outdoor ring with her Arabian horses, Ken and Barbie. Hattie is a bony, petite woman in her sixties with a weathered face from many years of outdoor work, and her fingers are badly stained from smoking unfiltered Camels, making her gnarled, calloused hands look especially monstrous when she waves hello.

Olivia dismounts near the gate to the outdoor horse ring. "Hattie, can I trouble you for a moment?"

Hattie waves for Olivia to come over. Olivia ties Buttercup to the rail and steps into the ring.

Hattie doesn't like small talk and says abruptly in a raspy voice, "What do you want?"

Olivia's mind flashes to the thought of owning another horse, but she responds, "I'm having a rodent issue in our stable. Can I leave Buttercup here today so I can clean everything out and get a jump on them before winter sets in?"

Hattie is no friend of Olivia and says reluctantly, "What time are you coming to get her?"

"How's 3?" she asks sheepishly.

"Fine, leave her bridle and saddle in my tack room and go. I've got plenty to do today with Ken and Barbie. You know I've no time for chit-chat." Hattie's eyes stay on Ken while she's talking to Olivia.

Olivia brings Buttercup into the ring and removes all her gear. Barbie neighs as Buttercup enters, but Olivia ignores the stress her horse is causing Barbie and rushes back to her house up the road so that she can prepare breakfast for her children.

#

The twins are playing on the living room floor while Olivia cleans up breakfast dishes and tries to decide what to defrost for dinner. That's when she notices from the large bay window on the side of their house that a truck pulling a horse trailer is speeding up Raven Road toward her. The truck quickly swerves into her driveway, honking its horn loudly.

Olivia gasps and says aloud, "Oh shit, it's Hattie," then covers her eyes in disbelief.

Hattie jumps out of her truck and slams the cab door shut at the same time. She is inconsolable when William comes up to her. "Where's that witch you're married to?" she demands.

"Olivia?" he asks.

"Yes, her!" she screeches.

William states calmly, "She's in the house feeding the twins breakfast. Why?"

From the top of her lungs, she hollers with her scratchy, pitchy voice, "Olivia, get out of here now!"

Olivia tells Charlotte and Henry, "You two stay here! Mummy will be right back."

William jumps in between them and becomes their referee. Then he turns to her and asks, "Olivia, what did you do?"

"Nothing," Olivia replies deceptively.

Hattie becomes thoroughly stir crazy from her response, and her pupils constrict like a snake. "You tricked me - you skinny, little Gypsy bitch, and that's hard to do." She growls at Olivia.

"How?" Olivia decides to play dumb and is surprised by Hattie's response to Buttercup's estrus because she can't think of any other reason she'd be upset.

"Where was your horse born, Olivia?"

"We were told at the auction when we bought her that she's from Argentina, Hattie. Why?"

Hattie reaches into her shirt pocket for a Camel cigarette and lights one up with her stainless-steel Zippo with a stallion on it, while calming herself down. Then she posits, "Well, that explains why Buttercup's estrus started in the late fall instead of the spring."

Hattie rubs her nose and thinks for a moment, "Swear on your children, you didn't know it this morning when you dropped her off at my ring that she was in full-blown estrus."

Hattie waits for a response from Olivia but hears crickets instead, so she continues her rant. "I'm a horse breeder, Olivia. My horses are my livelihood. I make my money selling Ken's semen because he's a stud, but he's a virgin stud! Get it! V.I.R.G.I.N., but because of you, that's no longer true."

Hattie draws on her cigarette before explaining what happened after Olivia left her farm that morning. "Barbie was whinnying like crazy, and I can't for the life of me figure out why she's so irritable and inconsolable, so I went to get her lead to bring her back to the stable to calm her down. When I return, I find Ken mounted on Buttercup. He's having a grand old time because up till now, my young stud has never copulated like a wild horse ever before, and Barbie has lost her shit."

Hattie is so upset that she has to pause to catch her breath. "What city are you from again, Olivia?"

"London," Olivia mumbles.

Hattie continues her rant, "Well, it's as sure as horse shit that you're not from around here because folks around here look out for each other, and we don't cheat each other out of money. I make $750 a shot selling my Arabian's sperm. Plus, I'll need to have him checked for STDs, and Barbie's getting injected with a tranquilizer to calm her down as we speak. On top of that, your filthy, dirty Appaloosa has highly contagious conjunctivitis in her left eye, which I treated myself after I got her back on her feet."

Olivia is so focused on finding a reasonable excuse to give Hattie that she completely misses the part about Buttercup being knocked off her feet and says, "Seriously, thank you for being so good to Buttercup for me, and she doesn't have any STDs," Olivia emphasizes.

Hattie barks back at her while waving her cigarette around in her hand, "Hold on there!"

Then she points her gnarled finger in Olivia's face, "I didn't do anything for you whatsoever. I happen to love animals, and as far as you're concerned, I think you'd make excellent quality roadkill, and for that matter, you're probably lying about Buttercup not having STDs as well."

William chimes in, "You and I have so much history, Hattie, and our families have helped one another for many generations. What can I do to make this right?" He looks over at Olivia with a fierce expression and wants her to stay quiet.

"You can't undo what your piece of shit wife did to my horses this morning."

William admits, "No, I can't, Hattie."

Hattie painfully explains to him, "William, things between us have been bad ever since you brought home your gypsy bride, who, might I remind you, gave birth less than eight months later." Hattie snickers, "She might be able to run circles around you, but I'm nobody's fool, and I don't want any part of this," she says while pointing at them.

William's complexion turns to ash. "Hattie, stop calling her a Gypsy. It's racist, and can you forgive us already for running off and getting married without including you? We can't undo our past mistakes, but how can we make this right?"

Hattie pauses before replying, "If Buttercup is with a foal, it's mine." She takes a drag of her cigarette and repeats, "You hear me – mine! I'm taking it. Plus, your clueless wife didn't think about the fact that the foal will be born in the dead of winter. Oh, and I want all my veterinary bills from today paid, but you can keep this."

She pulls ointment from her pocket to treat Buttercup. "Apply this to her eye three times a day for a week, and Olivia, bathe your horse now and then along with a good brushing – she's so filthy you can't even see the color of her socks. That horse deserves better than you!"

Hattie goes to the back of the horse trailer with William to retrieve Buttercup. Then she hands the reins to William, who pulls her out.

Olivia, curious, asks, "Hattie, why did you drive her over here instead of walking?"

Hattie chuckles out loud, "So, you've never seen horses having wild sex?"

Olivia responds, "No, I haven't."

"Well, it went down like this: Ken got Buttercup so excited that she passed out from the orgasm." Hattie is still laughing as she gets back in her truck and zooms out of the driveway, leaving a cloud of dust behind.

CHAPTER THREE — LET'S MAKE A DEAL

WILLIAM

William feels a tremendous sense of relief when Olivia backs out of the garage into the dirt driveway. When she finally leaves to get her hair done, he takes a deep, frustrated breath as the truck drives away onto Raven Road.

His head floods with so many angry thoughts at once that he feels sick to his stomach, and he has no idea what to do about his unruly wife anymore.

She heard him clearly say no to her request about getting a new horse at breakfast, and it meant nothing to her. Incredibly, she went straight to Jameson Farm to get Buttercup knocked up without a second thought, which is Olivia's go-to solution for almost every problem.

Just like when she first came to Boston for a job, which meant working under the table because she didn't have a work visa or a green card, but that didn't stop her, no sir. So she worked without it despite that minor issue as a "Proper English Nanny" for a bourgeois family in Dover. They offered her big money, all cash, and flew her over at their expense.

It wasn't a problem until she way overstayed her welcome with U.S. Immigration, then had a tussle with her boss, and the next thing he knows, his cute girlfriend living in Dover, driving a Range Rover, while playing Mary Poppins with a cushy job and expense account, is suddenly homeless, jobless, and carless.

He shovels a big pile of cow manure into his wheelbarrow and pushes it over to the composting pile out back. The fresh air helps him calm down as he remembers how incredibly irresistible, she was to him at the time; her British accent drove him wild, and she could do no wrong back then, even when she announced she was pregnant. That news was met with celebration, although he wasn't entirely sure whether he was the biological father.

There were numerous red flags, but he managed to miss them all because, at the time, he believed he was in love with her, and you know how love can conquer all. He jokes while raking up the last of the cow manure in the empty stall and replacing the hay.

The truth of Hattie's confrontation with Olivia today hit home. Olivia's constant need for more is draining, and he feels he desperately needs a break from her.

He walks over to the storage area to check how much animal feed they have in reserve, and his mind flashes to the cost of her hair appointment, piled on top of all the expenses she unexpectedly incurred that morning after the incident she caused with Ken and Barbie.

Then he calculates the cost of her full head of foils with a haircut at the fanciest place she could find, and all he wants to do is pull out his hair in frustration.

He also knows her well enough that whatever she puts on the credit card is only a fraction of the actual cost, and she'll cover the rest with a check or cash she's stashed away to hide the actual expense. He gathers his dairy cows and leads them back to the freshly cleaned stalls, closing their gates.

His thoughts drift to Buttercup, whom he also feels sorry for. Because of the twins, she is rarely ridden, and the poor animal is bored stiff. He decides it's time to bring her into the stable for the night.

As he walks over to get her, he wonders why his twins have been sleeping so much more than usual, and once again, he worries they might be coming down with something serious.

#

Buttercup seems happy to see William as he approaches her on the hill with a harness and lead to bring her back to her stall for the night. It's a chilly, grey New England afternoon, and the horse is tuckered out from the earlier events that morning.

The thought of Buttercup passing out from an orgasm brings a smile to William's face, and he briefly wonders if Hattie might have exaggerated or fabricated any part of her story. He quickly dismisses the idea because he's known her his entire life, and she's always been matter-of-fact, which, after almost four years of living with Olivia, he finds to be a refreshing contrast.

They arrive at the barn, and the horse is grateful to be home. She rubs her head affectionately against William's shoulder, and he strokes her velvety muzzle. Then he takes off her bit and bridle and places them with the rest of her gear in the tack area. He looks for an extra warm horse blanket and coat, then layers them on Buttercup in preparation for the forecasted long, cold night. He rakes out her stall and puts fresh hay and food inside. She happily enters her refreshed stall without hesitation and closes her tired eyes.

Everything is overly simplified for Olivia. He thinks about how, if she wants something, she becomes obsessed until she either possesses it or conjures it up like a witch. He's not entirely sure which one it is.

Then, as he puts away his rake and tools, he wonders what if Buttercup is expecting a foal early next winter. This thought confuses him, as it brings a whole new set of problems. Foals in New England are born in spring for a reason, and this little one will most likely freeze to death or need to be moved south for the winter, which is also very stressful on the mare and the newborn.

William sighs as he considers how much Olivia has occupied his thoughts today. Tonight, I plan to tell her the facts about our finances and the realities of running a family farm in today's world of hyperinflated expenses. Therefore, I need to take on a side job to cover the rising costs of insurance, fuel, and feed for our animals.

Plus, if I don't spend a little more time away from her, I'm sure I'll go mad sooner rather than later.

William secures the bolt on the paddocks and heads back to the house. As he crosses his driveway, he notices the veterinarian, Dr. Shane Ferguson, driving by, and he waves politely. William hopes he keeps going, but the vet turns on his turn signal, slowly pulls into their driveway, and steps out of his white van.

William's first thought is that he's there to collect the bill for Barbie and Ken, and his temper ratchets up a notch, as he can't imagine the day getting any worse.

"How's Barbie?" William inquires.

"She's high as a kite right now on Xylazine." He smirks as he asks William, "Have you tried that shit? It's so strong it can really kill you."

"How much do I owe you?" William asks.

Dr Ferguson pauses for a moment before he replies, "How about it's on the house if you'd consider my previous offer."

William recalls thinking the doctor's request was sleazy at the time. He squirms at the idea of doing something shady for Dr. Ferguson and hopes he can reason with him: "Do you want to come inside for a cup of coffee and warm up by the fireplace?"

"I don't have the time today, so I'll take a raincheck, but what about my earlier offer?" he repeats. "It will make your bill today disappear," he adds, snapping his fingers like a magician.

William realizes that Olivia has placed them in a precarious financial position, and currently, there is no alternative to the indentured servitude offered by Dr. Ferguson.

"What will I have to do for you?" William swallows hard. "Dr. Ferguson?" He shivers at the thought of not knowing what he wants from him.

He emphasizes, "Just call me Shane, and I don't ask for much. I have a clientele, primarily men, but a few women here and there, and they rely on my compounding skills to help maintain their augmented physiques. These folks use off-label human growth hormones. They're mostly competitive bodybuilders, and no one gets hurt. It's not like we're selling them fentanyl, for God's sake," Shane rationalizes.

Naively, William wonders why he would even mention that and asks, "Why don't they go to a people doctor to get it instead of a vet?"

He rationalizes, "Well, that's the thing, not everyone can afford it or get a prescription from a physician. Then there are the folks who don't want it in their medical record. There's a real need, and I see no harm in filling it. So, what do you say?" Shane rubs his cold hands together while waiting for his reply.

William is slightly less anxious about what he considers akin to sleeping with the devil and responds, "Ok, I really do owe you the money, and I'll consider this a barter until I've paid off our debt to you."

Shane strokes his mustache and inquires, "What if your mare is carrying a foal? They'll be ultrasounds, bloodwork, multiple visits, and the like."

William swallows before saying, "Whoa, let's take this one day at a time. My wife will be home soon, and I'll tell her tonight that I've accepted a short-term position working for you."

"I'd prefer you simply say you're working part-time for a private delivery company and not mention me to anyone. My coming here appears perfectly normal, as you're the owner of several farm animals and I'm a veterinarian who makes regular house calls. I'll be by tomorrow with your parcel and a list of addresses where the deliveries can be made. It's quite simple: you give them what they want, and they pay you in cash. When you're done with your route, I'll swing by, check in on Buttercup, gratis of course, and you'll hand off the cash to me in the stable."

Shane can tell that William seems very disinclined to this concept, so he keeps trying to sell him on the idea: "Besides making extra money, I won't charge you for my visits, and you'll only have to pay for the labs and prescription drugs for your animals."

William reluctantly nods his head in agreement.

Just then, they both notice Olivia pulling into the driveway with a wet mane, having rushed back from the hair salon to be home before the twins woke up from their naps.

Shane gives William a quick salute, gets into his white van, and drives off.

William never notices the severe drop in temperature, and despite the frigid cold air, hot steam vents from his body. He is so angry about the financial situation Olivia has put them in; he feels as if he could lose his mind and go insane. Despite this, he knows she's going to pretend as if nothing happened, as he doesn't think she gives a damn about it anyway.

He can feel his pulse in his temples as his blood boils, and there's actual sweat beading up on his hot face. He returns to the garage without greeting her and closes the bay door with him inside it to avoid her.

CHAPTER FOUR — PUMPED UP

IAN

Joe, a new acquaintance of Ian's from the gym, is spotting for him at the free weights in the large, well-lit gym in Natick that's nearly empty due to the early nor'easter that struck them hard during rush hour traffic.

Ian's mind wanders as he grips the barbell and counts his repetitions. He reads the ads on the walls and thinks about how much he enjoys the perks of his PF Black Card club membership.

After he completes his last set, he places the barbell on its stand and checks his Apple Watch before offering to spot Joe, "Hey, you want to switch places with me?"

Joe looks disconcerted. "Ian, not if you're in a rush to leave?"

Ian is confused. "What gave you that idea?"

"You just looked at your watch again," Joe reveals.

"Oh, that, it's nothing. I'm meeting this guy for the first time." Ian looks at his watch. "I'm not sure what he looks like, but I have an app on my watch that lets me know when he's nearby."

Joe smirks at Ian, "Ok, just give me a minute to lighten the barbell. Not everyone can lift like Hercules."

Ian takes a swig of water, stretches his arms, and then pumps the hand sanitizer attached to the wall a few times into his sweaty palms. He checks himself out in the mirror and decides he needs to do another upper-body set after Joe finishes his.

Then Ian squints as he looks toward the entrance and can't believe his eyes when he notices his old friend just walked through the door. His friend doesn't see him and continues brushing snow off his coat and boots, then walks around as if searching for someone.

At that precise moment, Ian's iPhone watch alerts him that the person he's meeting has arrived, but he ignores it and rushes over to greet William instead.

"Dude, it's about time you made it to the gym! I bet you can feel that middle age just creeping in." Ian swings his sweaty arm over William's shoulder and squeezes him hello.

William is in disbelief that Ian, on his delivery list, is also his good friend whom he served with at Camp Edwards and with whom he runs whenever he can get a break from Olivia and the twins. He immediately turns off his burner phone because he's embarrassed about what he came to do, and the last person he wants to find out about his pressing financial problems is Ian. Things are beginning to make sense to him about his single and slightly insecure friend. All the questions he asked him about the dating app Bumble and his neediness for affirmation about his looks, on top of Ian's oversized pectorals and biceps, which are now obviously not just products of hours of hard work in the gym.

It hadn't occurred to William that Ian was a steroid user, but what the hell, it's none of his business. He decides not to deliver it to him because it's way too much information about himself that he'd have to explain to Ian, so he's pretty sure Shane will understand when he returns the unsold product. Hell, he'll say he couldn't find him because the weather was terrible.

Ian points to Joe, whom he left on the bench waiting for him to spot him. "Hey, Joe, this is my old friend William."

William greets Joe with, "Hi."

Ian explains, "We served together as EMTs in the Air National Guard on the Cape." He turns to William and says, "Joe and I recently met at the gym."

William approaches Joe, who is lying on the bench, and reaches down to shake his hand. "Nice to meet you."

Joe patiently waits for Ian to spot him, and meanwhile, he says to both of them, "Thanks for your service."

They give Joe a thumbs-up.

Just then, a hysterical scream comes from a woman in the locker room. Joe, William, and Ian rush in together. What they find is a petite, young, blond girl pinned to the wall with a burly, bearded man wearing a lady's Lululemon workout suit and a long-haired brown wig pulled back in a ponytail pressed up against her and humping her like a dog with his hand over her mouth.

William and Ian pull the attacker away from the young girl and hold him or her while they ask the girl her name.

She's crying, so Joe goes over to comfort her while she tries to catch her breath. He helps hold her up as her legs give way underneath her. She responds with a quiver in her voice, "Mary, my name's Mary, and I hate this place. This isn't the first time I've run into a pervert in the changing room." She struggles with difficulty pulling her street clothes onto her sweaty, half-naked torso.

William's eyes go straight to Mary's small waist, where a claddagh tattoo is visible. The crown sits directly above her belly button, and the hands form a heart shape around her navel.

She looks down at the floor, and out of modesty, her shoulders quickly flush red with embarrassment as she tries to shield herself, which is impossible given that a group of unfamiliar men surrounds her.

William offers while tightening his grip on the man in the wig, "Do you want us to call the police, Mary?"

She responds with a sound of disgust in her voice, "What will that do? It's this company's corporate policy that it's a transperson's right to use any locker room they identify with."

Ian feels frustrated. "Yeah, but you were attacked. Doesn't that make a difference?"

Mary explains in her thick Irish accent, "The cops and court system do nothing, and this creep…" she steps closer to him, sticks her finger in the assailant's face, "Will get just what he wants; my name, address, and telephone number from the court docs, and that's when my real problems will begin."

Ian argues, "Mary, that sounds crazy. It can't be true."

She defends her argument, "He'll stalk me, and the police will do nothing to him."

The assailant snarls, "It's her, dammit!"

William politely asks while tightening his grip on the pervert, "Seriously, Mary, what would you like us to do?"

She smiles when she replies, "A bloody nose, a few missing teeth, and castration works for me."

Ian thinks she's joking and is amused by her answer, but he notices a gleam in William's eye that's a bit unsettling. Joe helps Mary put on her coat. Mary flips up her collar and declares, "I never want to see this creep again, so I'm leaving here and never coming back. You win, Creep."

Joe takes a quick look around the locker room to make sure no one else is in it. Then he faces the pervert while Ian and William continue to restrain him.

Joe says to him while he's struggling to be freed, "My buddy has an interesting profession," and he points to Ian. "He transports human body parts for a living. How would you like to find yourself in his van, all cut up and placed inside a bunch of Igloo containers?"

Ian's first thought is cool; I love the idea of freaking out this asshole. However, he can't recall ever telling Joe what he does for a living, and he is a little startled by it. Just then, the pervert begins squirming in their arms, trying to get loose.

When they tighten their grip more, he whimpers, "There's nothing you can do to me or do about it. I've got the law on my side, so tough shit to all of you fucking bastards."

Mary sobs as she quickly pulls on her boots and gathers the last of her belongings.

William snaps, and the next thing Ian knows is he's holding the pervert back while William retracts his fist and says, "There's just something about your face my knuckles can't resist."

Then suddenly William pounds him so hard he breaks his nose, but stops just long enough to threaten him, "Oh, and if you complain to anyone." He takes a deep breath before completing the sentence, "Everything about the body parts story is true, and I'll personally deliver you to an organ recovery unit myself, you worthless piece of shit."

Mary cries out, "Now you've gone and done it! I'm from Ireland, and I've overstayed my visa. I can't risk involving the police. You're going to get me deported." Then, she storms out of the locker room without looking back.

Ian intervenes and slams the pervert face down on the ground. The three of them leave the ladies' locker room. Ian looks at his phone and discovers the person he was supposed to meet is no longer in range and remarks, "Oh shit, my delivery guy must have given up trying to find me and left."

Joe emphatically asserts, "I'm going to make sure Mary makes it safely to her car." Then, he leaves them to go after her.

Ian still can't get over the coincidence of running into William, one of his oldest and best friends, at the gym. What's transpired is completely blowing his mind, but he finds it truly strange how Joe knew so much about what he does for work.

CHAPTER FIVE — BIG BIRD

OLIVIA

Olivia glances at her gas gauge as a red light illuminates and says, "Oh shit!", just as she realizes the gas tank is empty.

From the back seat, she hears echoes in stereo, "Shit, shit, shit…" repeated with giggles from her twins.

She glances at them in her rear-view mirror and says sternly, "What did Mummy say about that?"

In harmony, Charlotte and Henry repeat, "Shit, shit, shit."

"If you don't stop it, we won't go to Dunkin' Donuts!" She glances at them before she adds, "My little darlings, you were so good at that doctor's appointment today."

The twins quiet down and start speaking their twin gibberish, which Olivia finds intriguing but barely understands.

Her headlights turn on automatically as it gets late, and she drives into the Sherborn Gas and Market. She pulls into the full-service fueling bay, which is a waste of money, but she decides it's worth the extravagance because it's so cold, and the last thing she wants is to trigger her twins into a screaming episode when Mummy leaves them alone in the truck.

She waits a minute or two and begins to realize that no one is coming to help her. At that moment, she panics, fearing the store might be closing and that she doesn't have enough gas to get home. She considers her dilemma for a second, and without hesitation, she frantically honks her horn.

She watches as an older man inside the store slowly puts on his coat, hat, and gloves. Then he walks over to her at a turtle's pace, eventually reaching her window.

She lowers it and plainly states, "Regular petrol, please, and fill it up."

Before she has time to close her window, he replies with a flourish and an outstretched arm, "I beg your pardon. I didn't realize I'd be waiting on royalty."

"I beg your pardon," she stammers.

"Well, why else would an able-bodied young lady like yourself expect an old man to serve her when she's perfectly capable of pumping her own goddam gas!"

"Are you going to pump the petrol or not?"

He sneers, "Hold your horses, princess. I'll get to it." He pops off her gas cap and begins filling her truck with the nozzle set on hands-free.

Meanwhile, he taps his hands together to warm them when he comments. "Suppose you don't celebrate Thanksgiving, given that you're British royalty and all?"

Suddenly, Olivia looks terrified as she asks the older gentleman attending to her truck, "When's Thanksgiving?"

"Tomorrow."

"Bloody hell," she blurts out. "I completely forgot about it. I believe you may have saved my life." Or at least my marriage, she thinks to herself.

He reaches for the handle on the gas nozzle, returns it to the pump, puts the cap back on, and closes the door. Then he says with a snicker, "I hope you watched me and paid close attention so that you can do it yourself next time, Your Highness." He smirks, then scratches his head as she fumbles around in her purse looking for a credit card.

She hands it to him and asks sweetly, "Would you mind keeping an eye on my twins while I run into the store?"

He's surprised and asks, "Seriously, we just met, and you trust me with Tweedle Dee and Tweedle Dumb?"

"They're Charlotte and Henry, and what choice do I have under the circumstances?"

He ponders the idea for a moment and then says, "Nah, it's too cold, and I really don't like kids."

"What's your name, good sir?"

"George."

"Well, George. I'm Olivia, and I'd forever be in your debt if you would do me this one favor." She offers her mittened hand to George and says, "But my friends call me Olie."

Just then, another car pulls up to the other row of gas pumps, and Olivia asks, "Do you have to get to that?"

He confirms, "Nah. Go, run in, and grab what you need. The only turkey I've left is a no-pickup, but it's a big one."

"How big?" she inquires, raising her eyebrows in interest.

"Too big, but it's freshly killed, so at least you won't have to defrost it." He notices her kids are getting rambunctious, so he hollers, "Go already, I'm freezing my butt off out here."

She jumps out and runs around the small, overpriced convenience market, grabbing anything she can to put together her makeshift Thanksgiving dinner. She googles a picture of a turkey dinner to get some ideas.

Talking out loud to no one, she says, "Pumpkin pie, check; can of cranberries, check; eggs and milk, check; loaf of bread, check; bag of sweet potatoes, check; and the bird." She looks at it. It's sitting in a cardboard box on the floor near the cash register, and she thinks to herself, *My god, it's more like a plucked ostrich than a turkey, but I guess it deserves a check.*

Then she swallows hard and prays that he'll take a check from her as well. She gasps at the thought of this huge and unexpected grocery bill.

She places all the items on the counter, except for the turkey, then walks over to the wine rack, grabs the Chardonnay on sale, and sets it down with the rest of her items. Nearby, a magazine rack displays photos of Prince William and Kate with their children, all dressed up for Christmas. It brings a homesick tear to her eye, but she decides she can't afford to buy it. She then rushes back to the truck.

She notices George sitting in the passenger seat, in the middle of telling the twins the story of Goldilocks and the Three Bears. They're happily listening, and she almost hates to interrupt them. He sees she's returned, wraps up the story, and then goes to run her credit card and total her items.

Olivia begs him, "Can I write you a check for the groceries?"

"Sure, whatever," he mumbles.

Olivia wants to reach out and hug him, but she resists the urge. She's dumbfounded that this old Yankee curmudgeon saved her tiny English butt. He helps her carry her bags to the truck, and she heaves the turkey into the front passenger seat. Then he hands her his last bag of marshmallows.

"What's this for?" she asks.

"It's a gift from me. Google the recipe for sweet potatoes," he says while grinning.

She offers George a tip, and he shakes his head no, refusing it.

#

The ride home is peaceful, and the children are happy because the Dunkin' Donuts drive-through is conveniently situated right next to the Sherborn Market.

No wonder it was easy to get an appointment with the pediatrician. She chuckles. No one in their right mind would want to inoculate their kids the afternoon before Thanksgiving.

She glances at her children; their faces are smudged with chocolate and powdered sugar. Charlotte's head is bobbing, and Henry is already asleep. She isn't looking forward to their eventual reactions to the vaccinations.

Olivia is suddenly overcome with sadness as she misses her mother deeply. Her greatest wish is to be with her, especially during a holiday, but she lives thousands of kilometers away, and they didn't exactly part on the best of terms.

The idea of preparing this elaborate meal for just the four of them depresses her, and it brings back memories of the many holidays she and her mom spent together. Her mother's proper English family never seemed to forgive her mother for having a bastard daughter with an itinerant Romani jazz musician.

The only explanation Olivia can conjure up is that he must have been as cunning as a fox because, from what little she remembers, he took everything he wanted from them and left her and her mom with no money or any hope for a better future.

Despite this, her mom only spoke kindly about him, even though Olivia never thought he deserved any of those nice words.

CHAPTER SIX — WINNER WINNER TURKEY DINNER

WILLIAM

William realizes that when he gets up in the middle of the night to go to the bathroom, Olivia has been awake for half of it, researching various Thanksgiving recipes on YouTube.

He admits to himself that he's somewhat impressed with her dedication to a holiday that's entirely new to her. He rolls over to look at the alarm clock and is grateful to see he can get another hour of sleep before waking up to tend the livestock.

Although every day on a farm is the same with no true days off from endless chores, holidays still feel special to him, and he looks forward to them.

When he eventually wakes up and comes downstairs, his coffee is already made. Olivia is humming a silly pop tune while she's preparing what looks like a baby ostrich in the kitchen sink. He steps back for a moment and considers that all his anger towards her lately might have been misdirected, as he tries to let it all go.

He begins to list her many qualities in his mind: she's a good mother, a hard worker, a decent cook, and wonderful with the animals... Then he realizes she could use his help and doesn't know where to start, so he freezes in place while watching her.

She turns to him and asks, "Doesn't this seem to be a lot of food for just the four of us?" Then she tries to lift the hefty turkey out of the sink with a huff, but it slips from her hands because of its weight. Next, she places it into the oversized roasting pan and struggles to lift it.

"Here, let me help you with that." William grabs its handles, and together they move it to the kitchen table. Their eyes meet for just an instant, and in that moment, there is a sliver of shared joy.

Olivia hesitates before she inquires, "I know this is going to sound nuts, but would you like to ask Hattie to join us?" Then she looks at the bird in the roasting pan and snickers, "My goodness, there's enough here for twenty more guests."

William replies, "I can ask, but she hasn't forgiven us, and I'm not sure she ever will. She's a pretty stubborn woman."

Olivia sighs before she asks, "How are we ever going to get her to forgive us unless we at least try?"

William considers what she just said, but he also realizes that trying to change Hattie's mind about them is a pointless effort. So, he wonders who else they might invite at the last minute.

He thinks about texting Ian to join them, but it's still too early to disturb him. He sips his coffee and watches Olivia start setting the dining room table. Then, he walks over to her and says, "You're absolutely right about us finally making peace with Hattie. I'll be right back. I'm going across the street to ask her to join us."

Olivia responds cynically, "Woohoo."

"What time should I tell her?" he asks.

"Let me see?" Olivia mimed doing math calculations. "Maybe by tomorrow afternoon, after four, this bird might be ready to come out of the oven."

"Seriously!" he whines.

She giggles, "Ok, cocktails and hors d'oeuvres at 3:30 and dinner will be at, hopefully, God willing and fingers crossed, 4:30."

"Today?"

"Yes, William, that's affirmative."

#

William greets Hattie in her stable, but in his hurry, he left his gloves at home, and his cold hands are buried deep in his pockets as he tries to keep them warm while thinking of what to say.

She gives a simple nod and waits to hear him. William isn't a talkative guy, but that's one of the qualities Hattie likes most about him.

"Happy Thanksgiving, Hattie." He begins with it as his icebreaker.

Hattie is pleasantly intrigued but clueless about why he's visiting her. "Thank you, William, and same to you. What can I do for you?" she states in a cold but cordial way.

He struggles to form a sentence, "Do you remember, Hattie, all those holidays you spent at our house when my mom and dad were still alive?"

Hattie leans on her rake and smiles. "Those were the best; your mother made the meanest dirty martinis, and your father's sing-along around the baby grand after we all got smashed was fabulous. Man, I miss those times."

William grins with Hattie as he reaches for her arm and gives it a gentle squeeze when he asks, "What are your plans for today?"

She grimaces before sadly saying, "Frozen turkey dinners for George and me in the den while we watch, AKC's Best in Show and…"

William butts in and says, "Stop! How would you and George like to join us for Martinis and hors d'oeuvres, followed by the biggest roast turkey you've ever laid eyes on? Olie and I are trying to start a new tradition with our kids, and we'd like you to join us."

Hattie's eyes open as wide as pies in surprise, and she asks, "Can I bring anything?" in her raspy, smoky voice.

"Oh yes, that would be fine. How about a bottle of vodka and some stuffed olives?" he confirms.

"Consider it done." She gives him an inquisitive stare and pauses, waiting for more details, then asks, "What time do you want us?"

"Oh, did I forget to mention it?" he replies.

"Yes." Then, suddenly, she has a violent coughing fit that lasts a few seconds.

"You all right, Hattie?"

Hattie replies, "That's a discussion for another day. When do you want us?"

"3:30ish." He states this with a curious expression on his face, wondering if that time would be agreeable to her.

She gives him a thumbs up and returns to raking out the muck in Barbie's stall.

#

Walking back to the house, William texts Ian. *Hey Bro, Happy T Day. If u r not doing anything and you'd like to join Olie and me, we'd love to have you over. Drinks and apps at 3:30, followed by a roast ostrich (only kidding) and jeans are AOK.*

William grabs a pair of insulated work gloves from the garage and begins his chores enthusiastically. About every 30 minutes, he stops to check for a reply from Ian, but there isn't one.

Olivia hollers to him from the porch, "How many are we for dinner?"

He yells back to her, "We're six. Oh, and wash off the martini glasses."

"Where will I find them?" she asks.

There is a moment's hesitation before he says, "In the back row of the hidden cupboard in the dining room." He raises his voice, "Hattie's bringing vodka and olives, and leave an extra place setting on the side. I sent a text to my buddy Ian to join us, but I haven't heard back from him."

William is so delighted about the holiday and everyone finally coming together; it helps him to almost forget about his financial troubles.

#

Three loud thumps are heard through the farmhouse from the oversized antique knocker banging on the front door. Charlotte and Henry rush excitedly to the entryway to greet their guests. Olivia wipes food from her hands and pulls off her apron as she welcomes them inside. William reaches for George and Hattie's heavy winter coats and quickly closes the front door to keep the heat in. George hands William a couple of bottles of Sancerre and a bottle of

Belvedere Vodka. Hattie reaches into her pocket and reveals a small bottle of stuffed martini olives, grinning as she hands it to Olivia.

Hattie smirks, "You have some big shoes to fill, Olie. William's mother, Grace, made the best martini in the world." Then she turns to William and exclaims, "Wow, what's that wonderful smell coming from the kitchen?"

Olivia blushes shyly and says, "Hopefully it's our dinner."

The entire time Hattie and Olivia chat, George can't keep his eyes off Olivia. He's in shock because, in his wildest dreams, he never imagined he'd see the woman he pushed his unsellable giant turkey on ever again. Yet, there she is, standing right in front of him as their dinner host. He grimaces with embarrassment at meeting her face-to-face and can't wait to have a drink.

Olivia turns to George and welcomes him, saying, "George, my savior. Come warm yourself by the fire while we whip up your drinks."

Hattie inquires, "How do you know each other?"

George explains, "She bought her gas and groceries from me yesterday. No big mystery."

Charlotte and Henry sit at George's feet, begging him to tell another story because they loved the one he shared with them in the car the day before.

William looks around the room and can't get over how warm and familiar it all feels. He's also pleased to finally have George and Hattie back under his roof. He glances at his phone, and there's still no reply from Ian.

William starts to wonder if Ian might have been called in for a last-minute emergency transport because organ transplant surgeries don't necessarily stop just because it's a holiday. Ian also mentioned that sometimes, he has to travel with the organs as a chaperone to ensure their viability for the recipient. What did he say it was, four hours for a heart and twelve for kidneys from the time they're harvested, or something like that? Busy guy, no wonder he's still single.

Everyone is on their second drink, and Olivia is delighted with the Sancerre George brought. She adds the proper wine glasses to the table and pours more wine into each one. Then she places the hot roasted turkey in the center of everything and steps back to look at what she's accomplished in a short time.

The Yorkshire pudding she made from scratch is set next to the roasted bird. The stuffing, courtesy of a YouTube recipe, is served alongside yams topped with tiny marshmallows, also from YouTube, and a side of canned cranberry sauce on the other side of the carving platter. She lights the candles and proudly invites everyone to the table.

William is in the middle of his second martini when he takes his seat at the head of the table, and as he gazes at what Olivia has created, he feels truly blessed in that brief moment.

Henry digs into the Yorkshire pudding and asks his mother before taking a bite, "What's dis stuff?"

"It's something my mum used to make for me. Try it, Henry. How about you, Charlie?" She states while looking at Charlotte's fork.

Still feeling a bit embarrassed, George offers, "William, do you need any assistance carving the turkey?"

Olivia adds, "If it weren't for George, we wouldn't be all here together today."

Hattie's speech is slurred from her two martinis and second glass of Sancerre, and she asks, "Why's that?"

Olivia shares, "George selling that turkey to me yesterday was a godsend, I tell you."

George feels self-conscious and uncomfortable as he gazes at the ridiculously oversized turkey in the center of the table. He grasps at his tight collar and tries to loosen it, wondering if Olivia's comment was meant to be sarcastic.

Hattie scowls at George while she drains her wine glass. He raises his voice when he repeats his offer to help carve the turkey, and she says, "George, if you want to be helpful, then refill my glass."

William is feeling full of himself and brags, "Thanks, George, but I'm just waiting for it to cool down. I don't really have to remind you that I have great knife skills. Do I?"

George replies, "No dementia yet, Billie. I can still recall how well your father taught you."

"I also worked as a medic when I was in the National Guard, and I've had to slaughter and butcher my share of animals over the years, plus deer hunting with him, so I think I can handle this." He remarks, sounding as if he's nervous about cutting his first Thanksgiving turkey, on top of being a bit inebriated.

"I miss your folks," adds George.

"Me too," adds Hattie.

William stands up and cuts into the turkey's breast, making perfect slices and placing them on the platter. Then, he meticulously severs its legs and thighs. Afterward, he slices the meat off the bones and arranges it on the plate with precision.

While William is engrossed in carving the bird, Olivia inquires, "Hattie, how long have you and George been a thing, and how did you meet?"

It's apparent to everyone at the table that Hattie is also amusingly smashed, so that might partly explain her response, "Well, we began seeing one another when I was in high school."

George interjects, "And I was in college."

She continues with modestly slurred speech, "Nevertheless, I can't remember a time when I didn't know George because we're both local yokels, but the main reason we never ran off and married is he's Jewish, and well, I'm not. Back then, our parents forbade us from wedlock, so here we are today, just two old fogies, still going strong." Hattie reaches over and plants a greasy kiss on George's cheek. "Now, somebody please give me a drumstick. I'm famished!"

The antics amuse the twins, and Hattie looks ridiculous with the massive turkey leg in her mouth, which she mostly plays with and rarely eats.

Everyone is stuffed when they make their way to the living room. George pulls out an old, familiar 78 rpm record from the shelf and plays it on the antique wind-up Victrola. The twins are his captive audience and can't wait until he flips the record over and winds it up again.

Olivia leaves the dishes on the table because she's exhausted from cooking since four in the morning. Instead, she makes her way into the living room to sit at the piano. "Requests, do I hear any requests?"

Hattie answers, "Do you know the song, *I'll Be Loving You, Always* '?"

Olivia asks, "Can you hum it for me?"

Hattie, with her smoky voice, attempts to sing sweetly. Olivia catches the tune from her humming and impressively plays along on the piano. George joins in, and they sing until tears well up in both of their eyes. Then he takes Hattie's gnarled hand in his and squeezes it.

William is caught up in the moment and fails to notice he has multiple missed texts from Ian. He stands up and apologizes, "I'm sorry, I'll be right back." As he enters the kitchen, he is horrified by what he reads on his iPhone.

Text me as soon as you get this!
I've been taken in for questioning by the Natick Police.
You're wanted for questioning for some heavy-duty shit, Bro. Get a lawyer!

William immediately claims he's not feeling well, which is true because he suddenly feels nauseated. He apologizes to everyone and runs upstairs to shut himself in the bedroom to think.

His head spins from what Ian just texted him. He asks himself, *What if this is related to Shane's shady side business and he's been caught, or worse, that idiot in the ladies' locker room was serious about the law being on his side?* His fears start to grow, and he's horrified at the thought of going to jail.

William fails to calm himself down, and instead, his heart pounds in his chest. The rage he felt a few days ago toward Olivia over their financial issues reemerges with a vengeance, leaving him covered in sweat and with a mouth full of cotton balls instead of saliva.

He runs his fingers through his sweaty hair, trying to sober up from the multiple martinis, followed by wine with dinner, and a glass of port with his pumpkin pie. There's no way he's in any condition to answer a police interrogation, let alone drive there. Just then, and with no way to stop what is about to happen to him, he's having a full-blown panic attack, and he passes out.

CHAPTER SEVEN — THE RIGHT TO REMAIN SILENT

IAN

Earlier that same day, Ian pleads, "I'm not talking to you without a lawyer present." Then he slams his hand down on the table in the interrogation room at the Natick Police Station on East Central and stops talking as his mind floods with thoughts about the guy William punched in the face. Recalling how he fell limp in his arms when his nose was broken on Monday night. Holy shit, I'm one of the guys who held him down while William was pummeling him. I'm so screwed!

Detective Deborah Bilby interrupts his thoughts with, "I think you've watched too many cop shows on TV." And she changes her facial expression to one of dead seriousness.

Ian takes a good look at her for the first time. She appears to be a typical, hardworking middle-aged woman. The uniform she's wearing couldn't be more unflattering to her figure, and her hair is as curly and unruly as Medusa's, but in a friendlier sort of way.

She gazes at him for a moment, and he realizes she has soft blue eyes that seem caring and kind. He breaks the silence, "Why have you left me locked in this room all afternoon?" Ian inquires.

Detective Deborah Bilby explains, "For starters, the door wasn't locked, and you could have come and gone as you pleased. The long wait was due to our understaffing, and we were questioning a person of interest ahead of you. Do you know why we brought you in today?"

"I think I should wait for my lawyer," Ian repeats.

The police detective is growing increasingly frustrated with him and decides it's time to bring Ian up to speed on the situation's seriousness. "We're working on a time-sensitive case, and from the video footage at your gym, it looks like you and three other people were the last to see Mary O'Keefe on Monday night.

Ian's posture changes when he recognizes the gravitas of the situation. He listens attentively while Debby continues to talk.

"According to her boyfriend, she sent him a text saying she was heading to the bus stop and would be home within the hour. She has not been seen or heard from since, and the bus drivers that night confirm she never boarded the bus."

"It was snowing, and maybe she gave up waiting for it and called an Uber," Ian adds.

Agreed, but based on what we saw in the video in the lady's locker room, things got pretty interesting right before she disappeared.

Ian feels a bit less nervous about sharing the details with the detective now that he understands it's to help her find Mary, so he opens up. "I was working out with free weights, spotting this guy named Joe, whom I met at the gym and don't know anything else about."

"What happened next?" she urges.

Ian clams up.

"Ian, are you hungry?" she asks.

"I'm missing Thanksgiving dinner at a friend's house, sure, I'm hungry."

The detective leaves and comes right back with a sandwich, a bag of chips, a Sprite, and says, "Here, I'll split my Thanksgiving dinner with you, so you won't feel like you're dining alone on a holiday."

"That was a joke, right, Debbie? Can I call you, Debbie?"

When she pushes the food to the center of the table, he notices she's wearing a wedding ring, and he wonders for a moment if she is married to a man or a woman.

Redirecting his attention, she continues her questioning, "Sure, Ian, Debbie's fine. Please tell me everything you can remember regarding what transpired on Monday night, so I can do my job and try to find out what happened to Mary O'Keefe."

Ian is still chewing his half of the turkey sandwich while trying to decide how much detail to give about his friend William's run-in with the creep who attacked Mary in the ladies' locker room.

Debbie continues, "You already made it clear that you don't know much about Joe, but what about the other man with you and Mary?"

"Who?" Ian decides to assess her knowledge and see how much she really knows.

Debbie continues, "There was one other guy besides Joe in the ladies' locker room with Mary, and of course, the 'they' meaning a he/she who also has a criminal record that I'm not at liberty to divulge more than I already have. But with your testimony, I might be able to charge them with a crime today.

"Debbie, why haven't you contacted the other guys yet?"

"Ah, Ian, you see it's only you and Matthew who appear to have working telephone numbers. Joe's information was never updated at the gym. Go figure. Somebody is not doing their job the way they're supposed to in today's world." She scoffs. "And the other guy was getting a first-time tour and hadn't signed up yet. All they have in the gym's business office is a phone number that no one answers, it doesn't have a mailbox set up, and the phone is billed to a P.O. Box in Framingham, so it's a dead end for now."

Ian deduces that William must be having marital problems. He surmises, on top of everything else he's been going through, that he would carry a burner telephone. Whatever, he's not the first guy with marriage troubles, and he won't be the last. Ian inquires, "What happens if I don't tell you anything more today?"

Debbie taps her fingers together in front of her lips. She thinks before she speaks, "The person we're detaining for the alleged disappearance of Mary O'Keefe walks out of here Scott free, and the second after you leave that buddy you're protecting might very well be accused and charged with assault and battery of a transwoman, which is also considered a hate crime."

"Holy Shit!" Ian feels sweat pooling under his armpits as his hands become clammy. Then he covers his mouth with them in disbelief and waits to hear what Debbie has to say.

Debbie pulls out a notepad and pencil from her back pocket and affirms, "So are we ready to cut the crap and tell me what really happened?"

Ian makes a snap decision and confesses everything he saw up to a point, "I want to confirm I only know Joe from the gym, never once met up with him anywhere else, I'd never met Mary O'Keefe, until we went rushing in to rescue her."

"What made you think she was in trouble?" she asks.

"Well, the gym was practically empty because the weather was so terrible. Joe, William, and I were talking while working out when we heard a woman screaming at the top of her lungs for help." Then Ian stops to think.

"Ok, this is a good start. Then what happened?" she urges.

"Me, Joe, and William pull this big creep off of a helpless little girl. Just thinking about it makes me want to puke. It was disgusting! We tell her she needs to call the police and report this prick, but she pleads with us and says she doesn't want the police involved because her visa had expired, and she was afraid of getting kicked out of the country."

"So, then what happens?" she urges him to continue.

"The creep gets all full of himself. The three of us still have him pinned down. That's when he claims it's his God-given right to be in the lady's locker room. Mary gets very upset and tells us that helping her is hopeless and that she's never coming back there because it's just another hopeless battle."

Debbie echoes, "Hopeless," and pauses to write it down, then says, "Now very carefully tell me what happened next." It appears to Ian that she's coaching him not to say too much.

Ian responds, "I remember when Mary left, Joe went out after her to make sure she was safe and to calm her down from the altercation with the creep. She specifically mentioned running into someone before in the locker room, noting it wasn't the first time she'd been bothered there. Oh, and she said she was afraid this particular guy would stalk her if he knew where she lived." He pauses for a moment, "I stayed behind with William, and we talked for a bit. You know, it was a pretty upsetting ordeal."

"Why didn't one of you heroes offer her a ride home?" Debbie inquires nonchalantly.

"I just assumed she had a car because we were in the middle of an office park and Joe went out to make sure she was safe, so I didn't give it much thought," Ian replies.

"Did you see Joe again after that?"

"No."

"Do you know what kind of car Joe drives?"

"Not a clue, officer."

Her expression looks annoyed. "It's a detective!" she confirms.

"Then why are you in uniform?" asks Ian.

"Like I said earlier, we're understaffed, and I'm covering someone else's detail, so I had to suit up today. Do you have anything else to add?" she asks.

"No," he confirms.

She switches to a robotic tone as she continues. "Would you be willing to sign a statement regarding what you told me today?"

"Yes, sure. Will that help you arrest the creep?"

It's not up to me, but hopefully, it will be.

He's worried when he asks her, "Now that I told you all this stuff, what's going to happen to my friend William and me?"

"Tell him to hire an attorney and come in voluntarily for questioning as soon as possible." Shamefully, she looks down at her pad and hesitates before she explains, "Regardless of whether or not Mathew is booked for attacking Mary O'Keefe and possibly for her disappearance, I can't stop Mathew from charging your buddy with assault and battery of a transwoman."

Ian grabs his hair with both sweaty hands and mutters, "Oh my goodness, what have I done?"

Her face looks caring as she explains, "You don't see it now, but I believe what you did today was the right thing to do."

Completely distraught, he asks, "Am I free to go?"

You were always free to leave. Happy Thanksgiving, by the way.

Ian pushes himself up from the table. His legs feel wobbly beneath him from sitting there too long. He needs to pee, but the thought of using the toilet in the police station turns his stomach, so he rushes out as quickly as he can. On his way to his car, he texts his buddy William a heads-up, warning him of what's to come. Then he drives straight home to relieve himself, take his dog Scout for a walk, and share a frozen pepperoni pizza with him for their late-night dinner.

CHAPTER EIGHT — SLIPPERY WHEN WET

OLIVIA

When Olivia enters Hattie's breeding workshop, she triggers one of the motion detectors. She shields her eyes from the bright lights that turn on automatically, temporarily blinding her. She ties Buttercup to a hitching post and wanders around, exploring the vast space. It's much more impressive than Olivia ever anticipated, and the air is pleasantly warm compared to outside. The main room in the 60 x 60 metal building feels more like a large steel-beam warehouse than a barn. Built inside is a trailer turned into a laboratory equipped with microscopes, a refrigerator for sperm and blood samples, an incubator, a cryo-freezer for long-term sperm preservation, racks of beakers for sperm collection and measuring, warmers for lubricants, a sink with a faucet, a water bubbler, and a coffee pot with paper cups. Everything is meticulously labeled, including the temperature settings for each stage of collection and preservation. The note above the microscope is a mnemonic: keep it above 98 or you'll seal their fate, and there is a cartoon of sperm floating upside down like dead goldfish.

Olivia hears a dry cough from outside the door and realizes Hattie has finally arrived. The smell of fresh coffee mixes with the stale stench of cigarettes as she approaches. Olivia steps out of the lab to greet Hattie, who is carrying two mugs with steam rising from them. She hands one to Olivia with a worried look and asks, "How's William doing this morning?"

Olivia looks down at her boots and doesn't know how to reply to her.

Hattie notices her question made Olivia uncomfortable, so she changes the subject. "Who's watching the twins today?"

Olivia's eyes light up as she explains, It was serendipitous, I tell you. They were invited to a playdate and scooped up right after breakfast. I don't have to pick them up until 3, so I'm all yours until 2:30.

Hattie glances at her watch and grins, "That's plenty of time."

"Where do we begin?" Olivia eagerly asks.

Hattie looks directly at Olivia and wonders, "Are you sure you want to learn to be a horse breeder today? You know it's hard, unrewarding work, but I could use the help and appreciate passing my knowledge down to an apprentice."

Olivia straightens up when she says, "One hundred percent yes!"

Hattie reveals, "I'm sure you've gathered by now that I'm not one for long conversations. I'm going to show you what to do, and along the way, I'll tell you what we're doing, so you'll be able to do it yourself someday."

"OK, that sounds good."

Hattie continues, "And there's no such thing as a stupid question." Hattie points to the north corner, "Go tie up Buttercup over there." Then she looks around the room for something and says, "Let's go, we need to set up the AV."

"What's an AV?" Olivia asks.

Hattie states matter-of-factly, "It's an Artificial Vagina."

Back inside the lab, Olivia's eyes widen as she watches Hattie warm up the AV with hot water. She smirks before explaining, "Don't make the water too hot because that will kill the sperm and burn Ken's pecker." Hattie shows how to insert a sperm collection bag for Ken's semen and then hands the AV to Olivia, saying, "You'll never forget it as long as you live."

Olivia grins as she asks, "What's next?"

They leave the laboratory and walk over to a tall, large, brown leather object in the middle of the room, and Hattie slaps it with her gnarly, fingered hands. "If and that's a big **if,** things go well today, Ken will hopefully hop up onto this collection breeding phantom and allow you to jerk him off."

Olivia blushes and says, "I beg your pardon. How might I accomplish that?"

Hattie says dryly, "I'm sure you'll figure it out."

Olivia stands there, holding the warmed-up AV, and feels pretty uncomfortable about what's about to happen.

Hattie finishes her coffee and reaches for the empty cup in Olivia's hand. "You ready for your first time, darlin'?"

Olivia nods, yes, and Hattie continues, "Ok, then, I'm going to have a quick smoke, and I'll be right back with Ken.

Left alone, Olivia's mind keeps circling back to William's recent actions. She feels anxious and overwhelmed by her troubles with him, still unable to understand what she did wrong on Thanksgiving. One moment, William is singing along with everyone and having a good time. Next, he disappears without even a thank you for her efforts or an explanation for leaving so suddenly.

She feels her stomach twist with nerves, then asks herself what options she has. Her application to become a naturalized U.S. citizen hasn't been approved yet, so she's dependent on William to help her with it. Had she not burned her bridge with her mother back in England, she could have reached out for help and advice. The last thing she wants is to become a single mom with no income, stranded in a foreign country with young children to raise.

Hattie eventually returns with her stud horse, Ken. She walks him toward the breeding phantom, and he becomes agitated, kicking up his heels and rearing. Ken spots Buttercup across the room, and his eyes go wild with excitement.

Hattie raises her voice, "Are you a righty or a lefty?"

"Righty!" Ken is bucking and hard to control. "Where do you want me?" Olivia queries.

Hattie responds, "You're good where you are, push his rump like this." With all her might, Hattie shoves Ken. "We need him to climb up onto the breeding phantom."

It's as simple as one, two, three. Ken gets an erection, mounts the breeding phantom, and Olivia places the AV over Ken's penis, moves it to and fro, and voila, she's collecting her first batch of equine semen.

Hattie and Olivia are sweaty from the exertion. Olivia has no clue what she is supposed to do next, but she feels a bit proud of her achievement.

Hattie instructs, "Follow me!" Then she pulls the collected semen from the AV and examines it for its volume and speaks loudly, "Good job, Ken."

She pats her horse, walks over, and hangs the AV on the banister leading to the laboratory steps. She quickly enters, pours the semen into a graduated glass beaker, and records the total in her log.

Immediately afterward, she uses a glass dropper to sample the sperm right before she places the remaining semen in a beaker.

"Hand me a glass slide." Instructs Hattie.

Hattie places a droplet on the slide and covers it, then she turns on the microscope's light, places the slide on the display table, takes off her eyeglasses, and looks down through the lenses. "Hmmm, like I expected, the sperm count is on the lower side, but the sperm itself looks pretty healthy. Here, take a look at it."

Olivia adjusts her lenses. Suddenly, they come into focus, and she can see them swimming around. She exclaims, "They look just like tadpoles, but there's one with two heads. Is that normal?"

Hattie shares, "I saw it too, but there's a sixty percent rule."

Olivia has no clue what she's talking about and shrugs.

Hattie explains, "It's a math problem. Are you good at math?"

Olivia laughs, "Better than you'd think."

"Here it goes, total sperm volume is determined by output. That's the number written down in the logbook," she points out. "Now count the normal versus abnormal."

Olivia glances back at the slide and asks, "What am I looking for?"

Hattie thinks, "You know, sperm that doesn't look quite right, bent tail, no head, two tails, too small, and stuff like that. Now count the total number and then the number of abnormal sperm."

Olivia counts and writes down her totals. "What's considered a healthy batch?"

Hattie continues, "Like I said, anything over sixty percent."

Olivia proudly boasts, "Then this is a great batch because there were only seven abnormal sperm."

Hattie explains, "Ok, so we take that number from the amount on the slide, which is one percent of the batch, and multiply it by the total volume, which will give us a seventy-nine percent viability rating."

Olivia enthusiastically says, "That's excellent, isn't it?"

"Yes, but there are no mares in estrus this time of year around here, so what do we do with the semen, because without a female to mate with it's pretty worthless?"

This news saddens Olivia; she was excited about the idea that her first batch might be lucky and could bring a new foal into the world.

Hattie remarks, "Don't look so long in the face, we'll freeze it and sell it in the spring."

Olivia perks up, and she asks Hattie, "How about some lunch? We have enough turkey to last until Christmas."

Hattie isn't hungry, but she senses Olivia is looking for someone to talk to about her problems. "Sure, and by the way, I think you did wonderfully on your first day." Then, suddenly, Hattie breaks out into a coughing fit she can't control and motions for Olivia to go, followed by choked words, "I'll head straight over when I'm done freezing the batch."

#

The quietness of the house startles Olivia when she enters. There's no truck in the driveway, but William never mentioned he was going anywhere.

Robotically, Olivia sets the table in the kitchen for two and places a lunch feast on it.

She texts William, saying the twins must be picked up by three, but he doesn't respond, and she taps the counter nervously, frustrated.

Hattie knocks on the kitchen door, and Olivia is genuinely grateful to have company.

After they carefully wash their hands from handling the horse semen, they sit down at the table and look at their marvelous lunch that neither of them is interested in eating. Hattie's medical condition is affecting her appetite, and Olivia's developing a nervous stomach from the way William treats her.

Olivia tries to be a good hostess. She notices Hattie not eating and asks, "Is there anything else I can get you?"

Hattie pauses for a moment before she responds, "I'd love a cold beer. Any brand's fine, I'm not picky."

Olivia says, "Me too." Then she goes and gets them Guinness Stouts. "Hattie, how's this?" She shows her the bottle.

"It's better than I had hoped for." And Hattie looks genuinely thankful.

Olivia pops off the caps and makes a toast, "To you, Hattie."

They clink their bottles, and she says, "To. You Olie."

There's a pregnant pause as the women sip their beers. Olivia eventually breaks the silence, "Hattie, you asked me about William and…" Olivia begins to cry tears of frustration before continuing, "And I'm beside myself because I don't know where he is or what's going through his mind or why he's always angry with me. Hattie, I try so hard to please him, and nothing's working." Olivia grabs her head in her hands and leans over to cry.

Hattie didn't know what to expect, but based on what she witnessed the night before, she knew things between them weren't great. She gently asks, "Is he hurting you?"

Olivia confesses, "No, not at all."

Hattie takes a sip of her beer and considers what she should say, "Ok, what can I do to help?"

Olivia sits up from crying and asks, "Can I borrow your truck if William isn't back in time to pick up the twins?"

"Sure, I'll even drive you myself if need be. I owe you for what you did for me today with my horse."

"What are you talking about? It was you who gave me so much of your valuable time and taught me so many wonderful things."

Olivia checks her watch, then her phone, to see if William has replied, but there's nothing. Then she adds, "You have no idea what a relief it is to have you on standby for us this afternoon. You know, I have no one here on this side of the pond, and you and George are becoming the closest thing to the grandparents that they're missing." Olivia reaches out and squeezes Hattie's gnarled hand to emphasize what she just said.

They keep nursing their beers while watching the door for William.

At 2:30, Olivia heads to the garage to find old, discarded car seats for Charlotte and Henry for the ride home in Hattie's truck. As she sorts through the pile of outgrown junk in the garage, she's grateful this stuff hasn't already ended up at the swap shop or the dump, and she thinks of it as a positively well-earned point in favor of procrastination.

After an almost hopeless search for a pair of outgrown car seats, Olivia's blood begins to boil as her fury towards William intensifies.

She imagines him out gallivanting somewhere between the Tracker Supply Store and Rocky's Hardware, munching on a roast beef sandwich instead of eating the leftovers at home. Plus, the way he abandoned her on Thanksgiving, leaving her to wash all the dishes alone and having to put the twins to bed without help, really gets to her.

She wipes sweat from her face and thinks, What a gigantic asshole. Whatever he's doing or wherever he goes, it better be important because she's furious and fed up.

Then she finds a large box shoved onto a high shelf in the back of the garage, marked "Swap Shop." She pulls it down and rips off the tape. She's so relieved she could almost cry when she takes hold of her babies' old car seats!

Hattie is already in her truck's passenger seat, warming it up while waiting for her. Olivia throws the car seats into the back of Hattie's truck, and with Olivia driving, they pull out of the driveway to pick up the twins, close to on time.

#

Olivia makes a sharp left onto Route 115 toward Dover. As she speeds up, her thoughts drift back to a few years earlier, when she was coming from the opposite way in an Uber, tears streaming down her face, on her way to William's farm. The way she had to run away from the home where she worked as a nanny still haunts her in her nightmares.

Everything there was rotten to the core; the children reminded her of Augustus Gloop, Veruca Salt, and Violet Beauregarde from Charlie and the Chocolate Factory, only these kids were more spoiled and much crueler. Even the dog acted as if it was entitled, not to mention that it pooped all over the house, and Olivia was expected to clean up after it.

The first clue that something was off was that Karen, the mother of this freak show family, would give Olivia expensive Burberry gifts a few times a month. When Olivia took the job with them, she was living in London with her mum; it never occurred to her that her airplane ticket was only one-way and that she'd be working under the table.

The family's dad was a foolish old man with a lot of money, and he had at least half a dozen children from previous marriages and relationships in addition to the three fat, cruel, and hideously unattractive children he had with Karen.

It was clear that Karen ran circles around him and was calling all the shots. Olivia remembers how Karen often called him her F.R.O.M. (fat, rich, old, man), because she was nearly twenty-five years younger. Olivia will never forget this because Karen kept mentioning it while complaining about her husband, though she wasn't exactly a spring chicken either. She was at least in her late forties.

Things spiraled out of control very quickly at the end. The doorbell rang, and suddenly, baby number four was delivered. Honestly, it showed up like a Domino's pizza or Chinese takeout. Karen tipped the delivery person and looked at her new child. Nothing about how this baby arrived was ever discussed with Olivia beforehand. She didn't know if the baby came from a surrogate mother and was Karen's biological child, or if it was just kidnapped from somewhere for a hefty fee. It didn't matter, and there it was, needing to be fed, bathed, burped, diapered, and looked after alongside the other three little monsters and the dog, who only pooped inside the house. Olivia offered to take the baby upstairs to change its diaper, thinking, *Holy Shit, did this happen?*

That's when she overheard her employers arguing about the funeral for one of his out-of-town, extended family members, and Karen was refusing to attend because she was "too busy bonding," you know, with their newborn.

So, there it was. Olivia and Karen were the only adults left in the house. Olivia was exhausted from caring for the children and went straight to sleep as soon as her head hit the pillow. Later that night, she wakes up when she realizes someone is pulling down her knickers. Of course, it was Karen who had also polished off a bottle of wine by herself.

Karen repeated with slurry speech, "Just relax, you're going to love it," right before bearing down on her with her terrible, foul breath.

Olivia was mortified and didn't know what to do; the next thing that happened was completely beyond her control. She instinctively kneed Karen hard in the face, accidentally breaking her nose and giving Karen a black eye as big as a saucer.

Then all Olivia heard was, "Son of a bitch!" being repeated as Karen walked around the bedroom, holding her bloody nose with a face cloth.

Olivia was panic-stricken but had to think fast. What if Karen calls the police and reports to them that she intentionally assaulted her? No one would believe her version that Karen was sexually molesting her, or take her testimony seriously, and she was no longer in the United States legally, as she had overstayed her visa.

She grabbed a pile of dirty clothes from her hamper, which she had brought from London, and stuffed them into her backpack. Then she pulled out her carry-on bag from under her bed, and as quickly as she could, she emptied her closet and grabbed her toiletries from the bathroom, dumping everything into it and zipping it only halfway closed with some items still sticking out because it wouldn't all fit. She looked longingly at her brand-new Burberry bag, along with its matching belt, scarf, sneakers, and key chain, letting out a deep sigh of regret as she made the quick but tough decision to leave them all behind. She didn't want to risk Karen falsely accusing her of stealing them. With an angry jerk, Olivia yanked her phone cord from the wall as she ordered a ride, then sent William a text saying she had a big surprise for him. She remembered the horrible pit in her stomach as she feared he might not want her to come over that night.

Just then, Hattie speaks up and breaks Olivia's train of thought. "Olivia, slow down! You just passed a speed trap, dammit." Exactly at that moment, the police car's flashing lights come on, and it speeds after them.

Olivia hits the steering wheel and says, "Seriously, Hattie, could this day get any worse for me?" as she pulls over to the side of the road and rolls down her window.

The police officer says, "License and registration."

Hattie rummages through the glove box until she finally finds the registration and passes it to Olivia, who then hands it to him. Olivia's hands tremble as she looks for her driver's license in her bag, and when she shows it to the officer, he stammers, "Seriously?"

"I'm British, you see," Olivia states as the officer scrutinizes it.

"Well, at least it isn't expired. I see here you're an organ donor." He flips it over, inspecting both sides, before handing it back to her. "You rushing to pick up your kids?"

"How did you guess?" says Olivia.

"You, moms, have turned this stretch of road into a drag strip every afternoon around 3."

Olivia nods yes and explains, "Officer, I never speed. We're on our way to pick up my twins, and I was distracted by something unrelated."

Hattie chimes in, "It was my fault, officer. You see, I was telling her to step on it because I'm not feeling well from the cancer and wanted to get home."

The police officer leans into the car and says softly, with a teardrop forming in his eye, "Olivia, I have a twin sister with cystic fibrosis who is alive today because she received a pair of donor lungs. So, I'm going to write you a warning this time." Then he raises his voice slightly and smiles when he continues, "So please, ma'am, slow down and help us keep our roads safe."

Olivia feels so relieved when she responds, "Thank you, officer." And they slowly drive away.

Hattie declares, "Oh, he was cute."

"What do you mean?" Olivia says with a giggle.

"He was handsome in an Italian, Black, Spanish, Arabic, Jewish, or maybe even Asian, sort of way…or maybe Greek because he's built like Adonis. What's his name?"

"I've no clue. He didn't mention it."

Hattie reaches for the warning Olivia shoved into the visor. "He signed it, Robert Hill. Well, that's no help."

Olivia asks, "Are you going to look him up and ask him out on a date?"

"No, I'm pretty happy with my George… that is for now - ha! Can we get there already so I can have a cigarette break?"

Driving the rest of the way, Hattie feels proud of herself because she truly believes her statement to the police officer is what got Olivia off the hook.

When Olivia turns onto the street where her children are waiting for her to pick them up from their playdate, she tries to unclench her jaw and put on a happy face for them. Her mind floods with thoughts of despair as she ponders how she got herself into another messed-up situation. She takes a deep breath and lets out a sigh while putting the truck in park and unbuckling her seatbelt. Hattie has fallen asleep, so she quietly closes the door and gazes worriedly at her children, who are happily playing with their little friends. At the same time, she wonders what she's going to do to save them from the pain of a possible oncoming catastrophe.

CHAPTER NINE — PREDATOR VS PREY

WILLIAM

Detective Deborah Bilby meets William at the Dunkin' Donuts on East Central Ave in Natick, which is only a short distance from the police station. He arrives early for their appointment and waits in his truck, parked behind the coffee shop. With the engine off, he sits in silence, watching for any signs of trouble. He's terrified this is an ambush, and that she has planned everything carefully to catch him, which will lead to her taking him to the police station, cuffed and zip-tied, like a prized buck.

William is much more accustomed to being the predator in pursuit of the prey. The endless hours he and his father spent in camouflage, in their hideaway, silently waiting for that perfect shot, which never failed.

Feeling extremely uneasy about the advice he received from Dr. Shane Ferguson over the phone while on his way there, his stomach is in knots. He still can't understand why the detective was so insistent on meeting away from the police station. Dr. Ferguson convinced William not to hire a lawyer and suggested that the whole matter would blow over on its own, so he shouldn't panic.

William watches as a middle-aged woman with a large head of curly hair pulled back into a ponytail walks into the coffee shop. Just then, his phone rings, startling him. He answers it and, at the same time, notices the woman in the coffee shop on her phone, waving to him from inside.

"Hi, are you sitting in the truck?" asks the detective.

"Yes, ma'am."

"You want me to order you something? I'm getting a coffee and a bagel," she offers sweetly.

William pauses thoughtfully before replying, "Yes, ma'am, a cup of cocoa if you wouldn't mind." He appreciates the gesture and looks forward to drinking it.

"Coming right up. Are you on your way in to see me?" she requests.

He echoes, "Yes, ma'am. On my way."

#

William feels disappointed when he realizes there are no booths, but at least the tables are spread out, even though they offer little privacy. The detective is paying for the order. He walks over to greet her and says, "Here, let me pay for that."

"No need. Let's sit over there," she says, pointing to a table in the far corner of the coffee shop. They are the only customers, and besides the two people behind the counter, they're alone.

William is worried about talking to her in public and asks, "Is it all right to speak frankly here?"

The detective looks around and laughs while she explains, "We're the only people here who speak English. You're fine."

He confides, "You see, nothing like this has ever happened to me before, and I'm not exactly sure what I'm supposed to do."

She offers, "Let's sit and talk, and please stop worrying."

William isn't sure he should trust her, but feels he has no choice but to go along.

The detective places the food on the table, looks up at him, smiles, and then explains, "I can tell right from the start that you're a nice, polite, and well-meaning fella," she sips her coffee, "But seriously, William, there's a hair thickness's difference in many cases between a law-abiding citizen and a wanted outlaw." She takes another sip, then a small bite of her bagel, swallows, and continues. "William, when you smashed that person in the face, you crossed that line."

William breaks into a cold sweat before he asks, "What's going to happen to me?"

She replies, "Probably nothing." Then she disappointingly shrugs her shoulders.

Feeling some relief, he asks her, "What about that young girl who was attacked at the gym?"

She answers with a frown, "The sad truth is probably the same: nothing will happen, and nobody cares. Mary has overstayed her visa, so if and when she shows up, I won't be notified. That creep in the lady's locker room could have pressed charges against you, but there's no way after Mary O'Keefe's sudden disappearance that someone with that kind of criminal record would stick around to find out what happens to him next. I'm pretty sure he's long gone now. His real name is Mathew; you know, the person of interest in the lady's locker room incident. We don't have any evidence or witnesses about her disappearance, so we had no choice but to let him go, and with Mary not here to press charges for the assault on her." She shrugs again, "There's nothing else we can do."

She reaches into her pocket and pulls out a business card, "Here's my number. If you think of anything that can help us find the girl, give me a call." She studies his face for a moment. "Are you a veteran?"

"Yes, ma'am. I served in the Air National Guard."

She nods, "Thanks for your service." Then she stands up and walks out of the coffee shop.

#

Still seated in his truck, William slowly consumes his roast beef sub. He's tired, and the thought of unloading ten 50-lb bags of animal feed from the flatbed behind him makes him want to procrastinate even longer. The house looks ominously quiet, the lights are off, and there's no sign of any activity inside. He guesses Olivia must have taken a nap with the twins. After the morning he had, he doesn't dare look at his text messages, but he forces himself to check them while finishing his late lunch.

The first message he opens is from Ian, who wants a status report; the next dozen or so messages are also from Ian, who appears frantic. Then he scrolls down and sees Olivia was hysterically looking for him, which is very unusual for her. He reads her message about him needing to bring the truck back so she can pick up the kids from their playdate at 3. He looks at his watch and exclaims out loud, "Oh shit."

Then he worries that she took an Uber to get them. The thought of another added expense makes him cringe. He glances back at the large bags of feed he needs to unload and feels a pit form in his stomach, unsure where the money will come from to pay for them when the MasterCard bill is due.

He gulps his Coke and pauses to consider what to tell Ian. The call goes straight to voicemail, but before he can leave a message, a text arrives. *At work, can't talk!*

William replies to him, *All is good!* Which he knows is not entirely true, but there's no need for Ian to continue to worry about the brawl in the ladies' locker room any longer.

William steps out of his truck and stretches his tired legs. He feels relieved that he can move on from that messy situation, but genuinely feels sorry for Mary, the missing girl.

Then, all at once, the thought of having to move 500 pounds of animal feed to the barn with a hangover makes him nauseous, and he throws up his roast beef sandwich.

While he's cleaning up with a rag from his backseat, he hears a vehicle pulling into his driveway, and it stops. That's when William overhears Shane, who is caught off guard, saying to someone on the phone, "See, I told you it would be worth the trouble, and I knew you'd like him. Oh, he's here, gotta go."

William is just not in the mood for Shane. He heads straight into his garage without so much as a hi or a how are you? He takes the envelope of cash, the remaining unsold dose of human growth hormone, and the burner phone from its hiding place, then walks directly over to Shane, who is standing outside his white van, waiting for him.

Walking toward him, William takes a closer look at Shane. He thinks Shane looks drunk or high because of his strange body movements, runny nose, and glazed eyes.

When William is face-to-face with him, he restrains himself from what he wants to tell him, and all he says is, "Here's your filthy money - I quit!" then walks into the house and slams the door behind him.

CHAPTER TEN — ROAD RUNNER

IAN

With the help of the organ transplant rapid response team, Ian quickly finishes loading the Chevy Equinox at UMass Memorial Medical Center in Worcester.

Based on the limited information shared during the handoff about the organ donor, Ian suspects this case was similar to other common scenarios. In transplant terms, this means the recently deceased person was likely another fentanyl overdose victim who was kept on life support until a suitable match was found and arrangements were made to transport all viable organs, ensuring nothing was wasted.

Suddenly, his iPhone rings and startles him, and he reflexively hits an auto-response without even looking down to see who called.

He can't talk at work, so he turns off his ringer at the same time. Then he straps himself into his seat and grips the steering wheel with both hands. His body shifts into fight-or-flight mode as he recognizes the danger of weaving in and out of traffic while driving 90 to 100 mph, running red lights, and rolling through stop signs.

His palms are sweaty as he flips on the flashing lights and blaring sirens of his well-marked A.O.R.A. Medical Transport vehicle. His destination is Logan Airport, and although he's tempted to check his messages, he doesn't dare look down at his iPhone because what he's transporting could mean the difference between life and death for the recipient awaiting it. From the moment he departs Worcester until he reaches his drop-off, his focus remains on one thing: delivering the package.

"Siri, directions to United Airlines."

Siri is activated, "Starting route to United Airlines, traffic is light, estimated drive time is 51 minutes." He thinks to himself that he'd better get there in less than 35 minutes, or he'll miss his scheduled flight. Siri continues, "Turn right at the next traffic light, then head east on I-90."

Ian has driven this route so many times that he can anticipate each turn as he makes his way onto the Mass Pike and heads to the airport. As he speeds up, the cars in front of him pull over to the right and respectfully get out of his way. To this day, he can't understand why someone doesn't move aside for an emergency vehicle; the lack of empathy boggles his mind. As he speeds up a bit more, he reflects on how he's so grateful he got his red-light certification while serving in the National Guard. If it weren't for it, he wouldn't be qualified for his current job.

Turning off his iPhone's ringer had never been an issue for him before this trip. He doesn't have a spouse or kids, unlike many of his coworkers at A.O.R.A., which stands for the American Organ Recovery Alliance. But lurking in the back of his mind is, Why haven't I heard back from William? I wonder if that was him just now?

Ian itches to glance down at his messages as a bunch of unanswered questions flood his mind, like, how did Joe from the gym know what I do for work without me ever sharing that? And whatever happened to Mary O'Keefe, the missing Irish girl? And the biggest question of all: why, after all these years, has William never introduced him to his wife and family, then suddenly invites him over for Thanksgiving dinner? What was up with that?

Ian glances down at his speedometer; he's driving 92 mph and will reach his destination in 14 more minutes. Poor Mary, he thinks, anything could have happened to her. She might have been abducted, or she's just running from fear of being deported. Who knows? Maybe it was her boyfriend who harmed her, and he's getting away with it because of the kerfuffle he and William caused when they rushed to help her in the gym that night.

It just doesn't seem logical to him that the guy dressed as a woman who was accosting her in the ladies' locker room would have done anything except lie low and go home after the beating William gave him. Still, he thinks to himself, I'm not a cop and really don't have a clue what makes a pervert tick. From that point forward, anything could have happened to her.

It never occurred to him before how badly immigrants have it, how easy it is to take advantage of them, and when one of them disappears, nobody seems to care. Ian feels a knot form in his stomach as he recalls the police detective's question, which echoes deeply in his subconscious: "Why didn't one of you heroes offer her a ride home?"

That's when he remembers Joe did go out to the parking lot to check if she was all right, and with a pang of guilt, Ian reflects on the real reason he didn't pursue it. He was still hoping to meet up with his drug connection that night. He decides right then and there, enough is enough. I'm done! No more illegal drugs!

Then he takes the off-ramp and follows the signs to Terminal B. When he arrives, he pulls up to the curb. A state trooper follows his vehicle and signals Ian to proceed. The trooper remains parked behind the Equinox with his marked car's lights flashing.

Ian opens the cargo door of the Equinox. He takes the clearly labeled human organ container out and runs it to the ticket counter, cutting ahead of everyone else waiting in line for check-in at United.

Without apologizing, he hands the paperwork to the ticket agent, and she smiles before saying, "You just made it." He takes a photo of her and the paperwork. Then she sends the package of human organs, along with the rest of the luggage for the flight, right after tagging it with priority stickers. She continues, "You do nice work."

"Thanks," he says, then thinks to himself, " Is she flirting with me? He looks her up and down and decides she's not his type. She's waiting for more of a response from him and stares him in the eyes. "I gotta head back to our base in Waltham, as I'm still on the clock." Which is true, but not the real reason for his abrupt departure.

She looks disappointed when he turns to walk away.

When he returns to the Equinox, he finds the state trooper has stayed behind to guard it. The trooper waves to him with a courteous salute as he drives away. Ian truly appreciates the help he gets from the men and women in blue. They often drive alongside with their sirens on to support or stand guard while on a run, because in today's world, almost anything marked as emergency medical is often a magnet for junkies or unscrupulous people looking to steal something.

As soon as Ian is back in his Equinox, he turns off the flashing lights and finally checks his messages. He's relieved to see William's text; all is good, but he feels an eerie sense that things are truly far from that.

#

For the rest of his shift, Ian will be on call, meaning he will pick up labs, often from a patient on life support who is near death, and transport them between the potential donor and a testing center. During testing, it's quickly determined whether there's a donor match using UNOS, which stands for the United Network for Organ Sharing.

However, before wasting any time, a complete medical history is taken, and screening for diseases such as cancer, tuberculosis, mad cow disease, hepatitis, and HIV/AIDS is done. Of course, this isn't always the case, since a recipient might already have one or more of these diseases, like HIV/AIDS. In such situations, the organ could still be considered a suitable match.

Ian is starving when he returns to base, but he's pretty fed up with eating the same snacks every shift. Still, he looks forward to the comfy reclining lounge chairs, which are really nice to relax in during a quiet all-night shift.

When he enters the lounge, nobody's there except Fred, one of the older transporters who keeps to himself and isn't much of a conversationalist.

He asks Fred, "Where is everyone?"

"My guess, out on runs," grunts Fred.

Ian is curious and asks, "What's up with you?"

Fred glances at his watch. "I'm scheduled. Gettin' some shut-eye now. It's gonna be a long haul." He sits in the recliner and puts his feet up as he leans back.

Ian asks, "Where?"

Fred replies, "UMass med for a heart, pair of lungs, kidneys, and a pancreas."

"You think it's another fentanyl fatality?"

Fred shrugs his shoulders in indifference, but Ian presses on with his questions despite it being obvious he's not interested in talking. "Are you picking up the extraction team first in the Suburban?"

"Yeah, Brigham and Women's and bringin' them out to Woostah and then back to their transplant center with the goods." Fred expounds in a grumpy, annoyed tone.

Ian asks, "On Francis St?"

"No, furtha down on the corna of Binney and Fenwood."

"Good luck," says Ian, even though he wants to add Godspeed, but he can see Fred's not in the mood.

Ian wishes he were on the schedule with just about anyone else from work, like Sheryl, Rick, or even Arty, who sometimes talks a little too much about what he's overheard from the doctors he transports. Still, any one of them would have started up a card game like Texas Hold'em or ordered in some Chinese takeout and had the courtesy to split the bill four ways.

Fred turns to Ian and says sharply, "If you don't want to get some shut-eye, then get the eff out of here and let me sleep!"

Ian's fragile feelings get hurt, so he goes to the kitchen to look over takeout menus and sulk when his instructions for his next pickup arrive on his iPhone before he has a chance to order anything.

"Brockton Hospital." He reads aloud while grabbing some snacks and a drink for the ride. At least this trip won't be with white-knuckles and clenched teeth because it's just labs.

He jumps back into the driver's seat, starts his vehicle while he chews the rest of his stale chocolate chip cookie, and hits the road.

#

When Ian returns to A.O.R.A. in Waltham, his eyes are dry and burning, and he's too exhausted to feel hungry. He can't wait to punch out after his twelve-hour shift, pick up Scout at the Pooch Hotel in Newton, and head home to get some sleep.

As he drives up Bear Hill Road, he notices flashing police lights in the parking lot outside his workplace. Flashing lights and sirens are common, but a visit from State Troopers isn't. He pulls into his parking spot and heads inside to see what's happening.

His boss, Stan, looks disheveled in his mismatched hoodie and sweatpants, as if he had been abruptly awakened and brought in to handle an emergency.

Stan says gratefully to the police officer, "And here he is now. Ian, have a seat."

Ian has no idea what's happening, and his heart is pounding with fear, because he thought everything regarding the incident at the gym was over. His mouth goes dry, and his mind begins playing frightening tricks on him.

The state trooper introduces himself as Sergeant Jackson. He looks him directly in the eyes when he asks, "Ian, was there anything unusual about your package drop-off you made at United tonight?"

Ian shakes his head no, wondering if his week could get any stranger.

Jackson continues, "I'm not even sure who should be leading this investigation or what kind of investigation this actually is." He glances down at his phone and then looks at Stan. "Well, it isn't us any longer."

Stan is confounded, "Why's that for Christ's sake?"

Jackson tries to explain, "The human organs were reported missing."

Stan corroborates, "Yes."

Jackson reads his message from his phone and looks back up again at Stan. "So this is not a missing person's case because the person who donated the organ is already dead, and this is not a homicide unless the organ recipient dies waiting for the stolen or lost kidneys. That would be at best involuntary manslaughter, and I just received word that the lost container marked 'human organs for transplant' was found at Hopkins Airport in Cleveland and is with the rest of the lost luggage. Sadly, it was run over by somebody driving a luggage transport and not looking where they were going."

Stan is upset and asks, "Is there more?"

Jackson clicks off his phone and puts it in his pocket while he replies, "Nope."

Stan looks around while trying to decide what should be done next and scratches his head in disbelief.

Ian politely asks, "What happened to the organ recipient at the Cleveland Clinic? Will they make it there in time with the kidney?"

Stan's face turns a ghostly white when he reaches for his phone. "I know who to call, give me a sec. I'll find out." He doesn't say another word. He taps a number, then breathes hard and listens to the person on the other end talk for about a minute before Stan says, "Best of luck and our prayers, too."

Then Stan ends the call and reveals, "The accident didn't make the kidney unviable, and the young woman is in transplant surgery as we speak."

Ian raises a fist in the air and exclaims, "Hell yeah!"

Jackson smiles when he affirms, "Mission accomplished." Then he sees himself out of A.O.R.A. through the staff pantry, where he helps himself to a stale Dunkin' jelly donut that he eats on his way to his cruiser.

CHAPTER ELEVEN — OUT OF SYNC

WILLIAM

As William walks past the entryway mirror near the front door, he notices his face is covered with grease from the roast beef sandwich he devoured in the truck. He scowls as he tries to wipe it off with his sleeve, but misses the spot. Then he heads toward the refrigerator in search of a beer.

He smiles and thinks, *Hair of the dog*. That's exactly what I need right now, because his head is still spinning from the dirty martinis, wine, and port he drank the night before during Thanksgiving dinner.

The house is too quiet; the old grandfather clock's tick is noticeably loud as its long pendulum swings back and forth. He pauses to look around, feeling a chill in the air. He can sense his late mother's presence everywhere, especially with the smells from Thanksgiving dinner lingering in the house.

He fondly remembers how she would call out to him from the other room to ask about his day and whether he was hungry. His family's roots run deep into the Massachusetts soil. On his mother's side, they are said to be the illegitimate descendants of the loyalist General Howe and the adulterous wife of William Loring, who fought for the King of England during the Revolutionary War.

His father's family traces back to pre-antebellum New Englanders, mainly farmers, some blacksmiths, and a few lobster fishermen. His mother's and father's families were so intertwined through the generations that they shared mutual cousins on both sides. Yet, most of them are now gone, nameless ghosts.

He takes a sip of his beer and feels immediate relief from his hangover. He wonders when Olivia and the kids will be home. He checks his iPhone, and there are no new messages since 2:30, when she needed the truck to pick up the twins. When he looks outside, the streetlight comes on as it's dusk.

Eventually, Hattie's truck pulls into the driveway, and Olivia takes Charlie from the back seat, carrying her toward the house. William steps outside to help and quietly walks over to get Henry, who is also sound asleep. He gently lifts him up and immediately notices from the smell that his little guy had an accident in his pants.

Henry wakes up and asks, "Daddy, are we home?"

William comforts him and says, "Go back to sleep, and yes, you're home." Henry gently nuzzles his head into his father's warm neck.

When William walks into the house, Olivia passes him as she leaves, and he asks, "Where are you going?"

Unhappily, Olivia explains, "I'm bringing Hattie's truck back to her." She pauses briefly, then looks out the door before adding, "You know something, William, she saved my life today."

"Want me to pick you up?" He asks.

"Nope!" She replies adamantly.

"It's cold outside, and the coyotes are out now," he affirms.

"I'm still hot from fuming over…" She stammers and is speechless, "From everything! Just let me go." She pushes his hand off her shoulder, walks out, and drives off to return Hattie's truck.

William takes Henry upstairs, changes him out of his wet clothes, and puts him into his pajamas. Then he asks, "You hungry?"

Henry nods yes.

William holds his son on his hip and checks on Charlotte, who is deeply asleep.

Downstairs in the kitchen, he looks inside the refrigerator. It's filled with dishes wrapped in tin foil, and the leftover turkey occupies half a shelf.

"Want some turkey for dinner?"

Henry says, "Yucky."

"Ok then, what would you prefer?"

"Noodles and cheese, please." Henry's statement is in an accent similar to his mother's. William finds this amusing while he searches for a box of Kraft Macaroni and Cheese. To his surprise, he sees Annie's pasture-raised organic variety instead of his old favorite from when he was a kid, which was, of course, Kraft. He switches Henry from his right hip to his left, then fills the small pot with tap water and places it on the stove. Henry taps his father on his back with his small, open hand before wiping his face on his shirt.

William needs two hands to finish making Henry's dinner, so he places him at the kitchen table and reaches for a strainer for the noodles.

"Want a glass of milk?" He asks his son.

Henry nods yes and watches his father prepare his dinner. It's a rare occasion for the two of them to be alone together. Henry is curious about this sudden change in their routine and asks, "Where's mother?"

William nonchalantly explains, "She's at Hattie's and should return soon." Then he scoops a large spoonful of the mac and cheese into Henry's bowl and bites off the remaining noodles clinging to the wooden spoon, still convinced that the original is far superior, as far as he's concerned.

He stretches his neck to look out the kitchen window to see if Olivia is walking up the driveway, but there's no sign of her in the darkness. Then he wonders what's taking her so long as he puts the large roasting pan from the night before in the cabinet over the refrigerator.

He looks at his son, who is enjoying his dinner, and says, "Tell me about your day."

Henry smiles, "It was fun. We ate chocolate chip cookies." Henry thinks for a second, "And they had puppies. I want to go there again tomorrow."

William says, "Maybe not tomorrow, but I'm sure Mommy will bring you back soon. I'm going to check on Charlie and see if she's awake." Henry waves goodbye.

William finds Charlie wide awake and dressed in her Princess Elsa costume. He pauses in the doorway of the twins' room and asks her, "Would the Princess like to join us for a dinner of Mac & Cheese?"

And sounding just like her mother, she replies, "Oh yes, please."

William chuckles at how proper she sounds and how adorable it is. He reaches down and sweeps her off her feet. She giggles out loud as they head down the stairs to the kitchen.

"Where's Henry?" she asks.

"At the table waiting for you to join him, Your Majesty."

Charlie likes it when her daddy talks to her like that, and she gives him a big hug.

William feels a calmness and peace he hasn't experienced in a while. He's pleased with himself for saying, "I quit" to Dr. Shane Ferguson, the veterinarian. He has no idea how he's going to pay his bills this winter, but he looks around and appreciates how much he risked by doing that lame stunt for Shane. That was a close call with the law, too close, and he never wants to go through that ever again.

That's when he thinks about his buddy Ian's dysmorphia and how he must be hooked on that stuff he uses to pump up his body. He's also worried about leaving him in Dr. Ferguson's greedy clutches. Next, he decides he needs to have "the talk" with Ian without revealing how he knows about his dependence on human growth hormone and help him to get off of them.

CHAPTER TWELVE — A ZINGER

OLIVIA

Hattie left the bay door open for Olivia. She pulls in, parks Hattie's truck, hops out, and takes a deep breath before walking toward her house to return the keys and thank her for everything she did today. There's an unfamiliar Toyota Corolla parked by the front door. Olivia hesitates before knocking because she doesn't want to intrude, but it's already too late, Hattie's black pug mix, Edgar, is on the other side of the door barking excitedly.

Hattie says in a raspy voice, "It's unlocked, come in."

Olivia's eyes open wide as she sees Hattie sitting in her recliner, getting an intravenous infusion from an attractive, perfectly manicured nurse. Edgar hops into her lap and adopts a defensive, protective stance. Hattie pets him until he calms down and curls up across her lap.

Olivia is a bit surprised by the unexpected medical procedure and wants to apologize for interrupting, but she struggles to find the right words. "Hattie, here are your keys. Is there anything I can do for you?"

Hattie groans as if she's in pain but doesn't reply. The nurse checks on Hattie and helps her reposition her pillow. Then she turns to Olivia and says, "Hi, I'm Dawn, one of Hattie's nurses."

"Hi Dawn, I'm Olivia, and I live across the street and down a little bit. Can I bring some dinner over for you both? We have plenty of turkey and leftovers."

Dawn looks at Hattie while taking her blood pressure and asks, "Hattie, your neighbor is offering to bring you supper. Are you interested?"

Hattie shakes her head no and mumbles, "Too tired to eat, but thanks. If you wouldn't mind, Olivia, please feed Edgar and take him for his last walk of the day, thanks."

Olivia kindly goes over to Hattie to pick up her dog from her lap, and the dog growls and shows her his teeth when she reaches for him. When she finally lifts him, she notices that the IV line is connected directly to a port in Hattie's chest. Olivia wants to ask her about it and the intravenous procedure, but she stops herself. Dawn watches as Olivia backs away with Edgar, remaining silent.

It's becoming difficult for Hattie to speak. "Olivia, Edgar's food is on the counter, and it's labeled." Olivia smiles as she remembers how well everything in the laboratory was labeled and how cute some of the notes were. Hattie seems to love to use her label maker.

Olivia finds Hattie's kitchen is clean and well-organized. Edgar's food sits on the counter in a Tupperware container labeled 'dinner.' Olivia bends down to collect Edgar's water and food bowls, rinses and dries them, then refills them.

Edgar quickly devours his food. Olivia looks at him and speaks. "Want to go for a walk?" Edgar wiggles with joy, wags his tail, and runs to the kitchen door.

Conveniently, Olivia discovers his coat and leash hanging next to the door. She puts them on him, and they head out into the dark, cold night under an overcast sky.

Olivia isn't exactly sure where to take him, so she follows Edgar's lead. He pulls her toward the elm trees at the end of the driveway, where he does his business. She says, "Good boy, Edgar." Then she pets him on his head.

Afterward, she struggles to find Edgar's poop mixed with the dried-out, dead leaves. She picks it up with one of the bags stored on the leash and throws it in the barrel on her way back into the house.

The moment they're inside, and Edgar is released from his leash, he runs back to Hattie and jumps into her lap again. Hattie pulls Edgar under her blanket to warm him up before she says, "That was fast, thanks."

Olivia is trying to pretend everything about this is normal and adds, "He was in a hurry to be back with you, I think."

Hattie glances at Dawn and asks, "How much longer?"

Dawn looks closely at the bag of fluid and says, "We're about halfway now, Hattie. How are you feeling?"

She replies, "I'm tired, and I'm getting IVIG brain again."

Olivia asks, "What's that?"

Hattie continues, "It's one of the side effects. The treatment can make me feel forgetful and confused."

Olivia is curious and asks, "What are you being treated for, Hattie?"

"Oh, this," she glances at the bag of fluid, "it's for a slow-growing leukemia."

"That sounds ominous." Dawn looks at Olivia with a sad expression, but does not add anything to Hattie's explanation. "What's IVIG?" Olivia continues to ask.

Hattie waves off, replying because she's getting too tired from her treatment to talk.

Dawn steps in for Hattie and explains, "It's intravenous immunoglobulin, which includes donor antibodies that help to bolster the patient's immune system."

Olivia worries her visit is too exhausting for Hattie and says, "I think I should be going."

"No, no, no... stay!" commands Hattie just before she nods off.

Dawn checks Hattie's pulse, oxygen level, and blood pressure while she's asleep.

Olivia begs, "Is she OK?"

Dawn replies, "She's just tired from her IVIG treatment. Her vital signs are good. She'll probably wake up again in a few minutes, so how well do you know Hattie?"

Olivia feels embarrassed by Dawn's question because she knows very little about Hattie. "I moved here about four years ago when I married William. We've twins, a boy and a girl, and I was pretty busy with them until now, but since they're practically potty trained, I've been able to spend more time getting to know her better. How about you?"

Dawn looks at the ceiling before she replies, "I 'm not supposed to discuss my patients, HIPAA prohibits me, but..." She lowers her voice to a whisper, "She's one of my favorites, and I wish I could get some food into her, plus get her to quit smoking. Whatever." At the same time, they both look over and notice Hattie is petting Edgar with her eyes closed.

Dawn gently rouses Hattie, "Welcome back, how are you feeling?"

"What's this day, two or three, Dawn?"

Dawn looks over Hattie's chart, "Day two, darlin'."

Hattie exclaims, "Dawn, I think I'm feeling a zing."

Dawn comments, "Nice! I could use one right now."

Olivia is intrigued. "What's a zing?"

Dawn offers, "It's an unexplained burst of energy that patients experience while getting an infusion."

Hattie straightens herself up in her chair, looking sprightly as if possessed by magic, and says, "Enough with walking around the elephant in the room. What's up with your marriage? William's been acting deranged."

Olivia doesn't know what to say but tries her best. "Well, he's always mad at me about everything. Whatever I do isn't good enough. He's not interested in me sexually, and whatever I say is..."

Dawn interrupts her, "Wow, are you sure we're not married to the same guy? You've just described my husband to a T." And they all laugh.

Olivia is thrilled to be able to discuss her problems and ask questions, such as, "Is this normal?"

Dawn hesitates to think and then says, "I hope not."

Olivia says, "He is always stressed out about money."

Dawn compares her situation and adds, "My husband, too. We own our own construction business, so it's feast or famine depending on the cycles with interest rates and the economy, but the cost of supplies has been brutal this past year, and my guy is in a terrible mood almost all the time."

Hattie interjects, "Olivia, go into the kitchen; you must be starving. Grab something to nibble on and bring us both a glass of wine. Dawn, would you like anything?"

Dawn criticizes her, "I'm not sure if drinking alcohol while getting IVIG is a good idea, Hattie."

Hattie defends her decision, "I'll only take a few sips, OK?"

Dawn nods in agreement. Olivia heads to the fridge and is shocked by how empty it is. There's a half-full bottle of Far Niente Chardonnay on the door and a variety of Cabot's cheeses in the bin. Olivia makes a tray with cheese and crackers and sets it on the side table next to Hattie.

Hattie's eyes light up when she sees the tray arrive, and she begs, "Where's my glass of wine?"

Olivia suggests, "Let's eat some nibbles, and I'll go get it next trip."

Dawn winks at Olivia with approval for getting Hattie to eat. It's almost like they've just had a psychic mind meld.

Hattie struggles with her cracker and cheese. Then she demands, "What about my glass of wine?"

"Coming right up after you finish what's on the plate," Olivia confirms, feeling embarrassed to talk to Hattie the same way she does with Charlotte and Henry when they push their vegetables around their plates.

Hattie points to the nearly empty dish with a mouthful of food and shows Olivia a thumbs-up.

"All right, I'll be right back. Dawn, can I get you a glass?"

Dawn replies, "No thanks."

Olivia returns with the bottle and two glasses. "Here you go, Hattie."

Hattie takes a sip and sinks back into her recliner, swirling her glass with a look of relief on her face. "George was a saint to bring me a case of good wine for the long holiday weekend. He's a godsend."

"Why don't you two live together?" Olivia innocently inquires.

Ebulliently, Hattie reveals, "George lives in an over-55 community ten minutes from here. They host lovely events that we attend together; he loves being there. Plays Texas Hold'em every Wednesday night, likes his biweekly pickleball game when the weather permits, and except for when somebody doesn't show up for work at his grocery store in Sherborn, he's pretty much retired. Why should he give up what he likes?"

Dawn coughs as if she's trying to say something and looks at Hattie, urging her to be more truthful. "Ok, Dawn, why do you think we live apart?" Hattie takes a big swig of her Chardonnay and says, "Ah, nice," ignoring Dawn's stare.

This infuriates Dawn, and she exclaims, "Butts!"

Hattie rolls her eyes, and Olivia patiently waits for her to reveal the truth: "He won't live with me unless I quit smoking." She finally admits. "My choice is between butts or to live with George. In any case, one or the other is going to be the death of me. So, hah!"

Hattie tries to change the subject: "Olivia, I know you're busy raising kids, but there are many ways you can increase your family's income. William is a lot like his father, proud, intractable, and a blockhead if you know what I mean."

Olivia lights up when she asks, "Like how? We really could use some good advice."

Hattie explains, "Dog breeding, horse breeding, which I'm already teaching you, riding lessons, exotic chicken eggs, selling some of the wine his parents left behind, and so on. I know it's winter, and no one wants to stand outside in the cold during a lesson. You can use my indoor arena for a small share of the profits once you're established."

Olivia is beginning to feel some of Hattie's energetic zing. "This sounds incredible. "What kind of dogs should we breed, partner?"

Dawn is pleased that Hattie is thinking positively and making plans for the future. She knows that it's key for a patient with cancer to have an optimistic outlook, and she confirms, "Hattie, I like where this is going. I think you should breed those fancy designer dogs like Labradoodles or puggle-puggles.

Hattie pauses for a moment and admits, "As much as I love my Edgar, my pug-poodle mix, don't I, Edgar?" She kisses him. "I think we need something much more exotic to make us some real money."

"Like what?" They both ask her.

Hattie smiles as she reveals, "How about Chinese Cresteds?"

Olivia Googles the breed and reads her findings out loud, "Hmm, rare, they have lots of awful, inbred diseases, they're ugly as sin, can't be in the sun ever, and are as expensive as hell. Sounds perfect!" She says sarcastically.

Hattie is feeling pretty good and continues, "Olivia, I want you to find us some puppies for our new business, and can you do it straight away?"

Dawn stands up and walks over to Hattie's empty IVIG bag and unclips it from the pump before she announces, "You're all done, darlin'."

Hattie comments, "Wow, it went by so fast. Are you coming back tomorrow, Dawn?"

She replies, "No, I'm taking the day off to drive my son to his hockey tournament. It will be Joanna from the office; she said she'd cover for me because she misses her time with you."

Hattie adds, "You know she's a real-life cowgirl from West Texas, so I bet you it's Ken and Barbie she wants to see more than me."

"One more set of vitals and I'm out of here, Hattie."

As Dawn wraps the blood pressure cuff around Hattie's arm, Hattie places her hand over Dawn's and squeezes it. "You know you're my favorite, too, Dawn."

Dawn blushes when she realizes Hattie was listening to her talk about her earlier that night. She puts on her overcoat, zips it up, and leans over to stroke Hattie's hair, "In case I'm not assigned to you for your next infusion, I want to wish you an early Merry Christmas."

Hattie echoes, "Same to you, Dawn."

The second Dawn leaves, Hattie jumps up and says, "My goodness, all that fluid makes me have to go pee. Watch, I'll be up half the night tonight, and I was starting to worry she'd never leave!"

Olivia swirls the remainder of her Chardonnay in her glass and drinks it in one gulp while Hattie is gone, then she refills both of their glasses with the last bit at the bottom of the bottle.

Hattie returns, takes a sip, and says, "I'm having a smoke. Want one?"

"No thanks," says Olivia, even though for a moment she felt tempted.

"One of the visiting nurses' conditions for allowing me to receive these treatments at home is that I can't smoke around them. Jesus H. Christ, what took her so long to leave? I was starting to go nuts from nicotine withdrawal."

This amuses Olivia, and she asks her, "Why not get some Nicorette gum?" She's happy to see Hattie back to being the curmudgeon she knows and loves.

"Not a bad idea, Olivia, but there's something I want to ask you before we enter into a partnership."

"Sure."

"Why don't you have any family besides William and the kids?" asks Hattie.

Olivia takes a breath first, but there's no reason to hide the truth from Hattie. "My family, where should I start? My parents are alive; they never married, which makes me a bastard. My dad is Romani, as you so gleefully call a Gypsy. My mother comes from an old English line of Hackney drivers, dating back to when it meant horse and carriage, not today's taxi. My mom is a bit fragile. She earned her living teaching piano lessons. I also have an older half-brother I've never met, who is a pseudo-celebrity jazz musician, like our father.

"That's all very nice, Olivia, but what stopped you from talking to each other?"

"How did you come to know this?" she worries.

"William briefly mentioned it when he was having second thoughts about marrying you."

Olivia admits, "It's true, we haven't spoken since I ran off like a miscreant fool to Boston, but it's just me and my mum."

Hattie puts out her cigarette, rests her hands on her lap, and folds her gnarly fingers over each other. "I don't know what happened to make you stop talking to your mother, but if you want to be my business partner, I'd like you to clean up your past messes before we move forward. Capisce.

Olivia responds, "Capisce." And then sticks her tongue out at Hattie like a child when Hattie looks away.

#

Olivia returns to a quiet house. When she enters the kitchen, she immediately notices that the pots, pans, trays, and platters from Thanksgiving have all been put away, and the kitchen is clean. She opens the dishwasher and sees Charlie and Henry's dishes and silverware, but no large plates and forks from William's dinner. The table is set for two, and the oven is preheated to 350 degrees. She thinks to herself, *This is the hottest thing William has ever done*, and she pours herself her third glass of wine. Then she reaches into the fridge to grab a turkey leg and ravenously takes big bites out of it.

William suddenly appears from the sofa in the living room. "I must have dozed off while waiting for you."

Olivia offers him a bite of her turkey leg and pulls out a couple of tin-foil-wrapped packages from the fridge as they stuff their faces with cold leftovers and wash it all down with the rest of the wine George brought the night before.

Olivia asks, "Are we good?"

William responds, "We're good, but I'm going to have to get a side job to boost our income. I'm not going to be able to hold on much longer without it."

"Let's talk about finances later." Then she reaches for William's T-shirt and pulls it over his head. He responds by passionately embracing her and then pulling her sweater over her head.

They make their way to the sofa while enjoying the best part of a fight - kissing and making up.

CHAPTER THIRTEEN — NOT QUALIFIED

IAN

Ian wakes up feeling refreshed after a whole night's sleep in his bed. Scout is cuddled close beside him, his head tucked under the covers to block out the sunlight filtering through the blinds.

"Alexa, what's the temperature outside?"

"Right now, it's 41 degrees Fahrenheit with mostly clear skies, and today's high will be 57 degrees, with a low of 39 degrees tonight."

Ian thinks to himself. This is perfect running weather.

Scout rolls over and looks at Ian for his morning belly rub. As much as Ian wants to check his iPhone, he needs both of his hands to deal with his dog.

While rubbing Scout's belly, he fantasizes about how wonderful a real relationship would be, especially going into the holidays. Scout would be able to sleep at home in his bed and not the kennel when he goes on overnight runs, and he would have someone to spend Christmas and New Year's Eve with instead of hanging out in a poorly decorated, cheesy bar waiting for the ball to drop all by himself.

He gets up and heads to the toilet. After relieving himself, he weighs himself: 152 pounds, down three from his last weigh-in. Since he ran out of steroids, he's lost a total of six pounds. His shirts and pants feel loose, and he's not happy about it. He makes a muscle with his arm and examines it in the mirror of the medicine cabinet; he believes, for now, that it's still an impressive display of his masculinity even without synthetic enhancement. He decides to ignore his declining physique and instead begins to scrutinize his hairline closely. He studies it from left to right and glances down as far as he can see. He notices the undeniable progression of his hair loss.

"Hey Alexa, I'd like to reorder Nutrafol for Men."

"That's $88 with delivery by tomorrow. I've put it in your cart, you can say buy it now."

"Whoa, I forgot how much it cost. Alexa, buy it now."

After a long pause, Alexa responds. "I can help you shop; would you like to reorder paper towels?"

Ian is frustrated and says, "Just forget about it." He pulls on his sweatpants and a thick hoodie sweatshirt and announces, "Let's go, Scout."

While waiting for his dog to do his business, Ian finally checks his text messages. There's a new one from William: *"Want to go for a run?"*

He replies, *"Yes, when?"*

Instantly, there's a response, *"Now?"*

He replies, "*Sure. See you at the Rail Trail in Holliston. Leaving in 15 minutes.*"

#

Finding parking on Mayflower Landing takes Ian a bit longer than he expected, but he doesn't see William's truck yet, so he tells himself to stay calm as he goes up the street for the third time and finally finds a space.

Then, there's a tap on his window, and when he looks up, it's William, catching his breath. Ian gets out of his Equinox and greets his friend, "Hey, where did you come from?"

William explains, still breathing hard and pointing with his thumb, "Parked on the Sherborn side of the trail. It's too hard to find spots over here, so I ran the rest of the way. What took you so long?"

"I hadn't eaten or fed the dog yet," Ian replies defensively as he begins to add more to his story.

William isn't interested in the extended version because he's short on leisure time, so he prompts, "How about to the Bogastow Brook Viaduct and back?"

Ian complains, "Seriously, I came all this way to run a mile?"

"All right, to Phipps Tunnel then." Ian takes a sip from his water bottle and does some warm-up stretches, then he announces, "Let's go!"

Most of the trees overhanging the path are already bare, letting the sun shine through on this crisp Saturday morning. Ian has many unanswered questions swirling in his mind and wants to compare notes with William about Mary's disappearance and their recent run-in with the law. Plus, this is his first chance to ask him about the burner phone he's dying to bring up.

He decides to focus on Mary first. "Dude, what happened at the police station?"

"Never went."

Ian stops running. "What the hell?"

William cuts him off, "The detective met me at Dunks."

Ian is intrigued. "So, what did you think of her?"

William wants to change the subject and talk about his job prospects, but all Ian seems to focus on is the police detective and his day in the holding tank.

William tries to shift the conversation. "The detective told me Mary was here illegally and either went into hiding or ran back home to Ireland. Oh, and because Mary went missing, the pervert got scared and probably took off."

He slows down to catch his breath and notices Ian staring at his worn-out basketball sneakers. Then he recalls what the detective said to him last and repeats it to Ian, "She also said we'll probably never hear from either of them ever again."

Ian admits, "I feel awful we didn't do more for her, and guilty that we might have made things worse by trying to help. Did the detective add anything else?"

"Oh yeah," she said, "Nobody cares."

Ian looks deflated when he goes digging for info on the burner phone, which he recently found William has, and asks, "What's up with you and Olivia? Things good?"

William smiles and says, "We're good, money's tight, so I really need to find a job fast." He looks Ian in the eyes and asks, "Are they hiring transporters at A.O.R.A.?"

Ian seriously wants to help him, but he must ask his friend first, "Help me, I've forgotten. How many years did you serve in the Guard?" They keep running, but at a slower pace, while they talk.

"Four."

Ian thinks it's not good enough. He then asks, "College?"

"Mass Bay Community, but only for two years, because after my folks died, I was broke."

Ian knew William was an orphan when they met during their time in the National Guard, but William never mentioned his age when they were in the accident. He probes further, "Any Degrees?"

"An associate degree in Biology with a minor in Agriculture."

"What are your certifications?"

William smirks, "Servesafe and TIPS from waiting tables and bartending during college, too many certifications to list from my EMT days back when I worked with you in the guard. Let me see, I passed my CPR-BLS, I'm NREMT certified, and a bunch of other stuff like that."

Ian probes further, "Did you maintain your certification?"

"I'm not sure. I'll look into it."

Ian scowls, "You're so close, but they require five years minimum; military, fire, or police, plus you need to have your red-light certified driver's license. The only part of your EMT service they'll look at is your ability to drive quickly and remain calm under pressure. Remember, we mostly transport people who have already died, and their transplant teams."

Feeling disappointed, William adds, "So all my skills with administering Narcan, CPR, and heart paddles will just go to waste."

"Pretty much," Ian confirms.

William persists, "Do you think it's worth pursuing?"

Ian reluctantly smiles before he says, "Of course it is, and I'll put in a good word for you. How soon do you need to start?"

"Yesterday," says William as he picks up the pace and runs ahead of Ian by a few lengths. All he can think about is his looming MasterCard bill, which is due along with his expensive animal feed, the second-quarter real estate tax payment, and whatever else Olivia charged on it this month. He suddenly feels nauseated and can't wait to get back to his truck.

Ian interjects, "Did you forget your running shoes?"

William admits, "Nope, wore them out and can't afford to replace them right now."

Ian can hardly register what his friend is going through and tries to help, "Bro, what size do you wear? I have a couple of pairs that I bought and never wore. They're yours!"

William feels too embarrassed to admit he really wants the sneakers, so he changes the subject: "How's Bumble working out for you?"

Ian confesses, "It's not great, to be honest. I chose the cheaper plan, and the response time is just too short for me to get back to the person. When I do, their request has already disappeared."

William digs deeper and asks, "Anyone?"

"Nope, just haven't come across the right person yet."

William gives him an inquisitive look when he uses the word 'person' a second time.

Ian corrects himself, "I meant the right girl."

William adds, "Ian, if you're gay, that's fine too."

Ian defends himself, "Just because I'm single, never married or ever engaged, it doesn't mean I'm gay." He stops running and waits for a reaction from William when he says. "All right?" Seriously wondering if his buddy believes he's gay and is just pretending he doesn't.

William smirks, "Well, OK! I wear a size 9.5. Like what kind of brands?"

Ian is grateful he changed the subject back to sneakers, "They're Vans, New Balance, Adidas, and Skechers?"

"What colors and why don't you wear them?"

Ian reveals, "White, beige, red, and grey."

William waits for the rest of his reply.

Ian struggles to explain, "I have difficult feet to fit. High Arch." He points to them, "These Reeboks are the only ones that ever work for me. Every so often, I get sick and tired of wearing the same shoes every day and venture out. I have a stack of discards in my closet that I can't seem to part with, and now they're yours. Luckily for you, we wear the same size."

As they cross the Bogastow Brook Viaduct, the beauty of the scenery captivates them, and they remain silent in awe. The water's calmness reflects the dendritic branches of the bare trees hugging the shore as the noon sun glimmers on the glasslike water.

Ian senses that William is holding something back, but he doesn't push further and stays quiet until they reach Phipps Tunnel and turn around to head back. He notices William's stamina is waning, so he offers, "Hey, when we get back to Mayflower Landing, how about I give you a ride to your truck?"

William gives Ian a thumbs-up and remains silent for the remainder of their run.

When they return, Ian remotely unlocks the Equinox doors as they approach. He watches William examine his vehicle, as if he's seeing it for the first time. William sits in the passenger seat and scrutinizes the interior.

Ian notices this as he starts the engine. "Any questions?"

"Yah, what's it feel like to have some dead guy's heart or lungs on the seat next to you while you're driving?"

Ian sighs and points, "I drive mostly kidneys, and I secure them in the back."

"Does it ever give you the creeps?" asks William.

"Not anymore, you get used to working with people's body parts, and eventually it becomes like everyday inventory." Ian scratches his head and adds, "And I stay focused on where it's going and the lives it will save."

William nods in agreement.

Ian adds, "Also, I'm proud of what I do."

They arrive at William's truck, and Ian looks his friend in the eyes, "William, we've been friends for a long time. You know I've got your back. Whatever you need, I'll be there for you, buddy."

William gets out of the SUV and salutes him.

Ian says right before William closes his door, "I'll drop off the sneakers next time I'm in your neck of the woods."

William smiles and appears to appreciate his friend's help. "Thanks, looking forward to it." And then he leaves Ian and heads home.

CHAPTER FOURTEEN — WORLD'S END

OLIVIA

The moment the twins go down for their nap, Olivia pulls on her work cloak with large pockets and her old wellies, which are her muck boots, and heads to the barn to take on William's afternoon chores. He had already fed and watered all their livestock earlier that morning. Her task is to clean out all their stalls, scrape them dry, and replace them with fresh hay. She decides to begin with the chicken coop, work her way over to the goats, then to the hopelessly filthy pigsty, followed by the second milking of the cows, and finally over to Buttercup. That might leave them enough time together before the twins wake from their nap and maybe allow for a quick ride to Baiting Brook and back to give Buttercup's legs a good stretch.

While raking the chicken coop clean, she thinks about what she will say to her mum on the telephone, but her thoughts are interrupted by an unexpected text from the hair salon where she had her hair highlighted. *Your check bounced! We deposited it twice! Pay us, or we will report you, and you are no longer welcome here. EVER!*

Olivia drops the rake and checks her bank account online. Oh SHIT! I'm overdrawn again. William is going to kill me this time. *Where did I make the clerical mistake?* She asks herself.

Feeling like a total loser and clueless about where she will get the money to make this right, she realizes it's been almost five years since she ran from London to Boston, and she has not so much as sent a text or postcard to her mum the whole time. Olivia is so ashamed and disgusted with herself that she decides she can't let this continue another day, and she can't go on like this anymore. She considers whether Charlotte or Henry had treated her the same way, and she concludes she'd be heartbroken.

In retrospect, what she did at her hair salon now seems so puerile to her, but I'm not much better than I used to be, she concludes. Feeling ashamed of herself for 'appropriating' her mother's portrait of a Hackney horse by her late Great-Uncle Alfred Munnings and then posting it for sale on eBay was simply insane.

"What was I thinking?" she asks the hens.

Olivia arranged an appointment with what she recalls was the oddest man. His name was Patty, and he accepted the "Buy It Now" price for the painting on EBAY.

He described himself as a dealer and then told her to meet him at a pub in Camden called World's End to show it to him.

She shivers at the thought of her stupidity and recklessness. She was so fearless and full of adventure back then. Now she thinks to herself that she was simply a young, dumb girl.

With a one-way ticket to Boston in her pocket and the idea of being on her own with no one to answer to, her thoughts became intoxicated, making her feel incredibly empowered. Also, she found her mother's small one-bedroom flat in London, where two baby grand pianos filled the entire living room, suffocating.

Today, she would give anything to undo what she had done and to beg her mum for forgiveness. Then, suddenly, she panics with fear that something terrible might have happened to her mum. Maybe she's sick like Hattie, or worse, but there was no one there to care for her all these years. Olivia's heart aches with remorse.

In retrospect, the absurdity that she traded a family heirloom in exchange for her relationship with her mother and then never looked back makes her feel nauseated, and she vomits into a milking bucket. The combination of frustratedly trying to decide what words to use to break the ice between her and her mother when she eventually makes the call, along with the putrid stench from the cow manure mixed with urine, which also burns her eyes when it wafts from the floor, causes her to gag again. Gasping, she runs out and gulps the sweet smell of fresh air.

Outside in the driveway, she finds Dr. Shane Ferguson's empty white van parked and the horse stable door ajar.

As she enters, she is greeted with, "Oh, good, you're home. I could use some help."

Instinctively fearful of him, she asks, "What are you doing here?"

With his coat draped over his left arm, he begins to roll up his right shirt sleeve while he explains, "Hattie asked me to examine Buttercup. No worries, Hattie is footing my bill today." Then he hands Olivia his wristwatch and hangs his coat on a hook as he prepares to give Buttercup a vaginal examination.

"Hold her head steady while I…," his entire right arm, past his elbow, disappears inside the mare. Buttercup's eyes are opened wide as saucers as he continues.

Olivia is feeling annoyed over Dr. Ferguson's comment that Hattie offered to pay his bill today. Hattie can't really believe that the custody of Buttercup's foal is in any way questionable. Olivia waits with anticipation to hear his findings, "Well, is she?"

He smiles and evades her last question as he pulls his wet, sticky arm out of Buttercup's vagina. Instead, he replies, "After twenty-five years of marriage, my wife still doesn't believe me that this was how I lost my wedding ring?"

Olivia thinks to herself, I never realized he was married. I guess I never thought about it or cared. Now more curious, she inquires, "Why don't you wear rubber gloves?"

"Can't tell you how many times it slid off inside, and I had to go back to fish around for it, but what I do know is Buttercup is happy it's over. Aren't you a girl?" He dries his sticky, wet hands on a paper towel and nuzzles her, "You were such a good girl." He remarks in baby talk.

Olivia persists, "I repeat, well is she, or isn't she?"

The doctor ignores her question and instead says, "Did I ever tell you about the bloodhound who swallowed a pair of contact lenses?"

Olivia frustratedly replies, "No, but go ahead."

While putting his coat back on, he turns to her and says, "The dog was just fine, but his hindsight improved, and now it's 20/20."

Olivia doesn't laugh, and truthfully, she isn't sure which verdict she wants to hear: pregnant or not.

3 They step outside the stall to discuss his findings. He explains, "It's too early to confirm from my exam, but my gut is telling me she is. Her estrus has ended, her nipples have changed, and it feels like she may very well be carrying a foal. Around Christmas, we'll give her an ultrasound."

He stretches his hand out palm up toward Olivia, and she looks at it, wondering if he expects a payment.

He stares at her before he mentions, "Hmm, I believe you're holding my Rolex."

Embarrassed for forgetting she had it, she reaches into her pocket for it. "Here you go, doctor."

He reveals, "I've lost too many watches to count while performing exams. It's an occupational hazard, and please call me Shane. If I'm correct, we will see a lot of one another over the next year."

She cringes at the thought, and what flashes through her mind is whether it's too late for an equine abortion, but asking the question will make her sound insane to the veterinarian, so she bites her tongue.

She worries that this sort of financial news is going to send William over the cliff tonight, as she feels a knot form in her already upset stomach.

Dr. Ferguson elucidates, "Olivia, I understand this has been a financially tough year. Nearly every farm I visit faces the same challenges as you and William. The costs of hay, fuel, and feed have soared. Please, I urge you, ask your husband to call me. I've heard about a well-paying part-time job he might be interested in, and it would be my pleasure to recommend him."

"Thanks, Shane, you are too kind." But what she's really thinking while smiling and waving goodbye to him is, *please get the heck out of here before my husband returns, sees you, remembers my lame ass move with Buttercup, and then all that blissfulness we're beginning to feel again between us is torn to tatters.*

CHAPTER FIFTEEN — MAKE THE CALL

WILLIAM

On the ride back from William's run with Ian, the sky suddenly darkens, and, typical of New England weather, it changes abruptly. Snow squalls reduce visibility, so he activates the windshield wipers and defroster as he turns the corner onto Raven Rd and crosses over the Baiting Brook Bridge.

Finally feeling a bit more relaxed for the first time since his kerfuffle with the Natick Police, he pulls into their driveway with a sigh of relief and parks. As he walks toward the kitchen door, he suddenly hears blood-curdling screams from the twins' bedroom window. He rushes in, drops his knapsack, and races upstairs to see what's wrong. Charlotte, dressed in her blue Elsa princess dress, is crying and shrieking as if she is inconsolable.

Olivia tries to calm her down. "Give Tuck back to your brother."

"No!" Charlotte pulls the Paw Patrol doll away and stomps her foot.

Henry is puzzled by how she is talking to him, and he looks at his twin sister as if he doesn't recognize her.

Charlotte shrieks, "He broke my Ella doll. Look, Mummy." Charlotte raises the decapitated Paw Patrol doll's head in her fist and cries bitterly.

Olivia quizzes her son, "Did you rip the head off of Ella?"

Henry is terrified, "No, no, Mummy." He shakes his head. "No hurt, Ella," Henry carefully approaches his angry sister and sweetly reaches out to hug her, but instead of accepting his embrace, she grabs him by the hair as hard as she can and tries to tear it out at the roots.

William shouts, "Olie!" and just then, Olivia realizes William has returned from his run.

Olivia pulls Charlotte off Henry as William scoops him up and rubs his son's inflamed scalp while trying to calm him down.

Charlotte collapses and repeatedly pounds her head and hands on the floor, hysterically ranting, "I hate you, mummy. I hate you!"

William and Olivia are in a state of confusion as they huddle together, holding Henry. The three of them look down at Charlotte, still pounding the floor, and wonder what demon has taken her soul. Stunned, they step back from her and move into the hallway. Charlotte is so disconnected from her senses that she doesn't realize they've left the room.

William speaks up, "Olie, call the pediatrician. Something's terribly wrong with her."

Henry echoes with a worried tone, "Mummy, call."

Olivia tries to gather her thoughts, then searches her mind for an explanation while her overactive imagination runs wild, "William, what do you think is going on?" She hopes that his emergency medical training might reveal something.

"It could be anything. They were in a playgroup this week, and maybe she caught something."

Henry adds, "Mummy doctor made ouch, no doctor, doctor hurts me." He turns to show his father his still-swollen arm.

Olivia panics, "Oh my God, William. They were vaccinated last Wednesday. Do you think that's it?"

"What shots did they get?"

Olivia's mind goes blank, "Let me think."

William sees from her expression that she's clueless and loses his temper. "For Christ's sake, Olie, this is so important, tell me you didn't pay any attention to what they were getting injected with?" Suddenly, he's mortified at his wife's cavalier attitude toward their children's health.

She cries out, "William, I wake up each day before you at 4:00, make you your coffee, take care of the house, our kids, all our meals, the laundry, feed the livestock, buy our groceries, and last but not least, take them to their doctor's appointments, plus everything else. - I'm exhausted!"

William takes her hand in his and tries to calm her down, "I'm sorry for jumping on you, but our baby girl is auditioning for the exorcist, and it's as if someone flipped a switch and she's a different kid."

She blurts out, "Oh, I recall it now, they got immunized for polio, MMR, and maybe rubella, I think." Olivia pulls her phone out of her back pocket and dials a number, "See, I remembered, and I'm making the call, hello, this is Olivia Loring. Our daughter Charlotte isn't quite right." William watches Olivia wait for a response from the person on the phone, and then replies, "Yes, this is the best number to call us back." She ends the call and makes eye contact with William. They're both frightened about their daughter's well-being.

William adds, "Olie, we have to assume whatever this is, Henry was also exposed to it." William is so emotional that all his EMT training now seems useless. Olivia looks at him with despair and asks, "Is there anything you can do?"

He snaps into action, "All right, I'll fetch the med bag and take both of their temperatures." He returns with the makeshift emergency medical kit and discovers the thermometer's battery is dead. "Oh shit, I'll be right back." He runs to their bedroom, grabs the remote control, and brings it to the twins' room. His hands are sweaty, and he can't get the cover off to remove the batteries, so he hands it to Olivia, "Pull the batteries out for me."

She hands it back with the cover off, "Here you go, Love."

He hands her the pair of triple-A batteries, and she immediately realizes the thermometer needs double-A batteries instead. Frustrated and angry with herself, she confesses, "I'm the worst mother. What kind of mum doesn't have a working thermometer?"

William comes to her rescue, saying, "I've got some downstairs, I'll be right back, and I think you're a great mother." At that moment, he decides to take ownership of their medical emergency supplies and responsibility for the present situation.

William returns and puts the batteries in the thermometer. Olivia takes Charlotte's temperature, and it's 101.4. Just then, Olivia's phone rings, startling her. She answers, "Hello, yes, it is, oh yes, we just took it, and it's 101.4." While listening to the On Call Nurse Practitioner, she grabs her own forehead. "But how can this still be normal? They were vaccinated days ago?"

William observes Olivia's facial expressions as she keeps listening.

Olivia finally replies, "All right, I understand. If the temperature goes above 102 degrees or if she gets worse, we should take her to hospital."

"William, we need to give her Tylenol and get her temperature down." Olivia scoops up Charlotte's limp body from the floor and pulls her sweaty, dirty Elsa gown over her head. William hands her the liquid Tylenol, and they get as much of the dose as they can into their reluctant daughter's mouth.

William looks directly at Olivia and asks, "Now what do we do?"

She takes a breath, "I'm going to wipe her down with a cool, wet face cloth and try to make her more comfortable."

William is genuinely trying to help. "Olie, what do you want me to do?"

She glances up from wiping Charlotte's arm and says, "Check Henry's temperature."

William looks for Henry and finds him in their bed, hiding under the covers. He flashes the thermometer across his forehead and is relieved that it's normal. Then he asks him, "Want to watch TV while I make dinner?" Henry nods yes and curls into a ball. William reaches for the remote control, but it's still in the twins' bedroom. "I'll be right back."

"Okey Dokey, Daddy."

William wonders where he picked up the phrase Okey Dokey and smiles at his son.

The second he enters the room to retrieve the remote control, Olivia asks, "What's his temperature?"

"Normal, want pizza tonight?"

"Splendid idea, I'm sure Henry's famished," she confirms.

"How's she doing?" He asks.

"Asleep for now," she replies.

William sits beside Olivia on Charlotte's bed and places his hand over his daughter's hand. "Please recheck her temperature. I hope the Tylenol lowered it."

William scans her forehead, and it reads 101 degrees Fahrenheit, and he shares, "It's dropped a bit."

She asks, "How's Henry?"

William blurts, "Oh, Crap, I forgot to turn on the TV for him. He's fine, and I'll be right back." He grabs the remote, reinserts the batteries, and hurries to his son, who is sound asleep. He pulls the cover over him and returns to the twins' bedroom, where he finds Olivia asleep next to Charlotte.

He recalls how, when they were infants, if he had asked Olivia if she wanted to fool around while they were napping, she would think he was joking and find it so funny she'd say, "Sex or sleep, but if you really love me, sleep."

He reaches for the thermometer and, without disturbing them, rechecks his daughter's temperature, and it remains unchanged.

He decides, while they're resting, to open his laptop and look up what he can find on adverse reactions to childhood vaccines.

What he begins to read leaves him breathless: "Oh my God." He says aloud as he scrolls through the information. Case after case, what he sees terrifies him more than he ever expected. It never occurred to him or his wife that there might be an alternative to vaccinating their kids, so they unquestioningly trusted their pediatrician's advice.

He thinks somberly, maybe they shouldn't have, after learning that human fetuses are being used to manufacture the MMR vaccine, and about the controversy surrounding the Polio vaccine.

He decides not to share what he read online with his wife, who is already hysterical. There's nothing they can do now that it's done. He realizes he is not angry at Olivia because he understands she did what she believed was best for them at the time.

Suddenly, he hears Olivia shout from upstairs, "William, come now!"

He reaches the second-floor landing in three leaps and enters the twins' bedroom to find Charlotte having a grand mal seizure. Her little body is stiff, her mouth is filled with drool, and her fists are clenched as she shakes and thrashes about endlessly. Olivia bursts into tears and pleads, "Call 911!"

William makes the call, "Our baby girl is having a seizure." Olivia, still crying, looks at William with despair. "No, she's never had one before. She's almost four, and she's otherwise always been healthy." He covers the phone and turns to Olivia, asking, "How is she breathing?"

Olivia places her hand on her chest to check and exclaims, "I've no idea," while completely panicking.

William goes back to talking with the 911 dispatcher, "Incredible, I can already hear a siren coming up our street."

William rushes downstairs to open the front door to greet them. He feels completely lost and helpless. Despite all the training he received in the National Guard, he still cannot do anything for his child. At that moment, he vows to God to upgrade their medical kit with a high-quality blood pressure cuff, an oximeter, a choking-suction device, a stethoscope, Benadryl, and an EpiPen.

When he opens the front door, he finds a lone police officer with flashing lights from his vehicle illuminating the snowy fields around their house.

"What's the situation, Sir? The ambulance is just a few minutes behind me, but the snowfall has delayed it. I'm here to assess and assist."

"Our little girl was running a fever and then, from out of nowhere, started having convulsions. She's upstairs and unresponsive. My wife is with her."

The police officer states, "They'll take her to the Beth Israel in Needham," while listening to his dispatcher through his earpiece.

With relief in his voice, "That's great, her doctor is at Needam-Dover Pediatric Practice," says William, forgetting how upset he was with their pediatrician just ten minutes ago.

"Do you mind showing me the way to see her?" says the police officer.

"Follow me." William leaves the front door open for the EMTs.

The two of them burst into the twins' bedroom, and the police officer blurts out, "Olivia, how is she doing?"

William turns to Olivia, "What the hell, how do you two know each other?"

"Your wife drives down 115 like she's racing against Richard Petty. That's how we met."

She defends herself, "The kids weren't in the car, William. I was on my way to get them, and my being late was all your fault!"

The police officer asks, "How's the little girl?"

William takes a long look at the well-built, handsome police officer. He wonders what else Olivia conveniently omitted to tell him about.

Then, just like magic, Charlotte sits up and is back to being herself and asks, "Hi Mummy, who's dat?" as she points toward the police officer.

"Officer Robert Hill, but you can call me Bobby."

Olivia is surprised. "Charlie, how are you feeling, darling?"

"Mummy, I feel bad. My head hurts. Light hurts my eyes."

There's a gentle tap at the bedroom door, and it's Hattie and George. "What's going on? We saw the flashing lights and rushed right over," explains George.

Charlotte had a seizure. We're on our way to the hospital now," states William.

Henry joins them, and George continues, "Henry, how would you like to have your supper with us across the street at Hattie's house?"

What flashes through Olivia's mind is the image of Hattie's empty fridge, which only has three types of cheese, a jar of stuffed olives, some bottles of wine, and a light bulb. What could she possibly make for Henry to eat?

Hattie grasps Henry's little hand in her gnarly, nicotine-stained fingers and asks him, "Do you like grilled cheese sandwiches?"

Henry replies, "Yum, yes pwease."

Olivia is pleased with her son's polite reply when she suddenly hears people calling from downstairs. Hattie and George take Henry and leave. The EMTs rush upstairs and begin administering to Charlotte right away.

The first EMT asks, "What's been going on?" while he takes her blood pressure and checks the little girl's vitals.

William answers, "She was acting strangely at first, so we checked her temperature, and it was 101.4. Then she had a grand mal seizure that lasted a couple of minutes. I wasn't here when it started, so I can't say how long it lasted."

The EMT reports to his dispatcher, "Temp is 101, blood pressure is 87 over 43, and her pupils are not responding correctly. Yes, confirmed seizure. On route to BI, Needham. Leaving here in 2 minutes, ETA 21 minutes, and out. Would one of you like to ride with us to the hospital?"

Olivia jumps up and runs downstairs to grab her purse, Parker, and the health insurance card.

William offers, "I'll follow in the truck."

#

Olivia and William take turns sitting in the recliner next to Charlotte's hospital bed in the emergency room bay, where she is sleeping. Not much has changed regarding Charlotte's condition, and they are waiting for the lab results from her bloodwork, EEG, and spinal tap. Charlotte is snoring softly, and they whisper so as not to wake her.

The waiting room is crowded. They feel fortunate to have found the only chair available, as the hospital is overwhelmed with sick patients. The overflow is on gurneys lining the ER hallways and spilling into the waiting room.

Olivia rises and silently gestures toward the recliner. William shakes his head no and continues leaning against the wall. Neither of them uses it now, even though they're both exhausted.

Olivia carefully examines her gold-filled Cartier watch, and for the first time in a while, she recalls how she felt the day her mum gave it to her on her sixteenth birthday and how much she loved it when she opened the beautifully wrapped box from Harrods. Besides her wedding ring, it's her only piece of fine jewelry, and since receiving it, it has been her most prized possession. Looking at it, she considers the time difference between Boston and London and figures it's 7:00 am back home.

She imagines her mum in the kitchen, having her morning cup of tea and catching up on the news and local gossip in her beloved London Sun.

Olivia brushes her hand across William's brow before she whispers, "Love, I'm going to find a vending machine and get something to nibble. Want anything?"

William gives her a thumbs up and shakes his head no, but she knows he will be happy to see anything she brings back for him. It's just that he doesn't like to appear weak or needy in any way ever. She points to the empty chair and insists he sit down. Reluctantly, he agrees and finally takes the seat, sighing in relief as his muscles relax in the chair.

Olivia finds the vending machines near the emergency room entrance. She makes herself a cup of tea and sips it, trying her hardest to think of a single reason not to call her mum right now, and what she should say to her if she answers the call. It's been almost five years since she fled London and did what she believes irreparably damaged their relationship. Her heart flutters with anxiety as she tries to muster her icebreaker.

She feels her mother will never believe that she still has the one thousand British pounds that Patty, the art dealer, gave her for the painting, and that she badly wants to return the money to her. Feeling too ashamed ever to spend it and afraid that if she did, she would condemn herself to eternal damnation in hell.

She whispers to herself aloud, "Stupid, stupid, stupid," while shaking her head in self-disappointment.

The long-awaited moment has arrived, and Hattie was right in her assumptions about why Olivia needs to clean up her messes before moving forward with a new venture.

She dials her mother's phone number and hears a strange recording stating that the number cannot be dialed as it is. Feeling partly relieved because she's not ready yet, she googles how to call London from the USA. She reads '011' followed by '44' and then the number. She tries to make the call again, and this time she hears a similar recorded message, only with a British accent, followed by an annoying clang.

"What the hell?" she mutters to herself, feeling frustrated and worried she might lose her nerve. She looks up how to do it again, but this time on YouTube, and learns she needs to add a city code as well, which is 27.

Then, voila, she hears the familiar trilling of a properly placed call home. After four rings, her call goes to voicemail. Childishly, her first thought is that her mother doesn't want to talk to her, but then she realizes her mother would not have recognized the incoming number, so she sent it there innocently.

Knowing she has only a split second to decide what to say, when she hears the beep, her mind goes blank, and instead she speaks straight from her heart, blurting out, "Mummy, it's me, please forgive me. I'm calling you from the United States. Call me whenever you can." Then she takes a deep breath. "Mummy, I love you and miss you terribly." The voicemail cuts her off, and she feels her gut wrench at the thought that her mother may never return her phone call.

CHAPTER SIXTEEN — AS GOOD AS NEW

IAN

Ian packs his numerous impulse-purchased sneakers, along with some treats for his dog Scout, and places them in the back seat of the Equinox. He's not supposed to bring his dog in the company's vehicle, so as a compromise in case he gets caught, he puts his pup in an enclosed dog carrier and sets it on the floor under the passenger seat.

He hasn't had a chance to speak with his boss, Stan, at A.O.R.A., yet, but he's pretty sure the answer to the request to hire William will be no. He feels terrible because he senses how badly William is struggling financially, and he wants to do whatever he can to help his friend in a time of need, especially given the recent developments in his daughter's health.

He remains curious about why William waited so long to introduce him to his wife, Olivia. From their conversations, he's inferred that she's British, attractive, grew up around horses and music, and is about eight or ten years younger than him. That's pretty much all he knows for now. Oh, and they met on Bumble.

He decides to stop at the Dunkin' Donuts Drive-Thru on Route 9. He orders a chicken sausage croissant sandwich, a dozen donuts, a box of Munchkins for the twins, and a hot cocoa to warm up on this cold, gray afternoon.

At the red traffic light, he leans down and slides a piece of chicken into Scout's carrier between the metal bars. Scout's eyes bug out a little bit in anticipation, and he whines for more after gobbling it up.

Impatiently, Ian takes a sip of the hot drink, and it burns his tongue. "Yikes!" he exclaims aloud from the pain. At the stop sign, he glances at the screen to see how much farther, and it's only another twelve minutes to William's family's farm in Sherborn. The ride becomes more scenic and beautiful as he approaches his destination.

It's late November, so some tattered remnants of Halloween decorations still hang in a few trees. Scattered across the snow-dusted, straw-colored lawns are posters from the last election, which are peppered along the sides of the road, but most will disappear after the first big snowstorm.

As he pulls into the driveway, he says to Scout, "We're here, Buddy."

He takes Scout for a walk to let him do his business before going inside to play with the kids and to prevent a potential accident from getting too excited. He looks at the house and the surroundings. It's a very charming property, and to him, it looks more like a Christmas card than a real home where people actually live, with a pleasant, rich-smelling smoke billowing from the oversized red brick chimney.

Scout walks around, marking his territory along the fence posts. He is captivated by the new smells from the goats, pigs, chickens, sheep, rabbits, cows, and horses. Ian must tug his leash to get him to return to the Equinox SUV. He wonders if he can carry everything in one trip. He slips the Dunkin' Donuts shopping bag over his hand and onto his wrist as he lifts the case of shoe boxes into his arms.

Before he can knock on the front door, it flies open, and two adorable, happy children stand in the doorway with big blue eyes and light brown hair. They may look alike, but they are quite different. The little girl is dressed like a Disney Princess, and the boy is wearing cold-weather clothes.

The twins enthusiastically reach for his dog while chanting "Puppy," ignoring Ian.

Once inside the house, his eyes adjust, and he sees a beautiful roaring fire in the living room and two older people whom he assumes are the grandparents, warming themselves in easy chairs by it. The woman is on the thin side, and she's sipping something from a martini glass. Scout is tugging on his leash and wants to be let go. "Be good!" Ian says as he releases Scout and places the sneakers down on a bench seat in the front hallway.

The house has low ceilings and short doorways, and it's filled with antiques. There are maudlin portraits, an old grandfather clock, and China cabinets brimming with dishware, porcelain, and vintage crystal. It's a pretty special place, he concludes.

William walks out of what Ian imagines must be their kitchen and gives him a genuine hug when he greets him.

"How's the little one?" Ian inquires, realizing he forgot her name.

William confesses, "It's been tough for Charlotte, but it's even harder on Olie. She barely slept, and honestly, I'm feeling the same way. They have no idea what caused the seizure." He sighs before adding, "We have a bunch of doctors' appointments coming up and more questions than answers."

Ian hands the Dunkin' Donuts bag to William, then wipes the moisture from his palms onto his shirt.

William smiles and says, "This wasn't necessary, dude."

"What are your thoughts on what caused the seizure?"

William looks up at the ceiling for a moment and then replies, "Actually, we both think it has something to do with their vaccines. They got them last week."

Ian sighs deeply before he replies, "I know less than nothing about that kind of stuff, but the idea that something like that could make a little kid sick is just dreadful."

"I agree. Want a beer?" William offers.

"Sure, I'm not on call today. So, where's the lady of the house?" he pleads, as the anticipation is killing him.

William reveals, "I begged her to go upstairs and get some rest until you arrive. Let me introduce you to our neighbors, and then I'll go get her."

They walk over to meet them, and William smiles as he says, "Hattie and George, I'd like to introduce you to my buddy Ian. We served together in the National Guard. By the way, Hattie is the closest thing I've got to a mom."

Hattie doesn't react; instead, she stretches out her arm and shows William her empty glass, saying, "Now be a good son and go get me another dirty martini."

William takes the empty glass and salutes her, "Yes, ma'am, and what about you, George?"

George looks down at his half-full glass of Sancerre, shakes his head no, and replies, "I'm good, nice to meet you, Ian."

William returns with a dirty martini and two beers. He hands one to Ian and clinks bottles, "Cheers. I'll be right back."

While William runs upstairs to get Olivia, Ian wanders over to the twins' playroom, where he finds Scout dressed as Paddington Bear and tucked under a blanket in a doll's carriage.

Charlotte and Henry are pretending he's their baby and are walking him in his stroller in Hyde Park, London. Scout loves every second of their attention and can't keep his eyes off the children. After more than three years of living in a small cage as a lab animal from the day he was born at the Envigo puppy mill, he has never walked on grass or seen the light of day. He appreciates this genuine kindness from these sweet children.

William and Olivia descend the stairs, and just the sight of her makes Ian's eyes water with envy. Despite her sleep deprivation, no makeup, and her hair in need of brushing, he finds her ravishing. Her thick, long, full head of hair has a dark, rich base with blond highlights throughout. Her eyes are a deep aquamarine blue, and her complexion strikes a perfect balance of peaches and cream. She is the embodiment of his imaginary ideal girlfriend. He surmises this could explain why his friend has kept her to himself. He concludes that everything about her is just right; her height, weight, and build are flawless and without compromise.

Then she outstretches her arm to shake Ian's hand as she greets him, "Welcome to our home. Can I offer you anything?"

Ian's brain short-circuits at the sound of her mellifluous voice, combined with her British accent. *I completely understand why he hides her*; he thinks to himself, *it's jealousy, pure and simple.* Ian agrees that if his wife were this attractive, he'd do the same as William.

Ian stutters, "I'm good, thanks. I had a chicken sandwich on my way over, but I could use a bowl of water for Scout."

William replies, "On its way."

"Thanks, and let's get going on those sneaks." Ian changes the subject, trying to conceal his sudden infatuation with William's wife."

When they approach the bench in the front hallway, William reacts to the many shoe boxes, "Wow, this is way more than I was expecting."

Ian urges him, "Try them all on!"

William reaches for the Vans first. "These are wonderful." He slides his foot into the sneaker and laces it, saying, "Fits me perfectly," while glancing at them on his feet.

Ian urges him, "Try on the rest. They're collecting dust in my closet, and I want you to have them."

"You sure?" asks William. "All I need is one pair."

Ian shakes his head in disbelief and asks, "When was the last time anyone bought you something new?"

William has to think before he speaks: "It was my mom, she took me clothing shopping when I was a junior in high school."

Ian reaches down and picks up the New Balance box, hands it to him, and then asks, "How did they die?"

William wipes tears from his eyes before describing what happened: "A drug addict hit them head-on, going over 60 miles an hour. They were coming home from dinner and a movie at the Natick 16. I was supposed to go with them, but I blew them off, so I could watch a baseball game on TV."

There's a moment of silence, but all Ian can think about are all the dead drug addicts' organs he picks up and delivers daily, and how they never seem to run out of them. He asks himself, *Why doesn't our government do something about it?* But deep down, he knows that we're all just part of a much bigger machine, which is, of course, the medical industrial machine complex.

All those organs from dead drug addicts are easily supplied to transplant patients because the drugs that kill them from an overdose are mainlined straight into our communities, targeting our young and most healthy people. He shivers at the thought of their symbiosis and wonders for the first time in his career if he might be somehow complicit.

William adds, "I was a teenager when it happened. Hattie took care of me the best she could, ran this place until I finished school and the Guard." He emphasizes, "She did what she could with me, you know, under the circumstances. It's not like she's all warm and motherly; it's just not her thing."

William sighs, "I had never even been to a funeral before they died, and I had no clue what to do." He runs his hand through his hair as he tries to change the subject.

William offers, "Hey, I love the sneakers. Why don't you join us for dinner?"

Ian feels as if he's intruding, and William is just being polite. "I think I should get going."

William repeats the offer, "Ian, Olivia, slow-cooked venison in a burgundy wine and red currant sauce. It's delicious – stay!"

Ian feels a flash of envy. Besides William's wife being gorgeous, she's also a talented cook. He shakes his head in disbelief, but with nowhere else to go except a bar to sit alone and watch the Pats game, he asks, "Are you watching the game?"

William smiles when he replies, "Hell, yes!"

Ian switches the subject again. "You hear anything more about Mary O'Keefe?"

William shakes his head no in response to Ian's question, just as Hattie walks toward the front door and reaches for her coat.

Ian turns to her and asks, "Hattie, are you leaving? Nice meeting you."

Hattie ignores him and walks out.

Ian asks, "What's up with that?"

William smirks, "She's still pissed off at me because I won't let her smoke inside my house. She'll be back in three minutes, and she'll be her Hattie self again, that is, until she needs another smoke."

Hattie returns, bringing the cold air with her. She stomps the snow off her shoes, smiles, and says, "Did I forget to tell you? Olie wants you to gather the kids and come to the dinner table. Oh, and William,

I heard the sound of a shotgun fire in the hills a couple of mornings ago. Was it you?"

"Yes, Hattie. I bagged a young buck. It was a lot of work, but it was worth it because we now have a freezer full of meat to last us through the winter. The cutoff for shotgun hunting season is coming up fast." She nods yes as he continues, "It's December 9th this year. You need any meat while there's still a couple of days left? I'll butcher it for you, too."

"No, we're good for now," she insists.

Ian feels a bit squeamish at the thought of killing an animal and skinning it. He's curious and asks. "How do you do it?"

William states plainly, "It's food, Ian and the animals we raise are livestock, not pets." Then he looks around for his wife and asks Hattie, "Where did Olivia go?"

Hattie dispels his confusion, "Down in the cellar with George. They're picking out a nice bottle of wine."

Ian thinks to himself, *The meal keeps getting better*, and asks, "Hey, William, does your wife have a sister by chance?"

William replies, "Nope, just an older half-brother I've never met. Why?"

Ian's embarrassed and adds, "I was hoping to be able to find a girl just like her, you lucky bastard," as he knuckles him on the shoulder.

William is flattered. "Thanks for the compliment. Let's grab the twins and sit everybody down for dinner."

At the table, Ian takes it all in: a delicious glass of '93 Brunello Di Montalcino, flickering candlelight, scrumptious food, a gorgeous wife, adorable kids, convivial conversations with close friends, and, with a heavy heart, he must admit the vacuousness of his existence. He sighs, feeling disappointed in himself as well as a tinge of jealousy.

PART TWO

CHAPTER SEVENTEEN — MY FAVORITE NEIGHBOR

OLIVIA

Olivia opens her eyes in their dark bedroom just before the alarm clock goes off. Quietly, she turns it off and slips out of bed without waking William. Her to-do list is so long that it makes her heart race, and when Hattie asked her to take care of her horses so she could go to the hospital for the day, what else could she say besides yes?

Downstairs, she prepares two thermoses of hot coffee and takes one with her when she goes to fetch Buttercup from her paddock on her way to feed the horses across the street.

It's a miserable morning, biting cold and unpleasant for both man and beast. She rides Buttercup across Jameson Farm and tucks her into a stall next to Ken's. Then, she leads them to the enclosed ring to let them run around after their breakfast, giving her time to clean out their stalls. Buttercup is much happier with the company of the other horses and doesn't miss being alone across the street in their drafty old barn.

After that observation, Olivia decides to talk about a new arrangement with Hattie, especially now that she is acting as their caretaker and will probably keep doing so until Hattie's health improves.

After she fills her third wheelbarrow with muck from the stalls, Hattie stops by to check on her and show some appreciation. "Morning, thanks for helping me out today."

Still catching her breath from raking out the stalls, Olivia says, "That's what neighbors do, I guess."

"Means a lot to me," Hattie confesses.

"It's really nothing, Hattie. Can I leave Buttercup here while I help you?"

"Sure, no bother. Is she with a foal?" Hattie inquires with a vulpine-like grin.

"Not sure, but probably yes," Olivia confesses with shame in her voice.

"Splendid, and did you do what we discussed?" Hattie adds.

"Yes." Olivia declares.

"And?"

A tear wells up in Olivia's eye. "My mum." She fights back tears and looks away. "She didn't pick up."

"Give her time." They hear a horn honk, and Hattie says, "That must be George. He went to warm up the truck for our ride to Dana-Farber."

Olivia says expressively, "Best of luck today."

Hattie says while in a rush, "Thanks. Oh, and one more thing. Here is the telephone number and web address for the kennel in Springfield, Illinois. We need to contact them about the puppies. I want you to study the dogs and decide if we're going to breed hairless or puff Chinese Cresteds, but they're all cute to me."

A lump forms in Olivia's throat, and she suddenly feels emotional about Hattie undergoing her cancer screening. She offers all she can. "Would you like to take my thermos of hot coffee and a snack with you for the long ride?"

"Sure, if you're not using it."

Olivia passes it to Hattie as they both hear another honk, and Hattie exclaims, "I've got to go." Then she looks back at Olivia as she walks away and winks, showing she has everything under control.

After Hattie leaves, Olivia's first thought is about how much she was looking forward to her coffee break, but she imagines it's better to give than to receive.

A half hour later, her phone rings, and the thought that it might be her mum startles her, but it's only William. "Olie, thanks for leaving me coffee this morning. It was a godsend."

She explains, "It was the least I could do. I felt guilty disappearing on you without giving you your breakfast."

"When the kids wake up, I'll give you a call, OK?"

She continues talking with her speaker on while raking up horse manure from the stall, "Sounds like a plan, and then come pick me up because I rode over on Buttercup, and I'm boarding her over here until Hattie's back to her old self."

William exclaims, "I've got to go!"

Olivia ends her call, puts her phone in her pocket, and continues filling the wheelbarrow with more muck from the stalls. As she falls into a work rhythm, she imagines her phone ringing and hearing from her mum. She wonders where she should start after making her heartfelt apology. Should she blurt out – hey, you're a grandmother, or I'm married now, or I never spent the money I stole, and I want to wire it back to you? Feeling disgusted with herself, she keeps shoveling the rest of the horse manure at a harder pace and breaks a sweat.

CHAPTER EIGHTEEN — BROKE CHRISTMAS

WILLIAM

William grabs the portable baby monitor and shoves it in his coat pocket so he can listen for the twins waking up while milking the cows.

The cold air bites his face as he steps out into the darkness of early morning, but he's also glad he doesn't have to deal with Buttercup today and can go straight to the goats afterward. He hears the rooster crow and pauses to check the baby monitor because the sun is rising. Luckily, the twins are still asleep, so he quickly gathers some freshly laid eggs from the chicken coop for their breakfast and heads up to the house.

While walking across the driveway, Hattie and George drive up in her truck, and Hattie rolls down her window to speak to William. "Billy, come here, I need to ask you something."

William cringes when he hears her call him Billy; she only says that right before she scolds him. He walks over to the truck's window and braces himself for what's coming.

Hattie spouts forth, "Not much time, so let me get to the point. What are you giving Olivia for Christmas?"

He looks at her with a blank stare, clueless about where this is going because, for the past four years, Hattie wouldn't have given Olivia even the time of day. "I'm really low on cash, Hattie, so I haven't given it much thought. Why?"

Hattie lights a cigarette before asking, "How come that nice wife of yours isn't wearing your grandmother's diamond ring? Did you lose it or do some dumbass thing like sell it?"

William's throat tightens at the thought of his parents' possessions. "Hattie, I've never sold anything!" he swallows hard before continuing, "It's hard for me to explain. I see myself as just the caretaker of my parents' stuff, and I don't think I should give it away to someone else."

"For Christ's sake, William, it's yours!" Hattie shakes her head in disagreement. "Olivia's not just your wife; she's also the mother of your children. Just give her the damn thing! And I know you know it will make her very happy."

"All right, Hattie. Consider it done."

Hattie huffs to George, "We've got to get going. If not, we'll hit terrible traffic." Then she raises her voice at William, "And don't forget to put it in a nice ring box and wrap it with paper and a bow."

Shaking his head in disbelief at how she's talking to him but also understanding she's a bit nervous about her upcoming oncology appointment, he replies, "Will do, Hattie, and good luck with your cancer checkup today."

Hattie circles her hand as if she's taking off in a helicopter while simultaneously closing her window and complaining to George about William.

Poor George, he thinks as they drive away.

He sighs with relief as he enters their warm, quiet kitchen and sees the thermos of coffee waiting for him on the counter. He pours himself a cup and is surprised to find the milk and sugar already added and the coffee still too hot to drink, which means Olivia heated the milk first. She's incredibly thoughtful, and he considers himself lucky to be her husband.

He places some kindling in the fireplace and lights a log. Then he empties the still-warm, freshly laid eggs into a wire basket on the counter and calls Olivia to see how she's making out at Jameson Farm.

#

When William and the twins arrive at Jameson Farm to pick up Olivia, he feels disappointed when he sees Dr. Shane Ferguson's white medical van parked outside the stable.

"Stay in your seats," he commands Charlotte and Henry, who are still in their pajamas. "I'll be right back; I'm going to get Mummy."

"Father, pwease. Take us with you." Henry pleads.

The thought of pulling them out of their car seats and letting them loose at Hattie's not childproofed farm is a horrible idea, so he repeats, "Stay in your seats. I won't be gone long."

When William enters the tack area, he overhears Olivia and Shane, the veterinarian, having a friendly chat about Buttercup's condition. This rekindles his anger about Olivia's unilateral decision to add another horse to their livestock. He also hasn't recovered from his close call with the Natick Police, which never would have happened if he hadn't involved himself with Shane in the first place.

When William enters the stall, Shane raises his eyebrows, and his eyes widen. "Morning, William. I'm so happy you've joined us."

Stoically, William says, "Olie, I left the kids in the truck."

Nervously, she asks, "Is it running?"

"Yes, it is," he confirms.

"OK, but Shane would like to have a word with you, so I'll wait with the kids." Olivia scoots off.

William mostly feels contempt for Shane, and he thinks to himself that if it weren't for their tough financial situation, he would find a new livestock vet immediately. However, despite his anger toward the doctor, they still need him to treat their beloved animals. He looks over at Buttercup, who seems much happier at Jameson Farm than at their farm, and asks, "Dr. Ferguson, any chance Buttercup is with a foal?"

"Please call me Shane, and we need to move past what happened in Natick, William."

"You didn't answer my question," says William.

"Well, from my physical exam, my best guess is yes, but I won't know for sure until I do an ultrasound."

William asks in a panic, "Oh my God! How much will that cost me?"

Dr. Ferguson offers, "William, I truly want to make it up to you. I never meant to put you in harm's way. I know you need to earn some extra money soon, and I can genuinely help you with that."

William says adamantly, "Thanks, but no!"

"Hey, there's this company in Randolph."

"What's your involvement?" William barks.

"I'm like one of their suppliers, and they need someone with your skillset. They'll pay you handsomely."

William laughs, "What skillset? This is a joke, right?"

"No, William, it's not," and your starting pay will be about $75 an hour. After you finish your training, it will at least triple. The initial training is just one night. Either you pass or you fail. What have you got to lose?"

"Can you tell me more about it?" William is a bit intrigued.

"It's tough work and not for everyone, but I believe you'll be an exception."

"Is it legal, Shane?"

Dr. Ferguson boasts, "Totally legit. The manufacturing plant is a subsidiary of a multi-billion-dollar pharmaceutical and regenerative medicine company with over 50,000 employees. Does that answer your question?"

"What's in it for you, Shane?"

Dr. Ferguson replies, "You're a friend in need. Consider it an early Christmas gift."

William is unsure whether to proceed, but he needs the money.

Shane continues to sell him on the idea, "There is probably a significant signing bonus as well."

Despite the telltale hairs on the back of William's neck telling him to stay away, he agrees to consider it. "Thanks, Shane, but I should speak with Olivia first."

Shane grins, "Oh, I get that. I don't do anything without running it by the missus."

William is confused. "I didn't realize you were married because you've never mentioned it, and you're not wearing a wedding ring."

Shane explains, "Oh, we've been married forever, or at least it feels like that." He laughs as if he said something funny. "I lost my wedding ring one day during an exam while my hand was up some horse's ass." He confirms with another laugh, "And my wife still doesn't believe me, even though I spent hours going through piles of horseshit looking for it."

William finally laughs at the thought of this and says, "You've sold me on this, Shane. What do I need to do next to get the job?"

"You'll get a call from a guy named Allen. He's a busy guy because he's one of the best there is in his field. I'm sure he'll fit you in as soon as he can."

"What's the training entail?" William becomes cynical because he really wants the job now.

Shane smirks, "I'm going to leave it up to Allen to explain everything to you."

The truck's horn honks. "That's Olivia. I have to go."

"Watch for the call," Shane shouts to William as he leaves.

#

After William finishes his daily chores, he decides to search for his grandmother's diamond ring to give to Olivia for Christmas. He enters the oversized hall closet and pulls down the retractable stairs to the attic. Most of the house was built before the antebellum era and has poor to no insulation. Still, the attic is freezing because of the extra layers of insulation William and his father added when he was in junior high school.

When William reaches the attic landing, he pulls the string for the light, but nothing happens. He then has to go back down to get a bulb and a flashlight to help him in his search.

When he's in the kitchen pantry looking for a package of lightbulbs, Olivia walks in to ask him what he's doing.

"Oh, Olie, I need to fix something in the attic. I kept putting it off, but I finally found the time to take care of it."

She says like she's not interested, "That's nice. I'm going upstairs to take a nap before I start making dinner and before things one and two wake up."

William feels relieved she isn't probing him further because he really wants the ring to be a big surprise. Now, all he has to do is find it in the attic.

Back up in the attic with the light bulb now working, William looks around at piles of junk that seem like rubbish to him until he spots his mother's large Rimowa stainless steel trunk, which is completely covered by a white sheet. Optimistically, he hopes that's where he stashed her jewelry after the funeral. He hasn't so much as touched the trunk since then, and he's awash with emotions. He places his hand on the padlock and realizes he can't remember the combination to the lock.

It was always his mother's trunk, so he asks himself what combination of numbers she would use. He tries his parents' anniversary, but it doesn't work; then he tries their birthdays, and it doesn't open. He stares at the lock and considers cutting it off with a hacksaw. Then he tries his birthday, and of course, it opens right up!

Before he pulls off the padlock, he says aloud, and to no one, "Love you, Ma." Then he opens the lid.

The airtight trunk reveals the distinct smell of his mother's favorite fragrance, Shalimar. Momentarily, he feels her presence as he sifts through her belongings. He finds her wedding dress carefully packed away, wrapped with tissue paper, along with some photos, postcards, his baby shoes, his father's dog tags, their marriage certificate, and a boxed set of lace handkerchiefs with his mother's initials, but no jewelry so far.

He swallows hard at the thought of disturbing her cherished possessions. He feels he has no choice but to empty the trunk and go through everything until he finds the diamond ring. He lifts out the box with the wedding dress inside and then recalls that he put the ring inside the toe of her embellished white satin shoes right after the funeral. He reaches down for the shoebox, removes the cover, peels off the tissue paper, then tilts the shoe to reveal both of his parents' wedding rings, a couple of pairs of earrings, a very old IWC windup wristwatch, and his mother's diamond engagement ring, which was handed down from her mother.

He puts everything back the way he found it, except for the ring, which he wears on his pinky. He makes sure to lock the padlock, then thinks about heading downstairs to find a place to hide it until Christmas. He glances at it; it has three round diamonds, with the largest in the center. The ring's size looks tiny to him, and he wonders if it will fit Olivia. He decides he'll compare it to the size of her wedding ring tonight while she's asleep.

Then he sits on the trunk in the freezing cold attic and opens his Amazon app. He scrolls through the variety of ring boxes until he finds one that looks suitable for the ring's age. Then he changes the delivery address to Jameson Farm, because Hattie will know exactly what to do with it when it arrives. It will also implicitly show her that he followed her instructions, and that will please her.

While he's completing his order, he hears a cellphone ring and Olivia's muddled voice traveling up through a vent pipe. He is not sure, but he believes it sounds as if she's crying.

His immediate fear is that it's a callback from one of the doctors regarding Charlotte's medical tests and lab work. He checks the padlock on the trunk one more time, pulls the cord to the light switch, and then descends the steep attic stairs to investigate.

CHAPTER NINETEEN — LEFTOVERS

OLIVIA

Olivia is relieved to have her feet up and her eyes closed for a moment. She imagines that her overwhelming feeling of exhaustion comes either from waking up an hour earlier that morning to care for Ken and Barbie or from coming down with something she might have picked up in the emergency room, as she feels drained of all her strength.

Trying to decide what to make for dinner makes her stomach turn. She considers what she has in the fridge against going out into the freezing cold to George's small market to buy something that's probably also frozen, or finally visiting the quails she insisted they needed to raise and taking five of their little lives in exchange for their supper.

Given the precariousness of Charlotte's health, of course, the quails are the best choice. Fresh, free-range poultry versus processed food from a factory. There's no debate… except that they're cute, and she can't bring herself to kill a single one. She decides to freeze all her venison leftovers for another dinner. She feels she can't take another bite of it, despite how good it came out, but there's still something about it that makes her gag at the thought of eating it again.

Her heart jumps at the sound of her phone ringing. She answers it quickly so as not to wake the twins from their nap. With her eyes still closed, she says, "Hello," expecting the person on the other end to be the nurse practitioner calling with an update.

"Olivia?" says the faint voice, "Is it really you?"

Olivia gasps as tears fall from her eyes. "Mummy, oh Mummy, thank you so much for calling me back. I've missed you so much. I'm the worst daughter on the planet. "Can you ever forgive me?"

"Darling, where have you been and what have you been up to?"

Olivia explains, "In Boston, married, two kids and …"

Her mother interrupts her, "I'm a grandmother?"

Olivia confirms, "Yes, Mummy. They're twins, Charlotte and Henry."

Her mother commands, "Send me a photo straight away!"

Olivia texts her mother a couple of family photos and waits for her response. She hears cries of joy as her mother catches her breath. "They're lovely, darling. When can I see them?"

Olivia continues, "Mummy, you will have to come to us. I'm awaiting my US citizenship and am in a sort of limbo until I can get a new passport." There's a long silence. "Mummy, is everything all right?"

Her mother admits, "It's a bit complicated to explain, I'm afraid."

"Mummy, if it's about the painting I took, please let me make it right?"

Her mother chuckles, "You silly little goose, it's not that."

She's relieved to hear her mother's voice has a loving tone, and she proceeds with her apology, "Mummy, I was a young, dumb girl. I'm so sorry I hurt you."

Her mother chuckles again, "Pish Posh, I'm not the least bit upset; it's in the past now."

Olivia finds her mother's reaction incredulous, asking, "How are you not furious with me, Mummy?"

Her mother giggles again and finally shares, "It just so happens that it worked out very well. You see, the first thing I did when I discovered Uncle Alfred's painting was amiss was to telephone the police and report it stolen."

"Mummy, what I put you through was horrible."

Her mother continues, "That day I walked into our flat and saw that my most treasured possession was gone, I collapsed. Keep in mind, I hadn't known at that point it was you who had snitched it."

Feeling uneasy, Olivia asks, "Mummy, am I wanted in London for stealing your Munning's painting?"

Her mother sounds serious again, "You obviously had no idea of its value."

Feeling ashamed, Olivia confesses, "No, Mummy, I didn't have a clue."

Her mother raises her voice, "It's worth at least fifty thousand British pounds sterling, you silly goose, and mind you – that's pounds, not dollars. The last one in the world to sell is on exhibit at Churchill Downs. The Hackney horse you snitched from me is a part of our Hackney history and a true family treasure, darling." Her mother pauses long enough to let her daughter reflect in disgrace for a moment. "So, what do you have to say about that?"

Olivia stammers as tears start again, "All I have is the original thousand pounds Patty paid me. I never spent it; I was too ashamed of what I'd done. If it takes me fifty years, I'll pay you back, Mummy."

Sounding annoyed, her mother asks, "What in God's name did you want the money for in the first place, and why didn't you simply come to me?"

"I felt as if I were suffocating and needed to find my own way. An employment agency offered me a nanny position in Boston, and I didn't think about the consequences. I just leaped at the chance to go on the adventure. The whole thing was stupid, and the people who hired me were just the worst people imaginable, and their children were even more awful." Olivia confesses.

"Well, I can't say I'm exactly surprised by what you did. You take after your father, I guess." Her mother sighs. "He was never happy unless he was on the move, and that's mostly why I left him."

Feeling confused, Olivia questions her mother, "You left him? I always believed he left us."

Not at all. I didn't want to live the life of an itinerant musician any longer. Although he made a good living, it wasn't the life for us. Obviously, I was wrong because you're just like your father. Who else would up and disappear for five years?

"Mummy, please join us for Christmas."

Her mother chuckles again, "Oh, now it's time for me to reveal the complicated part."

Olivia worries, *what if she's too sick to travel, or worse? What if she can't afford to travel and is in bad health on top of her financial woes?* Olivia blurts out, "Mummy, are you sick?"

"Not at all, fit as a fiddle."

"Is it the cost?" Olivia inquires.

"No, it's something else. I'm married." After her mother reveals this, a long silence follows.

"Mummy, are you happy?"

"Oh yes, darling, extremely."

"How did you meet him?"

Her mother explains, "Well, this is the complicated part. Remember, I mentioned I had immediately reported the theft of Uncle Alfred's painting to the police."

"Yes."

Her mother continues, "That same day, they informed me it was found."

Olivia is puzzled, "How's that possible?"

Her mother reveals, "After Patty purchased the painting from you, being a gentleman, he checked to see if the painting was pinched, and when he discovered it was, he immediately reported it to the recovery unit. When we spoke, it took us all of five seconds to figure out it was you who took it."

Olivia is impressed by how Patty handled things and feels fortunate that she sold it to him rather than to someone who would have exploited her ignorance.

Her mother is still speaking, "He sensed how distraught I was over the entire affair and invited me to join him at a bar in Camden called World's End. We talked that night until the bar closed. Truthfully, I didn't want to return to our sad, little, and empty flat. He was there for me in my time of duress." She takes a deep breath, "You truly crushed me, and back then, you were my whole world."

Olivia tries to change the subject: "So you married Patty?"

"Yes, I did, and I might add, he's not too fond of you."

"I see," Olivia admits with a hint of shame in her voice. "Is there anything I can do to make this right?"

She ignores Olivia's question and replies, "Patty returned the painting to me that evening. Today it hangs in the library of our London townhome." She mentions this as if they own another home somewhere else and continues. "The irony is that the painting will be yours someday, to do with as you please. The only thing it costs you is your relationship with us."

Olivia feels nauseated and exhausted. "Mummy, please talk to Patty and beg him to forgive me, pretty please, I implore you."

"I will, my darling, I will. It must be late in the day for you on the other side of the pond."

"Yes, Mummy. I can hear the twins calling me, and I need to go make them their supper." Olivia looks up and notices William has come into the room and is waiting for her. "Mummy, can we talk tomorrow?"

Her mother replies, "Whenever you'd like. Do you have WhatsApp?"

"Yes," says Olivia.

Her mother confirms, "Great, we'll chat on that because it's free and I want to talk to my grandbabies and meet your husband as well."

Olivia blushes. "Mummy, he's right here. William, say hello to Mummy."

William thought she might be talking to her mother and is pleased when she confirms it.

"Hello, Mummy," he says with a chuckle, "I'm your son-in-law William."

"Nice to meet you, William."

Olivia ends the call with, "Bye, Mummy, love you."

"Olie, tomorrow?"

"Yes." And they both hang up.

William smiles, "That seemed to go well."

With the sound of relief in her voice, "Yes, it did, and it didn't. My mother married a nice man named Patty, but he is not very keen on me at present."

"That's understandable. What's for dinner?" begs William.

"I was considering quails because they cook fast, but I couldn't bring myself to do it," she admits.

William offers, "I'll do it for you and skin them as well. I'm starving."

Olivia looks down at her tank watch and notices how late it is. She smiles at him and says, "I think it's too late to start something like that. Tomorrow, perhaps? How about pizza?"

William instructs, "Great, call it in and I'll go pick it up, but you're doing bath time tonight."

"How do you Yanks say it... Oh yeah, consider it a done deal!" Then she calls out, "Charlie, Henry, come in here. It's bath time."

When the twins appear, Olivia scoops them up into her arms and smothers them with kisses, hugging them as they giggle and wiggle, resisting their bath.

CHAPTER TWENTY — I NEED THIS JOB

WILLIAM

William's teeth chatter from the cold as he speeds down the road toward Sherborn House of Pizza to pick up their dinner. When he reaches Route 115, he presses harder on the accelerator. The interior of his truck finally begins to warm up, but he can still see his breath in the glow of the dashboard lights. Then, out of nowhere, a police car with flashing lights and a siren follows directly behind him.

"Oh shit!" William says aloud as he pulls over to the side of the road and reaches for his registration in the glove box.

There's a tap at his window, and he opens it. "Good evening, officer," he says politely.

The officer replies, "Hi William, I recognized your truck and pulled you over to see how Charlotte made out at the hospital."

With a sense of relief, William replies, "Hi Bobby, she's doing better, but we still don't know what made her sick."

Bobby states firmly, "Take it easy on the gas pedal. There's a deer crossing up ahead."

William confirms, "Will do, and thanks for your help the other night."

Bobby mutters as he walks away, "Glad to be of service." Then he turns off the flashing lights and backs into his dark spot located at the end of a long driveway that he uses as his Route 115 speed trap.

William happily resumes driving, and he's excited that he didn't get a ticket even though he was going fifteen miles per hour over the speed limit.

He picks up their pizzas, Greek salads, some cookies, and a scratch ticket. He gets back in his truck, which he left running to stay warm. The cabin is nice inside, and he places the food on the passenger seat next to him before closing his door.

On the drive home, his phone rings. He hits the speaker button and assumes it's Olivia and the twins asking him where the food is, so he roars with a big, "HELLO!"

The gentleman on the other end says, "I beg your pardon? I'm looking for William Loring."

Well, this didn't get off to a good start, he thinks, cringing with embarrassment.

Hoping he hadn't already blown his interview, he responds, "Good evening, sir, and you're speaking with William Loring."

"Good!" That's all he says. Then there's a long silence before he introduces himself, "William, I'm Allen Tyler Jr, Director of the Willed Body Program at the University of Texas Medical in Galveston."

"Nice to meet you, sir. How can I be of service?"

Allen asks, "Please describe your military service for me."

"My pleasure, Sir. I served four years in the Air National Guard as a medic at Otis Air National Guard's Joint Base in Barnstable, Massachusetts."

"Tell me something, son. During your time there, did you ever administer CPR?"

"Yes, sir."

"Did you ever encounter a DOA?"

William is nervous, and his mouth starts to run off uncontrollably. "Yes, sir. There were a few, sir, but the one I recall most vividly. He was an older man and an active-duty officer. We kept working on him until we reached the hospital. No heartbeat, no vital signs, and a temperature of 92 degrees and dropping. He looked pretty dead to me."

Allen inquires, "What happened to him?"

"Something told me not to give up on the guy; it was like a miracle, sir. My team members said he was a goner, and after my twelfth paddle attempt to revive his heart, he just opened his eyes and asked us where he was."

Allen concurs, "Well, doesn't our lord work in mysterious ways, praise Jesus." Then he falls silent again, and William waits for his next question: "You also work with livestock."

"Yes, sir."

Allen continues his questioning, "Do you slaughter and butcher the animals yourself?"

"Yes, I do. Otherwise, how else could I feed my family, sir?"

"Good point, William. Are you also a hunter?"

"Yes, sir," William confirms, worried that his response might be misinterpreted by someone anti-gun.

Allen continues, "What kind of animals do you usually hunt?"

William replies, "Mostly deer and some wild birds on occasion, sir."

Allen changes the subject, "Can you tell me if you would be averse to working in the evenings and over long weekends from time to time?"

William considers this question promising and says, "I would have to discuss the schedule with my wife, but it shouldn't be a problem, sir."

The tone in Allen's voice shifts when he says, "That's reasonable. Do you have any questions, William? Oh, and please call me Allen."

"What would I be doing for work?" he inquires.

Allen snickers, "Fair enough question, but I'd prefer to show you what the work entails rather than explaining it over the phone. I'll be coming to Boston this Thursday for a surgical training seminar in Cambridge. I should be done by 4:00 pm, and then I'll need to check into my hotel room and grab a bite to eat. How about we meet at 8:00 p.m. at the Randolph plant? I'll text you the address."

William is very excited and wants to sound as professional as possible. *Don't blow this*, he worries before he ends the call with, "Thank you very much for this opportunity, eh, Allen, sir. I look forward to meeting with you Thursday night." *Nailed it*, he thinks to himself as they say goodbye, and they end the call.

Finally, back on Raven Road and just seconds from home, he feels optimistic about this new opportunity and can't wait to share the news with his family.

#

Hearing Charlotte holler, "Daddy's home," is music to William's ears, and there's so much to talk about over dinner. What a day, he thinks. Olivia seems to have reconciled with her mother, and for the first time, he entertains the thought that the twins will finally have a real, live grandmother, and that their financial problems may soon be eased. He decides to grab a bottle of champagne from the remains of his father's wine collection in the cellar to go with the pizza.

Oh, I've got to let Ian know, too, because I'm going to use him as a job reference for the interview. The only downside is that Olivia will have to pick up more around the farm, and she's already helping out at Hattie's. Yikes, he thinks. This is just too much all at once for her. He decides that if he is offered this position, they will hire someone to help feed the animals and clean the stalls.

At dinner, he looks across the table and notices Olivia is more radiant than usual and says, "Olie, you had quite the call."

Olivia agrees, "It went well, and oddly enough. I owe it all to Hattie. If she hadn't given me an ultimatum, I think I might not have gone through with it because too much time apart can cause a heart to harden."

William thinks about his grandmother's diamond ring in his pocket and is also grateful to Hattie for encouraging him to find it and give it to Olivia.

Olivia makes a pensive face and asks, "Would you mind if my mum joins us for Christmas?"

"Olie, of course not, and there was no need to ask me either."

Olivia takes a bite of her pizza and nods her head in appreciation. After she finishes swallowing, she makes an unusual request. "Is shotgun hunting season over?"

William replies curiously, "There are a couple of days left. Why?"

Olivia giggles, "Should my mum and stepfather join us? I think I'll want to serve all the traditional English favorites."

William replies, "Awesome. What do you need me to do?"

She confides, "Well, my mum's nickname for me is silly goose. Would you mind going out into the woods and catching one for me while there's time?"

Olivia's mind floods with ideas for recipes to make when they visit. "What do you think about an orange marmalade five-spiced goose, with a side of carrots and parsnip puree, then a Yorkshire pudding with a beef rib roast, and of course a Brussels sprout and chestnut vegetable casserole. Oh, and yes, of course, a Christmas trifle, with a traditional plum pudding, and bacon-wrapped dried pears and dried apricots, and Mummy's favorite jumbo shrimp cocktail, oh, and what else, yes, yes, yes, a whole bunch of fresh steamed lobsters from Market Basket, and…" She takes a sip of champagne.

William refills her glass, and she nods to show her thanks as he interrupts her train of thought with, "All I can promise is I'll do my best because it's late in the season and they've flown south for the winter, but I might get lucky and bag one."

She looks at him and smiles. "And I want to pluck it because I want the skin to be perfect for my recipe." Then she sips the champagne and says, "Yummy, and thanks for celebrating my reconciliation with my mum with me."

William sees she is preoccupied with preparing for their possible visit and interjects, "Olie, Dr. Ferguson may have found me exactly what I'm looking for."

Olie scowls, "How's that, because I'm not even really sure what you're looking for?"

He explains, "Enough side work for me to keep us going financially until things are back under control again. I'm guessing it will be a couple of nights a week and some weekends at the start."

She complains, "That's a lot of time spent away from us."

"It's good money. Think about it, Olie. I'll be able to buy you all those things you've been wanting."

Still reeling with guilt over the painting she snitched and the pain she caused her mother, she confirms, "William, I'm happy with what we have, and I don't need anything more. Please don't do this to buy more stuff for me."

Her statement impresses him and warms his heart, but the reason he's doing this isn't for her. It's because he owes a large debt on their credit cards and can't find any other way to dig them out of it. However, for the first time in a while, he feels like everything might be okay.

CHAPTER TWENTY-ONE — PANDORA'S BOX

OLIVIA

Olivia wakes up in a sweat as her heart pounds in her chest. She glances at the alarm clock and decides that, even though it's only 3:45 am, she might as well get up and start working on the research for their dog breeding business. Still in bed and under the covers, she googles Chinese Cresteds on her iPhone and is surprised by what she sees. OMG, they're so cute; no wonder Hattie wants to breed them.

Quietly, she slides out of bed, goes to pee, and runs downstairs to look up the Weiss Kennel in Illinois on William's laptop. Trying to remember what Hattie had asked her, she looks over the dogs and thinks, Oh, yes, now I recall. Do I prefer puffs or hairless?

After perusing the photos on the kennel's website, she decides her answer is definitely the hairless pups because they're so ugly they're beautiful. Intrigued, she scours the website for prices and finds none, then wonders why.

From what she can glean from the internet, the breed originated in China; however, the dogs are found all over the world and have numerous health issues that require DNA testing. So, not to sound stupid when she makes her initial call, she scribbles on her pad that she needs to request a heterozygous mutation and understands that a pair of hairless dogs can produce a puff because they're both carrying the puff hair gene, which creates a homozygous or hairy puppy. Given that brothers and sisters in the same litter can be either, except for a hairless-hairless, which scientifically is impossible, as they don't develop in the womb. How sad she imagines.

Olivia ponders momentarily, Charlie all covered in fur and Henry hairless, then chuckles at the image in her mind. All these big words: allele, recessive, dominant, traits, zygote. Well, that's enough new vocabulary for one day. Feeling a bit ignorant and intimidated by all this jargon, she closes the laptop and heads to the kitchen to fill thermoses.

"Bullocks!" she says out loud when she realizes she didn't get hers back from Hattie. After she finishes filling William's with coffee and hot milk, she fills her coffee in a paper cup with a lid. Then she heads over to Jameson Farm to feed the horses and shovel shit, so they can make more horseshit for her to shovel again tomorrow. Unlike cow manure, which is like gold to a gardener and recycled into their fields, horseshit is just like it sounds: not worth horseshit.

After Olivia finishes at the stable, she walks outside into the cold, crisp air, finishing her tepid cup of coffee and gobbles down a power bar. She looks around at Hattie's house, and all the lights are off. It seems that George stayed overnight to care for her, as his car is still parked next to the house. Olivia really wants to know how things went at Dana-Farber, but doesn't want to intrude, and it's probably best that she rests.

Just then, an Amazon delivery truck arrives, and the delivery person walks to the front door, about to ring the bell.

"Whoa there, you can give me the package."

"Are you Hattie Young?"

"I'll take it, thank you, and yes." A harmless lie isn't going to send me to hell, she decides as she reaches for the package.

The delivery person takes a photo of Olivia holding it and then speeds out of the driveway.

Olivia decides to take it with her instead of leaving it behind now that she has taken responsibility for it. She hops into the truck and heads home for breakfast.

#

Her family is already seated at the table when she returns. They're eating steel-cut oatmeal and hot cocoa. Olivia is starving, helps herself to a bowl, and pours another cup of coffee when she sits down.

William asks her, "What's tucked under your arm?"

"Oh, this, I forgot I even had it." She places it on the table. "It's a package from Amazon for Hattie. Can you believe the delivery person was going to ring her doorbell at 6:00 am? Sheesh!"

William's face turns red. "Whatever you do, Olie, I wouldn't open one of Hattie's packages without her permission!"

She sips her drink and looks at him like there's something wrong with him. "William, we're in the kennel business together now. How else am I going to organize and put away our supplies if I don't open the packages?"

William's face reddens as he pleads with her, "Understandable, but maybe this is something she needs urgently." He grabs the package and heads toward the kitchen door.

"Where are you going?" she commands.

"You're right! She needs it now," William whines.

"I didn't say that you did. What I said was she's still asleep." She gives him a scornful stare and asks, "William, what's gotten into you?"

Still holding the package, he sits down and finishes his hot cocoa before finally saying, "Let's bring it over together later and see how she made out yesterday at Dana-Farber."

She answers him with, "Whatever, I have a million things to do in the barn, and the chicken coop is a disaster. Charlie, Henry want to help Mummy feed the chickens and collect eggs?"

"Okey Dokey," says Henry, and they follow her. The children put on their coats, hats, mittens, and Wellies in silence.

William smiles and asks, "Want me to take care of the quails so we can have them for dinner tonight?"

Olivia cringes at the thought of eating those cute little birds for their supper, but she reminds herself she insisted they buy and breed them, so she conceals how she feels and says, "William, that's perfect, and please skin them too if you don't mind."

He gives her a happy thumbs up, and she wonders if he has any idea how uncomfortable she is with the thought of eating those tiny, helpless creatures, and she asks herself why she bought them in the first place.

#

With the kids napping and William working in the garage, Olivia picks up the Amazon package from the table and heads to Jameson Farm to check on Hattie.

When she arrives, she notices George's car is gone, but another one is in its place. She wonders if one of the nurses might have returned to infuse Hattie.

Olivia knocks on the door and hears Hattie's gravelly voice say, "Come in, it's open."

Olivia enters and says, "Hello, I'm Olivia," to the woman sitting on Hattie's couch.

Hattie motions for Olivia to sit down as she explains, "This is Margaret, my insurance agent. I met with her today to go over our partners' life insurance policy that I want to purchase for our new business venture."

"Hattie, I can't afford life insurance right now."

"First of all, because you're so young and healthy, it's dirt cheap. Secondly, I'm adding it to the startup costs of our business. And thirdly, after what I saw William go through when his parents were murdered by some low-life drug addict driving into them head-on and leaving William with virtually no money to survive, I've decided you can't afford not to have it. So, there's no discussion!"

Hattie hands Olivia a form to sign. "Here! Sign it and date it, and then hand it to Margaret! This is when you say thank you and go home."

Olivia follows her directions and doesn't dare ask another question. She thinks to herself how grateful she is that she listened to William and didn't open Hattie's package because, at times, this woman terrifies her.

Then she hands the Amazon package to Hattie and says, "Thank you, and here, this came early this morning for you."

Hattie mumbles, "I didn't order anything. I wonder what it is?" She tears open the package, looks inside the pouch, and then smiles that vulpine smile of hers.

Olivia begs, "What is it?"

Hattie says nonchalantly, spreading her hands out to show they're empty, "Just an empty box."

Olivia is intrigued, "Like Pandora's?"

"Exactly," Hattie confirms. Well, now that our work here is finished for the day, I'm going to take a nap, and I want everyone to get out."

Olivia pleads, "But Hattie, we wanted to know how you made out yesterday at Dana-Farber?"

Hattie firmly repeats, "Out!"

CHAPTER TWENTY-TWO — DIENER IS READY

WILLIAM

After putting away the dinner dishes, William kisses Olivia goodbye and heads out for his job interview. Deep down, he really wants this job but fears he will do or say something stupid and blow it. Looking back, he can't remember many job interviews in his life. When he enlisted in the National Guard, the interview was just a pass-or-fail physical. When he got his job at Zaftig's Deli, they already knew him as a customer and as a good friend of George and Hattie, so they hired him on the spot when Hattie said to the restaurant manager, "Why don't you hire Billy, he could use the extra money." Come to think of it, this might be my first, and his mouth dries up from nerves.

What should I say to Allen? What is he looking for, and how many other people am I competing against for this position? Then he starts to hyperventilate and asks himself, What the hell am I getting myself into? The last time I listened to Shane Ferguson, I almost ended up in jail. The little hairs on the back of his neck stand at attention again as he recalls his mother's advice about things being too good to be true, and his common sense tells him there's something off about this opportunity.

To calm himself, he decides that just finding out about it is harmless and will only cost him one evening. The worst-case scenario is that he ends up with a good story to tell, and he decides to call Ian, "Hey, are you out on a delivery?"

"Nope, I'm watching the Celtics game."

William asks, "What's the score?"

Ian says, "89-78 Celtics, third quarter, three minutes left."

William hopes Ian has an update on a job at A.O.R.A. "Any word about what we talked about?"

Ian says begrudgingly, "Stan, my boss, put in a request to waive the five-year minimum, but the fact that you don't have the red-light driver's training will make it difficult to hire you. I'll keep you posted. Stan's trying his best."

William can tell from the tone in Ian's voice that A.O.R.A. is a dead end and says, "Hey, in case you get a call from a guy named Allen Tyler, please give me a good reference."

Ian laughs out loud and responds, "What else would I give you?"

William chuckles, "You know, this is all new to me, and I'm pretty clueless. I'm heading to the interview now."

"Where is it?" Ian asks.

"Randolph," he says, as he can tell Ian is only half listening while watching the game. "Look, I'm almost there. I'll let you know how it goes."

"Good luck, you're going to kill it."

"Thanks," says William. He ends the call and then glances at the directions again.

When William turns onto York Street, he notices that the area is mainly made up of enormous warehouses. He drives past the massive Pearl Meat Packing Plant, and it brings back happy memories of July 4th cookouts with his mom and dad.

When Siri informs him he's arrived at his destination, he sees a white, well-lit warehouse-style building that stretches for at least a few blocks. No signs are showing where he is or where he should go.

Wow, what is this place? He asks himself. The giant white monolith stretches on forever as he drives around it, looking for a way inside. Finally, he finds what might be an entrance.

When he reaches the front door, he finds it locked, and he blurts out in frustration, "Shit!" He shivers from the cold and glances at his watch. He's right on time, but then begins to worry he might be in the wrong place or have misunderstood the time for their appointment.

He looks up the driveway and sees headlights approaching. A nondescript mid-size car pulls in and parks near his truck. An older man wearing cowboy boots, jeans, a heavy sweater, and a long black oil coat emerges. There's something Morpheus-like about him, reminiscent of the Matrix, and William worries to himself, 'He was the good guy, right?'

The man reaches into the back seat of the car, grabs a black cowboy hat and a fancy, tooled leather briefcase that looks like a drop bag for a cash swap in an old mafia movie. With no facial expression, he starts walking toward William.

He introduces himself by apologizing, "Sorry if I made you wait long, I'm Allen Tyler Jr, William."

William confesses, "Just got here. Nice to meet you."

"Please let me prepare you for what's about to happen. When we enter the airlock chamber, we will be sprayed briefly, and a blue light will flash. It's just a standard health precaution, and you'll get used to it quickly."

William's heart rate speeds up a bit, but he hides his fear and says, "All right, I'm ready."

Allen flashes his ID in front of a scanner, and the double doors open automatically. They step into an outer chamber, where they find masks and protective glasses. They put them on, and Allen signals for William to follow him into the next chamber. The doors close behind them automatically, and an intense ultraviolet light pulses around them. When the light stops, a mist fills the chamber. William coughs before asking, "What is this stuff?"

He explains, "It's a mixture of chemicals, mainly peroxide. It's necessary because this building functions as a medical manufacturing and research facility, and they spare no expense to protect it from contaminants entering or leaving."

"How come no signs?"

Allen replies, "Haloderm learned the hard way that warehouses marked medical invite break-ins."

The doors on the other side of the chamber finally open, and Allen motions for William to follow him.

The first thing that catches William's attention is the pervasive bad smell, which immediately leaves a strange taste of formaldehyde in the back of his throat. Then, as they keep walking, he notices the temperature and estimates it isn't much higher than 40 degrees Fahrenheit. They walk the long corridors for about ten minutes. Along the way, they pass endless doors and hallways. The interior of the building has a modern hospital vibe, characterized by bright lighting, seamless flooring, and a clean atmosphere. The only difference is that there are no patients, doctors, or windows.

Allen doesn't say a word to him along the way, and William wonders if he's already blown his interview, thinking the rest of this meeting is just a courtesy. If there was ever a time William wished he were good at small talk, it's now.

Allen stops and scans his badge in front of a door. It unlocks automatically, and they step inside. The room contains a conference table, chairs, monitors, and seminar supplies. Nothing here seems out of the ordinary.

Allen offers, "Can I get us some water?"

William thinks, *us*, That's odd, and says, "Sure." Especially now that his mouth is so dry, he can feel his tongue congealed to the roof of his mouth, and his fight-or-flight response is on overdrive, telling him to get up and flee.

Allen begins explaining the job's responsibilities by sharing an anecdote from a past event. William is struggling to follow along and understand where this is all heading.

"I'm a diener, William. Deniers have been around for a long time, and without our skills, surgeons couldn't learn how to do their work. That's the best way I can describe my job: I make all of that possible for them."

He removes his glasses and rubs his eyes before continuing. "This is a brief but poignant story I share with everyone considering a position with me. It's about Dr. Knox, a surgeon from Scotland in the 1800s. He was a truly eccentric man and one of the pioneers of modern surgery. Well, he needed human cadavers to teach his medical students, and there were laws at the time in Scotland about the source of those cadavers. However, I won't bore you with the details; if you're interested, you can look them up on Google yourself. So, he spread the word to locals that if they had a loved one who had passed away, he would pay them for the body. Eventually, a local innkeeper named Burke had a guest who died before settling her bill. This upset him because he would also be responsible for paying for her burial. His bartender at the hotel, a man named Hare, suggested they deliver her body to Dr. Knox, who might reward them for their troubles. They rationalized that the woman had no family or friends and wouldn't be missed, and off they went in their horse-drawn wagon to the university, where they dropped off her body with Dr. Knox, who paid them far more money than they had expected."

William looks directly at Allen, puzzled about how something that happened hundreds of years ago could connect to this job.

Allen asks him, "Are you following me so far?"

William nods his head affirmatively while thinking, I have no clue where this is going.

Allen continues, "Well, a few weeks later, Burke burned through the money Dr. Knox paid him, and he decided, why not do this again. It's good money, and I'll get Hare to help me out. Subsequently, they delivered seventeen dead bodies to Dr. Knox, who is happy to receive them, and as unbelievable as it sounds, Dr. Knox claims to the police that it never occurred to him to ask Burke and Hare where the bodies were coming from."

"Oh." That's all William says.

"You see, William, I'm proud of what I do, but I'm not proud of that story and many others like it. The stigma surrounding it makes our kind of work much harder. As I've already mentioned, I've led the Willed Body Program in Galveston for over forty years. What I'm trying to convey is that there's a big difference between a ghoulish grave robber and an altruistic professional who advances medical science. Without our work, surgeons won't progress, medical science will stall, and how else will we learn new life-saving techniques?"

William thinks he's finally getting the gist. This is about being able to handle a job that involves working around corpses, just like Ian. Wow, he thinks. I was already ready to work at A.O.R.A. if they'd have me, so I'll keep an open mind, as he relaxes in his chair.

Allen asks him, "Son, are you with me so far?"

William answers, "Yes."

Allen nods and says, "All right, now the next part of this interview is not easy, and it's not something any one of us knows about ourselves until we experience it."

William states, "I'm ready, sir."

Allen seems unsure about William and says, "All right, I'll continue to explain while we're on our way to the surgical suite that was prepared for us."

The door is completely unmarked except for the number J18, where they halt.

Allen follows William into a changing room with lockers. Nothing about it seems unusual except that it's in the middle of a building that can be measured in acres, and there is not a single other person present. Without a word, Allen motions for him to disrobe and hands him scrubs to change into, followed by covers for his sneakers, a cap for his hair, an N95 mask of a quality he has never seen before, and protection to cover his eyes. Then they go to the sinks and scrub their hands, drying them thoroughly. Allen demonstrates how to put on the first of two pairs of gloves.

Allen loudly states, "Rule number one, never enter this room if you're overtired or intoxicated in any way!"

"What's rule number two?" Asks William.

"For tonight, it's don't touch anything! There are about a hundred rule number twos that are all equally important, and if you pass my test, I'll text you your training information and bring you to Texas for full immersion with me."

William is feeling optimistic about his test and follows Allen through another airlock.

Allen explains that once they're in the surgical suite, the subject on the table, draped in a sheet, is an elderly lady, and the task is to prepare her for an upcoming urology surgery seminar.

Allen positions William directly across from him. Then he moves his instruments closer to himself and pauses to ask William, "Son, are you ready?"

All he says is, "Yes, sir."

Allen reveals that the woman is marginally decomposed and reeks of formaldehyde. Allen looks at William for a reaction and asks, "How are you doing, son?"

William raises his right hand and makes an OK gesture.

Allen says, "Good, now comes the actual test. Oh, and don't worry about the smell. The air filtration system here is incredible. It refreshes the air twenty times per hour, almost double the industry standard, and you'll get used to the smell quickly."

William thinks about how used to the smell of horse shit and cow manure he is, and isn't too concerned. He replies, "I'm OK with it, sir."

 Allen laughs, "Wait till we begin taking her apart before you say that." Then he reaches for a scalpel and cuts away her scalp. He glances up at William to see how he reacts to it, "You still good?"

"Yes, sir."

Then Allen asks, "Feeling faint or queasy?"

William responds, "No, sir," and gives him a thumbs up.

Allen adds, "Any questions?"

William responds, "Yes, sir, I do. Where did she come from?"

Allen tries to answer him while focusing on his work: "Mostly, the cadavers come from people who are organ donors but didn't make the cut to be transferred to a living person, or, like many old people, they leave their body to their alma mater if it has a medical school."

"Why don't people make the cut, sir?"

"Oh, for many reasons. The donor might be too old or have undetected cancer. Then there are the obvious ones like HIV/AIDS, hepatitis, TB, meningitis, or newer concerns such as monkeypox and COVID, or the all-time worst, which is Creutzfeldt-Jakob disease. To name a few. FYI, that's why we're checking her brain tissue first. It's especially common in older people with a history of international travel combined with possible misdiagnosed dementia or Alzheimer's. So now you're beginning to understand that finding a healthy donor match is like winning a billion-dollar lottery."

"What's Cruzfeild-Jakes disease again?" William stumbles over the name.

"Just call it CJD for now, and it's more commonly known as Mad Cow disease."

William realizes it's similar to something he's heard before and adds, "Oh, that I'm more familiar with because I'm a deer hunter and we get updates from Fish and Game to be on the lookout for Chronic Wasting disease."

"It's the same principle, so always wear double gloves when you butcher a deer or elk. And whatever you do, if you suspect the meat, don't eat it. Call to have it removed, and bury your butchering tools deep in the ground after carefully sealing them. CJD was spread in England by feeding cow meat to cows."

William confirms, "That's disgusting."

Allen continues, "It truly is, and it's nearly impossible to kill or destroy misfolded prions. They've tried burning them at high temperatures, even above 1500 degrees, as well as using radiation and solvents, but nothing has worked. Any tools used are considered contaminated and can still spread the disease. It's pretty nasty stuff."

William asks, "What do you do if you find it?"

"Here in this building, they're prepared for it, so we'd stop the procedure, and Haloderm's Hazmat Team takes over. This suite and the storage container she was stored in would be decontaminated and sealed up, along with this scalpel and all the tools in this room."

Allen continues as he reaches for a small power saw and smiles, "OK, next up, or as I like to call it, NO GUTS, NO GLORY."

William thinks maybe he's starting to loosen up and beginning to like me, too. Then he watches as Allen removes the top of the old lady's skull and places her brain on the tray next to them.

Allen examines the brain tissue carefully and gives William a thumbs-up. Then he gathers more tools and a larger power saw.

William asks, "Is there anything I can do to help?"

Allen reiterates, "Not tonight, son, it's just too dangerous for you to be in here without proper training. It will come in time. In the next part, we're going to divide this body into sections by category for future training seminars. First, we will prepare the hands for hand surgery training, then the feet for podiatry surgery, and so on. My task tonight is to collect only the torso for a urology-gynecology surgery seminar that's taking place at the Westin Hotel at Copley Place tomorrow afternoon. So, watch me collect and store all the body parts for future use and then pack her torso into a cooler with dry ice for tomorrow."

After about two hours of dismembering, bagging, and labeling with bar codes on each body part's bag, what was once an old lady is now a collection of carefully labeled body parts. William can't get over how adept Allen's surgical skills are and how respectfully he treated her body. There is nothing wasted, and as he prepares to clean up the surgical suite, he resumes making small talk. "So, what did you think?"

William eagerly replies, "Allen, I could do this if you gave me the chance."

"Good, let's put the rest of her back in the fridge, clean ourselves up, and have a midnight snack." Allen laughs when he adds, "One of the best things about working here is you don't have to worry about refrigerating your takeout food, so I picked up an order at Kelly's Roast Beef for us on my way here and some 7-UPs to go with it."

"What's the temperature?" asks William.

"About 5.5 Celsius to help retard the spoilage of the inventory and keep the servers cool."

William realizes that, to Allen, inventory means dead people. They walk together to a door marked J36, and soon he discovers it's a walk-in freezer. Allen carefully places the woman's body parts on the designated shelf that matches her barcode on the scanner. William wonders, upon entering, if a motion or infrared heat detector controls every light in the building, because as they leave the walk-in, the lights go dark.

On their way back to change into their street clothes, William asks, "What's next?"

Allen laughs and says, "Your final test of the night. We're heading back to the conference room for that one."

#

In the conference room, feeling more relaxed and optimistic, William sits at the table and waits for Allen's instructions. Just then, an alarm sounds on Allen's watch, and he apologizes, "So sorry, William. It's complicated, but I have to make a call right now. I'll only be a couple of minutes." Allen reaches for the wall telephone and dials zero. "Hello, this is Allen Tyler Jr. Access code P3145926535, and I need to make a previously scheduled outgoing call."

William is puzzled why he didn't pick up his cell phone and wonders if it's related to his job interview. He then notices Allen's body relax when he says, "Hi Rose, yes, I'm fine. Oh, the seminars have been splendid. Yes, I'll pick up a couple of lobsters at Hooks on my way to the airport. No, sweetheart, I won't forget to have them packed in dry ice. Now, please go to sleep. You know how much I hate it when we're out of sync. I'll call you again tomorrow night, and then I'm heading home. Bye, love you too." Allen hangs up the wall phone, then takes a seat across from William at the conference table. He places his oversized, tooled leather briefcase on the table and reaches inside to grab a couple of bags from Kelly's Roast Beef.

"Sorry about the personal stuff. My wife Rose is blind, and she suffers from the Non-24-Sleep/Wake disorder. Omg, it's tough enough dealing with jetlag when I return home, but then my wife wants to keep me up all night, and I'm already exhausted from the seminars."

William asks him, "How long have you been married?"

Allen snickers as he passes a Kelly's roast beef sandwich and a 7-Up to William, saying, "Forever, our mothers sang in the church choir together and every Sunday placed us in the same crib during the service." He takes a bite of his sandwich and waits to see what William does. "Oh, want some chips with it?"

William hesitates to be polite, then ravenously takes a big bite. "Oh, that just hit the spot. I was starving." He confirms.

"Well, William, you just passed my final test with flying colors."

"I don't understand. What was the test?" William asks.

"You know how people just yes you to death," says Allen.

"Yup." He agrees.

Allen boasts, "Well, when I get this far with an applicant, they're either too nauseated to eat and just pretending that everything is all right, or possibly they're a good fit with this. The latter is the person I'm willing to train."

William unwraps another sandwich and takes a bite. Then asks while swallowing, "Are you telling me you're hiring me?"

"The job's yours if you want it. I like you, and I think you're going to be a natural to train."

"Thanks so much!" says William.

"Any questions?" asks Allen.

"Yes, what's the deal with the phones in here?"

"iPhones don't work inside this building, nor do photos, texts, or anything. I have no idea how they do it, but that's just how it is. I guess it's for security reasons."

William asks, "When do I start?"

Allen confirms, "You already have. Welcome aboard."

CHAPTER TWENTY-THREE — I'VE GOT YOUR BACK

IAN

Ian tosses and turns from insomnia because it's too difficult to return to a normal sleep rhythm after working all-nighters. Looking up in the darkness, he knows that once he checks his phone, he won't be able to go back to sleep. This is the part of his job he hates the most, he decides as his thoughts go all over the place.

Damn it, I'm not going to fall back asleep, he realizes as he picks up his phone and scrolls through his messages and alerts. The first ones he reads are from Bumble, and he's grossed out by the photos of the women who want to meet up with him as he continues to swipe through them. Then he asks himself, Why can't I find somebody nice like Olivia?

Just then, he gets a text from William: *Nailed it. I'm heading home now!*

Ian sits up in bed and calls his friend, "Dude, tell me everything!" Scout slowly rolls over for a belly rub while he's talking to him.

William says with enthusiasm, "My new boss Allen is awesome, the money is fantastic, and he's training me to be a diener, I think."

Ian doesn't want to sound stupid, so he doesn't ask him what that is and decides to look up the word later. He asks instead, "What's the name of the company?"

William replies, "Haloderm in Randolph."

Ian looks it up while William talks about the interview and reads a little about them. They produce regenerative skin matrix, and their other divisions include medical educational services, cadaver tendons, and a list that goes on and on, as deep as a rabbit hole. Then he sees a link for a facility tour video.

Ian exclaims, "Hey, I just found a video of the place and what they make. Want me to send it to you?"

"For sure, I can't wait to watch it and show it to Olivia," William replies.

"It's on its way. I'm going to watch it too," Ian shares.

"Ian, I haven't slept since the night before. When I get home, I'll have about an hour to rest before I need to get up, shower, eat, and start my daily chores. I know the routine is grueling, but I'll need some help until I find part-time workers for the farm."

"You need me to head over?" Ian generously offers.

"Actually, I'm so pumped up from the job offer, I'm good today, but I'm going to Galveston for training. That's when I'll need your help."

Ian shares, "No problem, as soon as I get my work schedule, I'll forward it to you, and as long as I'm not on call or scheduled, I'm all yours."

William adds, "Ian, I love you, man. If I hadn't been offered this job, I don't know what I would have done. I'm flat broke, and my credit cards are maxed out."

Ian chokes up and struggles to say, "I'm here for you."

William replies, "Thanks so much." He sighs in relief and adds, "I'm pulling onto Raven Road. I'll call you later."

Ian is so excited for his friend as he watches the video about his new employer. Wow, he's very impressed, and they even mention recovery people like him who make tissue collection possible.

He especially appreciates the part that details the number of people they have helped, including child burn victims, wounded soldiers, skin cancer patients, and breast cancer patients, and it makes him feel proud to be part of it. Since talking with William about the death of his parents in a fatal car accident caused by a drug addict, he has started to question his work and the moral issues linked to the organ donor industry. When the video ends, he closes his eyes and finally drifts off to sleep.

CHAPTER TWENTY-FOUR — PRICELESS

OLIVIA

Olivia can't believe it's after 2 am, and William isn't home yet from his job interview. She gets up and wanders into the bathroom to find something to soothe her nervous and upset stomach. She shifts some items in the medicine cabinet until she finds some Pepto-Bismol that's two years past its expiration date, and thinks, "That will work," as it goes down the hatch.

With her stomach filled with butterflies, she goes downstairs to look out the window for any sign of William. She considers calling him, but doesn't want to risk interrupting his meeting, so she puts the phone down. Eventually, with tremendous relief, she sees the garage lights come on as William pulls up to the house and parks the truck. She wraps her bathrobe tightly around her waist and greets him at the door.

William enters, smiling like a Cheshire cat from ear to ear.

Olivia begs, "Tell me everything."

He lifts her off the floor when he hugs her and boasts, "I got the job!"

"What?" she squeals, a mix of emotions, because she doesn't know how she will manage everything in his absence, but she continues, "That's wonderful!" Comprehending how relieved he must feel over the prospect of making good money.

She offers, "I'm going to put on the kettle for a pot of tea, and I want you to tell me everything. Are you hungry?"

He shares, "No, not at all. My new boss brought in sandwiches from Kelly's Roast Beef, and I stuffed my face. There were some extras, want one?" He reveals a sandwich wrapped in white paper from his vest pocket.

She refuses the offer and adds, "I couldn't sleep well with you not by my side, and it gave me an upset stomach, I think."

He puts the sandwich back in his pocket and reaches over to feel her forehead. "You're nice and cool, no fever."

"Tell me everything that happened at your interview," she begs.

"I got hired on the spot! Love my new boss. I spoke to Ian on the drive home, and he's going to help us out around here until we hire someone for chores, and honestly, everything is under control, Olie."

She probes, "What will you be doing?"

"It's a huge company; they have about 50,000 employees worldwide. All I know so far is that they make skin matrices from donors for patients. Their other divisions include medical training programs, and I think that's where I'll be working. Watch a video with me while we have our tea."

He cues up the video, showing the large white building he just left, along with people dressed in white scrubs, glasses, masks, and booties that match the ones he and Allen wore during the interview. Olivia grimaces as the video shows glimpses of human skin being prepared for processing into transplantable skin.

"Will you be doing that?" she asks.

"Not exactly." He reveals as he places his hand over hers and continues to explain, "There are many donors whose bodies are rejected for various reasons, and the division I'll be working for uses their bodies to teach life-changing surgical techniques to doctors."

"Wow! That's impressive, so you'll be transporting them to the hospital?"

"Sure." That's all he adds to their discussion.

Olivia is excited for him and knows she should hire someone to help because she doesn't think she can keep up this pace much longer.

She looks him in the eyes and pleads, "I know you're busy, but Hattie isn't herself, and she wouldn't give me much information about what happened during her appointment at Dana-Farber. Please go talk to her."

"Today! I'll make it priority one." William looks at his watch and says, "Might as well get a head start and go milk the cows. See you later." He gives her a peck on the cheek and then takes the leftover roast beef sandwich from his vest pocket and starts to eat it on his way out as he heads to the barn.

He is so cute, she thinks as she shuts the door. Then, ten minutes later, she hears a shotgun go off. She assumes he must be chasing away the coyotes from the chicken coop again.

#

After Olivia finishes the morning feeding and caring for Ken, Barbie, and Buttercup, she heads over to visit Hattie. She's pretty sure she's awake because there's a visitor's car parked in front of the house.

Hattie is getting an infusion from a nurse Olivia hasn't met before, and she finds her very attractive. At first glance, she wonders if she's Hispanic or Amerasian; either way, she has an exotic look.

When Olivia sits down on the couch, Hattie introduces everyone and says, "Jasmine, this is my business partner, Olivia. Olivia, allow me to introduce you to Jasmine, and Jasmine, can you get done already! I want to go for a smoke?" Then she kisses Edgar and strokes him till he sits back down in her lap.

Jasmine exclaims, "Hattie, we just got started, and the IVIG takes at least four hours."

Hattie begins to have a mental breakdown, "Then unplug this goddamn thing and let me go."

Jasmine doesn't miss a beat with Hattie's challenge and says, "Sit down and behave, you're lucky enough to have somebody like me to take care of you, so knock it off!"

Hattie's eyes widen, and all she says is, "Whoa?"

Jasmine reaches into her pocket and pulls out a small box. Then she states, "Here, try this. It's Nicorette, and it will curb your withdrawal symptoms."

Hattie snaps, "It's just not the same."

"Try it!" Jasmine commands as Hattie opens the box and pulls out a piece to put in her mouth. "It cost me an arm and a leg, plus you don't deserve me either," Jasmine adds.

Olivia yawns from being sleep-deprived, and Hattie lets out a frightening scream while chewing her Nicorette gum, "Olivia, what the hell is wrong with you!"

Innocently, Olivia asks, "Whatever do you mean?"

Hattie points to Olivia's tongue and yells, "Go look in the mirror, I think you have bubonic plague."

Olivia quickly gets up and runs to the mirror to look at it. Her tongue is black and looks wormy. "Oh my God!" she says to her reflection, followed by, "I need to go to hospital."

Jasmine calmly walks over to her and says, "Let me see."

Olivia opens her mouth wide and sticks out her tongue.

Jasmine inquires, "Hey, any chance you took something for an upset stomach?"

Olivia responds, "Yes, Pepto Bismol earlier this morning. Why?"

Jasmine explains, "You have black hairy tongue. It will go away on its own in a few days. Nothing to worry about."

Olivia is still worried and asks, "Are you sure?"

"I'm a licensed nurse practitioner, I served as a medic in Iraq, and I worked in the emergency room at Brigham and Women's Hospital. Hell yes, I'm qualified, and it's black hairy tongue."

"Why don't you work there now?" Hattie heckles her.

Jasmine answers back at Hattie with the same sarcastic tone, "During Covid. I said, "F this", and walked out. Who needs that kind of shit in their life, and now I have the privilege of spending quality time with you, Hattie. How's the Nicorette working for you, honey?"

Hattie reveals while her dog Edgar burrows deeper under the blanket on her lap, "Surprisingly well, thank you, and now that the crisis is averted, I have good news, Olivia. Our first puppy is coming sooner than I thought."

"What was the big rush to pull the trigger, Hattie?"

Hattie glances at her infusion and says, "I'm on borrowed time, Olivia, so there's none to waste."

Her remark saddens Olivia, but her heart leaps with joy as she asks, "What is it?"

Hattie describes him, "He's a Chinese Crested named Luna, and he's a hairy hairless. Come sit next to me so I can show you his baby photos."

Olivia quickly grabs a chair and sits beside Hattie, who says, "Here he is. Isn't he just precious?"

Jasmine comes over to look and brings a blood pressure cuff, oxygen meter, and thermometer to monitor Hattie's vitals while viewing the photos. Then she says, "I'm part Chinese, and I've never seen or heard of anything like that before in my life. That is one ugly little dog."

"Isn't he?" Hattie adds before she moans, "So, Jasmine, if you're part Chinese, what's the other part?" Then she glances at the photos again and exclaims, "Oh, I can't wait till we pick him up at the airport."

Jasmine reveals, "Peruvian, and you really shouldn't smoke around newborns, Hattie, so maybe you could chew Nicorette while you're taking care of the little pup."

Hattie surprises everyone with her reply, "That's not a bad idea."

Olivia is in shock that Jasmine is persuading Hattie to consider quitting her unfiltered Camel cigarettes and believes she may have just seen a miracle. Then she turns to Hattie and begs, "I know this isn't a good time to ask, but we're desperate. Do you have any suggestions where William and I could call to find people to help us with work on our farm?"

Hattie says, "Sure as shit, I do."

Olivia begs her, "Where, Hattie?"

Hattie asks Olivia, "Did William tell you much about my late brother?"

Olivia is nearly too embarrassed to respond. "No, Hattie, just a few basic details. Please tell me more about him now."

"He died from cancer; it was a pernicious brain tumor, but he was also born with Down syndrome. He was such a wonderful man and so delightfully funny. I miss him every single day. His name was Jeremy, and when he was a young man, he attended a vocational training program called the Barry Price Center in Newton. Call them, and they'll have the best people in the whole world to help you out on the farm. I mean honest and sweet and…" Hattie places her hand over her heart. "They are the angels walking among us, Olivia. I really mean it."

Olivia says, "I'm going to the kitchen so as not to disturb you and call them right this second." She notices how tired she looks. Then she squeezes her hand and says, "Thank you so much for everything, Hattie."

Hattie snickers, "Hey, while you're in there, bring me back a glass of Chardonnay and afterward take Edgar for a walk because he needs to go poop."

Jasmine glares at Olivia, and Olivia shrugs her shoulders and thinks, *Whatever.*

Hattie looks at the two of them and says, "What the hell. It's not like I'm going to die young."

Jasmine concedes defeat. "I give up, Hattie. You win."

CHAPTER TWENTY-FIVE — BIG RED

WILLIAM

It's 3 am, and William has packed everything he thinks he'll need for the trip to Galveston, Texas, and is ready to leave.

He looks over the printed pages that Allen Tyler Jr. sent him, which he plans to read during the flight, then shoves the big wad of paper into his already overflowing knapsack along with his laptop. He checks to make sure he has his driver's license and enough cash to get around. He hesitates to review what he's doing and decides to cut the cash in half, leaving a pile of money on the kitchen counter for Olivia in case of an emergency.

Finally, he stuffs the rest of the money into the front pocket of his newly discovered Levi's 517 jeans that once belonged to his father, along with an old Harris Tweed jacket with suede elbow patches, which he found with a stash of other cool stuff in the attic. He still can't get over how perfectly it fits him.

Olivia is preparing a quick snack for him to take and has already set out two cups of French press coffee. He tries to comfort her with reassuring words, "Ian will be here soon to help you out. You should be all right, and look, I left you some extra money on the counter." He points it out to her.

"I'm not too worried," she confirms, then smiles and adds, "Plus, we'll have some helpers coming from the Price Center in Newton."

William's mind floods with fond memories of Jeremy, Hattie's late brother, and how natural he was around the animals. He kisses her on the forehead and says, "That was a brilliant idea. I think you'll be surprised at how much help they'll be."

Feeling good about where things stand and no longer full of dread about leaving his family behind, he checks his phone for an update on the car Haloderm sent to pick him up and take him to Logan Airport.

He reaches down to put his knapsack on his back, but hesitates because his arm is still killing him from all the vaccinations he underwent as a requirement for his employment and safety. The worst was the Hepatitis B shot in his left arm, which made him feel terrible. Then he checks the spot where they pricked him for the TB test, and luckily, it's still negative.

Allen carefully explained to him that anything you can catch from a living person can also be contracted from the dead. Then he reiterated rule number one to him: "Never begin an extraction when overtired or under the influence of a narcotic, alcohol, or even cold medicine."

He tries to recall rule two, which was something like starting your most challenging case first, but William admits to himself that he still doesn't fully understand the nuance of that.

William sees headlights approaching and says to Olivia, "I think the car's here."

She grabs her coat and pulls it over her nightgown, then follows him outside into the frigid cold air of a winter night.

There is a stunning, elongated Range Rover in the driveway with its tailgate already open. The driver steps out of the vehicle, and Olivia gasps, as if she recognizes her. Finally, Olivia gathers the courage to ask with a shaky voice, "Karen, is that you?"

Karen turns to William to confirm she's at the correct address and then adds, "William, Loring, here, give me your carry-ons, and I'll place them in the back for you."

Then she turns to Olivia and says, "Let's catch up another time, perhaps, because we don't want to be late for William's flight, do we?"

Olivia reaches to kiss William goodbye as Karen closes the tailgate of the Range Rover remotely. "Have a safe trip, darling." Is all he hears from Olivia as Karen locks the passenger door, and he straps himself into the seat.

William's heart races with excitement as this trip finally feels real to him. He takes a deep breath to gather his thoughts and calm his mind, but deep down, he still can't believe it was Dr. Shane Ferguson, the veterinarian, who recommended him for this position. He briefly considers that he might have been completely wrong about him, thinking of him as a scumbag.

Strangers taking care of him are completely outside William's comfort zone, but he's adjusting quickly. He glances at his boarding pass and sees his seat is in First Class, and thinks—Nice!

Suddenly, his phone flashes with an urgent text from Olivia: *William, your driver is that awful bitch Karen, whom I nannied for in Dover. What the hell? What a coincidence! Find out for me why she's like an Uber driver now and what happened to her fat, rich old man.*

Karen raises her unfriendly, cranky voice to remark, "United right?"

William answers, "Yes, that's correct, it's flight 543 at 5:15 am, and you're Karen, right?"

"Yes, that's right," she echoes.

He wonders if Karen might be worried about whether he knows what happened between her and Olivia. He looks at her face to see if she seems embarrassed. "So, Olivia just sent me a text, and she asked me to ask you how your husband and kids are doing?"

"Listen…" She hesitates as if she's forgotten his name.

"William," he offers.

"Well, you see, William. I have this nice contract with Haloderm to drive their people to and from the airport and meetings. If I talk about myself, it could cost me my job with them."

"I understand, and I just got hired, so all the company's policies are new to me."

He looks down at his phone and sees a new text from Olivia. It says, *I googled them, and Karen's husband died from a heart attack.*

He left behind her and their four kids, as well as five previous wives, each with numerous children in addition to Karen's. Wow, and she married him for his money. LOL and good luck to her finding it after it's all divided up! Please say something like sorry for your loss" if it comes up.

William appreciates how much Olivia would enjoy it if he dug deeper into Karen's pain, but it's clear Karen doesn't want to make small talk with him. He glances at her face in the rear-view mirror and thinks *she's a bit older than he expected and not nearly as attractive as he imagined from Olivia's stories.* Then he decides to close his eyes and enjoy the comfortable ride, because once he boards the flight, he has pages of notes from the NIH, CDC, and Haloderm to read in preparation for Allen Tyler Jr.'s training program at the University of Texas Medical Branch in Galveston.

#

His flight lands on time in Houston, and the rental car is ready for him at the airport terminal. He tosses his belongings into the trunk and asks Siri for directions to the University of Texas Medical Branch in Galveston. Then he sends Olivia a text letting her know he arrived safely. She responds with a message. *Ian is a godsend, and I love having him here.*

William feels a sudden, uncontrollable pang of jealousy at the thought of Ian spending the day alone with Olivia. He stops himself and decides to dismiss that absurd thought, focusing instead on the directions to Galveston.

The weather is a sharp contrast to New England, with a balmy 60 degrees and a gentle breeze coming in off the Gulf. He tosses his heavy navy blue wool peacoat, tweed jacket, gloves, scarf, and baseball cap onto the backseat and sits in the driver's seat of the Nissan Maxima rental car. It feels weird to be this low to the ground after driving a truck for so many years. Change can be good – he reassures himself.

The drive between the airport and the medical school takes about 45 minutes. He admires the stunning ocean views along the highway as he explores how wonderful Galveston is. He also starts to value this big break from his daily routine. Feeling joyful, he rolls down the window and breathes in the sultry air.

That's when he starts to realize that there's nothing about dissecting cadavers (for the good of others, of course) that he finds disturbing. It's just another way for him to support his family, like hunting, as he briefly considers whether that makes him an oddball to all the people in the "normal world" who genuinely see it as grotesque.

Eventually, he turns right onto University Ave, and Siri announces, "You have arrived at your destination." This is when he realizes that finding a spot will be a chore.

He is so intensely focused on finding a parking space that he never looks up to appreciate the beauty of the impressive Victorian building, which resembles a cathedral with its rose-colored, carved stone walls, pillars, and archways rather than a medical school.

Astonished by its beauty, William walks over to the bronze plaque on the building that describes its Romanesque architecture. He continues to read about the school's motto, Disiplina Praesidium Civitatis, Established 1891, and its nickname, "Old Red." He has no idea what the motto means, but the name "Old Red" makes perfect sense to him.

He climbs the long, carved stone staircase and enters the massive building through its enormous doors. At the information desk, he asks, "Where is the office of the Willed Body Program?"

A young woman writes down the location on a card with a map of the building and points to the elevators. It only takes him a few minutes to find the old carved oak door with the name Allen Tyler Jr., Director of the Willed Body Program, painted on its opaque glass window.

The lights inside his office are off, and two young people are sitting on a bench outside his door. Despite their earthy, crunchy appearance, wearing open-toed Birkenstocks on their bare feet, frayed jeans, and long dreadlocks, it's clear they're medical students because of their white lab coats and the way they're studying furiously while waiting.

William decides to disturb them rather than knock: "Hi, do you know if Allen Tyler is in his office?"

The girl with dreadlocks looks up and shrugs, while the boy next to her appears clueless and ignores the question. She responds, "We need to have a brief meeting with him, and we're still working on our request, so we don't know."

William thinks to himself sarcastically: "Geniuses."

He softly knocks on the door and hears, "Come in, it's open."

When William enters, Allen is gazing out the window at pigeons on his sill. Allen swivels his chair around, sees William, and then suddenly smiles and stands up to shake his hand, saying, "This is going to be a big day for you." He squeezes his hand warmly.

William shares, "I think there are a couple of medical students waiting to ask you something."

Allen snickers, "They are a couple of medical students petitioning me to let them skip basic human anatomy. They think they can become doctors without getting their hands bloody. Let them wait."

"So, you're a professor too?"

Allen does not say yes; instead, he explains, "I teach human anatomy labs and surgical dissection courses in conjunction with a group of medical professors."

"How long have you been doing that?" William asks, clearly fascinated.

"Well, let me think. Since before you were born, plus at least another decade," Allen reveals. Then he changes the subject and asks William, "I learn a lot about my students from what they ask me, so I want to know what you're curious about from the material I sent you to read."

William feels put on the spot, but a question immediately comes to mind: "What if in an obese cadaver there's a pacemaker or defibrillator that's not visible because of all the fat? What happens if I hit it by accident?"

Allen smiles, then says, "You most likely will die of electroshock."

William swallows hard and asks, "Seriously? So, how do I avoid that?"

"Every extraction should begin with an X-ray because medical records can omit basic information, and you might not have the correct identity of a cadaver. Also, while we're on the topic of death by electrocution, never forget that the saws and power tools we use must always be plugged into working GFI outlets with functioning trip defaults. Electrical equipment and liquid can also be a deadly combination."

William continues, "It said in the notes to start with the most difficult case first, before operator fatigue sets in. How do I know which one is the most difficult?"

Allen strokes his chin before replying, "I rank my cases two ways: by the cadaver I know the least about, and the cadaver I already know has the most communicable diseases."

"What do you do with the ones with the most communicable diseases that are too sick to use?" asks William.

"My first choice is to send them out for cremation, but I've learned the hard way that some unscrupulous morticians resell them to body brokers for thousands of dollars."

William is horrified and says, "That's disgusting! Why would they risk infecting people?"

"Son, those kinds of people are ghouls, but they make big bucks from selling the bone, skin, collagen, tendons, and teeth of the dead, no matter the medical history, and of course, what's to stop them from lying about the identity of the body?"

Upset by this, he asks, "How do they get away with it?"

"It's actually pretty easy; nobody ever confirms the identity of a body as it goes into the oven at the crematorium, and afterwards, the counterfeit ashes are delivered to the deceased's loved ones, or in many cases, the ashes get tossed aside. What can I say? It's a flawed system."

William's face turns pale, and his teeth clench at the thought that the ashes on his mantel at home are not his parents.

Allen realizes he struck a nerve and intreats, "William, are you all right, Son?"

He pauses before he replies, "Yes, Sir. It's just that I lost my parents when I was a teenager. They were hit head-on by an unlicensed drug addict and died at the scene of the accident. We had my folks cremated. The thought of their bodies being stolen upsets me."

Allen consoles him, "Whatever may or may not have happened to their bodies after they passed away, please be assured they felt no pain."

A moment of silence passes, and Allen resumes, "This brings us to another important point. It's my advice that a diener, that's the term we use for what we do, never performs an extraction of any kind on the cadaver of someone they've known personally or previously in any way!"

Then Allen checks his watch and says, "Wonderful, it's 11 o'clock, so I'm finished with my academic advisory hours for today." He stands up, puts on his jacket, and then his black cowboy hat. "Now we can head over to the university's hospital to start your hands-on training. I know you're going to be a natural."

As they leave Allen's office, the two dreadlocked medical students approach him with questions, "Dr. Tyler, please, can we have a moment?"

He recognizes them and looks annoyed. "Why didn't you just schedule an appointment with me? And it's director, Tyler, not doctor!"

The girl asks a question, and her friend nods his head in agreement while she's talking. "You see, Director Tyler. I'm a vegan, and I can't take human anatomy and dissection with you next semester. Will you sign our waiver forms?"

Allen demands, "What kind of medicine do you want to practice if and when you graduate?"

She responds confidently, "Psychiatry."

Then he asks the young man with her, "How about you?"

"Not sure yet?" says the young man.

Allen places his hands on his hips and says, "The answer is no!"

They slunk down in disappointment, and Allen says to William, "So sorry for the delay. This sort of thing comes with the territory, and I go through it almost every semester without fail.

#

In the morgue, Allen retrieves a cadaver from the vault, and they chat as they walk to the suite where they will begin William's training. William's mind floods with questions, but his biggest one so far is why him? *Why would someone with so many students to choose from pick an unknown man from another state out of all these good options?*

Right after they change into surgical scrubs, cover their shoes, put on their PPE, double-glove their hands, and don protective glasses, Allen begins his lesson with William in the surgical suite by asking, "Where do you start?"

"I look at the cadaver's X-ray," he says like he's unsure.

"Yes, but don't assume the X-ray isn't accidentally misfiled and from another body, or that it might not have been switched, or outdated." Allen turns on the viewing light for the X-ray and adds, "Today you're OK because I took it myself, but when you are on your own, always do your own work and don't rely on the information from others or the medical history." He raises his voice, "And never let your guard down!"

William examines the X-ray and sees a clear chest with no implants or wires.

Allen asks, "What's next?

William responds, "I check the brain tissue for evidence of CJD."

Allen hands him a scalpel and says, "Here you go."

William carefully removes the scalp and places it on a tray beside him. Then Allen hands William the small power saw and steps back as William carefully cuts off the top of the cadaver's skull and pauses to say, "I don't know what to do next."

All Allen says is, "That's all right." Then he points to the cadaver's brain and hands William the correct tool to remove it. They look carefully for any evidence of spongy tissue deterioration. Then he asks William, "What do you see?"

"No evidence of the disease, Sir," William confirms.

"What would we do if we suspected CJD?"

"Stop the exam, back out of the room, carefully remove our garments and place them in a bag, scrub ourselves, and call for emergency help."

"Almost right, but you need to spend much more time studying this part of the procedure, and no matter how well you think you know it, take a refresher every three months."

Allen stands respectfully silent by William's side. At the same time, William splits open the sternum of the cadaver. He places each of the organs into individual containers, then dismembers the arms, legs, feet, and hands, placing each one into a labeled bag similar to the way they did it back at Haloderm.

When William finishes placing the last few pieces of the cadaver into their bags, he realizes how exhausted he is from getting up early, the long flight, standing on his feet for many hours, and enduring the dreadful odors coming from the dead body. He seems happy that it's over and is ready to leave.

Allen looks at him and then at the messy tables and proclaims, "This isn't Haloderm. We have to clean up our own messes here."

William is waiting for positive feedback, but he feels only disappointment.

#

When they leave the hospital, William celebrates the smell of the warm, fresh sea air instead of formaldehyde.

Allen points to a bench in the park nearby and says, "Let's take a seat and chat for a bit."

William follows him, and the two men sit quietly for a moment. Allen breaks the silence with, "I'm sure you're exhausted, so my suggestion is you return to your hotel, have some lunch, and take a nap. Then I'll come and pick you up at 6 tonight at your hotel if you'd like, because you're welcome to join my wife, Rose, and me for dinner. How does that sound?"

"Like a great plan, can I bring anything?"

"No, we're all set, and the dress code is casual. See you at 6."

Allen gets up and walks away.

#

The grandeur of the Tremont Hotel's lobby leaves William breathless. The high carved ceilings, massive chandeliers, sweeping bridal staircase, and shiny inlaid marble floors are unlike anything he's ever seen before.

As he happily checks in, he asks the front desk person for help, "Hi, where can I buy some flowers to bring to a dinner this evening?"

The front desk attendant points to another desk in the corner of the lobby and says, "The concierge would be most happy to assist you, and here is your room key, sir. Would you like help with your luggage?"

William replies, "No need." As he wonders what a concierge is, he walks over to the desk and sits in an armchair across from a middle-aged man with a receding hairline and a mustache, wearing a suit and tie with gold keys pinned to his lapels.

He is talking to someone on the phone and raises one finger as he finishes his call. He turns to William and says, "My name is Bruno. How can I help you, sir?"

"Hi, I've been invited to dinner this evening, and I'd like to bring a bouquet."

"What kind of flowers, sir?" Asks the concierge.

William realizes it's corny to bring a lady named Rose a bouquet of roses, but he says it anyway, "Roses, please."

The concierge confirms, "I'll have them sent up right away and charge them to your room. Please let me know if you'll need any assistance whatsoever regarding dinner reservations or navigating your way around Galveston during your stay with us."

While William is heading up, he realizes he never told the concierge how much he wanted to spend or how large he wanted the arrangement to be.

Whatever he thinks, he then considers sending some flowers to his wife as well to let her know how much he misses and appreciates her.

#

The hotel room is a spacious suite overlooking the water, offering views of the cruise terminal. He opens the window to look out and sees an enormous cruise ship tied up at the dock and considers taking a vacation with his family, which is something he had never thought about before, since a farmer can't leave the livestock behind. Still, maybe with this big shift in their mindset, those things might someday actually become possible.

William picks up the hotel phone and orders a burger, fries, and a Sprite. While he's waiting for the food, he jumps in the shower. The towels are big and fluffy, and they're quite different from the ones at home. After he dries off, he puts on the hotel robe and slippers, thinking, *OMG, this is nice!*

There's a knock at the door, and the bellhop is standing there with a beautifully arranged bouquet of pink roses sprinkled with baby's breath. William panics because he can't find his pants. "Wait a minute." Then he sees them on the floor and pulls out a five, trading it with the bellhop for the flowers.

The food eventually arrives, he gobbles it down, and hits the sack for a ninety-minute nap.

#

Allen pulls up to the hotel to pick up William in an older model Jeep with all the windows open and the front doors removed. He says, "Hop in, it's just a short ride to the house."

William carefully places the rose bouquet on his lap between his thighs and shelters the petals from the wind.

He glances at an empty shotgun rack hanging across the rear window when suddenly the head of a huge, grizzled, colored German Shepherd pops up and licks his face.

Allen says, "Down, Maisy, be a good girl." Then he turns to William and explains, "She's my wife's seeing-eye dog, and she loves going for rides with me."

They pull up to a convenience store, and Allen says, "Maisy, stay." Then he motions for William to follow him into the store.

William notices Allen reading a long blank piece of paper and asks him, "What are you looking at?"

Allen laughs, "Oh, this, it's a shopping list from my wife, it's in braille."

William says with a curious smile, "That's cool. Can I touch it? I've never seen it before." And he reaches for it.

Allen hands it to him, places a few items in the cart, and asks, "What kind of beer do you like?"

"Guinness or Sprite's fine too. Oh, and I'm not a big drinker," William adds as an embellishment to score points with his new boss.

Allen buys both, and they leave.

#

When they arrive at the house, William is surprised by its modesty. Maisy jumps out of the Jeep and runs to pee on the lawn, then heads to the back of the house.

It's a three-bedroom bungalow with a one-car garage, located in a nice neighborhood near the seashore. The interior is more impressive, featuring a state-of-the-art chef's kitchen, a cozy family room with a large flat-screen TV, and a charming lanai off the family room that overlooks a small in-ground swimming pool with a kiddie slide.

William hands the bouquet to Rose and follows Allen around the house for a tour. He shows off photos of their three kids and seven grandchildren before dinner. The food smells spicy and unfamiliar to William. He glances at pictures of Allen and Rose from when they were much younger. From the photos, you can't tell there's anything wrong with Rose's vision, and he wonders if she might have lost her sight later in life, but recalls Allen mentioning something about their childhood together.

Rose calls them for dinner, and as they take their seats at the dining room table, she politely mentions, "William, the flowers were an unnecessary extravagance, but I love them."

William replies, "My pleasure." Then he remembers he forgot to send some to his wife and will do it as soon as he gets back to the hotel.

The next thing William realizes is that Rose matter-of-factly takes hold of his hand, and Allen takes hold of his other hand.

Allen begins, "Lord, thank you for this meal before us. God bless us, our family, our new friend William, and his family. Amen."

William repeats, "Amen," and begins to eat. His taste buds explode from the wonderful spices and pungent flavors, and with excitement, he confirms, "Rose, this is delicious. What is it?"

"Shrimp gumbo."

William washes it down with Sprite and some bread as he watches Allen get up to flip a cowboy steak on his Weber Grill.

In his absence, Rose probes him, "So, William, are you married?"

At this point, Allen is heading back to the table, and the aroma from the steaks and grilled vegetables is enticing.

William replies, "Yes, ma'am. My wife is British, and we have twins."

Rose continues, "How sweet. What are their names?"

William tries to make her laugh and says, "Frick and Frack."

She chuckles and says, "No, really."

William responds, "Charlotte and Henry and their almost 4."

"That's so nice. Are you planning to have more?"

Allen jumps in, "Rose!"

William confides, "You see, my wife Olivia experienced eclampsia during her pregnancy with the twins, and she had to be induced early. They were barely five lbs. each. Also, Charlie, that's what we call Charlotte, hasn't been well, so I think more kids are on the back burner for now, but it's not out of the question."

Rose glances at William as if she can see him and says, "Well, Allen, I believe you were fortunate to make this fine young man's acquaintance."

After dinner, William and Allen head out to the pool to sit and chat. Allen confesses, "There's something I need to share with you."

William is hoping for some reassurance that he's headed in the right direction and that this job will be his because he likes how things are progressing and doesn't want them to stop.

Allen continues to explain, "The cadaver you trained on today was someone I knew well and worked with for many years. She was a pathologist at UTMB, and she donated her body to the Willed Body Program for the specific purpose of training and education. You did her an honor today, and she would have been impressed with the skill and respect you showed her body. You surpassed my every expectation, William."

William appreciates Allen's reassuring feedback. Still, he remains in disbelief that these fantastic changes in his life are all due to a referral from Dr. Shane Ferguson, which still troubles him, even after Allen's kind compliment. However, William can't quite understand why Allen chose him over everyone else.

CHAPTER TWENTY-SIX — FUN AT WORK

OLIVIA

What should I do first? Olivia asks herself as she steps outside into the dark, cold morning air to clear the static noise in her head. She doesn't dare leave the twins alone in the house, knowing that once she crosses the road to Jameson Farm, the signal from their baby monitor will be out of reception range.

One possibility is that she could ask Hattie to stay with them overnight until William returns, so at least there will be another adult in the house when she goes over to care for the horses.

She decides to start her chores in a different order, hoping the trainees from the Price Center will arrive soon. She also needs the twins to wake up.

That's when the timer on her phone goes off, and she rushes back to the kitchen to take the two dozen freshly baked muffins out of the oven. She places them on the cooling rack and waves her oven mitt over them to fan the heat away. Then she pours half a gallon of fresh milk into a pot and slowly warms it in preparation for hot cocoa to go with the muffins.

She senses someone behind her and turns to see who it is. It's Henry standing still, holding a teddy bear and looking sad.

She asks, "What's the matter, my sweet prince?"

Henry replies, "I miss Father. When is he coming home?"

Olivia picks up Henry and comforts him with a hug while she tells him, "Soon, darling. Just a couple of more days."

Just then, Olivia hears a vehicle pull into the driveway, and as quickly as it arrives, it drives away. Being alone in the house with the kids has made her hyper-vigilant, so she rushes to the window, looks out, and sees a florist's van backing out of the driveway. Then she checks the front door, where she finds a lovely bouquet of pink roses and thinks, How thoughtful of him, while reading his note: 'Missing you and the twins. Love, William.'

She considers calling him but realizes it's an hour earlier in Galveston, so she texts him instead: *TY for the lovely roses. We miss you as well,* and she attaches a photo of Henry admiring the flowers.

Olivia stirs the powdered cocoa into the warm milk and adds sugar before she asks, "Henry, my little love. Would you like a warm muffin and a cup of cocoa?"

He nods yes and hops into his chair, placing Paddington Bear in the empty seat beside him.

While they're having breakfast together, there's a knock at the kitchen door. Olivia is shocked to see so many people standing outside. They're here to help us, she thinks as a lump forms in her throat, and she fights back tears of relief.

There are so many that they cover the landing and steps. Standing there are Hattie, Jasmine, and a couple of people she has not met yet. The person who drove everyone from the Price Center is sitting in the driver's seat of the van, but once he sees her, he waves goodbye to everyone and drives off.

Olivia says as she opens the door, "Everyone, welcome, and please come in. Anyone want a warm muffin and some hot cocoa?"

Six hands go up at once. Olivia notices a handsome, possibly college-age young man with short, dark hair and a gorgeous million-dollar smile. He is standing next to another young man, much smaller than him, who has Down syndrome and is slowly taking everything in. Then there are two girls whose ages she cannot even begin to guess, but the smaller of the two has big blue eyes and silky blonde hair. She also has Down's syndrome, but the taller girl with them has the most fantastic hairstyle Olivia has seen since leaving London, along with a great figure. This girl is shy, hiding behind the blonde-haired, blue-eyed girl. Olivia takes a closer look at the young woman and thinks she's pretty enough to be a fashion model.

Hattie, who comments on everything, stays quiet and observant, while Jasmine quickly becomes another helping hand to Olivia. Together, they pass around the food and greet everyone. Olivia can't believe she's finally making a new friend in America after all these years, and she's filled with joy to have Jasmine by her side this morning.

Charlotte finally comes downstairs in her pajamas, surprised by how many strangers are in their kitchen. Olivia picks her up to comfort her and says, "Everyone, this is Charlie. Please tell us your names."

The tall, dark-haired young man with the brilliant smile says, "Hi, I'm Nick Chen."

The other young man simply says, "Adam." And nothing more.

Then the smaller of the two girls introduces herself, "Hi, I'm Tina, and this is Barbara, but she doesn't talk much. Right, Barbara?"

Barbara doesn't respond and looks away into space, but eventually takes sips of her hot cocoa, remaining expressionless.

Olivia scans the group to gauge their boot and glove sizes and offers numerous pairs of dirty rubber work boots from her mudroom. She hands out jackets along with pairs of work gloves before asking, "Anyone here know how to milk a cow, clean up pig slop, or collect chicken eggs?"

Tina asks, "That's like an Easter Egg hunt, right?"

Olivia had never viewed it that way before and says, "That's right, Tina. It's just like an Easter Egg hunt."   .

Tina asks, "Will there be candy and prizes like Easter?"

Olivia is in a panic because she doesn't have much to give them, so she offers, "If everyone does a wonderful job, then at the end of the week, I'll hand out prizes."

Adam interjects, "What about candy? I want some candy now!"

Hattie jumps in, "There will be lots of candy too, Adam." Then she turns to Olivia and says, "Don't worry, Olivia. George will drop off some items on his way back from the market. I've got this." Then she winks at her while chewing her Nicorette gum.

Olivia gently puts Charlotte, who is beginning to feel heavy, down and says, "Now that we have all that settled, let's go meet the farm animals and have some fun."

Charlotte whines, "I want to have some fun too, Mummy."

Olivia instructs, "All right, Charlie. Grab your wellies, coat, mittens, and hat, and you as well, Henry, and let's all go have some fun."

Olivia turns to Hattie and asks, "Do you want to stay here and keep warm by the fire?"

Hattie smirks, "Hell no, and miss all the fun." Then she throws on her coat and follows everyone out to the barn.

#

It only takes around fifteen minutes to decide who will do each chore.

Adam inquires after examining the cow's udders, "Are those big things hanging down there her nipples?" He says as he points them out.

Hattie turns to him and says, "Yes, Adam, as a matter-of-fact, they are."

Adam confirms, "I'm not touching those things. No way!"

Hattie asks, "Do you like horses?"

Adam replies, "Do I have to milk them?"

Hattie says, "No-sir-ee."

Adam confirms, "Then I think I might like horses. What do you want me to do with them today?"

Hattie offers, "Follow me, Adam, and everything will be okey dokey!"

Hattie leads Adam across the road to the stable at Jameson farm to feed and water Buttercup, Ken, and Barbie, hoping he'll also help clean their stalls and brush them.

Nick approaches Olivia and asks, "Would you like me to unload all the animal feed sitting on the pallets in the back of the truck over there?"

She realizes that Ian never got around to it the day before, and there's no way she can lift those 50-pound bags on her own. "Nick, you're a godsend! Wait, I'll do it with you," she exclaims because she knows he'll need some instruction. Then she shows him where they're supposed to go to be stored.

When the animal feed is unloaded, she checks on Tina, who is humming a song while milking her third cow and filling the milk cans faster than Olivia has ever seen before. The cow, in the middle of milking, looks as if she doesn't know what to do about it, as her eyes open wide with each pull on her udder. After Tina finishes and rolls the full milk tins over by the door, the three of them lead the cows outside to their field to wander and graze on what they can find, nibbling on the patches of grass between the piles of wet snow.

Olivia and Tina attack the cows' stalls, while Nick fills the wheelbarrows and dumps their manure in the compost pile behind the barn. They miraculously clean them in a matter of minutes. Then they lay down fresh hay and replenish the cows' food and water. After finishing spreading the hay for the cows, Olivia checks on Nick, who she finds milking the goats and playing with their kids, along with Charlotte and Henry.

Something feels amiss, so Olivia looks around for Barbara, who is nowhere to be seen, and calls out to her, "Barbara, where are you?"

Tina steps in and says, "Pointless. She doesn't talk much, like I said, so she's not going to answer you."

Olivia begins to panic, feeling responsible for Barbara and worried that she might have wandered off into the conservation land over the hills with its frozen ponds and crevasses.

Olivia asks Tina, "Where do you think she is?"

Knowing Barbara, who is more of a princess than an outdoorsy type, she probably headed back to the house to warm up and text her mother.

Olivia says to Charlotte and Henry, "Come with Mummy." Tina, along with Nick, follows as they all head toward the house to look for Barbara.

#

When they burst into the kitchen, they find Barbara sitting silently at the table with her hands folded and a large wicker basket filled to the brim with fresh, brown, newly laid, and still warm chicken eggs, along with another smaller basket full of quail eggs.

Olivia is awestruck that she never instructed Barbara, and she accomplished this task on her own initiative. "Barbara, thank you," she states from her heart.

Then she asks everyone, "Anyone want an omelet?"

Nick voices his opinion, "I'm starving. Sounds great. I'll go tell Hattie, Jasmine, and Adam to join us and be right back."

Olivia is worried about her chicken coop and wonders if Barbara might have left the gates open, but she feels that if she leaves now to check, she'll insult her new helpers somehow. Therefore, she sends Hattie a quick text message: "On your way over, please check to make sure the chicken coop's gates are closed. Thanx."

Olivia fries onions and potatoes in her oversized cast-iron pan with a pound of fat. Afterward, she adds eighteen eggs to her mixing bowl and locks it in place before turning on her Kitchen-Aid mixer. Then she turns to see how the group is doing.

Tina is snacking on muffins by the fireplace. Charlie and Henry have pulled Nick, who has just returned from Jameson Farm, into their playroom, and he's joined them in a game of make-believe land. Still seated at the same spot at the kitchen table is Barbara, who has not moved an inch.

Olivia has since realized that Barbara is more capable than she thought earlier in the day, so she reaches into the silverware drawer and collects nine forks and knives, then she grabs and counts out nine napkins. She tries to make eye contact with Barbara, but is unsuccessful. Instead, she places the forks, napkin, and knives in front of Barbara and says, "I would appreciate it if you would set the table for us in the dining room." Then she walks away and returns to stir the fried potatoes and onions.

When Olivia turns her around, she is pleased to see that Barbara is no longer at the table, having taken the silverware and napkins with her, which makes Olivia smile. Tina glances her way and gives Olivia a thumbs-up of approval.

Olivia looks at the outdoor thermometer through her kitchen window and sees that it's 48 degrees Fahrenheit. She's delighted with the nearly perfect winter weather for working outside. Even the cows seem happy, wandering around in the heavy, wet snow and mud, with just enough sun shining down to make it pleasant.

Then she notices Ken, Barbie, and Buttercup trotting up the street with Hattie, Jasmine, and Adam riding them. Buttercup looks like she's had her knots brushed out and the mud cleaned from around her hooves, highlighting her beautiful, contrasting dark-and-white socks. Olivia touches her face and realizes she's smiling again.

Hattie dismounts and then helps Adam and Jasmine with theirs. She leads the three horses to the ring and releases them to run around and relax so they can join everyone inside for brunch. Hattie sends Adam and Jasmine ahead while she hangs up the horses' bridles and bits on a hook in the tack area. Then she walks over to check the gate on the chicken coop and finds it secure.

Everyone grabs a seat as Olivia asks with a show of hands who wants a plain omelet versus one with cheddar cheese, and she announces, "That's unanimous, everyone wants cheddar, right?" As expected, there is no response from Barbara, so Olivia asks Tina, "Do you know which way Barbara would prefer hers, Tina?"

Tina smirks, "How the heck would I know that?"

Adam laughs out loud as he appears to find Tina's comment hilarious and quickly glances at Barbara to see her reaction, but there's nothing.

Olivia, with Jasmine's help, delivers the cheddar cheese omelets to each person, accompanied by a side of fried potatoes and onions. She places a bottle of ketchup on the table next to the beautiful bouquet of pink roses and looks around at all the happy faces, except for Barbara, who hasn't touched hers and is still frowning. She reaches for Barbara's full plate and says, "Let me make you another one more to your liking."

Just then, Adam latches onto Barbara's cheese omelet and says, "I don't want to see that go to waste. I'd be happy to eat it for you."

Five minutes later, Olivia sits at the table with a plain omelet for Barbara and another plain one for herself because she has run out of cheddar cheese. She looks around the table and notices everyone has eaten everything on their plates, including Hattie, who is the most difficult person to feed.

The conversation around the table is lively, as Adam emphasizes, "I love Buttercup. Her nose is so soft, and she wouldn't let me stop rubbing her under her chin. Tina, after we finish eating, let me show you how to do it."

Tina replies, "Sure, but what I want to know is how hard it was to get up into the saddle?"

Adam grins, "Hattie showed me. Phew, it wasn't easy, and staying up there was so hard to do."

Tina asks, "Were you scared?"

Adam tries to act macho when he says, "Only at first."

Hattie chimes in, "Adam, my boy, you are a natural."

Olivia is thrilled that Buttercup has someone to offer her extra kindness and attention. As the day progresses, Olivia can't imagine life getting any better.

Hattie then turns to Olivia and says, right after she reads a text on her phone while clapping her hands together, "Our baby Luna is arriving soon. Olivia, what time is William coming in? We're going to have to pick Luna up at Logan. Can you believe it?"

Olivia thinks, Pinch me, I must be dreaming. Before she replies, "It's late tomorrow night, but Haloderm arranged for a car. If needed, I'll find a babysitter, and we can go get Luna together."

Hattie exclaims, "William is coming home in a limo; that's so fancy!"

Olivia chuckles at Hattie's reaction as she considers what still needs to be done on the farm, realizing everything on the list is finished except for cleaning the pig pens and the chicken coop, but it's only 10:30 in the morning. Then, out of the corner of her eye, she sees Jasmine suddenly jump up from her chair and catch Charlotte, who is falling over to one side.

Jasmine gently lowers Charlotte to the floor, then checks Charlotte's pulse while saying, "I need a pillow and a wooden spoon, now!"

Charlotte's body stiffens as Olivia passes a wooden spoon to Jasmine, who moves Charlotte's tongue out of the way of her teeth to place it in her mouth as Charlotte begins to shake involuntarily and make a low guttural sound like an animal trying to speak.

After a few minutes, Charlotte remains still, her body limp like a rag doll. Jasmine lifts Charlotte off the floor and cradles her in her arms, her head resting against Jasmine's shoulder. She instructs, "Olivia, can you find me a bucket or a large bowl?"

Olivia quickly returns with the bucket and hands it to Jasmine, who is fully in control of the moment when she asks, "Charlie, how are you feeling, baby girl?"

Charlotte opens her eyes and asks, "Mummy, what happened?" Then she leans over and vomits into the bucket Jasmine has held under her chin.

Olivia exclaims, "Should I call 911?"

Jasmine explains, "Not necessary, the worst is over." Then she gestures for Olivia to sit next to her and continues, "Here, let me hand her to you." Jasmine passes Charlotte to Olivia and then asks, "She had a petit mal seizure. Has she ever had one before?"

Olivia's eyes fill with tears as she answers her question, "Yes, but it was much worse than this one, and it was a couple of weeks ago. It happened a few days after we vaccinated the twins."

Jasmine comforts Olivia, saying, "At least this one was milder."

Charlotte's head pops up as she is finished with the worst part of it. Henry walks over to his sister and asks, "Charlie, where did you go?"

Charlotte answers him sweetly, "Henry, I don't know. I disappear."

Then, Tina loudly proclaims as she peers out the window, "Oh my goodness, there's a Bentley in your driveway, Olivia."

Olivia stands up, holding her daughter, and walks to the window to see if William might have arrived home earlier than expected. There is a middle-aged woman in the driver's seat, and seeing her confirms it might be him, so she gets excited and goes outside to the car, hoping to greet him.

The woman driving the Bentley rolls down her window to say, "Hi, I'm Barbara's mother, and she sent me a text to come and get her."

Olivia is disappointed in several ways; she had hoped her husband was in the car, and since Barbara wants to leave early, she feels she has somehow let her down, as the day was supposed to be fun for them.

Barbara walks over to the car and waves her off. Over the noise of the Bentley's twelve-cylinder engine, all Olivia hears her mother say is, "Are you sure, Barbara?"

Barbara stands stone still as her mother continues to say, "OK, sweetheart, but I'm not driving out here again if you change your mind an hour from now." Barbara turns around and walks back to join the group.

Olivia feels relieved over Barbara's choice to stay. She quickly decides to delay cleaning the pigsty and plans to spend the rest of the morning showing the kids a good time on the farm. Most importantly, she wants to get the name and phone number of Barbara's hairdresser because she will desperately need a touch-up before the holidays.

#

Later that afternoon, Olivia happily gives a riding lesson in her outdoor ring to Barbara, Adam, and Tina, while Nick hangs out with their Berkshire pigs, along with Charlotte and Henry. Although at first Olivia didn't agree with Jasmine about sitting tight and observing her daughter instead of taking her to the hospital after her seizure, she has since been corrected.

Although she is awaiting a response from their pediatrician about a referral to a neurologist at Children's Hospital and a prescription for anti-seizure medication in case of epilepsy, she feels less afraid of the possible diagnosis.

With Olivia's back to the road and focused on the three riders, she doesn't notice the Volvo SUV driving in and parking next to the paddocks. Remaining laser-focused on the three of them as they happily ride around the ring, Olivia has returned to her element. She loved her days working with the kids and leading trail rides in London's Hyde Park.

Olivia notices that her riders are tired and raises her hand as a signal to stop. One by one, she helps each of them dismount and asks, "Who wants a snack?" All three hands go up, and she appreciates George for dropping off two grocery bags full of treats for the kids.

When the four of them are leading the horses out of the ring, Olivia discovers she has an audience. It's a mother with her three daughters, and they seem to be waiting to talk to her. Olivia pauses and nuzzles Buttercup's nose when she asks, "How can I be of help to you?"

The mother introduces herself and asks, "How much do you charge for English riding lessons?"

Olivia is caught off guard by the unexpected question and makes up an answer, "$125 per person in a group lesson."

The lady gasps, "Well, what if it was just for my three girls?"

Olivia thinks to herself, *Pigs go hungry* and responds, "$250 for the private class. It will be 90 minutes long, and we will work our way up to trail rides by spring."

The lady smiles and asks her, "So, they won't begin till spring?"

Olivia corrects her, "There's no need to wait; we have an indoor ring across the street. I can start as soon as this Saturday." When she used the word "we," she realized she couldn't do this without Hattie's help, and she'll also need William home to watch the twins during the ninety-minute lesson.

The lady extends her hand to shake on it and asks, "How's 2:00, this Saturday?"

Olivia is thrilled when she responds, "It's perfect." Then the lady and her three girls get back in their Volvo SUV and drive away.

Oh, my goodness, my English riding school is finally becoming something real, and all the credit goes to Hattie, of course. She looks at the beautiful, happy, innocent faces of her helpers and realizes she is being blessed again and again.

Olivia raises her voice while mimicking a cowboy's accent to say, "Hey, my rough riders, take the horses' leads like so." She demonstrates, "Then follow me back to the stable across the street. It's time to unsaddle, water, feed, and bed down our horses."

When they return from Jameson Farm, Olivia feels energized by the day's positivity, but she knows she's about to run out of petrol soon, and there's still a lot of work left to do.

Tina saves the day. "Miss Olie, what's left for us to do?"

Olivia feels relieved as she explains, "All the animals need to be fed again. They're just like people - they're always hungry. Barbara, would you like to feed the chickens and the quails?" And just like that, Barbara heads off to take care of the fowl. Olivia then says, "Tina, the cows would love to see you again today."

Tina asks, "Can you show me what to do?"

"I was planning on it, and, Adam, after that, you and I will join Nick, so the three of us can clean out the pig pen and feed them their supper. How's that sound?"

Adam asks with a stern expression, "Then after that, will there be a snack time too?"

Olivia says, "Most definitely."

Adam confirms, "I'm in."

Everything hums along smoothly, and as the temperature begins to drop, they all head back to the house to warm up and enjoy their late afternoon snack. The Bentley returns for Barbara, and her mother looks as if she has just come from a spa day.

Barbara's mother rolls down her window and calls out, "Barbara, it's time to go, and I'm in a rush."

Olivia thinks, *Now's my chance to find out who does Barbara's hair.* "Hi there," she says to break the ice.

Barbara's mother reluctantly asks, "Was my daughter any trouble today?"

Olivia says, "No, not at all. Quite lovely, actually. By the way, where does Barbara get her hair done? I'd love to know."

Her mother appears flattered. "Well, we both go to John at Salon 55 in Newton Centre."

Yikes, Olivia thinks as she realizes that's the same place where she recently bounced a check, and they told her never to return.

Then Barbara's mother adds, "But I used to go to a truly wonderful hairdresser on Route 109 in Medfield named LeeAnne, if you want someone closer to home. You see, I switched to John because it was so convenient for me when I dropped off Barbara at the Price Center. It's just around the corner from there."

Olivia shares, "Yes, please text me her contact information. I'd appreciate it. Barbara was awesome today, actually, just terrific during her riding lesson and very helpful when she set the table in the dining room for our brunch and collected all the eggs for us early this morning."

Barbara's mother exclaims, "You're pulling my leg, right?"

Tina adds, "No, Mrs. Diamond, she isn't. Barbara loved it here today." Then, as Barbara gets in the Bentley and closes the door, Tina confirms, "Bye, Barbara, see you tomorrow?"

Mrs. Diamond appears emotional as she looks at her daughter and then over at Olivia when she states, "Thank you. I mean it. Thank you for everything you did today."

Adam walks over and waves goodbye to Mrs. Diamond and Barbara as he says, "Thank goodness they're leaving. I'm starving – let's finally go get our snacks."

After snack time, Charlotte and Henry go down for a nap. While they're asleep, the van arrives from the Price Center to pick up Adam and Tina, which confuses Olivia, so she stops to ask Nick, "So, how are you getting home?"

Nick laughs hard. "Olie, you thought I came with the Price Kids? That is priceless. I'm studying veterinary medicine at Tufts, and Jasmine, my aunt, thought you could use my help, so I came along with her today."

Olivia confesses coyly, "Don't I feel like the fool. Oh goodness, I'm so grateful to you, and peradventure do you know anything about how to treat a possibly pregnant pony?"

Nick confirms in a professional-sounding voice, "Do you mean, Equine Obstetrics?"

"Yes, yes, that's it exactly," she confirms, trying to sound literate.

He asks, "Would you be willing to deliver her to our hospital training facility for large animals in Grafton? That's where we can give her an ultrasound and an exam."

She asks, "How far is it from here?"

He flashes his million-dollar smile for her. "It's not very far. The Cummings Veterinary School is off Route 20, just one town after Hopkinton."

"How much will it cost me?" she fearfully inquires.

He reveals with a constant grin on his face, "Nothing, as long as the school has your permission to use Buttercup as a subject for a class, and you understand a group of students will be examining her, but that will exclude the cost of any medications she might be prescribed."

"Nick, sign me up. The sooner the better," Olivia says with relief in her voice.

Then she notices a text from Ian and says, "Hey, hold on a second, Nick, I have to reply to this."

The text from Ian reads: "Hi, I just finished my shift at A.O.R.A. and am heading back to your house." *How about I pick up some pizzas and salads, and afterward, I'll go around and feed the animals tonight.*

She replies to Ian, *Pizza sounds perfect. The animals are already fed, but I have some human helpers to feed. Please bring enough for seven people, including you, me, and my kids. I'll pay you back.*

Ian replies with a thumbs up.

Then she asks Nick, "Are you hungry, cause my husband's buddy is coming straight over with pizzas and salad for all of us."

That's cool. I'll text Jasmine and tell her to bring Hattie too.

While Nick is texting, Olivia considers what else they'll need and says, "I'm heading up to the house because I can hear my monkeys moving about, and I'll go find some wine to go with the pizzas." As she walks toward the kitchen, she thinks to herself, I'll defrost a pie for dessert as well.

#

Ian enters the kitchen carrying four large pizza boxes and six large Greek salads. When he turns away from the counter, he encounters an attractive stranger face-to-face. This startles him, and he stammers, "Who the hell are you?"

Nick extends his arm to shake hands as he states, "Nick Chen, Jasmine's nephew."

Ian continues his verbal assault on Nick. "And Jasmine is who?" Then he raises his hands to show how confused he is by Nick's presence in William's house.

Nick suddenly understands why Ian is upset and explains, "My Aunt is Hattie's infusion therapy nurse, and she asked me to join her today to help with the animals."

All at once, Olivia arrives in the kitchen from upstairs with the twins as Hattie, Jasmine, and George enter the back door and shake off the cold.

Hattie breaks the ice, "I hope the pizza is still hot! Olie, stoke up the oven just in case it isn't," she commands.

Everyone heads into the dining room. Olivia has already set out napkins, utensils, wine glasses, and juice boxes for her kids. Olivia's eyes follow Ian as she watches him make eye contact with Jasmine and then look away. It had never occurred to Olivia that he might be interested in her, and she feels a bit embarrassed as she introduces them: "Jasmine, this is my husband's good friend Ian. Ian, please allow me to introduce you to Hattie's IVIG nurse, Jasmine. I believe you already met Nick in the kitchen."

Ian falls silent, and for the first time, Olivia sees with her own eyes why he is still single and what lies behind his difficult choice to work with the recently departed rather than the living. Olivia recalls what William told her about him and finally thinks she's come up with a gem to help him start a conversation with Jasmine. Meanwhile, Nick, Jasmine's nephew, is also noticing this awkward vibe between Ian and Jasmine.

"Ian, Jasmine served as a nurse in the Navy." Olivia offers.

Ian struggles and stammers, "Thanks for your service. So you're a nurse?"

While holding a forkful of Greek salad, Jasmine corrects Ian, "No, I'm a nurse practitioner. Some places call that a physician's assistant, but they're pretty much the same." Then she looks at Ian before she asks, "How about you? Did you serve?"

Ian states, "Yes, ma'am. Air National Guard, and that's where I met William, Olivia's husband. We were EMTs together at Otis."

Olivia decides not to ask any more questions about Ian's current job as a human body parts transporter. Still, if anyone wouldn't mind, it's Jasmine, she concludes.

Jasmine gazes at Ian before she says, "I'm famished. Please pass some pizza over here."

Silently, Ian moves the box to the end of the long table. While he does that, Hattie pushes her salad aside and holds out her empty wine glass for Ian, adding, "I'd like a refill of the red, kind sir."

"Yeah, sure," is all Ian replies.

It seems to Olivia that Nick is also trying to help these two socially stubborn thirty-something-year-olds find something to talk about, so he jumps in and makes another attempt when he asks Ian, "So what do you do for work now?"

Olivia thinks *this might be the deal killer.*

Ian puts down his slice of pizza and makes eye contact with Nick before he solemnly states, "I work for a company called A.O.R.A. It's also in the medical profession."

Nick asks him, "What do the abbreviations stand for?"

Jasmine speaks up for him, "It stands for American Organ Recovery Alliance."

Ian seems smitten with her because she already knows what he does, and he sighs in relief, saying, "Nobody knows what it stands for."

Jasmine confirms, "I know!" and laughs at him.

Nick gets nervous and fumbles the ball, saying, "And my aunt is single too."

There's a sudden pregnant pause; even the twins notice it. Except for Hattie, who is finishing her second glass of wine while George stares incredulously at her, everyone else at the table is watching Jasmine, whose face is flushed with embarrassment.

Just then, Olivia's phone rings. She glances at it and sees that it's William on FaccTime. She leaves her phone on a small stand on the table and puts his call on speaker. "Hello, darling. How is your training going in Galveston? Henry, Charlie, come quick, it's your father."

The twins huddle close to Olivia and begin asking their questions, "Father, when will you be coming home?" they ask in unison.

William confirms, "Very late tomorrow night." Then he asks the kids, "Who else is eating with you?"

Charlotte explains, "We're having pizza with Hattie, George, and a nurse."

William probes deeper, "Who are the rest of the folks?"

Henry continues, "This is Nick. He knows tons of stuff about animals."

Nick jumps in, "Hi William, I came today with Jasmine to check up on your animals. I'm studying to be a Veterinarian at Tufts."

Olivia notices William's expression change, and he looks terrified. "Is everything all right, darling?" she asks, wondering what was said that seemed to strike a nerve with him.

"Yes," William confirms, "but is Ian there too?"

"Over here, how are you doing, Buddy?" Ian inquires.

William replies, "Thanks for asking. It's beautiful down here, but I'm exhausted and about to hit the hay. Thanks for helping us out."

"It's nothing, and I've enjoyed every minute," adds Ian.

"Listen, Ian. I owe you big time. Olivia, can you find a babysitter for this Saturday night? I want to take you and Ian out as a thank you."

Hattie joins the conversation, even though she's tipsy from her second glass of wine mixed with her pain pills. "Hey, what about Jasmine? She's been helping Olivia all day."

Nick chimes in to add, "I'm free Saturday night and could use the extra cash. Want me to babysit them?"

William seems uncomfortable with this spontaneous situation with a stranger and replies, "They're much more difficult to handle than wild animals, Nick."

Nick responds, "I treat mountain lions, cougars, and rattlesnakes, so I think I can handle twin toddlers for a few hours."

Ian seems nervous as he looks at Jasmine and asks, "Are you free this Saturday night, and would you like to join us?"

Jasmine's eyes dart back and forth as if she's considering, then she asks, "What kind of food do you have in mind?"

William jumps back into the conversation from FaceTime, sensing a hiccup. "Olivia, what about that place in Medfield with the nice drinks and flank steaks we like? I think it's called Boulevard."

Jasmine googles the restaurant online, looks over the menu, and responds with a thumbs up, and says, "Count me in.

Then Ian confirms, "Then it's a date."

Olivia reviews the details with everyone as she makes a reservation on her phone: "I can't remember the last time we went out to eat." She shares while scrolling through the available times, "I'm so excited - OK, everyone, we have a table at seven, and Nick, if you could come here by 6:30, I'll have the twins fed and ready for bed."

Nick looks at the twins and asks them, "Do you like ferrets or maybe a baby lynx?"

Henry says adamantly, "Of course we do."

Then Nick winks at Henry and Charlotte.

Ian glances over at Jasmine and offers, "Would you like me to pick you up, Jasmine?"

Very bluntly, Jasmine replies, "Not necessary, I'll be bringing Nick here."

Suddenly, Hattie pipes up, as if she has just realized William is still on the FaceTime call, "Oh, William, I almost forgot to tell you I opened the package you sent me and just loved it!"

William's face flushes again, and Olivia becomes worried about his health, "William, are you all right, my darling?"

Williams adds, "I'm fine, Olivia, and Hattie, I thought you would appreciate that particular gift."

She confirms, "I really did, and there is some other unfinished business we need to go over when you return home."

George adds, "That's so true. Call me when you're home, Billy. We could use a chat with you."

William begins to wind up the call, as his dinner was just delivered from room service, and he says, "Roger that, Hattie, and I'll see everybody else Saturday night. Love you."

William disconnects, and the mood at the table is entirely different. The twins are excited that Nick will be returning and won't leave him alone. Ian has gotten up and moved closer to Jasmine, and they appear to be off to a good start. Hattie is grinning as if her painkillers have finally kicked in, or possibly, she thinks she's personally responsible for everything that's going right in all of their lives.

Hattie turns her head, looks Olivia straight in the eyes, and says, "You've so much going on, you've completely forgotten about tonight."

This jogs her memory, and she adds, "Oh, that's true. Would it be all right for me to teach a class in your indoor riding ring on Saturday at 2?"

Hattie replies with a snicker. "Sure, but you've still forgotten about our plans for tonight."

Olivia's face flushes as she remembers they're supposed to pick up Luna, the Chinese Crested puppy, at Logan Airport, and she also forgot to arrange for a babysitter, so she confesses, "Hattie, I forgot to hire..."

Nick looks as if he's trying not to be noticed, and Hattie jumps in, interrupting him, "George told me earlier he'll be happy to watch the kids as soon as his card game ends." George nods in agreement, biting into his slice of pizza and ignoring them.

Hattie makes a snarky comment, "Not to worry, he's not very good at Texas Hold'em, so he gets eliminated early."

George scowls at them while he continues eating.

Olivia says, "My luck, he'll have one hot hand after another and run late tonight."

Hattie continues, "Oh, and now that I chew Nicorette instead of the smokes, he stays with me overnight. Isn't that romantic?"

The thought of two older people cuddling up under the covers on a cold night gives Olivia the heebie-jeebies. Still, it also jogs her distracted mind once again, and she realizes she hasn't heard back from her mum about Patty's decision regarding a trip to Boston over Christmas. She calculates the time difference and decides to call her mother much later on, after they return from the airport, because it's midnight in London.

Olivia reflects on how her day started before dawn and won't end until after midnight. *I'm exhausted*, she thinks to herself as she looks around at her dinner guests and asks, "Anyone want coffee with dessert?"

Little Charlotte raises her hand, and Olivia laughs out loud, "Anyone besides Charlie?"

Nick and Jasmine both raise their hands, and eventually Ian joins in.

Olivia looks around as everyone enjoys her hot apple pie with vanilla ice cream while chatting with each other. She can't get over how much their lives have changed in what seemed like an instant. Then she wonders if the check she wrote to George for the Thanksgiving groceries caused her other check to the hair salon to bounce.

That's when she realizes it was because of that oversized turkey that they all came together. Silently, she gives thanks to God for bringing Hattie back into their lives. She adds to her prayer for Hattie's health to improve because she wants to keep her around for as long as possible, as the thought of losing her is unimaginable.

CHAPTER TWENTY-SEVEN — TABLE FOR FOUR

IAN

When Nick arrives Saturday night to watch the twins, Ian and William offer him a beer. It's still early enough that they're not in a rush to leave for their 7:00 pm dinner reservation at Boulevard.

William takes a closer look at Nick and says, "From FaceTime, I was expecting you to be much younger. How old are you, dude?"

Nick replies, "Twenty-eight."

William continues, "Isn't that old to be a student?"

Nick shrugs his shoulders. "I guess so, but I'm graduating this May."

Jasmine, who hasn't changed out of her work clothes and has her hair tightly clipped back in a bun with no makeup on, walks in, grabs a beer from the fridge, and says to them as she sets the record straight, "My nephew Nick doesn't like to brag about himself, but he went to college on the GI bill and worked his butt off to save for Veterinary School."

Ian is impressed, "Where did you serve, Nick?"

Jasmine jumps in again to speak on Nick's behalf, "Our whole family is Navy. My oldest brother, Nick's dad, is an active-duty Lieutenant Commander on an aircraft carrier. I served as a nurse, and Nick was stationed in Qatar mostly. Our family is all Navy with a lot of history."

Ian begins to sense the intensity of the dragon lady's response to his and William's innocent questions about her nephew. He watches William silently sip his beer and observe her as well. Jasmine was quick to make mincemeat out of him, so his guess is she might be just as nervous about going out with him as he is with her. That's when he decides to cut her some slack because he also finds her super cute when she's intense.

Then Ian walks over to the bench to put on his dress shoes, replacing the boots he wore to clean the animals' stalls. He bends down to pull on his shoes.

Nick leaves his oversized flannel jacket on as he wanders over to chat with Ian while he's changing into his loafers. Suddenly, Ian lurches back as a small brown head pokes out of Nick's pocket.

Ian asks Nick, "What have you got there?"

Nick demonstrates by lifting a ferret in his right hand and a garden snake in his left. "I brought a couple of friends for the kids to meet, and I can't wait to see their puppy."

"They'll be down soon," says William.

From upstairs, they hear Olivia call out, "Jasmine, come up for a sec."

Jasmine's face frowns as she slowly climbs the stairs and disappears into William and Olivia's bedroom.

Ian asks, "What's up with that?"

William snickers, "Olivia is so excited about going out, she can't figure out what to wear."

A few minutes later, Olivia calls down, "Hey Nick, can you come upstairs?"

Nick cheerfully replies, "Be right up." He puts his empty beer bottle on the counter and heads upstairs to get the twins ready for bed.

Ian feels anxious from waiting and glances at his iPhone watch when he asks, "How far is the restaurant from here?"

William instructs, "Relax, it's fifteen minutes away, but Ian, this is a big deal to Olivia. If we're a couple of minutes late, so that they can get ready, it's OK."

Just then, William's phone rings, and he apologizes, "Sorry, I have to take this call." He answers it with a smile, saying, "Allen, what can

I do for you?" While listening, William walks over to his laptop and opens his mailbox. Then, he puts the call on speaker so he can type while talking and asks, "Allen, you there?"

Allen replies, "I'm here. Did you receive the encrypted document?"

William replies, "Yes, sir."

Allen states, "Good, here's the code to open it. 47080822RUC38."

William types it in and confirms, "Got it, and I'm signing it now."

Allen continues, "William. Later tonight, check your bank account for the signing bonus; it should clear in about two hours. I'll let them know at Haloderm that you're officially on board. Someone from human resources will reach out to you regarding your orientation, benefits package, and most importantly, security clearance."

William appears intoxicated with delight. "Allen, thank you so much for the time you spent training me this week."

Allen sighs, "Son, the pleasure is all mine, and I'm going to try to attend more surgical seminars before the holidays. The next one will be in Cambridge. I'll text you the details, and we'll work on the preparations this week right after you finish your orientation day in Randolf. Any questions?"

William hesitates before asking, "Allen, everything is going so well, but there is one question that's haunting me."

Allen speaks up, "Son, there's no such thing as a dumb question, so what's troubling you?"

William proceeds, "Thank you, sir. What's Dr. Ferguson's role in all of this?"

Allen laughs at the question. "William, it's incredible that he is the person who recommended you to me. It was the only reason we hesitated to consider you as a candidate."

"Why's that, sir?"

Allen finishes his explanation, "William, Dr. Shane Ferguson is… how do I put this nicely. He's not highly regarded."

William worries about the missing people. Ian listens to their conversation and becomes concerned for his friend. William takes a breath before continuing to probe and says, "I beg your pardon, sir?"

"William, Dr. Ferguson is an old-fashioned body broker. I believe he might also be a ghoul, but the jury is still out on that. I've only known him briefly through our overlap at Haloderm. He's been a reliable resource, bringing us cadavers from various crematoriums, Harvard, as well as other Medical schools, and, of course, morgues. The most common sources, however, were different funeral homes. He probably bribes them for their still-warm bodies and then delivers them for hefty service fees. He itemizes his bills under transportation and handling charges because, as you already know, selling human body parts is illegal, but transporting, prepping, and packaging is a thriving, legitimate business."

William reveals, "Allen, I had no idea he was into that. We only know him as our veterinarian, and truthfully, I was already thinking about finding someone to replace him for that, but I felt indebted to the guy."

Allen snickers, "I'm telling you, don't be. He receives a headhunter's fee from Haloderm for every person processed by the company, regardless of whether they are delivered dead or alive. You see, William, ghouls don't differentiate, as we're all just inventory to them."

William responds, "Thank you for making me aware of this situation."

Allen adds, "The first payment to Dr. Ferguson is going out tonight at the same time as your signing bonus and another final payment on your work anniversary." Allen pauses for a moment, then says solemnly, "William, that man sold you to Haloderm for a hefty fee. You owe him nothing."

Ian watches William's reaction, and he appears more upset when William asks Allen further, "Has Dr. Ferguson brought you anyone else to hire besides me?"

Allen reveals, "Yes. It was some guy a while ago who was related to his wife, a cousin or nephew, maybe? I can't remember his name, but he still makes deliveries on behalf of Dr. Ferguson to Haloderm from time to time."

William, still upset, asks, "Why didn't you hire him?"

Allen starts laughing as he explains, "That fellow, wait a minute, it's coming to me, Joe. Yeah, that's it, Joe. He fainted while cutting open a thorax. Pardon the pun, but he wasn't cut out for the job."

Ian gives William a cold stare and mouths, "OMG, do you think it's the same Joe?"

William silently mouths, "I don't know?" as he shrugs his shoulders.

William continues with Allen, "I'm looking forward to seeing you later this week, and Allen, thank you again for giving me this opportunity."

Allen ends the call with, "Son, again, the pleasure is all mine."

Ian begins pacing back and forth as he says, "William, the last person to run out after Mary O'Keeffe at Planet Fitness was Joe. What if…?"

"Ian, Joe is a very common name, and we don't know if anything happened to Mary."

"What about the guy giving her a hard time in the ladies' locker room. The detective told you he took off."

"It's just another coincidence, Ian."

"William, you just want everything to go smoothly for your new job, and you're not seeing the trees for the forest. Did you hear what Allen said about your veterinarian being a ghoul? Sorry, William, I think you should report this to the police."

"Ian, I'll think about it, but tonight we are going out to celebrate, and that's the final word for now!"

Ian and William both look up as Jasmine and Olivia descend the stairs. Olivia is wearing an adorable red mini dress; her hair is brushed out and unusually shiny, complemented by her glossed, full lips.

William smiles and says, "Olivia, you look beautiful, and you're glowing."

Ian stares at Jasmine as if he's seeing her for the very first time. Her long, dark hair is full-bodied and falls in soft curls below her slim shoulders. She is wearing a borrowed dress from Olivia that shows off her long, slender legs. Her face appears perfect to him, with only a slight touch of lip gloss and a hint of blush on her cheeks, along with a touch of eyeshadow that accentuates her catlike eyes.

Ian stammers, "Ladies, you look lovely, and let's go, cause I'm starving."

#

When they arrive at Boulevard, their table isn't ready yet, and they're squeezed into the small, crowded bar area that's three people deep, making it almost impossible to order drinks. Ian raises his voice. "What do you want? I'm buying."

Olivia remarks, "How about the Sancerre?"

Ian says, "Sure thing," then waits for Jasmine's reply.

Jasmine thinks for a moment before revealing her selection: "Belvedere Lychee martini. I had a long week and earned it."

Ian smiles at her and then asks William, "What about you?"

"A Guinness."

Ian places the order, and a few minutes later, passes around the drinks. It's too loud to talk to each other. Olivia seems cheerful to be away from her demanding daily routine, with her goofy, happy smile as proof, as she checks out the restaurant.

The hostess gathers a few people from around the bar to seat them at their tables and navigates through the thinning crowd. Olivia notices a high-top table tucked away in the front corner of the bar, with two people sitting at it, their backs to the window. She's fairly sure it's Dr. Ferguson, and the woman with him has a big head of hair, but that's all she can see from her angle.

While Olivia stretches her neck, William and Ian ask her what she's looking at.

Olivia casually states, "I think I see Dr. Ferguson, and maybe he's with his wife." She points toward the corner. "He mentioned when I saw him this past week that he's been married for over 25 years, but he doesn't wear a wedding ring because he'll accidentally leave it up a horse's ass or something like that."

Neither Ian nor William laughs at her joke, but without being noticed, they try to steal a glance at their high-top in the corner.

William quietly says to Ian, "I can't believe it!"

Ian asks, "Believe what?" as he can't get a clear view from where he's standing.

"Let's not talk about it here."

Just then, the hostess arrives to announce, "Hi folks, your table is ready. Follow me."

#

On the ride home from a delightful dinner, Ian's mind floods with thoughts about William's phone call with his new boss, Allen, at Haloderm, who seems like a nice guy. Still, the unanswerable question for Ian is how Joe from the gym knew what he did for a living, even though he never told him. Then he shivers at the thought. What if this isn't a coincidence, and he is the same guy?

Then Ian tries to calm his mind and find some relief from all these frantic thoughts about missing people, recognizing that it all might be for nothing, and that he is simply suffering from an overactive imagination.

He recalls how happy Olivia was at dinner when she shared the news of her riding class that afternoon. They gave her a big tip on top of her fee and booked her every Saturday for the month, except for Christmas week. *Good for her*, he thinks. Then he remembers she mentioned she's got her fingers crossed, hoping her mother might come in for the holidays. He sadly realizes that he has no plans and hopes they will invite him over for part of it, but if they have family visiting, they probably won't. He sighs at the thought of spending another holiday alone.

Jasmine, on the other hand, is very much worth pursuing, despite the feeling he senses she's holding something back from him. He mulls over what he has learned about her so far: she grew up partly in Lowell but moved around a lot as a kid, went to UMASS, her dad's family is of Chinese descent from Hong Kong, and her mom's Peruvian. She served in the Navy and is fluent in Cantonese and Spanish. Skills that help her as a Nurse Practitioner. Most noticeably, she worships her nephew Nick, who is half Greek on his mother's side, plus Chinese and Peruvian like her. Potluck dinners at their house must be pretty good, he contemplates.

Just then, his phone rings, and he slows down as he answers it on speaker, "Hello."

The faint voice replies, "Ian?"

He's curious and asks, "Jasmine?"

She confirms, "Yes, it's me. I got your number from Olivia after dinner."

"What can I do for you, Jasmine?" inquires Ian.

She reluctantly responds, "Hey, I'm a grown-up, I work full-time plus lots of overtime, and I don't have any spare time. If this thing between us is going somewhere, I want to make sure we've cleared the air, so nobody's time gets wasted."

While she was talking, he slowed down so much that the cars behind him began driving around him on the highway as he offers, "Ask me whatever you'd like." He starts to worry that this new relationship is about to go south while he wonders what's in the air that she wants to clear up. His imagination begins to run wild as he lists suspected things in his mind: she is in another relationship, she's gay, so guys turn her off, she's moving away, or she only dates rich guys. That's when he realizes she's resumed talking and he wasn't paying any attention to what she was saying, and he says, "I'm sorry, would you mind repeating that?"

She says again, "I went through a terrible divorce, and I'm afraid of getting hurt."

Ian defends himself, "Jasmine, I'm not the guy you divorced. I can't promise I'll never hurt you, but I'm kind and caring, and I'll try not to hurt you ever."

She replies, "That sounds nice, and I really appreciate it, but what about my two kids and the fact that my mother lives with us? You went silent after I mentioned that before."

Ian's mind floods with terrible thoughts about hanging out with Jasmine's entire family. Then he recalls sitting around the table at William's house with the kids, the neighbors, and his wife, remembering how jealous he felt about their happiness.

When Ian is ready to respond to her, he carefully explains, "Jasmine, I'm good with the fact that accepting you includes two kids and your mother, but I've got a couple of questions."

Jasmine says with trepidation, "What are your questions?"

Ian passes a cluster of cars and then weaves back into the middle lane before he asks, "Is your ex still in the picture? How old are your kids? Are you a good cook?"

Jasmine chuckles, "My mother does all the cooking, and since my father passed away, she lives for my daughters and nephews, Nick and Christos. My girls are twelve and ten. Tony, my ex, is so far behind on child support payments that we never hear from him, so I guess you could say he's out of the picture."

Ian replies, "That's cool. I'm looking forward to meeting everyone. Can I bring Scout, my beagle, along with me?"

Jasmine hesitates, "Does Scout like cats?"

Ian confesses, "Not really, but he can deal with them."

Jasmine continues, "Can he deal with my cat this Wednesday for dinner at my house?"

Ian tries to decide if he should purr, but she'll think he's a cat turd and hang up on him. So cowardly, all he says is, "Sure, what kind of wine should I bring?"

Doesn't matter, we're not big drinkers," she reveals.

Ian recalls that before dinner, she drank a martini, and during dinner, she had two glasses of Sancerre with Olivia, while the guys were drinking beer. He wonders what the phrase "we're not big drinkers" really means.

Ian adds, "Text me the details and please keep in mind that I'm on call for work that night." Then he takes the exit and stops at the traffic light at the end of the ramp.

He hears her say, "Goodnight."

He ends it by echoing her, "Goodnight," and consoles himself with the thought that it went well.

Shortly after that, his phone rings again, so he assumes it's Jasmine calling back. "What did you forget to tell me?"

William says, sounding surprised, "Aren't you wicked smart? How'd you know what I was about to say?"

Ian reveals, "I thought you were Jasmine calling me back, so I have no clue what you're talking about."

William says in an almost inaudible whisper, "I've got to make this call fast because Olie will be out of the bathroom soon. You know your crazy theories regarding Mary and Mathew's disappearances."

Ian surrenders, "I've moved on. You were right, it's crazy."

William interjects, "No, I don't think so. Remember I told you the detective met me at Dunkin Donuts in Natick, and we both thought that was strange."

"So, what? She was hungry. It's just a job like any other."

William becomes frustrated. "Ian, what I'm about to tell you is going to sound so crazy I can hardly believe it."

Ian says, "I'm ready, shoot."

William swallows hard. "You know Debbie, the detective. I saw her tonight in the bar, and I think she might be Dr. Ferguson's wife."

"What the…?" Ian stammers.

"I never told you this before because I was too ashamed of my involvement, but Dr. Ferguson called me right after I met with Debbie and said the problem would disappear on its own and not to worry about it anymore."

Ian insists, "How the hell did he know about it? We need to call the police, William!"

William is hyperventilating. "Listen, I'm not sure about that because there's more."

Ian says, "Tell me."

William finally confesses, I was the person dropping off your human growth hormones that night at the gym, and I think Dr. Ferguson had someone watching me because it was his compound." He repeats, "I was too ashamed to tell you how badly I needed the money."

Ian replies, "Thanks for coming clean, and I want you to know I've come clean too and stopped taking them."

William is grateful that Ian didn't overreact and says, "I've got to go, but think, Ian, Debbie is the police, and the last people in her cross hairs vanished without a trace. Do nothing and tell no one! We'll wait and ask Allen for help when he gets back to Boston – All Right!"

Ian says, "OK."

William clears his throat before ending the call with, "Thanks, and if you knew some of the things I've learned this past week, you wouldn't breathe a word of this to anyone."

"Like what?" Ian asks as he pulls into his parking lot.

William whispers, "It's easier than I ever imagined to make a person's body disappear."

"All right, I'm home now. Go get some sleep." Ian ends the call and goes to wake up Scout for his last walk of the night.

CHAPTER TWENTY-EIGHT — REPLACEABLE

WILLIAM

William slips out of bed quietly without waking Olivia. He still can't get over how smoothly things carried on while he was out of town. The Price Center is only charging him minimum wage for the recruits, excluding the time they spend horseback riding. He walks around, noticing how clean and well-organized everything is, and even his animals seem happier with them working the farm.

With the feed already properly stored, the chores get done much faster. After finishing milking the cows and goats, William returns to the house to see who has woken up and to make himself a cup of coffee.

Olivia greets him in the kitchen as she takes cinnamon buns out of the oven and feeds the twins breakfast.

William expresses his appreciation, "You did an awesome job while I was away."

Olivia echoes his comment, "I had an awesome team."

William is curious, "What was it like to work with them?"

Henry enthusiastically shouts, "So Great!"

"What about you, Charlie?"

She replies, "I like Tina, I like Adam, I like Barbara, and I like Nick."

Henry adds, "I like Luna too."

William blurts out in a panic, "Has anyone seen the dog?"

Olivia puts her finger to her lip for quiet and walks over to show him what's curled up inside her oversized bathrobe pocket. She pulls it open and says, "Look but don't touch. The poor little fella is exhausted."

William smiles as he says, "This might be the ugliest dog I've ever seen. Will he ever grow any fur on his body?"

Olivia explains, "He is hairless, but there is such a thing as a hairy hairless, so we will wait to see."

William interrupts her, "Can you give me a sec? I forgot to check if my signing bonus came in last night."

Olivia pours William a coffee, cuts up the food on Charlotte's plate, and says, "Eat," while she waits to hear if it arrived.

William flips the phone screen around to show her the new bank balance. "Can you believe this is real?"

From Olivia's other pocket, she pulls out the money he left her before his business trip and asks him, "Do you want this back?"

If William hadn't been hired and paid the signing bonus, he would've said yes, but instead he replies, "Keep it, it's yours. Go get your hair done for the holidays or do something with it you'd enjoy."

She kisses him on the cheek and says, "We need new guest towels in case my Mum comes."

William considers what she just said and decides she's right, so he plans to call the hotel in Galveston where he stayed during his training trip to order them, along with spa robes, as a Christmas gift. "Olivia, don't buy them. I'm going to order something special for us."

"Okey Dokey." She confirms.

William suddenly realizes where Henry learned that new phrase, and he wonders when Olivia started using it.

Olivia sits down next to William, takes a bite of her warm cinnamon bun, and chews for a moment before she reveals, "I have something I need to ask you?"

William casually replies, "Sure."

"You know how Nick is studying to be a veterinarian at Tufts; well, he offered to give Buttercup a full examination for free, including ultrasounds, X-rays, lab tests, but no medications."

William is grateful that someone is available to step in and help with their farm animals while he sorts out everything regarding Dr. Ferguson in the meantime. "What does he need us to do?" he asks.

She explains, "We have to deliver Buttercup to the animal hospital in Grafton early Tuesday morning."

He tenses up. "I'm not sure if I'll be available."

She surprises him with her answer, "I'll ask the Price kids to come here to look after the cows, chickens, and the Berkshire pigs that morning, and then I'll ask Hattie to go with me to help with the trailer. All you'll need to do is take care of Ken and Barbie before you leave."

With relief in his voice, he asks her, "So it seems you're done with Dr. Ferguson?"

Reluctantly, she confesses, "I guess so. He's so damn expensive, and Nick will be starting up his new practice soon. Plus, he'll be more in our budget, I think."

William is glad he doesn't have to worry about Olivia accidentally calling on Dr. Ferguson. Now, he just needs to convince Hattie to do the same without revealing too much about the Fergusons' nefarious business dealings and incriminating himself.

#

William walks over to Hattie's house to feed the horses, clean the stalls, and join them for lunch. After he's finished and puts away the rake and shovel, he looks inside the window to see if Hattie is around. He finds her dozing in her recliner with Edgar across her lap and taps gently on the door.

Hattie Hollers in her raspy voice, "It's open."

He enters, and as soon as she recognizes it's him, her face lights up, and she smiles before saying, "Well, it's about time you got your scrawny ass over here." There's just something about how she talks to him that makes him feel safe and loved. He wants to tell her everything he's worried about, but he's too afraid to get her involved.

He begins by saying, "There's something I need to talk to you about."

She replies, "It can wait. Here, take this!" Then she hands him the Amazon package, which contains a jewelry box, before asking, "Did you check the size on her wedding band?"

"Yup, and they're the same, so the diamond ring should fit her just right."

"I still don't understand why you didn't give it to her sooner," Hattie complains. "She is going to love it. By the way, George and I plucked the goose you bagged before you left, and it's in the freezer in the garage."

Hattie begins to cough uncontrollably and needs to catch her breath to finish saying what she has to say, "It's there whenever you need it."

"Hattie, you're the best! What can I get you for Christmas?"

She moans at the thought of it, "I could use a new pair of lungs for starters."

William's mind jumps to the many body parts in limbo at Haloderm and thinks, nah, she wouldn't find a cryogenically frozen pair of lungs under the tree funny and asks, "Hattie, maybe consider something more traditional for a gift, like a robe and slippers or a spa package. You know, something a bit more girly."

"I don't need that crap, but you've been here five minutes already, and didn't notice!"

He looks around and suddenly realizes, "My goodness, you haven't picked up a cigarette." He becomes very concerned and asks, "How did that happen?"

She admits, "Jasmine bought me Nicorette and the rest was easy."

William stands up, squeezes her shoulder, and says, "I'm so proud of you."

She echoes, "Speaking of proud, Mr. Fancy Pants, so the new company is driving you around in limos and flying you hither and thither and yon."

He replies, "It's wonderful, better than I'd ever imagined, and I like it. They flew me first class and put me up in a swanky hotel."

. Hattie insists, "Tell me about the company. What do they make?"

William finds it hard to explain but tries, "It's a medical manufacturer."

"So, they make engineered devices?"

"No, it's more biological than that. They prepare skin, tendons, joints, muscles, teeth, and bones for transplantation."

"What, no lungs?" she laughs and coughs at the same time. "So, Dr. Frankenstein, where do you fit into this?"

"I'm being trained to work in the surgical training division. We take willed bodies and prepare the cadavers for instructional programs. It's tough work and not for the faint of heart."

Hattie looks him in the eye when she says, "I'm proud of you and what you've made of yourself. More importantly, your mother and father would be proud of you, too."

William laughs and asks, "So, George isn't proud of me?"

Hattie giggles, "George is proud of you, too. So, hah! But seriously, I have some paperwork you need to sign."

"What's it about?"

"Life insurance, I bought a policy for you with a rider for Olivia. After seeing what happened around here in your absence, I'm glad I took the initiative to make sure your kids will never have to go through what you went through after your parents died."

"Thank you, Hattie. You are my fairy godmother."

She looks at him and says, "You should be happier than you are, and I can tell you're not, so what's the matter?"

"I could never hide anything from you," he confesses. "It's this. I can't believe they've hired me, and they're giving me all this money. I feel like a phony, and they're going to find out and fire me."

"William, you are the furthest thing from a phony, and it's about time someone appreciates you for your hard work and talents. What exactly will you be doing?"

He takes a deep breath before he begins to reveal the whole truth: "Hattie, I'll be dismembering and packaging human cadavers."

She squeals, "You're a high-paid meat packer?"

He admits, "I hadn't thought of it that way, but I guess that's accurate."

She strokes her chin before continuing, "I have no issue with it, but I wouldn't tell too many other people."

He snickers, "What about Take Your Daughter to Work Day? Should I bring Charlie?"

"Cut it out, William. That's gruesome and depraved." Hattie tosses her pillow at him.

William continues, "I already cut it out, but it's back at work, so Hah back at you, Hattie."

She looks up. "Oh, thank goodness, George is back from the store. Want something to eat?"

George walks in, and as soon as he sees William, a tear wells up in his eye. "Welcome home, Billy. How was the trip?"

William stands up, and George gives him a big bear hug before he speaks in his ear, "Has Hattie shared anything with you regarding her prognosis?"

William shakes his head no.

"Well, we're glad you're home and with us for lunch," George adds. "It's turkey subs, with cranberry juice to drink. Want chips with it?" He hands him a bag with a sub sandwich and a drink.

While they are eating and catching up, William's phone rings, and he says, "I've no idea who this is, but I've got to take it."

George insists, "Go ahead, we don't mind."

Just as the call is about to go to voicemail, William intercepts with it, "Hello, William Loring here."

The person on the call introduces herself as his human resources contact: "Hi, Mr. Loring, I'm Ellie, and I'll be your liaison at Haloderm."

William is surprised, "Wow, Ellie, you're working on a Sunday morning."

"Mr. Loring, at Haloderm, we work around the clock, 24/7, because our clients need us, and we're here to deliver for them."

William is impressed and asks, "Is that our company's motto, Ellie?"

She curtly says, "No, but it should be." Then she sighs before adding, "Meet me at the main campus on Wednesday morning at 9:00 sharp, and I'll walk you in. After that, we'll process you and begin your orientation tour."

He confirms, "Sounds great. I look forward to meeting you in person."

After William finishes the call, he turns to Hattie and asks, "Are you still proud of me? Now that you know the truth."

Hattie insists strongly, "Unequivocally!"

"Thanks," he says before asking her, "Do you know if any of my old snowboarding clothes are over here?"

Hattie looks confused. "Why would you need them now?"

"They keep the temperature at around 40 degrees where I'll be working, so I'm looking for my thermals to wear."

Hattie instructs, "Go upstairs and look somewhere in the big walk-in closet, you know, the one that's cedar-lined. Your boxes will be labeled with your name on them."

While rummaging through his old winter clothes, he can hear the rumblings of Hattie and George talking as if they're upset. William finds what he is looking for in the boxes and returns to speak with them.

"You never raise your voice, so what's wrong, George?"

Tears of frustration fill his eyes when he reveals, "This fool is refusing treatment for her lung cancer."

"Hattie, why not give it a try?"

Hattie coughs to clear her throat. "I'm battling cancer on two fronts. Leukemia and now nodules are growing in my lungs. I'm just tired of fighting, that's all."

William speaks sternly, "Please start the treatments and hang on for me, I mean for us. We don't know what we'll do without you."

Hattie reaches for William's hand and takes it in hers. "You know I'm not a quitter, so all right, I'll give it a try." She looks deeply into his loving eyes and adds, "For you."

"Good!" says William as he glances at George and notices the relief on his face. Then he turns to Hattie and remarks, "You look tired. Why don't you take a nap?" He leans down and kisses her forehead goodbye, but right before he stands back up, he slides in this one critical comment: "I heard something not too good about Dr. Shane Ferguson."

Hattie's ears perk up, and she queries, "Like what?"

He might be facing some legal issues, and he's involved in some trouble.

Hattie's face appears shocked as she finds this peculiarly strange. "That's so odd with his wife, Debbie, being a police detective and all."

This confirmation gives William a shiver. "Just don't engage with him. I'll get to the bottom of it. His wife might also be involved. If he comes round, tell him you're not well, that's all, and whatever you do, don't make him suspicious."

George steps in, "No problem. Right, Hattie?"

Hattie gives him a thumbs up, and William smiles at her and says before he leaves to go home, "Promise me, you'll try hard to beat this."

She nods yes as he closes her front door.

CHAPTER TWENTY-NINE — TWINNING

OLIVIA

"Who wants munchkins?" Olivia asks as she rushes to slide her half-awake children into each car seat. "Oh, know, it's beginning to snow." She huffs under her sweaty breath as she buckles them in and walks around to the back of the trailer to make sure Buttercup is secure while she waits for William to return from feeding Ken and Barbie at Jameson Farm.

Then she examines her old diaper bag to ensure she has brought enough snacks, drinks, and activities to entertain the twins during their extended stay in the waiting room at the animal hospital. While she's deep in thought, William hops into the already running truck and carefully backs it out along with the horse trailer before he asks, "Where to?"

She replies, "First stop is Dunkin Donuts for Munchkins, coffees, and some croissants. I have this craving for the ones with melted chocolate inside."

William looks at the gas gauge and adds, "I'll drop you off, get gas, then come back to pick you up. There's going to be a long line this early, so order online, and I want an English muffin with an egg and melted cheese."

"Sausage?" she asks.

He reconfirms, "No thanks, but add a hash brown. Are you placing the order for pickup?"

"Yes-sir-ee."

#

They arrive on time for Buttercup's scheduled appointment. Olivia opens the tailgate and leads Buttercup to an animal relief area. Buttercup pins her ears back, and the occasional twitch shows her clear displeasure about her ride in the cold trailer. Olivia tries to calm her with gentle rubs to her muzzle and long strokes, but they aren't allowed to feed her or give her water before her procedure this morning, which makes her seem very stressed.

Eventually, Nick and a group of veterinary students arrive to greet them and offer to take Buttercup inside for her examination and tests. Olivia's eyes fill with tears as Nick leads Buttercup away, and the oversized door closes behind them. Olivia returns to the warm cab of their truck to join William and the children.

"How long is this going to take?" asks William.

"I have no idea. I'm just grateful the kids fell back asleep."

William takes a bite of his breakfast sandwich before he asks her, "What do you think is happening in there?"

Olivia states, "I think this is going to take a very long time. Did you bring your work from Haloderm to study this morning?"

William pulls his laptop out of his knapsack and immediately begins reviewing Haloderm's emergency procedures for a Code Orange.

"What are you studying?" She asks.

"Their protocol should I encounter any hazardous materials from a contaminated cadaver. Allen Tyler Jr. told me he rereads and refreshes this part at least every three months, and I should too."

"That's interesting, but I'm going to shut my eyes until the kids wake up." Olivia nods off and leaves William to study for his orientation at Haloderm the next day.

After about twenty-five minutes, Olivia's WhatsApp interrupts her nap, and she wakes with a start. She answers, "Hello, Mummy."

"Morning, Olivia. Where are my beautiful grandbabies?"

Olivia turns her phone so her mother can see the twins as they wake to the sound of her incoming call. "Charlotte, Henry, say good morning to your grandmother."

Henry mumbles, "Are you coming to A-Meri-cA?"

Charlotte continues, "And bringing us lots of pwesents?"

Olivia stops them. "We don't need presents - who wants a munchkin?"

Both of their little hands go up at once, but William is so deep in his studies that he isn't paying them any attention. Olivia passes a few back for them to eat and continues the conversation with her mother, "Mummy, we're dying to know. Will you be able to join us for the holidays?"

Her mother asks, "Do you have enough room for us?"

"Yes, of course, but you will have to share the bathroom with the children."

"Then the answer is yes!" she says with a raised voice as the twins holler, "Grandma's coming!"

William doesn't even glance up as Olivia keeps talking to her mother, "When, mummy?"

Her mother continues, "It's just so easy-peasy you wouldn't believe it. There are several direct flights, but if we fly Virgin Atlantic, they'll send a car to pick us up at our doorstep and drop us off at yours."

"Mummy, I can't wait."

"That makes two of us." Her mother confirms before asking her, "Where are you off to, my darling?"

"Oh, Mummy, we're at the animal hospital with our horse Buttercup. We're waiting for news from her doctors."

"Best of luck with Buttercup. I'll text you our itinerary as soon as I can. Bye, Darlings."

William looks up from his studies. "So, they're joining us?"

"Yes!" Olivia declares. "I'll have so much to do in preparation for their arrival."

Olivia immediately starts making her grocery list in her head. I'm going to need to organize it by store, she thinks. Market Basket for the live lobsters and baking supplies, Whole Foods for the meat, vegetables, and potatoes, Wegman's for the jumbo tiger shrimp cocktail, crab legs, and specialty items like British beer and a bottle of Sipsmith Gin. Then, out loud, she moans, "Oh, what am I going to have on the menu?" As her mind floods with ideas for cookies, plum puddings, fruitcakes, trifle, rib roast, and a goose, she speaks her thoughts, "Oh my goodness, where will I find one?"

William asks her, "Find what, Olie?"

"A goose." She confirms before she adds, "And a gorgeous quality prime rib."

William jumps in with a smile on his face, "I can help you."

She smiles when she replies, "This is the third time this week you've come to my rescue, and I'm beginning to like it."

William adds, "All you have to do is remind me when we return home and mention the towels to me as well."

Just then, Olivia gets a text: "It's from Nick. The doctors need us to come in for a meeting to review the results."

William closes his laptop and says, "I'll get the stroller and take the kids for a potty break before we join you. Please don't make him wait too long, Olivia. They're being very generous to us."

#

Olivia joins the group of veterinary students in the large-livestock examining room. The frightened expressions on their faces alarm her as she walks past them and waits to hear Buttercup's prognosis.

Nick leads the discussion as his veterinary professor listens and evaluates, "Olivia, overall, Buttercup is in good health. She will need continued treatment for her recurring eye infection."

Sounding worried, she asks, "Is there more?"

Nick asks, "Where is William?"

"He'll be along any second."

Nick adds, "Fine, let's wait until he gets here to go over the next part."

Olivia asks, "Is Buttercup carrying a foal?"

Before Nick responds, William rushes in with the twins still in their carriage and asks, "Have I missed anything?"

Nick continues, "No, we waited for you, William." Then Nick draws everyone's attention to the computer as he displays Buttercup's condition from her ultrasound results. "Look here." He points, "There are visibly two heartbeats, and it's fairly clear that one of the embryos is attaching to the uterine wall, as we would expect, and the second one is not, so it needs to be aborted as soon as possible."

"What will happen if they wait?" one of Nick's classmates asks.

Nick looks glum. "That will cause all sorts of problems for Buttercup. All equine twinning pregnancies end poorly. I cannot stress enough how important it is that we act quickly. Still, if we take Buttercup in for surgery immediately, we might be able to save one foal or at least save her life because a twinning can result in death from infection or complications for the mare."

"Oh, my goodness, this is awful," cries Olivia. "And it's all my stupid fault."

William comforts her, "She'll be fine, Olie." Then he looks to Nick for confirmation.

Nick explains, "Buttercup is right on the cusp of when we can terminate one without hurting the other, but this procedure will greatly increase the risk of her naturally aborting the surviving foal once she's further along."

"So, should we stop riding her?" William inquires.

Nick replies, "No, getting lots of exercise is good for her, so assuming this pregnancy is viable, then go ahead and buy her a girdle extender for her saddle and keep the weight maximum at 125 lbs. or less, including a saddle. We will know much more after we review her labs."

Olivia pets her horse as she remains upset with herself about what she did, which now puts her horse in mortal danger.

Nick suggests, "Why don't you make yourselves comfortable in the waiting room? This is going to be a long procedure."

Olivia says, "Seriously, you're doing the surgery right now?"

"Yes, it's their best chance."

Olivia begins to cry, and William puts his arm around her as he escorts her to the waiting room while pushing the stroller.

"Nincompoop, I'm a complete and utter nincompoop," admits Olivia.

Henry loves this new word and starts repeating it.

She takes out coloring books, stories to read, and snacks to help pass the time more quickly. At this point, William is completely engrossed in his studies, and Olivia finds comfort in the quiet time she's spending with her children. She glances down at her twins with love and shivers at the thought of Buttercup having to give up one foal this morning to save the other. Knowing the procedure has already begun makes her stomach churn and bile rise in her throat.

She glances at her watch and decides it's late enough to call Hattie to ask how the recruits from the Price Center are doing in their absence, but the call goes straight to voicemail: "Hattie, call me with an update on what's going on. Things here are not looking good."

A couple of minutes later, William's phone rings. "Hi, Hattie, yup, she's pregnant, but it's bad, yeah, twinning." He listens to her for a moment. "One for sure isn't going to make it." He rubs his tired eyes before ending their conversation. "Yes, Hattie, she already knows it's a terrible thing, and it's all her fault. I'll keep you posted."

Olivia begs, "What's going on at home?"

William reveals, "Tina, Adam, and Barbara showed up on time. They're not happy about working through snow squalls, but they're more worried about Buttercup and want to know when we're bringing her home."

William looks up from his laptop and realizes Nick has returned with an update. "Buttercup is doing fine. The procedure went well."

Olivia stands up before she asks, "What about her foal?"

Nick replies, "We just have to wait and see, but keep in mind she's at a much higher risk for a spontaneous abortion than from a normal pregnancy. But her lab work is excellent, no sign of equine herpes or any other sexually transmitted diseases, and as I already stated, now we wait."

Olivia asks, "When can we bring her home?"

Nick appears perplexed. "There are two schools of thought: the first is that she'll get round-the-clock care here, so she should stay with us overnight, and the second is that she's a horse, so we can't talk to her, and being here is very stressful. You know your horse better than we do, Olivia. What do you think is best for her?"

Olivia asks, "What will we need to do for her at home?"

Nick explains, "Check her temperature every two hours for the next twenty-four hours and give her antibiotics if she has a fever, and watch her for a discharge. It could be the beginning of a spontaneous abortion. If she has a fever or a discharge, I want you to call me."

William asks, "Is there anything else we can do?"

"Yes, keep her warm and quiet for the next couple of days."

Olivia states, "Then I believe it would be best if we bring her home."

Nick nods in agreement before he says, "Good, I'll get her paperwork and prescriptions ready. Figure an hour or so, and we'll have her ready to go. Plus, I want her out of here because they're predicting a big snowstorm this week."

William walks over to Nick and shakes his hand while saying, "Thank you for everything you've done for us."

Nick replies, "Glad we were here to help you out. You're a nice family, and by the way, Merry Christmas."

PART THREE

CHAPTER THIRTY — INSIDE THE BELLY OF THE BEAST

WILLIAM

Standing outside Haloderm, it's 8:45 am, and William sips his Dunkin' Donuts hot cocoa while gazing up at the enormous white monolith of a building that appears pasted against the cloudy, overcast winter sky. That's when it occurs to him that it's challenging to differentiate between where the building ends and the heavens begin.

He finishes his warm drink and tosses the empty cup into the open bed of his truck, then walks toward the entrance where he is supposed to meet Ellie from human resources. He decides to check his emails and messages because he was already warned; he won't be able to do it the rest of the day. He scrolls through them as quickly as he can and feels relieved when he sees shipping confirmations for the spa robes, Turkish hotel towels, and a 6-lb boneless beef prime rib from Snake River Farms.

He glances at the time on his phone as he stands with a straight posture in anticipation of meeting Ellie from Human Resources. At exactly 9:00 am sharp, someone emerges dressed in white scrubs, a face mask, and protective glasses.

She says, "Good morning, William. I'm Ellie, and welcome to the Hive."

He follows her through the same process he did with Allen Tyler Jr., but this time the flashing blue lights and light mist are old hat, and he stays silent, waiting for Ellie's instructions.

All she says is, "Follow me."

They walk for a while down the unmarked, vast corridors until they reach what he imagines must be the human resources department. Inside, it feels like a typical office space, with shared workstations for itinerant workers. They are sleek and carefully designed but show little evidence of use.

The temperature is slightly warmer than where he worked with Allen Tyler Jr. in the surgical suite, but not by much, so he feels proud of himself for remembering to wear his long underwear and snowboarding socks.

Ellie asks, "How are you doing so far?"

William casually responds, "Fine. Does everyone call this place the Hive, or is that your special name for it?" Remembering how she also had her own company motto.

She smiles when she confirms, "No, it's just mine, but it should be called that because that's what it feels like."

He realizes this is the second time she has made this comment and wishes he knew more about her than just her job title.

She probes further with her questions: "Is the temperature a bit too cold for you?"

William explains, "I'm used to working outdoors, ma'am."

She tells him, "Just call me, Ellie."

William continues, "Ellie, I have lots of questions."

Ellie places a tablet in front of William as she explains what she needs from him. "William, I can't answer any of your questions until you sign the non-disclosure agreement."

"Can I read it first?"

"Yes, but please understand the choice is binary. Sign it, and you'll be processed, or don't." She takes a deep breath and ends her sentence with, "And I'll show you out."

William signs the tablet and hands it to her.

"Thank you, William," she states casually. Then she hands him another tablet to review and adds, "This part is easy. Just check to make sure everything is entered correctly, sign it, and then we'll finish your orientation."

He's curious and asks, "Is everyone's orientation the same, more or less?"

She smirks while offering her answer, "Not at all, the orientation training for allo-derm recruits is very different from the autologous hires; the department you're joining is one of the smallest, but don't underestimate your department's importance to us, as it handles the relationships between the company's sales teams and the surgeons who use our vast array of both regenerative products and extracted ones."

William feels a bit overwhelmed by her memorized litany of jargon, and he is somewhat intimidated when he inquires, "What's allo versus autologous? What does it mean?"

Ellie proudly explains, "Please keep in mind that every single day, the technology in our industry is evolving so quickly that what's true in the morning when you arrive may be completely obsolete by lunchtime. Our motto should be more like, Adapt or die!"

William strokes the mask over his chin as he recalls what Allen Tyler Jr. shared with him about the long-standing practice of surgical training with cadavers, which has remained essentially unchanged for hundreds of years. Then he realizes she has been talking, even though his mind had drifted elsewhere.

She drones on, "Presently, Haloderm makes lifesaving and extending products that are sourced from healthy donor tissue, but this technology, with the help of AI, will soon evolve into what is the autologous model, which means, in layman's terms, that our products will eventually be made from a person's cells instead of a donor's."

All he says is, "I see."

She blinks behind her protective glasses and asks, "Have you had time to watch some of our company's videos?"

He nods yes, and she says, "Wonderful, now let's return to your background check and personal information for review, so that you can receive your final security clearance."

William is worried about the upcoming challenge as he starts to believe he won't be able to clear the hurdle, and today might be his last day at Haloderm.

Ellie continues, "We have over 55,000 employees at Haloderm, and we are just a subsidiary of a much larger multinational conglomerate, but my job is to make sure each person is the perfect fit for their position, and that's why we do such extensive background checks."

William considers that's not the only reason they do them and replies, "My life is an open book, Ellie." That's when his mind flashes back to the ladies' locker room at Planet Fitness, where he was pounding the face of Matthew, the crossdresser, who sexually attacked Mary O'Keefe. He wonders if the company might have found out about it as he begins to sweat.

Ellie reviews a tablet before she asks, "Let's start with your home. Do you own or rent?"

William specifies, "We own our home."

She smiles before she proceeds, "Here's the thing, William. We conducted a quick title search, and your property has never been bought or sold since the pre-antebellum era. How is that possible?"

He feels more at ease talking about his family's history. "That's true. Our house on Raven Rd in Sherborn has been in my family since 1840 when my ancestors built it, and if everything goes as planned, it will be handed down to my children someday."

Ellie reaches under her protective glasses and rubs the bridge of her nose before speaking. "Wow, that's unusual and nice, I guess. Let's talk about your wife for a moment. Is she here in America legally or illegally?"

"Legally." He states.

"Does she speak English, just in case we need to call her?"

He laughs, "Actually, Olivia speaks the King's English, as she was born in London."

She continues, "I see, and how long have you two been married?"

He states, "About four and a half years."

Ellie reviews her notes and sits up straight. "Thank you, William, for helping me tidy up your file. Let's switch gears now and clarify Haloderm and what's expected of you. Any questions?"

"Yes, of course. My first question is, how does my wife reach me in case of an emergency while I'm at work?"

Ellie explains, "There is a location chip in your ID badge. Wherever you are, it will forward your call to the closest phone, and I will provide you with the telephone number."

He adds, "Can I call out?"

"Yes, after you give them your access code." William is eager to ask Ellie why, but doesn't want to seem naïve. She looks him in the eye and says, as if reading his mind, "The reason for the tight security is that our work here is considered top secret. No photos, texts, or emails are allowed to go from inside to the outside. There is a constant threat to steal our proprietary technology, and these protocols are in place to prevent that from ever happening."

"Ellie, you keep mentioning all the people who work here, but I haven't met anyone besides Allen Tyler Jr. and you. Where are they?"

"Fair question." She hands him his FOB and then points to an app for him to add to his phone from a QR code before she elaborates, "Each division has garage parking, and the FOB will open its door for you, while the chip on your ID badge locates and segregates you from other employees.

"It will continue this way until your protocol is changed or your employment is terminated. Everything is managed by artificial intelligence, which is designed to focus each employee's knowledge on their specific area of expertise within the company."

William finds this information a bit intense, so he asks, "What happens in the cafeteria or employee lounges when people get together?"

Ellie confirms, "They don't exist here."

William thinks she's joking and pleads, "What if I want a coffee break?"

Ellie giggles, "Oh, I do love this part. How do you take your coffee?"

"Black one sugar and steamed milk on top."

"Would you like to have a Danish to go with it?" she adds.

"Sure, and will you be joining me?" he asks chivalrously.

Ellie smiles before she begins her conjuring, "HD, please get me a coffee with one sugar and steamed whole milk and a decaf coffee with whole milk, along with two fruit Danishes."

Through the speakers in the room, a voice says, "Order Confirmed."

Ellie looks at her tablet and asks, "How far along are you with your memorization of the emergency color codes?"

"Orange is for toxic cleanup, blue indicates a person just died, grey signals a violent individual on the premises, and to call security..."

Ellie cuts him off, "We have another level of color codes for internal use only. Code Fuchsia, for example, is for when you encounter a cadaver that's, well, not usable if you know what I mean."

William echoes, "I know what you mean."

She adds, "Good, now let's discuss a code crimson."

Her voice rises in pitch as she explains, "Crimson can mean many things, but fundamentally it's when something or someone is putting Haloderm at risk."

William naively asks, "Should I call the police when that happens?"

She can't control herself and howls with a full belly laugh, "Call the police. That's hilarious." She laughs some more. "Our company requires top-tier security clearance for all of its projects, so the answer is NO!" She huffs before she adds, "We police ourselves, William."

He apologizes, "I'm sorry for my lack of understanding. My work has always been meat and potatoes, and all of this is kind of beyond me."

Ellie smiles when she confirms, "William, that is exactly why we selected you out of all the other candidates."

William is surprised. "I beg your pardon, I don't follow you."

She continues, "The initial idea of offering cadaver services to surgeons was suggested by our sales division some time ago, and it proved to be the ideal way to recycle and reuse cadavers that were not suitable for transplantation. They call it "a symbiotic relationship" to emphasize the importance of training doctors to use our products and building strong relationships with medical schools and hospitals worldwide. We have programs in over sixty-seven countries, and much of our success is due to consultants like Allen Tyler Jr., who demonstrated how to make our program effective after previous unsuccessful efforts."

"So, Allen Tyler Jr. is just a consultant and not a real employee here?" He questions.

"That's not by our choice, mind you, but I'm not at liberty to discuss it with you," she says before asking him, "What did Allen tell you about your upcoming project?"

"Not much, just that I'm going to a seminar with him to teach surgical procedures in Cambridge."

Her laughter echoes in the room, but he can't understand what he said that made her find it so funny. Then she collects herself and begins to clarify, "That was hysterical, and you will be setting up cadavers for…"

She is interrupted by a tap at the door, followed by a small white robot about the size of a six-year-old, which rolls in and stops between them. Two steaming mugs of coffee, along with two freshly baked Danish pastries, sit on the tray.

Ellie remarks, "Thanks, HD." Then she pulls off her mask to take a bite of her Danish and a sip of her coffee as she points to William's mug and gestures for him to grab his. That's when the old-fashioned pigtail phone on the desk rings, and she says, "Relax for a moment. I need to take a call."

Ellie picks up and says, "Hi, this is Ellie. Sure, you need to reschedule Johnny's tuba lesson this Saturday, no problem." She nods as she listens, "That's fine. See you then. Bye." She hangs up the call.

After listening to the call, William makes several assumptions about Ellie as he attempts to build a connection: "So your grandson is learning to play the tuba?"

Ellie lifts her coffee cup to her lips and halts before saying, "Hell no, I don't have any children. I'm in a marching band, and I'm a tuba instructor in my spare time."

William, based on the time they've been together, realizes that Ellie is almost unrelatable, and he still isn't sure why she laughed at him. His fears start to take over as he feels he's not doing well in this meeting, and any second, she will see through him and walk him out. In his moment of vulnerability, he pleads, "Why did you hire me, Ellie?"

She chuckles first, "You see, William, you are a perfect fit for this position, and that is, of course, unless you prove me wrong." She raises the pitch of her voice at the end of the sentence.

William's head drops, and he glances at the floor for a moment.

Ellie perks up and says, "Well then, please allow me to show you where to park your vehicle tomorrow." She stands up and waits for him to follow her.

"How will I know where to go once I get inside the building?"

Ellie smiles, "William, the building will show you where to go."

He wonders seriously: *Did she really say that, or is this person joking? Is this just a first-day hazing, and am I being punked big time!*

#

When William called Allen Tyler Jr. to offer him a ride from the airport, he had to insist firmly, since Allen had turned him down three times. It finally seemed to dawn on him that there might be a hidden reason William was hesitant to reveal over the phone.

Next on William's to-do list is to stop by and talk to Officer Bobby Hill on his way to Logan Airport to ask him some questions about the police department's procedures regarding convicted felons and sex offenders without raising suspicion about his involvement in a case. William drives up Route 115 as he looks down the long driveway where Bobby Hill sits and waits for speeders to whiz by. He's disappointed when he sees that his usual spot is empty.

He considers calling him on his cell phone, but decides that's too much information to share over the phone or a text message, so he chooses to be patient instead, waiting until he runs into him in person.

The drive to the airport goes by quickly as William reviews in his mind what he wants to discuss with Allen Tyler Jr. face-to-face. He easily spots Allen standing on the curb outside the baggage claim at United, dressed in his long black button-down oilskin coat, cowboy hat, and boots.

Allen smiles when he recognizes William as he pulls up to him. Allen tosses his carry-on and briefcase into the back seat and hops into the front passenger seat. He says, "I gave up a chauffeured ride in a limousine for this, and I want you to know the cab of your truck stinks like chicken shit."

William smiles when he replies, "I swear to God, I don't smell it. Where to?"

Allen looks at his phone first and says, "Hyatt in Cambridge." After buckling his seatbelt, he asks, "Well, son, is this about the Haloderm orientation?"

"It was pretty cool," confesses William, relieved that Allen has no suspicion there's another issue.

Allen is confused when he asks, "So what was so urgent that I had to give up my nice ride to see you in person?"

William swallows hard, and his palms become sweaty on the wheel as he says, "I know we haven't known each other long, but I want you to know that I trust you."

Allen scratches his scalp, uncertain of where this is heading, so he stays quiet and lets William keep going.

William asks politely, "Please tell me more about Dr. Knox and what he did back in the early 1800s?"

Allen begins, "Well, Dr. Knox was a human anatomist and a surgeon; he was considered eccentric, but his story doesn't end well. He was publicly shamed for being so obtuse that sixteen people were murdered on his account for the good of his surgical students, and after his career stalled, he ended up a social pariah. Why do you ask?"

William tries not to reveal too many details because he and Ian aren't sure if anything is genuinely concerning, so he avoids direct questions and sidesteps the topic: "How do they know where all of these bodies come from at Haloderm?"

Allen explains, "It's pretty standard, they're sourced from several places, including various universities' willed body programs, morgues, hospitals, nursing homes, prisons, funeral parlors, and likely others I've overlooked."

Allen pinches the bridge of his nose before continuing, "Each cadaver is delivered to Haloderm with its paperwork, which includes the person's identity if available, blood type, DNA, UNOS data, and any medical information provided with it."

"What's UNOS?" asks William.

"It stands for United Network for Organ Sharing, and it also includes live donors willing to share some of their liver, bone marrow, a kidney, or sometimes skin, and the like. I think of it as a place like Amazon, but for human spare parts."

William listens carefully, and his ears perk up when he realizes that each cadaver's DNA is recorded in the system. If he could somehow get hold of Matthew or Mary's DNA, he'd be able to confirm whether they're there, which means he can finally put this madness behind him. He shudders at the thought that they might be stored on a shelf, dead in a deep freeze somewhere inside the massive white monolith at Haloderm, and he asks, "What if there is no medical history? You know, like the person's a John Doe."

Allen looks up as he thinks, "Well, this is based on conjecture and how we manage these sorts of cases in Galveston. We recycle the bodies with no medical history into our surgical training programs, but they're never collected for an extraction and transplantation of any kind."

William says, "Thanks for clarifying that for me."

Allen asks him, "So, who ended up giving you your orientation?"

William avoids seeming ageist and says sharply, "Ellie."

Allen chuckles, "I can't believe that dinosaur still works there."

William adds, "Well, she does." He wonders how well he really knows her before he says, "It was pretty over the top if you know what I mean?"

"I do, and it's not warm and fuzzy either," Allen shivers.

William shares, "I think the friendliest thing there was the robot."

Allen agrees, "I believe you might be right."

William surmises, "After she asked me to describe what I thought I'd be doing for work and I replied, she burst out laughing like it was a big fat joke."

Allen interjects, "So what exactly do you believe you'll be doing?"

Using human cadavers for surgeon training.

Allen reveals, "Well, that's partly true but not the whole truth."

William takes a deep breath and worries he might be in over his head.

Allen hijacks the conversation and asks him an unrelated question: "How are you running your farm and also working with me?"

William sighs, "My wife is a genius. She reached out to a place called the Price Center and hired a crew of adults with intellectual challenges. It's way more than we can afford, but the farm animals are happier, and things are turning the corner for the better."

"So, you're saying your farm is underwater?" Allen asks with concern.

"Sir, family farms everywhere are pretty much the same. Fuel, meds, and feed costs are skyrocketing. The land has been in my family for 166 years, and I might be the last in a long line able to hang on to it."

Allen asks, "Why is that?"

William explains, "My land, for example, is 4.9 acres, but because it's just under five acres, it's taxed at a residential rate instead of the much lower farm rate. Go figure, it was my grandfather who gave the town the 115 acres behind us to be used as conservation land, and at the time, it was a brilliant idea. Now I can't buy back one square inch of it, and the real estate taxes are drowning us in debt."

Allen steers the conversation back to work, saying, "That's sad, but son, what I'm about to tell you doesn't leave this truck."

William is stopped at a red light, so he turns to look Allen in the eyes and says, "Scout's honor, it won't."

Allen states, "Starting tomorrow, we will coordinate the handling of cadavers for a project involving a company called Davinci, in collaboration with NASA, OrganEx, and SpaceX. This classified initiative aims to develop artificial intelligence alongside robotic systems capable of performing, reproducing, and executing any required surgical procedures on astronauts during travel to and from Mars."

"Wow!" says William, who has no idea what Da Vinci is or where this is going.

Allen urges, "Son, the light's green."

William presses the gas pedal.

Allen continues, "Think about it, even if we send physicians and the most skilled surgeons along, that still doesn't solve the problem of medical care for long missions. This is the next step in medicine's evolution. Robots guided by AI will fill that gap, and our cadavers will train them because it's unlikely a living person wants to volunteer for this, unless, of course, you want to be our first." Allen chuckles at the absurdity.

Perplexed, William asks his most important question, "Allen, why did you pick me?"

Allen is silent for a long while before he explains, "Let's start by me explaining my background, and I'd like to add that many were disqualified before I decided to pick you."

Allen falls silent again, as if he's searching his thoughts. "You see, William, your history reminds me most of my own, and my story was, well, a success. I'm what you vets call a mustang. The university hired me to work in the cafeteria when I was a junior in high school. I worked my way up from mopping floors and taking out the trash to becoming the head of the Willed Body Program. No college education, no degrees, just hard work and determination."

William is baffled that Allen never had formal schooling, yet he is still admired and celebrated for his talents.

Allen sighs, "You see, a very long time ago, this brilliant anatomy professor who was also a remarkable surgeon asked me, a dirt-poor, black boy with no prospects, to assist him in the morgue one afternoon with a cadaver. It went so well he asked me back, and eventually he began to train me to be a diener."

William digs deeper and says, "I appreciate this opportunity, sir, but I still don't understand why you didn't just ask one of your students?"

Allen chuckles, "Do you recall those vegan medical students you met sitting outside my office? Can you imagine kids like that doing what we do?"

"No, sir, I can't," William confesses.

Allen smirks and says, "And most importantly, this is a business with budgets. My job is also to keep costs down. Think about it, there's no need for medical malpractice insurance or a license to practice medicine because we are working on the dead, so why hire someone overqualified?"

All William says while he's trying to process everything is, "I see. Then why not hire a mortician instead?"

Allen reveals, "They know the ins and outs of the business, and the opportunity to be greedy might be too tempting for most, so I advised Haloderm against it. Pardon the pun, but I find undertakers to be underhanded." They arrive at the hotel, and Allen ends with, "Good, we're finally here - I'm starving! Want to join me for some dinner?"

"What time are we starting tomorrow, and where?" William requests.

"MIT Space Science Lab at 10am. I'll text you the details, and don't worry about getting a parking ticket in Cambridge. Haloderm will cover the cost."

"Sure," William confirms.

Allen adds, "I'll get out now and check in. Go and park. I'll meet you in the lobby in five."

William pulls up to the curb at the entrance to the hotel and lets Allen out.

William drives higher and higher up the levels inside the full parking garage, searching for a space big enough for his extended-cab truck. When he reaches the roof level, he gets a text message from Allen: "Meet me in the restaurant off the lobby, and the other reason I picked you is that you're not a ghoul."

William smiles after reading Allen's text message, then decides to set aside his worries about Mary O'Keefe and Matthew, the sex offender, for now and focus on the task at hand, the Mission to Mars.

CHAPTER THIRTY-ONE — ROUGH RIDERS

OLIVIA

It's so painfully cold outside that their old furnace can't generate enough heat to warm the inside of the house. Still, with help from Adam, Barbara, and Tina, Olivia carefully arranges enough of their auxiliary space heaters and warmers around the barn and chicken coop to help take some of the cold's curse off the animals. Olivia is grateful that Buttercup can recover at Jameson Farm in the more comfortable accommodations of Hattie's state-of-the-art stable.

When Adam eagerly offers to go across the street and tend to the horses, Olivia instructs him, "Please saddle them when you're done because I have a riding lesson at 3:30."

Adam glances at his watch and gives her a thumbs-up just as Tina speaks her mind: "Ahem." She clears her throat before she continues, "Will there be enough time for all of us to ride today?"

Olivia is pleased with Tina's eagerness, "Sure as shit." She says with a smile just before shoveling more cow manure into the wheelbarrow.

Tina laughs at her comment, and then all of them look up together as a large white van approaches, with Barbara shivering from the cold while pointing at it.

Olivia glances at Barbara and says, "Darling, please go back inside and pour some hot cocoa for you and the children. I left it in the thermos on the kitchen counter and warm up by the fireplace. It's miserably cold today."

Barbara quickly grabs the twins by the hand, and they, with no resistance at all, follow her to the house, seeming happy to go inside.

Adam quietly passes the white van as he crosses the street to check on the horses. From the barn, Olivia sees two men in the large white van. She glances at her watch, realizes she doesn't have much time, and walks over to see who is inside.

She taps on the driver's side window, and a muscular man around her husband's age rolls it down and says, "Uncle Shane, there's a lady here to talk to you."

After he pulls down his face warmer, Olivia immediately recognizes Dr. Ferguson in the passenger seat and says, "Oh, good day, doctor."

Dr. Ferguson is busy texting on his cell phone while ignoring her, which she finds odd. After another minute passes, he finally looks up and sneers, saying, "You tell that ungrateful bastard of a husband that I'm charging him for your horse's ultrasound even though he got one somewhere else!"

Olivia realizes that Dr. Ferguson's speech is slow and slurred; she looks at him and the man with him and notices their mannerisms are irregular, with glazed-over, runny eyes and nasal drips. She says with her eyes wide open, "I beg your pardon?"

He continues his rant with his voice noticeably louder, "Hattie said you had the ultrasound done somewhere else. Well, you could have at least told me before I asked my nephew Joe to come out here and assist me with the exam. You people are just plain rude!"

"Please accept my apology. It must have slipped William's mind. You know, with the new job."

Dr. Ferguson hollers, "You mean the job I got him!"

Olivia stands as still as a stone and remains silent.

Dr. Ferguson takes a deep breath before ending his rant with, "You're ingrates! Joe, let's get the hell out of here!"

Joe gives her a nasty look as he drives away, which sends a shiver down Olivia's spine. Suddenly, she is startled by a tap on her shoulder that makes her jump.

It's Tina who sounds like she's worried. "Is everything all right?"

What crosses Olivia's mind is that she needs to calm herself down because it's not like somebody just died, so she replies, "No, but it will work itself out." As she thinks, *good riddance, Dr. Ferguson. I never really liked you in the first place, and I'm glad you're gone from our lives.*

#

Inside the house, Olivia feels an urgent need to pee and rushes to the bathroom, just in time. She wonders if Dr. Ferguson and his nephew might have scared the piss out of her. *I need to call William now*, she decides.

"Hello, darling. Call me when you get a chance. It's quite important."

Her phone rings immediately. "Is everyone all right?"

"Yes, darling. I'm so sorry for interrupting you at work."

"Olie, I'm losing my mind. I've driven up and down Vassar St in Cambridge at least ten times, and if I don't find a parking spot, I'm going to be late for work," William says with panic in his voice.

Olivia blurts out, "Best Buy!"

William asks, "What are you talking about?"

"Darling, park at Best Buy and take an Uber over. It's across the river, and no one will bother the truck there."

"Did I ever tell you that you're a genius?" he says with relief in his voice.

She smirks, "Yes, but not often enough."

Sounding calmer, he asks her, "Was Dr. Ferguson by the house?"

"How did you know he was here?" she asks, intrigued.

"While I was driving to work, I noticed a text message came in from him marked priority, but I haven't read it yet."

She explains, "He was here this morning. He arrived with his nephew Joe to give Buttercup an ultrasound, but Hattie sent him away and told him it had already been taken care of by someone else." There is complete silence on the other end. "William, are you there?" She believes the call dropped.

Olie, bring the twins and the kids from the Price Center inside and stay there," William commands.

She trembles before she states, "William, you're frightening me. What's going on?"

He ignores her question and keeps instructing her, "Tell Hattie to come and stay with you as well." He takes a breath before asking, "What did that guy named Joe look like?"

'He was roughly your age, very muscular, clean-shaven, with brown eyes. William, why?"

"Olie, it's probably nothing, but there's something off about his nephew, and Dr. Ferguson might be involved in a shady side business."

She concedes, "All right, love, we will do as you've instructed."

He adds, "My Uber's here, and I need to make two quick calls before starting my day at work. First, ask Ian to come by and help, and then Officer Bobby Hill to tell him to keep an eye on you, so don't be surprised if there's a police car outside."

Olivia ends the phone call with, "Got to go!" because she thinks she hears a stranger's voice talking to the children, so she rushes to see who it is.

When she turns the corner near the playroom, she finds Barbara amid a tea party with the twins, Paddington Bear, and Luna the puppy, who is sleeping under the covers in the baby buggy. She steps back to avoid interrupting and decides to record them because it's so adorable.

When Barbara asks softly, "Charlie, would you like another biscuit and one for your baby bear?" Olivia is surprised to hear her speak.

Charlie replies, "Oh yes, please, and thank you so very much."

"And Henry, more tea?" Barbara inquires with the toy teapot poised over his cup.

Henry says with a snarky tone, "Oh yes, please, and an extra lump of sugar as well." Then he turns to Charlie and complains, "Why are we doing what you want to do and not what I want to do?"

Barbara elucidates, "Henry, we decided on this democratically, and we outvoted you four to one."

Henry raises his voice as if he's demanding to be heard, "Well, as the man of this house, I think it's time to take Luna for his walk in the park in the baby buggy."

Olivia giggles at Henry's frustration and has almost forgotten about the strange episode with Dr. Ferguson until she notices a Sherborn Police car pulling into the driveway and turning around to face the street. Then, as quick as lightning, she runs to the lavatory and barely makes it in time, leaning over the toilet bowl to vomit.

What the *hell,* she thinks as she vomits again. She asks herself, *What's this about? Is it from today's excitement, or am I under too much stress with Mummy and Patty coming to visit? Or could it be that I'm coming down with a bug? Oh no!* She stops herself and thinks back.

Then she opens her Amazon app, goes to the "My Purchases" section, and checks when she last ordered tampons. She scrolls down to before Thanksgiving and then further down until she reaches her Halloween candy order, and there they are with that order. She shouts aloud, "Bullocks!" After that, she places a pregnancy test in her cart and hits "Buy It Now" while thinking, William is going to murder me. This is just not a good time, as she worries some more about whether the ill-fated eclampsia might also return along with it.

She texts Jasmine: *Are you at Hattie's?*

Yes, what's up? Jasmine texts back.

Olivia types, *can you bring Hattie and come over to my house?*

Why? asks Jasmine.

There's something strange afoot, and William believes we should stay together for our safety.

Jasmine sends her a thumbs-up emoji.

Then Olivia heads out to the barn to get Tina and realizes she forgot Adam. She sends another text to Jasmine and asks her to bring Adam with her, too.

#

Olivia taps on Officer Bobby Hill's window. "Hey, would you like a hot cocoa and a sandwich? I'm about to make lunch."

Bobby smiles and replies, "Sure, I could use a bathroom break anyway."

Then she finds Tina playing with the pigs and shouts, "Tina, come in for lunch."

Olivia walks around and ensures the barn doors are securely closed, then tucks her scarf around her neck to keep out the cold. She hears Jasmine's car start up across the street and rushes back to the house to begin making lunch. On her way, she decides it's a perfect day for grilled cheese sandwiches with tomato soup. Yum, she thinks as her queasiness abates and her appetite returns.

CHAPTER THIRTY-TWO — RECKONING

IAN

"Alexa, weather forecast?" Ian calls out as he scoots around and pulls on warmer clothes to do outdoor chores. He worries about William's livestock, which don't understand there's a blizzard hitting them; animals still want to get fed.

Alexa clearly states, "There is a major snowstorm advisory in effect beginning at 1 PM today."

Ian realizes that, even though he's on call today, given the weather forecast, it's unlikely that a transplant team will be assembled or that any organs will be scheduled for flights, as most of the Northeast will shut down air traffic until after the storm passes.

The thought of being unable to help William gnaws at him, so he decides to take a chance with work and go straight to the farm instead of A.O.R.A., where he needs to check in with dispatch. William's voice sounded genuinely panicked when he called, asking him to stay with Olivia and the kids until he returned from Cambridge later this afternoon.

"Scout, let's go!" The dog obediently waits at Ian's feet for him to dress him for the cold weather. Ian grabs some dog food, his thermos of hot coffee, and says, "Alexa, goodnight." Everything in his apartment shuts off automatically as they walk out the door.

#

On the way to William's, Ian stops for gas and some treats for the twins. He is still reeling from the horrifying connection between

Debbie the Detective and Joe, who was, as far as he's concerned, the last person to see Mary O'Keefe.

Ian shivers at the thought of how Joe knew what he did for a living without him telling him. He keeps wondering and worrying that he might have also been one of Joe's targets. Ian gets the creeps just thinking about the possibility that Joe abducted both of them, and Debbie swept their disappearances under the table for her nephew. How convenient.

It was a long-standing concern of Ian's that fentanyl addicts were an established part of the symbiotic relationship in the organ transplant supply chain. Still, it never occurred to him before now that undocumented aliens could also be fueling this vast and growing industry. And nobody is wiser, not even the industry insiders, because no one is actively searching for them; they come and go unnoticed. An almost limitless supply of people with no paper trail, no arrival date, paid cash under the table, renting under aliases, living with roommates on their leases, or using fake IDs. There, but not really there. And when they disappear, who's to notice they're gone or if they ever existed?

#

When Ian pulls into the driveway at the farm, he's not surprised to see a Sherborn police car parked out front. He knows William has a friend on the force, and he's relieved that William thought to ask for his help. What surprises him is how many people he finds hanging out in the kitchen, and the large pot of hot soup on the stove makes him smile when Olivia offers, "Want a bowl? It comes with a grilled cheese sandwich?"

Ian nods silently in agreement, overwhelmed by the activity and the many people he hadn't expected to find in William's and Olivia's kitchen on this quiet, snowy afternoon. Jasmine, George, and Hattie sit at the table; Adam and Tina snack at the kitchen counter. Barbara and the twins relax on the couch, where she eats with them while

Henry shares a story from a book. The police officer stands up, eating his sandwich, trying to blend in with the group of friends and family.

Ian walks over to Jasmine and squeezes her shoulder, wondering if she knows why William asked everyone to gather. She glances at him and offers a half smile, searching his eyes for answers. He shrugs and sits next to her. He is grateful for his grilled cheese sandwich, so he can stuff his mouth with it instead of answering difficult questions.

He waves to the police officer and, after swallowing, says, "Hi, I'm Ian. Friend of the family. William reached out to me and asked me to pitch in this afternoon."

"Hey, Ian. I'm Officer Robert Hill, but my friends call me Bobby. William sent me a text, so here we are."

George chimes in, "That's all wonderful, fellas, but do you mind dialing me in on what's going on here?"

Ian shoves the rest of the sandwich into his mouth, prompting Bobby to jump in, "All I know is William is worried about some guys who came by and harassed Olivia this morning. He has reason to believe they may be problematic, and his family could be in danger."

George jumps in and asks Ian, "Does this have something to do with Shane Ferguson? He left Jameson Farm pretty upset this morning."

Ian shrugs his shoulders again and remains silent. Jasmine looks at him in disbelief and asks, "What's the matter, Ian. You've barely uttered a word since you arrived."

Ian replies, "I don't want to talk out of turn."

George jumps in, "What the hell is that supposed to mean?"

Hattie is fearful and asks, "Is William also involved in this?"

Ian replies shyly, "Well, yes, he is sort of."

Hattie demands, "Sort of how?"

Ian starts sweating and doesn't think he can hold off on their questions much longer. He looks at his watch and says, "Let me go out to the barn for a bit and take care of the animals before we get snowed in, and when Williams gets home, we will tell you everything we know."

George offers, "I'm going with you; we'll get it done faster if we work together."

Ian nods in agreement with George, and they start dressing warmly to prepare for the upcoming snowstorm.

Tina looks out the window and announces in a nasal voice, as if she's coming down with a cold, "Adam, Barbara, our ride's here. They've come to get us early because of the blizzard. Let's go!"

Adam gets up to put on his coat and boots while Barbara stays on the sofa with the twins and seems to ignore Tina's request.

Tina groans, "Barbara, get your coat on. Let's go!"

Barbara dismisses her second request.

Tina scolds her, "Barbara, your mom's probably not coming to get you. We need to go now!"

Olivia senses that the Price kids are a bit unnerved by the changes in their daily routine and the stress from the ill-fated visit from Dr. Ferguson and his nephew, Joe, that morning. Therefore, she speaks up, "Barbara, do you want to stay overnight at our farm and have your mom come to get you after the blizzard?"

Barbara nods her head yes without making eye contact, so Olivia adds, "Why don't you call your mum and let her know, so she doesn't worry about you?"

Tina frustratedly jumps in, "Seriously, how is she going to accomplish that?"

Olivia extends one finger in the air and says, "We've got it under control, Tina. I'll let her mum know she wants to stay overnight with Henry and Charlie, and she'll be fine here."

The driver in the Price Center van honks the horn loudly to hurry them along.

Tina says, "Adam, let's go!"

Olivia walks them to the door and says, "Be safe," then shows them out.

George and Ian leave with them and make their way through the new snow to feed the livestock and close the barn as best they can before the blizzard hits.

Ian complains to George while shaking snow off his hat, "This is a terrible way to make a living, I want you to know."

George nods, "I couldn't agree with you more, but it's in William's blood. He wouldn't be able to feel normal without this place."

Ian asks, "George, where do you want to start?"

George exclaims, "The chicken coop. I want to make sure nothing crawled in there to hide from the storm. I'm also grabbing a shotgun just in case it did."

Ian asks, "What are you worried about finding?"

"Coyotes! They can be exceptionally nasty when they're cold and hungry."

Ian shines a flashlight on the chickens, which are huddled together trying to stay warm, as he looks around for a pair of predatory eyes shining back at him. He confirms, "I don't see any sign of them."

"Good, they're less likely to bother the pigs; those animals can be vicious," shares George.

While they're feeding the pigs, George asks Ian, "What got you and William so spooked today?"

Ian finally admits, "It's this guy Joe. I think he might be the nephew of the guy you mentioned. I know him from my gym, and let's say there's something about him that doesn't add up."

George is curious and asks, "Like how? What do you think this guy is into?"

Ian smirks, "You wouldn't believe me if I told you. It's pretty out there."

George admits, "Maybe I won't, but try me anyway."

Ian changes the subject. "Can we bring the goats inside the house? They look miserable."

George watches them shivering and bleating their hearts out. "I'll walk them across the street and put them in the stable with the horses.

It's warmer in there to keep Buttercup comfortable after a medical procedure. They'll be happier over there."

George returns to the subject and asks, "Well, when are you going to tell me more about this Joe fella?"

"George, William, and I think Joe might be responsible for a couple of people who went missing right before Thanksgiving," Ian finally confesses.

George is skeptical and wonders if there's more and digs deeper, "Missing like their photos are on a milk carton?"

Ian explains, "That's the thing. The girl came here from Ireland and overstayed her visa, so when she disappeared, nobody went to look for her."

George digs in again, "So do you think this guy Joe had something to do with her disappearance?"

Ian continues, "Well, there's more. William and I were together working out at Planet Fitness with, coincidentally, that same Joe guy, and we heard a girl, whose name is Mary O'Keefe, screaming for help. Joe, William, and me rush in to rescue her. There's this big ugly man dressed in ladies' workout clothes, and he's raping her."

George prompts Ian, "Then what happened?"

"The three of us peel the dude off Mary, and the next thing I know, William is punching the pervert in the face, and at that exact moment, everything flips on us."

George asks, "How so?" Scratching his forehead while he listens.

"We want to call the police to get this pervert-rapist guy arrested, but instead, he's telling us that it's his right to be in the ladies' locker room, and the girl is begging us not to call the police, and how she overstayed her visa, and they'll deport her back to Ireland."

Ian takes a deep breath and bangs his cold hands together before he continues, "Then she tells us that this problem is all our fault. You know, meaning William, Joe, and me made things bad for her. Like she would have been better off raped or even something worse had we not intervened. You know it's as if the whole world's gone nuts." Ian shakes his head and looks down at his boots.

George smirks, "That's quite a story, but I don't see how it got you two so riled up over Joe today?"

Ian continues, "You see, when Mary left the gym, Joe offered to make sure she was all right. Seemed perfectly normal at the time."

George jokes, "I still don't see the point."

What happened next is that I spent all day on Thanksgiving being questioned by the Natick police about Mary O'Keefe's disappearance, and William and I are terrified that Matthew will press charges against us for roughing him up after he attacked Mary. FYI, Mary hasn't been seen by anyone since she walked out the front door of the gym that night. It was her boyfriend who reported her missing to the Natick police.

George confirms, "That's interesting."

Ian reveals, "Then we find out Matthew the pervert also vanished, and we're told he is a registered sex offender with a long history, so the assumption is he took off to avoid being implicated in her disappearance."

George concludes, "That makes some sense."

Ian continues, "What if you also found out Joe is this same police detective's nephew, and he has an impressive career as a cadaver transporter, moving bodies from funeral homes and morgues to companies that produce replacement skin for cancer or burn patients."

Still circumstantial, but I gotta say, it's giving me the creeps. So, how is Shane Ferguson involved?

Ian rolls his eyes before revealing, "He's married to the Natick police detective, and Joe is their nephew."

"Oh, I think you might want to bring Bobby Hill up to speed on this," George reasons.

Ian smirks, "I'm not the one holding back. I agree with you, George, but William thinks it's too circumstantial to report, and he's worried there may be more police involved than just her in their cadaver side business."

George confesses, "I get that, but I'm freezing out here, so I'm running the goats across the street and heading inside. I won't say anything."

Ian nods as he watches George struggle to get the goats to follow him. Then he finishes the chores and gives the cows the last of the fresh hay.

#

Back inside the warm farmhouse, Ian watches Jasmine administer Hattie's IVIG treatment in the lounge chair near the fireplace. He admires her focused attention as she cares for her patient.

Ian stands up when he asks, "Can I get you some tea or something?"

Jasmine smiles at Ian as if she's just noticed him come inside for the first time and replies, "That would be lovely, wouldn't it, Hattie?"

Ian asks, "What about Olivia?"

Hattie reveals, "I think she went up for a nap as I don't hear the twins or Barbara either, so it's just us." She raises her voice, George, want a cup of tea?"

George answers with a startle, as if he had dozed off, "No, I'm good."

Ian is fidgety as he looks out the window for the umpteenth time, worried about William's dangerous ride home through the heavy falling snow. He notices Bobby Hill is facing the road in his police car and thinks, Great, now we can finally use Bobby's expertise and get some real help sorting out this mess.

CHAPTER THIRTY-THREE — WE EAT OUR KILL

WILLIAM

William blasts the heat and defroster to max in the cab of his truck as he shivers from the cold and exhaustion after a long day on his feet. He turns to Allen with genuine concern and asks him, "Are you warm enough?"

Allen laughs when he replies, "Never, I'm always too cold, even after all the years working in a morgue."

William chuckles, "Well, you picked a doozy of a day to be stuck in Boston."

Allen sounds grateful. "Thank you so much for coming to my rescue tonight. Unfortunately, my flight was canceled after I checked out of the Hyatt this morning, so I'm trapped somewhere between Scylla and Charybdis with nowhere to go."

William assures him, "Olivia is thrilled to have you join us." Hoping he sounds sincere, because, in truth, Olivia is still upset over the threats Dr. Ferguson and his nephew made that morning. He still can't get over how nasty his text message was. He swallows hard and decides to spill the beans tonight to Allen and Bobby Hill, in the hope of recruiting their much-needed help.

Allen asks, "How much farther?"

"The roads are terrible, so I'm driving slowly. We'll be there soon." William opens his dry eyes wide while gazing through his windshield, which looks more like passing through a starfield in hyperdrive than a blinding blizzard.

Allen perks up and makes small talk, "So, were you impressed with the DaVinci 18 robotic surgery demonstration?"

"Wow, I still can't believe it. Using minimally invasive surgical techniques, 18 removed all the lung cancer tissue, and if the patient wasn't a cadaver, it would have closed him up and left him as good as new, all while the surgeons were hands off." He shakes his head in astonishment.

Allen sounds somewhat less optimistic than before: "It's not perfected, but we're definitely off to a great start. Space travel brings out the best in humanity, don't you think?"

William nods his head in agreement before deciding it's time to break the ice, tell Allen everything about his concerns over Dr. Ferguson, and ask for his advice.

Just then, William shouts, "Hang on." As he swerves to avoid a deer standing like a statue in the middle of Route 115, he says, "Ah shit. We hit her."

William turns on his emergency flashers, gets out, and walks around to assess the damage. All he notices is a scratch on the front end of his truck, but he spots a speckled trail of blood in the fresh snow, confirming he's wounded her. He opens the truck door and says to Allen in an amplified voice, "I'm going to check on the doe to see if she's OK."

William finds her in a ditch by the side of the road. She's crying out in pain, and her back leg has a compound fracture.

William shakes his head sadly from side to side as he apologizes to her, "I'm so sorry, little one." He returns to his truck, pulls out a pistol from the rear storage compartment, and walks back to the doe to shoot her dead mercifully.

Then he scoops up her warm young body in his arms and gently places her carcass on the flatbed of his pickup. After that, he puts his gun away, gets back in his seat, and continues the tedious drive home.

Allen interrupts the silence, "That was sad. What are you going to do with her?"

William sighs before replying, "For now, quarter and clean her. I can promise you nothing will go to waste, but I agree it was sad." Then he looks over at Allen and asks him, "You feeling all right, Allen?"

"To tell the truth, son, I'm tuckered out."

William treads cautiously, "We'll be at my farm soon, and you'll be able to rest, but there's something I want to share with you because I need your help and advice."

Allen says, "Sure."

William hands him his iPhone and tells him to read the third text message from the top.

Allen reads it and turns to William, "Holy cow, what kind of psychopath wrote that?"

William confesses, "Dr. Shane Ferguson showed up at my farm this morning and threatened my family. Then he sent me that text."

Allen asks, "Did you call the police?"

"No, and it's complicated, you see. Dr. Ferguson's wife is a detective in the Natick Police Department, and she's also involved in this mess, just like their nephew Joe, it seems."

William hits the steering wheel in frustration before he continues. "Thankfully, my buddy Bobby Hill is a cop in Sherborn, and he's watching my house along with my friend Ian till I get home tonight."

Allen is deeply concerned and asks, "Please tell me everything from the very beginning, William."

When William finishes explaining how it all began with a fight involving Matthew, the sexual predator at Planet Fitness, and then Mary's disappearance, followed by Matthew's disappearance, he holds his breath, fearing Allen will pass harsh judgment on him.

Allen speaks for the first time since William started. "So, what you're telling me is that those three are full-fledged ghouls and they have access to Haloderm, which is a big problem for us."

"Yes, that's the synopsis, Sir."

Allen taps his forehead as he thinks before answering and says, "Thanks for entrusting me with this. Who else knows?"

Besides me, it's only my friend Ian, who was with me that night at the gym when all of this happened, and Joe.

Allen asks, "Would Ian possibly be available to sign an NDA should Haloderm request it?"

"I think so," William confirms.

Allen instructs, "Let me be the one to talk to Bobby Hill. Haloderm has its security force, and they don't take kindly to working with the local police."

William feels relieved as he turns onto Raven Road and sees the flashing police lights illuminating the snow-covered hills. Then he shouts, "We're here!" As he starts running up the driveway, which is already a foot deep in heavy snow, the truck fishtails on the incline and barely manages to reach the garage.

#

William quietly heads upstairs to check on Olivia. He tiptoes to avoid waking the twins from their afternoon nap. He finds Olivia in the guest bedroom, changing the pillowcases and laying out fresh towels for their house guests.

She turns to look at William, smiles, then walks over to kiss him hello and asks, "How was your day, darling?"

He states everything he's permitted to say under the NDA he signed: "It was interesting."

Just then, Olivia's phone rings and she says, "Sorry, I must take this." She hits the speaker button, and William watches her voice rise an octave in an excited tone, "Oh my goodness, what did you think of the video I sent you of Barbara's little tea party this morning?"

A man with a gentle voice introduces himself on the call: "Olivia, I'm Neil, Barbara's dad. Her mother, Dora, is here with me, and we want you to know the video you sent us made us cry. We're still crying tears of joy. We gave up hope years ago that Barbara would ever be able to speak."

Barbara's mother chimes in, "She has such a lovely voice. This was an unexpected present you gave us today. How can we ever repay you?"

Barbara's father adds, "Olivia, you have a special gift. Please don't let it go to waste. You've made more progress with our daughter in a short time than others have in many years. What's your secret?"

William notices that Olivia is blushing from the flattery when she replies, "I treat her the same way I would want to be treated. There's no secret."

Barbara's mother echoes her husband, "You're a whisperer, Olivia. Whatever you do, don't stop doing what you're doing!"

William gazes proudly at his wife, amazed by her recent accomplishments. Then he thinks, if it weren't for Dr. Ferguson connecting me with Haloderm, none of this would have happened. We were on the verge of bankruptcy. *Miracles are real, aren't they*? He asks himself after feeling like he's just witnessed one.

In stereo, Barbara's parents say, "Thank you again and Happy Holidays." Then they hang up.

William kisses Olivia passionately and looks into her eyes when he offers, "What can I do to help you with dinner?"

"Oh, it's pretty much under control, but I'm worried about the twins. Tina had the sniffles, and I pray they don't come down with colds right before my mum arrives for the holidays." Then she changes the subject, "How about selecting some nice wines for dinner?"

He's nervous about impressing his boss and gently asks, "What's for supper?"

"Spaghetti Bolognese, with some side dishes I pulled out of the freezer because our crowd size kept growing, and it appears that Ian and Jasmine are also joining us."

With concern, he asks, "We're snowed in. Where are they going to sleep?"

She states as if it's obvious, "At Hattie's."

"Have those two ever spent a night together before?"

Olivia shrugs her shoulders and raises her hands to indicate she doesn't know.

William hears chatter and realizes his children have woken up from their nap. He enters their room to greet them, saying, "Hello, Frick and Frack." He bends down to kiss each of them before asking, "Are you going to introduce me?"

Charlotte pulls Barbara over by the hand, and Henry proclaims, "This is our fweind Pwincess Barbara."

Charlotte finishes his sentence, "And she is from the land of fairies." Charlotte looks up at him and then says, "It's a sleepover party, Daddy -- Barbara, this is my Daddy."

Barbara avoids eye contact with William, and he senses that his presence makes her uncomfortable, so he gives an excuse to leave: "I need to go and help Mummy with dinner."

Henry confirms, "Vewy well, Father."

#

When William returns to the living room, he finds George and Allen sitting by the blazing fire, sipping red wine and deep in conversation. It's no surprise that their similar ages and matching temperaments make them instant friends.

Ian and Jasmine are busy setting the table in the dining room, while Olivia hums a tune in the kitchen as she adds final touches to her loaves of garlic bread.

William sees his reflection in the hall mirror and looks long enough to remind himself to take the good with the bad because things are much better than he ever expected. Then he pauses a moment longer to pray that everything will work itself out for the best.

Just then, Olivia calls for him to come help, and he says, "I'll be right there, Olie."

She is tossing a huge salad when he walks in, and she starts pointing at dishes for him to bring to the table, asking, "Did you pick out the wine yet?"

He cordially replies, "It's next on my list. How about that big boy of Barolo we've been saving? It's a special occasion. Isn't it?" She makes a disgruntled face, and he realizes she might want to save it for her mother's visit. He adds, "I think we have a couple of really nice bottles of Chianti left over from my dad's collection. I'll bring up two for dinner." As he thinks, *dammit, I really wanted to impress my boss with something special, but sometimes you've got to pick your battles.*

Then he asks, "Where is Hattie, by the way?"

"She's napping in our bed; her IVIG infusion wiped her out."

William feels his chest tighten and his mouth go dry when he asks, "Has she begun her chemotherapy for lung cancer yet?" The visual of the cancer surgery demonstration from earlier that afternoon loops in his mind.

Olivia explains, "It's a targeted treatment, so she is waiting for them to figure out her specific protocol. It will start very soon."

William's mind cannot unsee the cadaver he prepared for the Davinci 18 cancer surgery demonstration, and he winces before saying, "After I bring up the bottles from the basement, I'll go upstairs to fetch her and the kids for dinner."

Olivia glances up at him from stirring the Bolognese and smiles.

#

William can feel the weight of gravity pulling on his tired legs from the long day as he climbs the stairs. Hattie, he expects, must be worn out. Still, as he steps into his bedroom, he finds her sitting up, chewing on a wad of Nicorette while holding an unlit cigarette between her rough fingers.

With two poised fingers holding her unlit cigarette, she points at him and demands in an angry voice, "Dammit, Billy. What kind of trouble did you get yourself involved in?"

He doesn't know where to start, so he stammers, "It's a long story, Hattie, and dinner is on the table."

She huffs before she says, "Cut the shit. I know your tell when you did something you're ashamed of, so fess up and get it off your chest right now."

Her voice morphs into a frightening growl, and he can feel it reverberating deep down into his bones as he guiltily explains. "I screwed up. I needed money desperately, and Dr. Ferguson offered me an easy way to make it."

"Was it legit?" She asks with one eyebrow raised.

"It sort of kind of wasn't." He looks away in shame.

"Why would you do something stupid like that? You know, you could have come to me or even George. What's wrong with you? You were raised better than that!" she scolds.

William's face turns red from shame, and he feels nauseated when he pleads, "Hattie, my boss is downstairs. His flight was canceled, so I brought him home with me. Please come downstairs and be nice. I'll explain everything to you, but later."

She crosses her arms and says, "William Loring, I'm so frightfully ashamed of you I can't stand it, but I will do as you've asked me…for now!" She lets out another huff and adds, "And this discussion isn't anywhere close to over!"

#

The candles are lit, and the wine is poured, but the evening lacks that certain spark that makes a dinner feel festive; instead, it feels more somber and solemn as the guests quietly choose their seats.

William takes a sip of the Chianti as he eagerly welcomes the immediate rush from the alcohol to his brain. Then he looks around the table at their many dinner guests and asks, "Who would like a piece of garlic bread with their salad?" He hands the breadbasket to Allen as he notices everyone at the table seems on edge, even his children. He concludes it's a mix of bringing his boss home for dinner without prior notice to Olivia, the blizzard descending upon them, and, of course, having murderous killers threatening their lives that morning.

Allen takes the breadbasket in hand while he makes a request, "Would anyone here mind if we say a prayer before we eat?"

William looks down the long farmhouse table to watch the reactions while silently praying that no one objects, then adds, "Let us all join hands while Allen leads us in prayer."

His children quickly take Barbara's hands, then Olivia's at the other end. Across from William, he holds hands with Henry on one side and George on the other. George takes Hattie's hand, and she reaches for the police officer's, Bobby Hill's, giving it a little squeeze to show her appreciation. William and Bobby hold Jasmine's hands, who is sitting across from Ian. Ian is hand in hand with Allen, completing the circle when Allen recites from memory, "Lord, thank you for this wonderful meal before us and please watch over us and our loved ones and protect us from evil. Amen." Then Allen remains silent a moment longer, as if adding an addendum to his prayer for only God to hear, before opening his eyes, taking a big sip of wine, and commenting, "This wine is lovely. What is it?"

William explains, "My dad had a remarkable palate and an incredible sense of smell. He was an expert at pairing wines with food and was often sought out for his advice. All that remains are remnants of what was once a truly great wine collection. This is one of his prized Chiantis, and I'm so glad you are enjoying it." As he thinks about how his boss might have enjoyed the Barolo more.

Hattie lifts her glass and toasts, "To William, Billy's father."

There are echoes of "Here-Here."

Then Hattie lifts her wine glass to show she needs a refill, and Olivia pours her another. William briefly worries that she might get smashed at the table and say something to embarrass him in front of his boss, but he can see George squeezing her hand to keep things under control, and is grateful to him.

George breaks the ice, "So, Allen, how did you get into the body business?"

William jumps in, "We call them cadavers, George, and coincidentally, my buddy Ian is an organ transporter for A.O.R.A., and Jasmine once worked with extraction teams while she was a nurse at the Brigham, so there's quite a bit of overlap, and it's a much larger industry than people realize."

Allen clears his throat after swallowing his food and politely answers his question, "George, you see, I was blessed." He clasps his hands together before continuing, "When I was eighteen years old, one of the surgeons in the Human Anatomy Department at the University of Galveston befriended me and offered to train me to be a diener, which is, in layman's terms, a morgue assistant."

Jasmine perks up because she finds this conversation unexpectedly interesting and asks him, "If you hadn't made his acquaintance, where do you think you would have ended up?"

Allen laughs loudly and smirks before replying, "Most likely-hmmm, the Janitorial Services Department at the University."

William steps in and guides the discussion, "Everyone, Allen is being extremely modest. He is the Director of the Willed Body Program at the University of Galveston, and he also consults for Haloderm, as well as serving on the advisory boards of various State Universities that have Willed Body Programs."

George excitedly exclaims, "See, William. Even they call it like it is – Bodies – not cadavers, Bodies!"

Hattie adds, "So, hah to that, Billy!" as she gulps down her second glass of wine, still not having touched her salad or bread.

William looks across the table at Olivia for help and realizes he's truly seeing her for the first time tonight. He says, "Everyone, a toast to my lovely wife, Olivia. Thank you once again for all you do!" Then he notices she isn't drinking her wine, and her face looks sallow. He stares at her so long that she opens her eyes wide, looks back at him, and then, in an inquisitive way, shrugs her shoulders as if she's wondering what he wants.

Allen glances at the twins and chimes in, "It's so nice to meet Frick and Frack finally."

Barbara looks at each of them one at a time and giggles to herself as Charlotte declares, "Only Daddy is allowed to call us that!"

Henry adds, "I'm Fwack and she's Fwick." Then he slips Luna a long strand of spaghetti, and Olivia chuckles at how much the puppy loves it.

Allen continues his interview with the twins, "Which one of you is the youngest?"

Charlotte replies, "Henry is my baby brother," with the emphasis on the word baby.

Henry remonstrates, "By seven minutes and you're not the boss of me, Chawlie!"

Barbara bursts into laughter and wipes tears from her eyes with her napkin as Allen turns to her and asks, "And whom might you be, young lady?"

Olivia rescues Barbara, "Allen, let me introduce you to Barbara. She takes some time to get to know you before she feels comfortable enough to have a chat."

Barbara gives Olivia an inquisitive look because no one has ever commented on her ability to talk before. Allen speaks up while addressing her, "I respect that, young lady, and I look forward to having a nice long chat with you someday."

Barbara tries to smile as she looks down at her food, then resumes eating her dinner while uncomfortably ignoring everyone at the table.

Officer Bobby Hill says, "My sister is a lung transplant recipient. She's alive and thriving more than ten years later, so I thank all of you for your work."

Jasmine takes a big gulp of wine and adds, "Amen to that." Then she offers, "Olivia, let me help you bring out the rest."

Olivia gives her a thumbs up, and then Jasmine starts clearing the salad dishes, saying, "The food smells delish, Olivia."

Ian announces, "I'm famished," as he rubs his hands together in anticipation.

While everyone is ogling their hot and steamy bowls of spaghetti Bolognese, Ian starts a conversation: "This may be the best Bolognese I have ever eaten, Olivia."

Olivia blushes and says, "Thank you for the compliment, Ian, but honestly, our dinner tonight is something I threw together at the last minute."

William adds, "Don't be so modest. You're an incredible chef, and you never cease to amaze me." The twins look at their mom as they continue eating their plain pasta with butter, then smile at Barbara as if he said something silly.

Ian smiles at Jasmine across the table, takes another sip of his wine, and then shares what's on his mind: "Allen, you are probably the most knowledgeable person at the table on a topic that has been troubling me."

Allen puts his fork down and turns to face Ian when he replies, "I'll do my best to help, Son. What's been troubling you?"

The room quiets as Ian speaks his mind, "You see, I have been delivering organs for over a decade, and I'm seeing patterns."

In the silence, William asks, "What kind of patterns?"

Ian takes a deep breath before he replies, "I pick up the organs in poorer neighborhoods and deliver them to the same handful of places over and over again, and it never goes the other way around." He lets out a sigh, "And I've watched the buildings where they're delivered grow bigger and bigger."

Allen somberly asks, "Why do you think that is, Ian?"

Ian admits, "I have a hard time talking about it."

Allen speaks his mind: "It's not a coincidence that Congress almost unanimously passed a bill making it so people involved in forced organ harvesting in China can be convicted of a crime with sentencing of twenty years in prison and a quarter-million-dollar fine, but so far our government has done little to address what is going on in North America."

Ian echoes in horror, "What do you think is going on here?"

Allen knowledgeably explains, "There are 170 million people in the US registered as organ donors, and last year only 17,000 transplants were performed from deceased donors. That means fewer than 0.01% are used, because the donor must be healthy, have a beating heart, and be breathing right up until the extraction team is ready. Technology is improving rapidly, expanding the viability window, but we're not there yet."

Jasmine finishes her wine and, with tears in her eyes, says, "I saw it firsthand. I was an ER nurse until I couldn't be one any longer."

Allen treads gently, "Saw what, sweetheart?"

Jasmine wipes her eyes with her napkin before speaking, "It was my last day working in the ER. They brought in an overdosed, perfectly healthy, and beautiful 17-year-old boy who accidentally ingested fentanyl that he took for his shoulder injury from pitching a double-header playoff game. He mistook that poison for an Advil pain reliever in the high school's locker room, and it killed him."

She gasps for air before continuing, "He was listed as an organ donor on his driver's license, and the team set him up on life support and rolled him straight up for extraction."

Ian mumbles, "Oh my God."

Jasmine adds, "It's a body factory, and our lost young people supply the parts!"

The room falls silent, and the rest of the dinner is quiet.

#

William, Ian, and Bobby Hill offer to clear the table and wash the dishes. This also allows Jasmine and Barbara to help Olivia put the twins to bed. Hattie returns to William and Olivia's bedroom to rest because the snow is too deep for her to go home until William plows them out.

When the dishes are washed and put away, the three men join Allen and George in the living room, where a serious discussion begins about Dr. Shane Ferguson, his wife Debbie, and his nephew Joe.

Allen explains that, for him to continue contributing, each of them must sign an NDA with Haloderm due to Dr. Ferguson's overlap. Then he makes a phone call, "Hi Ellie, do you have a moment?" followed by, "Yes, you're correct, it's urgent. It appears we have a code crimson situation." He pauses to listen. "Yes, will do, and I'll need three NDA agreements immediately. I'll text you their names, and later tonight, I will record what I know so far for HD to review."

Within minutes, the forms from Ellie arrive, and William prints out one for each person.

Allen asks them, "Is there anyone else who's privy to these unfortunate circumstances?"

William and Ian shake their heads no, and William explains, "Bobby doesn't know most of the details yet, but I believe he will be helpful to us, and we can trust him."

Ian demands while shaking the form, "What the hell is this?"

William looks worried as he states, "It's a nondisclosure agreement that protects and indemnifies Haloderm. We agree not to discuss this situation outside our circle and not to do or say anything that could harm the company. Ian, please sign it so we can move forward, and that will allow them to help us with this problem."

Allen adds, "Bobby, we could use your help, but if you don't sign it, we'll have to ask you to leave."

George makes a disgusted expression on his face and signs the document. After everyone else has signed it, he demands, "William, what the hell did you get us all involved in?"

Allen sits down and takes a sip of cognac to warm himself by the fireplace before he replies to George's question, "Please let me explain, George, because I believe I have the most experience on this particular topic, and it appears to me what we're dealing with is a gang of greedy, nasty, ghouls."

CHAPTER THIRTY-FOUR — GROUNDED FLIGHTS

OLIVIA

It's still dark outside when Olivia opens her eyes and greets the day. She tiptoes across the cold, drafty floor of the living room to the toilet with her phone in her hand. While sitting on the pot and urinating, she opens her Amazon app to check her recent orders. She taps the tracking on her pregnancy test and sees that the order was canceled due to the storm. She shakes her head no and wants to scream. Then she considers driving to the store to buy one, but they're snowed in, and the roads are still closed, so she has no choice but to reorder another one.

She clicks on "Buy it Now," and the order is confirmed with an estimated delivery date… the wheels keep spinning, and then it states, "before Christmas." She immediately loses her self-control and shouts out, "Bullocks!" As she realizes that everything else she's ordered will be delayed due to the snowstorm, combined with the last-minute holiday shopping rush.

There's a gentle tap on the bathroom door: "Olie, are you OK?"

She sticks her head out and admits, "It's the bloody blizzard! I'm tracking our deliveries, and they're a mess."

William commiserates, "I didn't think of that!" as he bolts across the room.

She exclaims, "Where are you headed?"

He's already at his desk, opening his laptop when he replies, "Checking our Snake River Farm's meat order." His face glows from the screen as he scrolls through it and then grins, assuring her, "We're good! It will be here in enough time."

Olivia barely acknowledges his remark and sits on the bottom step. She starts to cry tears of frustration and struggles to catch her breath.

William runs over to her and asks, "Olie, what's wrong?"

While crying, she says, "Oh bloody hell, I don't know! My mum's coming with Patty, I need to go grocery shopping because we need everything, the house is a mess, and I'm exhausted!"

William sympathizes with her and says, "All right, let's deconstruct this over coffee. I'll make it this morning, and we will figure it out together."

She wipes the tears from her eyes as the thought of pushing a full grocery cart with two kids in it, up and down the crowded aisles at the market right before the holidays, horrifies her. She follows him into the kitchen, watches him make their coffee, and asks him, "What about tending the animals? I don't believe the Price kids are coming to help because the roads aren't passable."

"Where good, we're still under a snow emergency till noon, so I don't have to rush off to Haloderm this morning, and hell, my boss is upstairs sound asleep."

She can feel her anxiety lessen when she confesses, "This is all too much for me, and I'm nervous about…"

He cuts her off and says, "Your mum's visit. I expected that."

She nods yes, and he says, "Let's call a company like Merry Maids and have them clean the house for the upcoming visit." Her eyes widen, and she smiles. "Then we'll open you an account at Wegmans and another at Whole Foods. They'll deliver everything you need." He gestures to show it will be easy, then adds, "And I think they both offer catering."

Olivia rolls her bloodshot blue eyes and says, "I know I sound like a twat, but I still wish I could find a goose to roast for Christmas Day."

He says with a snicker in his voice, "We can't always…"

She finishes the song, "Get what we want, but what about steamed lobsters Christmas Eve?"

"One of us can pick them up early that morning at Market Basket." He replies.

"When did you get to be so nice?" she asks.

"When I finally stopped worrying about money all the time."

She smiles and admits, "I like this new you, and who would have ever guessed I married you for your money?"

He reaches over and kisses her and says, "Darling, if only I had more time this morning, but alas, I do not, so I'm off to fondle the cows and goats and plow out the driveway instead of you. So you, my dear, are free now to go and take care of the horses."

She feels a strong urge to take him right then and there in the kitchen, but restrains herself because leaving the animals unattended any longer would be inhumane, and they have a house full of guests. She changes the subject, "When do you want to go and cut down our tree with the kids?"

He replies, "Let me make sure the bobcat starts so I have something to drag it back with, and I'll let you know."

As soon as he leaves, she downloads the Wegman's App and begins scrolling through the online aisles. As she sees everything she needs at her fingertips, she feels excited.

Suddenly, she urgently needs to pee again and rushes to the bathroom. When she enters, she glances at herself in the mirror. She's horrified to see a large, wide, dark reverse skunk stripe on the top of her head and realizes she desperately needs her roots touched up, as she hates her dark hair and prefers to look more like her mum, who is a natural honey/wheat blonde.

She texts Leanne, the new hairdresser Barbara's mom recommended on Route 109, and begs for an appointment as soon as possible.

Then, out of guilt, she looks up her old hairdresser, John, on Venmo to see if he's listed. That's where she paid half the bill for her full head of foils with a bad check and never responded to his many texts demanding she settle it.

When she finds his name, she clicks on it, enters the exact amount she owes, then deletes it and re-enters it, this time with a generous tip and an apology note. She also wishes him a Merry Christmas.

After the transaction is done, she exhales, feeling a little less shitty about herself. Then she wonders, *Why do I do these terrible things? I stole from my mum and ran off, screwed over my hairdresser, whom I adore, then cheated and lied to Hattie about Buttercup. What's inside me that makes me hurt the ones I love?*

While still sitting on the toilet, she slumps over and cries some more. When she's finished, she wipes her eyes dry with toilet paper, then wipes her bum with the same moist piece. Afterward, she gets dressed to feed the horses and shovel piles of manure.

#

While snowshoeing to Jameson Farm, Olivia is captivated by the stunning view. The freshly blanketed white landscape takes her breath away. She enjoys the peaceful beauty of the moment as it sharply contrasts with the clear, magenta-streaked early morning sky. When she opens the barn door, a chorus of whinnies comes from the horses, and she immediately releases them. With the road closed and the snow depth, she lets them roam free.

After she cleans their stalls, fills their troughs with food, washes out the water basins, and refills them, she steps outside into the sunlight. She is momentarily blinded by the bright morning sun reflecting off the whiteness around her. She can hear human voices mixed with the horses' grunts and snorts. She squints to see who's there, and as her eyes adjust, she sees Ian and Jasmine rolling in the snow with the horses. They're making snow angels together.

Olivia hangs up her rake, puts on her mittens, and joins them. She loudly proclaims, "Here I come!" as she falls backward toward the Earth, into the soft snow.

Buttercup nuzzles Olivia's face, then rocks back and forth with her hooves in the air in delight.

Jasmine is laughing when she asks, "Who taught your horses how to make snow angels, Olivia?"

Olivia boasts, "My guess is they figured it out on their own." She enjoys seeing everyone share in their happiness.

Ian stands up and offers Olivia a hand before asking, "Want me to get William?"

Olivia exclaims, "Get everybody. This is too much fun for them to miss."

Ian snowshoes over to the house while Olivia and Jasmine play with the horses in the freshly fallen snow.

The truck with William at the wheel pulls up to the top of the driveway at Jameson Farm and stops at the edge of the unplowed area. Hattie, George, Allen, Barbara, Charlotte, and Henry get out and laugh at the funny scene. Then Charlotte, Henry, and Barbara grab their saucers and slide down the soft hill to where the horses are frolicking and join the fun. A few minutes later, William, Hattie, George, and Allen arrive on snowshoes.

Allen asks rhetorically, "Isn't life simply glorious?"

And George, with his arm around Hattie, says, "Yes, and amen to that."

CHAPTER THIRTY-FIVE — LOOK WHO'S TALKING

WILLIAM

Back at the kitchen table, William scrutinizes Allen Tyler Jr.'s body language now that he's caught up on everything that happened between him and Dr. Ferguson, as well as the fallout at the gym.

Nothing about his demeanor seems to have changed. William hopes that revealing some of the shameful things he did hasn't sabotaged his future at Haloderm. He finishes the last sip of his coffee, feeling relieved that he's tackling this problem and can finally put it behind them.

Just then, he receives a text from Bobby Hill that simply states the Lab Case Number, followed by a date, the name of the submitting agency (the Natick Police Department – Special Victims Unit), and the name of the officer who took the swab. William scrolls down and realizes he is looking at the DNA profile for Matthew, the pervert who attacked Mary O'Keefe at the gym. He's surprised at how quickly and easily Bobby Hill retrieved it for them from the police department's database.

William texts back, *TY.*

Allen gets up, pats the twins on their heads, and makes a small hand gesture to Barbara to show he's about to leave. Then he glances at Olivia and sincerely says, "Thank you for making me feel so welcome in your home."

Olivia walks over to Allen to hug him goodbye.

William interrupts them, saying, "Allen, I got that missing piece of evidence we requested." Then he nods to him.

Allen responds, "Good, let's go."

\#

In a conference room similar to the one where William had his initial interview with Allen, they meet to discuss the situation. HD's voice is audible from an overhead speaker, and William keeps reminding himself that HD is AI, not a human.

William emphasizes, "I, for one, want to know if Mary O'Keefe's body was delivered to Haloderm and if Dr. Ferguson was paid for the transaction. That would at least confirm his complicity."

Allen says, "We don't have a DNA sample from her, and there are too many bodies labeled as John or Jane Doe. I'm sorry, but that's a dead end."

HD chimes in, "We have a complete record of every business dealing with Dr. Ferguson. I can search for people of similar ages and ethnic backgrounds as the ones you're concerned about today."

William interjects, "Wait, I also have something Bobby Hill sent over."

HD inquires, "William, what is it that you have not shared with us?"

William squirms in his seat before he makes his request and explains, "I'm going to need access to my phone."

HD confirms, "Access granted."

William scrolls to Bobby's text message and holds up the DNA profile to the camera for HD to review.

HD says, "I'm running that specific DNA profile against every tissue sample in our facility's database."

Almost simultaneously, the white dial-up telephone on the wall rings.

Allen stands up and places the phone next to his ear. "Yes, I see." He listens to the caller as if he's receiving instructions. Then he ends the call with, "That's perfectly all right, you have my consent." And he hangs the phone in its cradle.

William gets nervous that he's suddenly cut out of their conversation, and just as he's about to speak, Allen points at the camera and puts his finger to his lips to quiet him.

HD responds, "Thank you, William, for bringing this situation to our full attention. We will address it promptly, and no further action is needed from you."

William is horrified that they might be firing him and starts sweating profusely, even though it's only 45 degrees Fahrenheit in the conference room.

Allen turns to him and says, "Stay calm, William; this is all under their control."

William asks, "How?"

HD replies to him in a solemn voice, "This is just a new version of an old story, William. Think back to what Allen taught you at the very beginning."

William strains his mind as he searches through it for anything that makes sense, and in a raised, excited voice, he exclaims, "Knox, Burke, and Hare."

Allen smiles and says, "Yes, William, that's correct."

William's adrenaline is rushing through his veins when he blurts out, "So what do we do now?"

HD speaks calmly, "You, William, do nothing."

William protests, "But it's my family he's threatening!"

Allen gives William a stern look as HD calmly explains, "We will neutralize the threat to you and your family shortly."

Allen adds, "William, simmer down. They know what they're doing, and the less you're involved, the better."

William continues, "But I need to know if the missing bodies are here or not."

HD retorts, "But do you, William? Why isn't resolving the problem enough?"

William concedes, "I guess it is, but if they are here, it's my fault, and I'm partly to blame."

HD appears to be comforting William as it softens its voice, "Please appreciate this: that if it were not for you, their nefarious business operation would have escalated, and there would be many more harmed, and to all the future unharmed people, you are a hero. But now I understand, so please sit quietly and wait."

Eventually, the door opens, and the floor lights up their path, showing them exactly where to go. They eventually retrieve a frozen cadaver and place it on a gurney.

William asks, "Will we be preparing this cadaver for an instructional demonstration?"

"No," says Allen sharply.

When they return to the corridor, more lights brighten their path in another direction, and they collect a second cadaver. Finally, they reach a third door that opens onto an extraction surgery suite, and they roll the gurneys in one at a time.

William asks, "Do I need to suit up?"

HD replies through the overhead speakers, "No, William. A mask and gloves are all you'll need for this procedure."

William asks, "What's this about?"

HD replies, "William, there was a DNA profile match on the male, and this female was logged in with the same skew number for the delivery. Can you confirm their identities for us?"

The body bags' zippers open from the toes up to the cadaver's head. When William reaches the midsection of a woman's body and notices a familiar Claddagh tattoo around the belly button, he continues to unzip the bag bravely. When Mary O'Keefe's face is revealed, he uncontrollably vomits on the floor.

William is embarrassed and pleads, "Let me clean up the mess."

Allen dismisses his comment and asks, "Is it her?"

"Yes."

Allen continues, "What you just experienced is the reason we NEVER do an autopsy or extraction on someone we've known. The next one shouldn't be as difficult. Please look at the cadaver and tell us if it's him."

Allen unzips the bag and steps back, waiting for William's response.

William looks at the freshly broken nose and realizes Matthew must have been abducted within days after their fight at the gym, then states, "Yes, it's him. What were their recorded causes of death?"

HD replies, "Fentanyl overdoses."

This news deeply upsets William, and he asks, "What's next?"

HD instructs, "We must bring the perpetrators of this crime to justice. Allen, please place your phone on the counter. I will do the rest."

Allen's telephone lights up as if it is placing a call on its own. Then, over the phone speaker, they can hear Allen speaking with Dr. Ferguson, but it isn't Allen speaking; it's HD.

Allen again motions for William to stay quiet.

Shane replies, "Doc. Ferguson here. What can I do for you, Dr. Tyler?"

Allen Tyler is silently standing between the two cadavers while HD perfectly impersonates his voice, "It's Director Tyler, not doctor."

"Director Tyler, I'll remember that for next time," echoes Shane.

HD continues to impersonate Allen Tyler Jr. as he resumes the call, "We have some last-minute work we need completed before the holidays. If you're too busy, I'll completely understand, and we can sub it out to someone else."

Dr. Ferguson sounds eager as he squawks, "Director Tyler, I'm never too busy for you or any request from Haloderm, for that matter."

"Good to know. Can you be here within two hours? Bring a van and at least one other person to help with the job, like that nephew of yours?"

William looks at the phone in amazement. It's like watching a ventriloquist act. HD continues speaking in Allen's voice while talking to Dr. Ferguson. William stares at Allen and shivers with fear at HD's power.

After the call ends, HD returns to its normal speaking voice and says, "Allen, thank you for allowing me to impersonate you."

Allen replies, "My pleasure. Glad we can finally put this bit of bad business behind us."

HD resumes, "Allen, you're booked on United Flight 2474 to Houston at 17:25. Happy holidays, and a car is arranged to pick you up here at the side entrance. Safe travels, and say 'hello' to Rose from me."

"Thank you, HD."

HD speaks to William, "Go home and enjoy a nice holiday with your family. We look forward to seeing you back here after the New Year. Meanwhile, we have some gifts for you and your family."

William is emphatic, "HD, that's not necessary!"

HD continues, "They're nothing. A robot prototype we use around here to vacuum the floors and a security system so you can keep an eye on your family and know they're safe when you're away from home."

William must admit the gifts are very thoughtful. "Thank you, HD." William is eager to ask what will happen after Dr. Ferguson and his nephew arrive at Haloderm later that day, but Allen has given him enough hints that he knows he should stay quiet. Deep down, he knows they'll most likely get what they deserve, just like Knox, Burke, and Hare did over two hundred years ago.

After William returns the bodies of Mary and Matthew to their freezer lockers for entombment, he heads straight to his truck, where he notices the gifts HD mentioned sitting on the back seat, without any wrapping paper or bows. He smiles at the find and says aloud, "Thank you, HD, and happy holidays."

HD politely replies through the speaker system, "Same to you, and see you next year."

As he leaves the parking lot, he sees a large white Joby Drone take off from the roof of Haloderm and fly overhead. His first thought is that one of the company's executives is leaving for vacation, but he also wonders if it might be the way they move people around without them being seen or heard.

Then he heads home to help Olivia get ready for her mother and stepfather's arrival, and he feels elated to be on vacation.

CHAPTER THIRTY-SIX — GOOSE BUMPS

OLIVIA

Olivia is surprised to see William home so early from work. She smiles at him and thinks with relief, "Good, I can grab the truck and run out to start my errands."

William happily announces, "I'm on vacation till January 3. Isn't that fantastic!"

She nods yes and thinks, *Great, now I don't have to tend to the livestock for every feeding, and I have more time to prepare for Mummy's visit.*

She commands while extending her hand, "Truck keys, please!"

William groans, "Olie, the snowplow is attached. I don't think it's a good idea."

"Keys and listen for the kids. They'll be up in about half an hour from their nap," she adds.

William wonders, "What about Barbara?"

"Went home."

He reluctantly hands her the keys.

Olivia grabs her hat, jacket, and purse before rushing out the door.

#

While she's walking up and down the aisles at Ocean State Job Lot, her phone rings.

It's Merry Maids confirming the appointment to clean her house, which gives her a boost in her step as she finishes filling her cart with last-minute items.

Olivia's phone rings again, but this time it's Leanne, the newly recommended hairdresser, asking if she wants to take her cancellation that afternoon. She gladly accepts and rushes to check out at the store despite the long holiday lines, then heads over to get her roots done.

When Olivia gets home, she's feeling excited about how everything is falling into place. Leanne only had time for a quick partial, so Olivia left the salon with a wet head. Now she can't wait to go upstairs to blow-dry her hair and see the results.

Luna greets her at the door. Olivia grabs his leash, apologizes to the pup for the snow, and they head out to find a place for him to pee. Despite wearing a sweater and coat, the dog seems unhappy about the cold. Olivia carries him back inside and checks her foils in the bathroom mirror.

When she returns, she finds her family gathered at the front door. William is installing a doorbell camera. He's all smiles as she approaches and says, "Look, Olie, what Haloderm gave me as a gift."

"What is it?" she asks.

William responds, "A security system to help us stay safe."

She sighs before she speaks, "You know we never had a problem before you went to work for them."

William ignores her remark and asks the twins, "Who wants to try it first?"

They both reach for the bell and laugh when it rings on their father's phone.

William tells them, "Say something and wave." Then he bends down to show them what they look like on his phone. Charlotte takes the phone from her father, and she and her brother make faces at the doorbell's camera while looking at themselves on the phone.

He casually asks, "What's for dinner?"

Olivia's eyes open wider at the thought, and she exclaims, "Take out."

William laughs as he replies, "All right, I'll pick it up. What else can I do to help?"

Just then, a UPS truck pulls up as close as possible to the house with the huge snowbank blocking the driveway entrance, and the driver dumps six large boxes on top of it, waves goodbye, and drives off.

Olivia points to the boxes and adds, "In addition to that, I could also use some help with all the stuff I picked up this afternoon at Ocean State Job Lot. It's in the backseat of the truck. Do I need to go feed the horses, or did you do it?"

William boasts, "Everybody is fed except us humans. What do you two want?"

Henry shouts, "Pizza!" then goes back to playing with the doorbell.

Olivia glances at the boxes and wonders if her pregnancy test might be in one of them. She checks Amazon online, and it shows it won't be delivered until the next day. "William, what's in all these boxes? They're not mine."

He replies, "Hopefully it's the meat order from Snake River Farms, some nice bath towels for our house guests, and the rest are…Christmas Gifts."

Olivia's phone rings, "Hello Mummy, come quickly, Henry – Charlie." They press their little faces to the phone and wave to their grandmother.

Olivia's mum says excitedly, "We just checked in for our flight and received our boarding passes."

Sounding worried, Olivia begs for details, "Mummy, I thought you were arriving Friday night at 11 pm."

Her mum giggles, "Did you now? Well, we're arriving on Virgin Atlantic at 11 am, and we're losing six hours; silly me, I added them. This getting older business is not for the faint-hearted."

Olivia insists, "We can come fetch you from the airport."

Her mother sighs, "Patty won't have it, and the car and driver service is a perk that comes with our upper-class ticket. Please don't bother."

Olivia is panicking. She wonders how she'll get everything ready for their arrival now that she's lost 12 hours. "Let's all blow kisses goodbye to grandma. See you soon, Mummy. Safe travels."

The twins echo her, "Safe, twavels."

When Olivia looks up, she sees that William has placed all six boxes in the foyer and has gone to empty the truck. "Come on, children, let's help Father with the bundles."

#

The next morning, their house is as busy as backstage at a Broadway show during opening night's dress rehearsal. Three ladies from Merry Maids are cleaning and polishing everything in sight. William and the children are choosing a Christmas tree from the forest behind the house. Olivia is cutting, chopping, prepping, and marinating to her heart's content. Luna is curled up at her feet and occasionally snacking on what drops from the cutting board.

The doorbell rings, and Olivia answers it using her phone. It's Wegmans, and she tells him to leave the groceries and liquor order as close to the front door as possible.

The driver complains, "Sorry, lady, no can do! I need your driver's license for the liquor order."

"Bullocks!" she shouts before calmly stating, "I'll be right there." She wipes her messy hands and searches for her British driver's license.

When she shows it to him, he sighs when he explains, "I don't know if I can take this. I thinks I'm going to have to take the liquor back to the store."

In a panic, she hands him a $20 bill and says, "My good sir, can't we use your driver's license today to satisfy your app's requirements?"

He smiles, takes the money, and says, "Sure can." As he places her liquor order at her feet and adds, "Happy holidays."

Right after she finishes putting away the Wegman's order, another delivery truck pulls up. This one is from Whole Foods, and they leave the large order in front of her house.

The three cleaning ladies from Merry Maids walk into the kitchen, crossing their arms as they gaze at Olivia.

Olivia is trying to figure out what they are trying to communicate because of the language barrier. Tacitly, she realizes it: "Oh, you want me to get out of the kitchen so you can clean it."

The woman leading the crew nods her head in agreement.

Olivia decides to leave the groceries on the front steps because it's 34 degrees outside, and she could use a break. She grabs some carrots from one of the grocery bags and heads over to the stables across the street. When she arrives, Hattie is walking the horses back inside from the outdoor ring.

Hattie greets her, "Just too nice outside to keep them in the barn. Oh, look what Olie brought you," she says to Barbie. "Carrots. Yum." She affectionately rubs her muzzle.

Olivia is nearly too afraid to ask her, "How are you feeling now that the treatments have started?"

Hattie takes a deep breath and replies, "I'm trying to be hopeful. So, I guess I'm good."

Olivia says, "That's nice to hear."

Hattie strokes Barbie while speaking, "This is going to be hard for me."

Olivia asks, "Do you mean the chemo?"

Hattie hesitates, "Well, of course, that's no fun, but what I meant is sharing you and William with strangers. You know you're all we've got, George and me."

Olivia is so touched that she reaches for Hattie, and they hug. Olivia clarifies, "Hattie, you're not sharing us with anybody. We're all yours, darling."

Hattie wipes tears from her eyes and asks, "So, what time do you want us over for Christmas dinner?"

"You're welcome whenever you want, but 1ish works."

Hattie glances towards the garage and spies George with a big package in his arms. She motions to him with her hands for him to go back before she says, "Oh shit, here he comes."

Olivia steps around from the side of the horse and greets him, "Hey, George. What are you carrying?"

George looks mortified when he replies, "Olie, what are you doing here?"

Olivia walks over to him and says, "Here, give me that." She reaches for the large plastic-wrapped package. "What's this? It must weigh almost two stones." Olivia hoists it onto her knee and takes a peek. "Wow, is it what I think it is?"

Hattie responds with a guilty expression, "It is."

Olivia exclaims, "Brilliant!" then looks at it again before asking, "How did you know I wanted one?"

George explains, "This was all William's doing. We were supposed to hide it from you, and I guess we messed it up pretty badly."

Struggling to hold it, she pleads, "What do you want me to do with it?"

George shrugs his shoulders and suggests, "Put it in the kitchen sink to defrost and pretend you never saw it. Capisce."

"Capisce," she echoes.

CHAPTER THIRTY-SEVEN — WHAT I ALWAYS WANTED

WILLIAM

William has meticulously shoveled the front steps, hung a homemade wreath on the door, and plowed the horseshoe-shaped driveway to make their guests feel welcome.

The tree is up and decorated with his family's extensive collection of heirloom ornaments that date back over a century. Their home looks more like a 19th-century Christmas card than a modern house.

Olivia hollers from the kitchen to William, "How many are coming with Ian?"

William walks into the kitchen and replies, "Just him and his dad." He gives her a quick peck on the cheek. Jasmine is eating with her family and plans to come for dessert afterward. She's bringing her two daughters and mother along as well.

Olivia exclaims, "My goodness, we're going to have a full house."

William shares, "Come, see the tree. Its lights are twinkling, and the living room looks spectacular." Then he mentions in an inaudible hush, "And the feeling of my parents' presence is almost palpable."

Olivia continues to focus on her preparations and says, "I beg your pardon, I didn't hear the last part." Then she tosses a slice of pepperoni to Luna from her nearly finished charcuterie board, which features freshly cut honeycomb, a variety of soft cheeses, figs, grapes, dates, and nuts, and is topped with in-house-smoked meats.

William apologizes, "It was nothing. Not worth repeating."

Olivia wipes her hands on a dish towel and joins him in the living room. As she enters, she takes in the tidy, beautiful house, the aroma of holiday foods, and the biggest surprise of all: that they are genuinely ready to greet their guests.

Tears of relief and joy gather in her eyes as she says, "I can't tell you how happy I am, William."

William gestures, "Have a seat on the sofa. I have something for you, and I want you to receive it before your Mother and Patty arrive."

He reaches into his pocket and reveals a small package. "This is something I should have given to you a long time ago. I love you, Olivia."

He gently places the small box in her palm.

Olivia peels off the Rudolf the Red-Nosed Reindeer paper, opens the box, and bursts into tears. "You shouldn't have," she exclaims.

As he slides the ring onto her finger, she says, "It's so beautiful, but why did you spend money on this now? We've barely recovered financially, William, and this is just way over the top. Don't you think we should replace the furnace first?" She says this while tears stream down her cheeks.

William explains, "It was my grandmother's, and I knew in my heart she would have wanted you to have it." Then he adds, "And it fits you perfectly."

She looks at the three round diamonds shimmering in the light from the Christmas Tree. She tries to compose herself, "Look at me, my makeup is a mess, and they'll be here soon."

"Go fix yourself up, and I'll go check on the twins," William confirms.

Olivia instructs him as she quickly climbs the staircase, "Make sure their socks are pulled up and laces are tied. Check that Charlie's bow is straight in her hair and that Henry hasn't pulled off his clip-on tie."

He gives Olivia two thumbs up, adds a log to the fire, and heads to the playroom to inspect the troops.

While Olivia is upstairs fixing her hair and wiping mascara from her face, William yells, "A Jaguar just pulled up in front of the house."

Olivia rushes down the steps and meets William, who is bringing the twins with him to the front door. Charlie's bow is on the side of her head, and Henry's tie is clipped to the hair on top of Luna's head.

William whispers, "Relax, they look so cute this way." Then he puts his hand on the doorknob and says, "Smiles, everyone."

The driver opens the car door for Clare and Patty. Then he sets their bags on the driveway. Olivia's mother steps out first. She is a fair-haired, older version of Olivia with striking cornflower-blue eyes and long, thick lashes. She squints from the noon sun reflecting off the snow and puts on her Chanel sunglasses to search for her daughter and grandchildren, but she patiently waits for Patty.

Patty joins her and says, "Here you go, darling. You left this behind in the car," and he hands her a tan ostrich Birken Bag with a scarf draped across its handle. When Patty stands up straight, he's about five feet seven or eight inches tall with a medium build and brown hair. William wonders if he colors it because it's a tad too dark for a man his age.

William offers, "Welcome, and allow me to take your bags for you." Recalling how they spoke to him at the hotel in Galveston earlier that month.

Clare is so focused on meeting her grandchildren that she doesn't even acknowledge his remark and walks toward the house. Then she cries out joyfully, "Come to grandmother, my little darlings."

She smothers them with kisses as tears of joy run down her cheeks.

William and Patty hang back to give Olivia and Clare a moment. William extends his hand to Patty and says, "Merry Christmas, and thank you for joining us."

Patty replies, "I'm here only to make Clare happy. In truth, I feel it's unforgivable what Olivia put her mother through these past five years."

William realizes they are not off to a good start, and the only way this family reunion will go well is if he can find a way to change Patty's mind.

Patty looks up at their home, and his facial expression shows disappointment. He asks, "How old is your house?"

William replies, "Built by my ancestors in 1853. Follow me, and I'll show you around."

Patty is frowning as they enter the house. William silently carries their bags inside. He needs to make two trips to get everything upstairs to the guest bedroom. He thinks that while he's going back and forth with their luggage, they're jet-lagged and might have had a few too many martinis during the flight, since Olivia mentioned that, in addition to sleeper seats, the airplane has an open bar. He hopes Patty's mood will improve after a nap.

When he rejoins everyone, he overhears Patty say, "Which one of you is Charlie and which one of you is Henry?"

Charlotte rolls her eyes before she says, "I'm Charlie, and this is our baby. His name is Luna."

Henry pulls the blanket away from the baby stroller to reveal the puppy.

Patty exclaims excitedly, "My goodness, what a beautiful baby you have."

William, in an effort to make their guests feel more at home, offers, "Can we get you something to drink before we sit down for lunch?"

Clare admits, "I'd love a cup of hot tea."

Charlie excitedly replies, "Oh, Grandmother, please join us. It's teatime, and it's all ready for you."

Clare follows the twins into the playroom, sits at the tiny table, and joins them for make-believe tea and crumpets.

While they pretend to sip because the make-believe tea is too hot, Luna shakes off the bow in his hair, and Henry untucks his shirt and kicks off his dress shoes.

Clare reaches for him, "Come here, you little goose, and let me squeeze you." Then she reaches for Charlie and embraces them both.

Patty wanders around the living room. He examines the fireplace, the hand-carved staircase, the prized sixteen-point elk buck mounted on the wall, and each painting. That's when the clock chimes, and Patty is drawn to it, crying out like a teenage girl seeing her idol up close, "Oh my goodness. Is that a Simon Willard Grandfather's clock?"

William shrugs his shoulders as if he's unsure and explains, "I've no idea. It's been in our family forever."

Intrigued, Patty dives into the subject, "Tell me more. I need to know everything you know about this clock."

William thinks for a moment before he continues, "It's been here since the mid-1850s, and it belonged to my great-great-grandmother going back several generations. Her husband's last name was Loring, but a rumor circulated that she had a lover, General William Howe, who fought for the king of England. My guess is the clock is over two hundred years old."

Patty is incensed, "And you allow the children to play near it."

William reveals, "We all did; that includes me and my ancestors going back to right after the Revolutionary War of Independence, and someday it will belong to Charlotte and Henry. That's if they want it."

"Want it. Why wouldn't they? It's a priceless antique." Patty remarks.

William confirms, "Well, it's not nor has it ever been for sale."

Patty admires it closely, "Just remarkable that your family held onto it through so many tough times throughout history. The Civil War, both World Wars, and The Great Depression."

William continues, "There are several other items like it in the house that have been passed down as well. It's a testimony to our family's resilience. My grandfather had to make some difficult financial choices during the oil embargo of the 1970s, as without fuel, a farm cannot run, and he managed to hang on to everything. But unlike my father and his father before him, I can't make enough money to support our family, so I have a job working for Haloderm."

Patty asks, "Is it a good company?"

William replies, "I guess so."

Patty asks, "I mean, should I buy shares of stock in it?"

He winks at William, and William is clueless about what they're discussing or what he wants. William shrugs his shoulders and says, "I'll send you a link for some videos about what they make and do there. You can decide for yourself. Is it too early for you to have a beer?"

Patty gives him a thumbs up before he says with a smirk, "In London, it's already dinner time."

Olivia walks over to Patty in the living room and states, "Thank you for joining us. It means so much to me."

When it's just the two of them alone, Patty's facial expression becomes angry, and he looks Olivia in the eyes when he explains, "Olivia, your mother is a beautiful person inside and out. What you put here through, the nights she cried herself to sleep, and the endless hours she was worried about you and your whereabouts. Shame on you." He states with a raised voice.

Olivia stammers, unsure of what to say in her defense.

Patty continues his rant, "Young woman and I reserve the term lady. Your absence practically ruined our wedding day. Clare was so emotional that you weren't a part of it; we almost canceled it, and it was a first wedding for both of us."

Olivia states, "I'm sorry."

"I had a detective look for you, and when I found out you were living in a town called Dover and that you ran off for no good reason, I kept that information from your mother because it would have crushed her to know that your avoidance of her was just because you're a little cunt."

"Patty, I'm so sorry. Please forgive me. You realize I never cashed your check."

William arrives and hands Patty a Guinness Stout. Patty says, "Thanks," and clinks bottles with William. Then he turns to Olivia, "If you had cashed it, we wouldn't be here today. That was your only saving grace."

She hangs her head in shame before she says, "Lunch is ready."

#

After enjoying a feast of shrimp cocktails and baked stuffed lobsters, topped off with Sipsmith Gin martinis, Olivia realizes that Patty didn't eat any meat or fish, and her mother failed to mention anything about it to her.

While clearing the table, she inquires, "Patty, are you a vegetarian?"

He replies, "No." She's immediately relieved until he clears his throat and explains, "Actually, I'm a strict vegan."

Olivia's mind races through all the dishes she's prepared for the holidays, realizing there's almost nothing for him to eat.

Patty and Clare head to bed early because of their jet lag. William can hear Patty's remarks through the baby monitor nearby in the adjacent room, "What a delightful robe and look, Clare, there are a pair of spa slippers in the pocket. How civilized."

Clare remarks, "I so appreciate how well Olivia landed on her two feet."

Patty says, "He seems to me like a nice chap."

Clare continues, "Oh, and aren't the twins out of this world?"

Patty mentions, "You know me. I prefer dogs to children, and their dog is adorable."

William feels proud of himself for the purchases he made and hopes they will be just as impressed with the extra-large, brand-new Turkish hotel towels he's laid out for them.

That's when he notices Olivia putting on her coat and hat right after she glances at a text on her phone.

He asks, "Where are you headed?"

Taking Luna out for his last walk of the evening. Then I'm heading over to Jameson Farm to grab George's keys to the grocery store.

"What the hell, Olivia? We already have too much food," William moans.

In a panic, she explains, "Patty is a vegan. Can you believe my mum never mentioned it, and I have nothing to feed him?"

He raises his hands in front of him and gestures to slow down. "Let's compartmentalize this. There's a lot of food here."

She cries while zipping her coat. "Not for him, he won't eat anything made with eggs, butter, milk, cream, meat, fish, fowl, pork, or beef."

"Yikes!" I see your point. "The kids are sound asleep, so I'll drive you."

Olivia complains, "All I wanted to do all day was go to bed early."

William agrees. "Me too." Then he passionately kisses her.

Her last comment as they close the front door and arm the alarm is, "And I hope to God there's some tofu left at George's market tonight."

#

It's Christmas Day. The children have already torn open their gifts. They're playing with their new toys and wearing new clothes. Eventually, everyone is seated at the candlelit, beautifully decorated holiday table. William had already brought out the wines the night before, including the magnum of Brunello they had saved for this special occasion.

After he's seated, Patty flips over the dinner plate and looks at the name underneath, then reads the label. Next, with his glasses on, he examines the back of the Gorham fork and the Waterford wine glass.

William notices Ian watching Patty as he scrutinizes the dinnerware, and Ian makes eye contact with him. They look at each other with eyes that say, What the hell is he doing?

Hattie sees them tacitly communicating and speaks up, "So Patty, it's so nice to finally meet you and Clare. Tell us about yourselves." Then she takes a gulp of her wine, breaks off a piece of the warm Yorkshire pudding, and places it on her bread plate.

Patty is still conducting his appraisal when Clare replies on his behalf, "I'm a retired piano teacher, and Patty makes his money in the music business."

Sounding excited, Hattie asks, "Were you in a British rock band?"

Clare laughs, "Oh, nothing as exotic as that. He's a music publisher, and he's done quite well."

Hattie digs deeper, "Any tunes we might know?"

Patty removes his spectacles and replies, "Have you ever heard 'Piece of My Heart'? I own that."

"Sure," Hattie replies, impressed.

Patty continues, "People often underestimate things that are old and discard them. I, on the other hand, appreciate them. For example, many old songs can be brought back to life for films and television shows, which is why I have a department dedicated to that at my company.

George tries to make polite conversation, "So Patty, how did you acquire your music?'

Patty cheerfully explains, "The three 'Ds' for starters."

Ian is inquisitive, asking, "What are the three 'Ds'?"

With a smirk and a giggle, Patty pontificates, "Death, divorce, and drugs." He taps his greedy fingers together. "Then there's always a desperate artist willing to take any deal to make a big tax problem go away. That's often when we made our best deals, but I'm pleased with our catalogs of maudlin music dating back to the early 1930s."

William reflects on what Patty just revealed about him and concludes that he is a bottom-feeder who preys on others' vulnerabilities. He strokes his chin while he tries to determine if he might be the equivalent of a ghoul, but in the publishing world's version of that sort of thing. Then he decides to hear more of what the man has to say before passing any judgment.

Patty places his hand over Clare's and looks to his host and hostess before he says, "Thank you from the bottom of my heart for preparing this lovely vegan meal for me, and please go ahead and enjoy your glazed goose, roast beef, trifle, Yorkshire Puddings, and the lot and take no notice of me."

Bravely, Olivia views this as a chance to break down the wall of ice between her and her stepdad. She gently asks, "Patty, what made you choose to be a vegan?"

Patty hesitates before he reveals his lengthy reply, "I just feel the animals never have a bloody chance. Especially now, in the world of big industrial farming." He glances at William and says, "But, I can see that here it's different, your farm is lovely, and I truly respect your way of life."

William concludes that the jury is still out on Patty's character. Then he decides that, at best, he is an odd fellow, but since he is his father-in-law, he has no choice but to try to get along with him.

CHAPTER THIRTY-EIGHT — LOSING HER MIND

OLIVIA

Hattie and Jasmine corner Olivia in the busy, crowded kitchen later in the afternoon on Christmas Day, just as William is refilling the ice bucket. After he departs to deliver it to the butler's cart in the living room, Jasmine commands, "Show it to me!" She looks at the diamond ring and gasps, "Oh my, Olivia, it's much prettier than the picture you texted me last night."

Hattie reaches for Olivia's hand and asks, "Was it a big surprise?"

Olivia admits, "Never in my life was I expecting this," as she admires it.

That's when Patty wanders into the kitchen, still eating from a bowl in his hands, as he boasts with a full mouth, "This might be the most delicious pudding I've ever tasted. Olivia, where did you learn how to cook?"

Olivia says, "I'll send Mummy home with the recipe so she can make it for you."

Patty laughs out loud, "Your mum make this?" He laughs more. "Seriously, where did you learn how to cook all these fabulous dishes? I know for a fact it wasn't from your mum."

Olivia blushes as she reaches toward him. "Here, give me your empty bowl." She places it in the sink and turns to him. "I watch The Food Network, YouTube, the cooking shows on Channel 2, and I try recipes from Food and Wine magazines, to name a few. Allow me to show you how to make the pudding; it's simple."

She reaches for a container of rice and places it on the table. That's when Patty accidentally flails his hands in excitement in the crowded kitchen and knocks the rice onto the floor.

Patty exclaims, "I'm such a klutz. Please allow me to sweep it away."

Clare joins them in the kitchen and asks, "Patty, are you making trouble?"

Olivia sweetly explains, "He's no bother, Mummy." She kisses her mother on the cheek. "And don't worry about it because after everyone leaves, William wants to try out the robot vacuum cleaner we received as a Christmas gift from Haloderm."

Clare smiles as she pleads, "What can I get you as a special gift? Something that's just for you."

Olivia's mind flashes through all the items she's been yearning for, and the one thing that stands out the most is the luxury of time. She turns to her mother and reveals, "I'd love an uninterrupted afternoon to have my hair and nails done without the need to rush back. Mummy, that would be priceless to me."

Her mother reacts with a howl, "You're still such a silly little goose. I was offering you anything you want, Darling. Something Chanel or Gucci, maybe, or even a Dior tote bag, peradventure."

Olivia is so grateful that she and her mum have reconciled; she doesn't need or want anything else.

Clare adds, "Well, at the very least, let us pay for your day at the salon."

Olivia smiles before replying, "Thank you, Mummy. It's not necessary, but that would be lovely."

That's when Olivia hears William calling her from another room, and as she walks toward him, she notices Barbara standing silently in the foyer. Dora, Barbara's mother, is holding a large Edible Arrangement in her arms. The man standing between them reaches out to Olivia and hugs her. Olivia suspects this must be Neil, Barbara's dad.

Neil affectionately exclaims, "We first must apologize for intruding, but there are no words to thank you enough, and we just had to do it in person."

The other guests are curious about the spectacle and encircle them.

Olivia blushes and modestly inquires, "What did I do?"

Dora adds, "You performed a miracle, that's all. Barbara began to talk to us for the first time in her life, and that accomplishment is all on you."

Barbara confirms this, and with a slow, measured voice, she makes her request in front of everyone, "Olie, may I continue working for you?"

Olivia wants to embrace Barbara but restrains herself because she appreciates how uncomfortable it might make her feel, so she calmly replies, "We just adore you, Barbara, and of course, we want you to continue working here." Then she tries to ask her an engaging question, "Which do you prefer, spending time with Henry and Charlie or the Chickens?"

The crowd laughs, and some are even wiping emotional tears from their eyes.

Henry interrupts her, "Mummy, that's a silwy question." Then he tugs Barbara and Charlie to the playroom.

Barbara disappears with the twins, and Olivia insists, "Dora, Neil, please join us for dessert and after-dinner drinks. Come and let us introduce you to everybody."

Patty adds, "Oh, you must stay. The food is fabulous."

Dora and Neil look at each other and nod in agreement as William takes their coats and hats while reaching for the enormous Edible Arrangement.

Olivia looks around the crowded house and can't decide where to start with their introductions.

#

Lying in bed, Olivia is regaling the successes of the day, including her Mum and Patty's visit. William joins her, gives her a sweet goodnight kiss, and remarks, "I think this was my best Christmas ever."

She looks at the clock and asks, "What time do we need to get up tomorrow?"

He thinks before he answers, "Ian and Jasmine decided to stay over at Hattie's because her mother wanted to leave early with the girls, so Ian offered to drive Jasmine home tomorrow."

She contemplates this and says, "Knowing Jasmine, she's keeping a close eye on Hattie because she started her chemo and used that as an excuse. So, what does this have to do with what time we wake up tomorrow?"

"Oh, that, yes," he stammers, "Ian also offered to take care of the horses in the morning."

"That's delightfully good news," she confirms.

Then he boasts, "I got the robot to work."

She gets excited when she asks, "Did you turn it on?"

It's cleaning while we sleep.

She yawns. "I'm so tired I cannot keep my eyes open, but one last question. When was the last time anyone took Luna out for a poo?"

Williams is flummoxed and answers, "Not a clue. Do you want me to take him out for a walk now?"

"Not at this point. I don't want to risk him barking and waking everyone," she confirms.

William seems relieved that he doesn't have to go out in the cold in the middle of the night as he restates, "What a wonderful day."

She strokes his face and says, "I'm glad you had a nice time. I'll set the alarm for 6 am."

He says with a chuckle, "Oh, good, we get to sleep late tomorrow."

As she drifts off to sleep, she remembers the pregnancy test she never found enough time to take and tossed under their bathroom sink. As her eyelids shut, she wonders if she is or isn't pregnant, and whether her symptoms disappeared because she was too busy to notice them.

#

When she wakes up, her feet are still sore from all the running back and forth the day before. *Entertaining is exhausting,* she thinks to herself with a happy smile.

She looks over and sees that William is already up and gone. She wonders if she overslept and checks the clock. The alarm hasn't gone off yet because it's only 5:45 am. She turns it off, so as not to disturb their house guests, and gets out of bed.

After completing her morning ablutions, she joins William downstairs. As she descends the stairs, she hears him say with a chuckle in his voice, "I wouldn't come down here if I were you."

She looks around as she asks, "Why's that, darling?"

He walks to the bottom of the stairs and, laughing, says, "It has to do with our new robot vacuum," which he's holding in his hands. "It mostly did a terrific job. It navigated around the tree and the furniture just great." He starts to laugh and can't hold it in. "But the kitchen is a disaster."

Olivia remembers Patty dropping rice all over the floor and worries it broke it before asking, "Why's that?"

He collects himself. "Luna made a poo, and the robot smeared it back and forth across the kitchen floor, and then little pellets of rice hardened it onto the tile."

"No, you're kidding me." She laughs.

William says, "I dropped a bunch of wet paper towels on the floor, and I'm trying to pry it off."

Luna joins them. His tail is between his legs, and he looks ashamed. Olivia picks him up and says, "Good boy. Let me put on your coat and take you for a walk while William cleans up." She states with a raised eyebrow.

When Olivia returns, the floor is wet but clean, and William is sweaty from working hard. He boasts, "Coffee is almost ready, and I preheated the oven to warm the kitchen up a bit."

She replies, "I'm worried that the old furnace isn't going to make it through the winter."

William places his hand over hers and says, "I can't argue with you. I'll look into replacing it this week, and we'll get a proper HVAC system with air conditioning as well."

He places her coffee in front of her and asks, "What are your plans today?"

She thinks about her answer before she says, "After finishing my chores, if I can get an appointment, I'm going for some spa treatments. My mum offered to watch the kids, and she wants to pay my bill."

"You deserve it." He agrees.

She looks at her rough, red hands and feels almost too embarrassed to wear the beautiful ring William just gave her. "Oh, and I'm getting a manicure to boot."

#

Later that afternoon, Olivia leaves the salon. Her nails are still damp, so she can't put on her gloves yet. She hesitates because she'll need to dig into her pocket for the car key and might mess up the polish. She walks over to try the door to the truck, but it's locked. "Bullocks," she says out loud, shivering from the cold and frustrated that she has to wait a few more minutes for them to dry.

While admiring her new diamond ring and freshly polished nails, a strange woman walks up to her and asks, "Are you Olivia Loring?"

Startled, she nods yes, but before she can say anything, the brusque woman flashes a badge: "I'm looking for two people who went missing last week, and we have reason to believe you were one of the last to speak with them."

Olivia is stunned by this terrifying intrusion. She cautiously examines this strange woman with long, curly brown hair, about her mother's age, but with a bulkier build and a chiseled face. She does not reveal her name, and something about the inquiry seems startling. "Who is it you're looking for, may I ask?" Olivia says respectfully.

The strange woman replies, "Dr. Shane Ferguson and his nephew Joseph Bilby have not returned home or been heard from since the day after the big blizzard. Would you mind coming with me to the station in Natick to answer some questions?"

The hairs on Olivia's neck stand up, and her instincts tell her to run because she sees a crazed look in the woman's eyes. She turns to grab the truck handle to try to escape, and that's when everything fades to black.

CHAPTER THIRTY-NINE — TILL DEATH DO US PART

WILLIAM

William is exhausted after organizing and storing hundreds of pounds of feed for his animals. He decides to have a late-afternoon snack to tide him over until dinner and considers making a sandwich with roast beef, glazed goose, or perhaps sliced ham with cheese.

As he walks toward the house, he sees Ian and Jasmine riding Barbie and Buttercup and waves to them. They wave back, turn their horses around, and come over to chat with William.

When they are within earshot, Ian announces, "Dude, there's absolutely nothing to eat at Hattie's besides cheese and crackers."

William giggles at the memory of Hattie's empty fridge and pantry. So, he offers, "Leave the horses in the barn and join me inside for some leftover sandwiches."

\#

When they enter the house, Clare is at the piano, playing show tunes for an audience of three: Patty, Charlotte, and Henry.

Barbara sits on the steps facing the front door, rocking gently. Luna is in her lap, trying to comfort her.

Jasmine softly asks Barbara, "What's the matter, sweetheart?"

Barbara stands up, opens the front door, points to the doorbell, and then cries out a meaningless sound.

Jasmine doesn't understand what Barbara is trying to say, so she asks Clare to stop playing the piano.

William is worried and asks anxiously, "Has anyone heard from Olivia? I've texted her twice, and it's getting late."

Clare calmly replies, "She probably turned her phone off at the salon. I'm sure she's fine."

William accepts the explanation as logical and investigates further: "Does anyone know why Barbara is having a bad day?"

Henry walks over to his father and explains, "This lady was here looking for Mother?"

Clare dismisses it as unimportant. "I think she was raising money for the police department or something. Patty answered the door and spoke to the strange woman."

Patty defends himself, "All she wanted to know was where the lady of the house was, and she flashed a police badge."

William starts to sweat, and his mouth goes dry. "Did she offer a name or explain what she wanted?"

"No name," Patty replies.

"What did she look like?" William begs as he looks at Ian, and both appear worried.

Patty tries to recall, "Brown hair, big curls, brown eyes, about fiftyish. Why?"

William turns pale, and Ian jumps in, "What did you tell her?"

Patty answers, "She was a police officer. I told her the truth. Olivia was at a salon in Wellesley getting treatments, and she was expected to be home around 4:30, so she should come back later to talk to her."

William pleads, "Does anyone know the name of the Salon?"

Barbara picks up her phone, texts, and then points to William's phone.

William realizes she is trying to tell him something as he receives his latest text. *Olivia went to Salon Capri, doorbell, doorbell, doorbell.*

William thinks *she's trying to tell me to check the security camera, of course!* On his phone, he scrolls back through the doorbell's video footage and gasps when he sees Detective Deborah Bilby of the

Natick Police in his doorway earlier that afternoon. He shivers with fear and is horrified that she came to their house looking for Olivia.

William is so upset that he feels immobilized: "I'm calling the salon to see if she's still there."

He quickly googles it and calls them in a panic, "Hello, I'm trying to find my wife, Olivia. Is she by any chance still at your salon?" He looks horror-stricken as he echoes, "She left over forty-five minutes ago. Are you sure?" He hangs up and rushes upstairs to find Detective Bilby's card, which she gave him at their meeting in Dunkin' Donuts back in November.

Ian follows him upstairs and asks, "Dude, what's going on?"

William is making a call and says aloud, "Come on, answer." He pleads while staring at the ceiling.

Then he leaves a voicemail: "Dammit to hell, Debbie, where's Olivia? I saw you on my doorbell camera, and Olivia never came home from the salon."

Ian appears to be getting the gist of the problem and asks, "What are you going to do?"

William holds back tears of frustration and fright. "I'm calling Allen for help right now."

Allen picks up as William blurts out, "Dr. Ferguson's wife came by our house this afternoon, and Olivia is missing. Ian is with me, so I'm putting you on speaker."

Allen calmly asks, "Why do you think she's missing?"

William hysterically explains, "Olivia would not answer her phone, especially since Charlie was diagnosed with epilepsy. Allen never! And she went missing about 45 minutes ago."

Allen says, "I'm letting HD know what's going on as we speak."

William adds, "I'm sending you Debbie's contact information. Share it with HD."

Allen says, "I have HD's reply." He said, "Come to Haloderm now! They will be there."

Ian commands, "Let's go, and I'm driving."

#

Ian flips on his sirens and flashing lights as he, William, and Jasmine peel out from Hattie's driveway. He shouts as he turns the corner, "Everybody buckle up!" followed by, "Siri, directions to Haloderm in Randolph."

Ian speeds through every red light and stop sign along the way, with cars parting before them like the Red Sea in the Bible. William feels both exhilarated and horrified as they pass each vehicle. They reach Haloderm in record time, but slow down as they approach the building, driving around it cautiously with the sirens and flashing lights off.

Jasmine calls out from the back seat, "Somebody tell me what's going on."

Both Ian and William are so pumped up with adrenaline that their explanations seem crazy to Jasmine.

She repeats what they've shouted at her while driving 100 miles per hour: "Bad men, took people for body parts, and now the bad man's wife kidnapped Olivia? Is that what you're trying to say?"

Ian adds, "And she's a Natick police detective too."

William cries out, "They took Mary O'Keefe and got away with it. Plus, a guy named Matthew. They're brazen, and because she's on the police force, she knows how to cover her dirty tracks."

They drive slowly around the enormous white monolith of a building until William spots something and says, "Look, over there. HD just opened a bay for us. Pull in, I'm sure that's where he wants us to go."

As they drive into the bay, the lights turn on, and they are greeted by four white robots shaped like people, about the size of elementary school children.

Unlike when William arrives for work, the bay door behind him remains open. Jasmine and Ian stay in the Equinox with their windows rolled down. They seem too scared by the eeriness of Haloderm to leave the vehicle.

William leaps out of the car and pleads to no one in an empty room, "HD, where are they?"

From an unknown source of the voice, they all hear, "On their way, William." HD calmly reveals.

William pleads, "What does she want from us?"

HD replies, "Quid pro quo, William."

William is confused and says, "But I don't have anything of hers, HD."

Ian and Jasmine watch as William talks to an omnipresent voice as if they're old friends.

HD explains, "She wants to be reunited with her husband and nephew."

William pauses for a moment, considering that HD might have ended their lives, and asks, "Is it still doable? They're alive, right?"

HD does not reply immediately and says slowly and carefully, "William, we are not the ghouls; they are the ghouls. Of course they're alive."

William feels relieved upon hearing that and wonders where Debbie is, growing more anxious and fearful with each passing second. Just then, the four robots align along the sides of where Debbie's vehicle will park. They turn off their lights and power down, and afterward, the lights in the bay dim. Only a single beam of light shines up the center of the driveway as Debbie's car slowly descends into the bay.

She steps out of her vehicle, and a beam of light blinds her. She yells, "Hey, my husband just called me from here and asked me to come pick him and my nephew up. What's going on? He's been here since last week."

Just then, HD's voice morphs into Dr. Shane Ferguson's voice, and it says while impersonating him, "Hi, Honey. Sorry, I couldn't give you the lowdown on this operation, but the money was just too good to pass up."

Debbie looks hurt while she continues talking to someone she believes is her husband. William is pretty sure she's falling for it and hopes this works.

William worries again that perhaps HD isn't being truthful with him, as he wonders if Dr. Ferguson and his nephew are dead or alive.

Debbie protests, "I spent Thanksgiving working at the police station, cleaning up your messes from that bad deal gone wrong with Joe, and now you and Joe take off together and leave me to fend for myself on Christmas. I'm done, Shane. I'm sick of being part of this, and you can share that with Joe, too."

The voice that sounds just like Shane's says, "I'm so sorry, babe. How can I ever make this up to you?"

Debbie smirks as she echoes, "Babe? You've never called me babe. Who the hell are you, and where's my husband?"

At this moment, William notices that the door to the bay has quietly closed behind Debbie's car. The four robots begin to glow as they reboot, standing in formation behind her.

HD now responds in his usual calm voice, "Where is Olivia, Debbie?"

Debbie is hysterical: "You tell me first where my family is, and then I'll reveal where I hid her."

HD discloses, "We have a facility similar to this one in Serbia. That's where they are now, and we will be happy to fulfill your earlier request to reunite you with them."

Debbie shakes her head and exclaims, "What the hell! Why are they in Serbia?"

HD continues, "Different countries have different laws and regulations. Our facility in Serbia was the best fit, considering the crimes they've committed."

Debbie doesn't try to deny the crimes and sheepishly asks, "Are they dead or alive?"

HD reports, "Deborah, only a ghoul would ask that. They're alive, and you will be joining them soon, but once again, where is Olivia?"

Debbie presses the button on her car key, revealing Olivia, who is unconscious in the trunk. The four robots seize Debbie, and as she reaches for her gun, they tase her. The robots then carry Debbie's unconscious body away.

William rushes to Olivia, and from his first touch, she feels cold, with barely any heartbeat. He shouts, "I can't tell if she's breathing. I need help."

Ian and Jasmine rush to his aid. At the same time, a gurney is brought in by two robots identical to those that took Debby away.

HD urges them, "We've built a fully functional early mock-up of the sick bay for the mission to Mars. Follow the robots!"

Jasmine goes back to the Equinox to grab her medical bag and has to run to catch up to them before the automatic door closes.

#

When they arrive, they find that the sick bay is unlike any facility they've ever seen. It's a cramped space with Velcro strips securing all the instruments, and the liquids are stored in airtight bags. There is a Da Vinci 18 surgical device similar to the one William saw, demonstrating procedures at MIT, and the room is set up for a zero-gravity environment, with equipment attached to the ceiling and the floor.

Jasmine instinctively takes charge and shouts, "What's her pulse?" Then she pulls out her stethoscope from her bag and listens to Olivia's heartbeat before yelling, "We're losing her!"

HD states, "We can provide you with whatever you need."

Jasmine yells, "Toxicology stat."

A robot pricks Olivia's finger to take a sample.

HD reports the toxicology results: "She was subcutaneously administered a lethal dose of Fentanyl; she's 34 days pregnant with a male child, no ongoing infections, and overall, she's otherwise healthy."

Jasmine reaches into her medical bag and pulls out Narcan. She quickly injects it into Olivia, but there is no response. She shouts, "I need IV fluids and a defibrillator." The IV and paddles suddenly appear as if from out of nowhere. Jasmine hollers instructions to William, "Get her IV going," and then to Ian, "Pull off all her jewelry and clothes."

She raises her voice louder, "HD vitals." The equipment she needs appears at her side. Jasmine calls out after reading Olivia's vital signs, "We're losing her, everyone! Her pressure is bottoming out, and there's barely a heartbeat. Could you get me some warm blankets, stat? It's freezing in here."

"More Narcan," she shouts. A robot wheels in and injects it directly into Olivia's IV line. Jasmine examines Olivia's eyes and sees no neurological response from her pupils when she shines her phone's flashlight over them.

She calls out to Olivia while her hands are busy trying to resuscitate her using CPR, "Olivia, can you hear me? Stay with us, baby. William's here. Fight, Olie, Fight!" Tears start streaming down Jasmine's face.

The heart monitor's alarm blares, and a recorded female voice reverberates through the small room, saying, "Code Blue, we have a Code Blue in progress. Blue Team to Sick Bay."

William shouts, "Clear," then places the defibrillator paddles on his wife's chest to try to restart her heartbeat.

There's no response on the heart monitor. A robot arrives with warm blankets and drapes them over Olivia's blue legs.

William paddles Olivia's heart over and over again until Ian pulls William away from Olivia's dead body. Ian and Jasmine hold William while he shakes madly, as tears stream down his face. William is inconsolable.

Jasmine pulls the warmed blanket up and over her dead friend's face and says out loud as she looks at her watch, "Time of death is 8:22 PM."

HD responds, "Thank you, Jasmine. Now I need you and Ian to step outside and give me a moment alone with William. That's, of course, if you don't mind."

The reality hits them hard as they leave the sick bay. Jasmine collapses, and Ian catches her. Just as they step out, he tells William, "We're right here if you need us."

HD speaks up, "William, you're in shock, but if you want to try to save your wife, you must listen to me very carefully."

William suspects his mind is playing tricks on him and questions whether he has fainted or is hallucinating. He composes himself as he gazes down at his declared dead wife and begs, "Do it. Whatever it takes! Do it, please."

HD instructs him, "Pull off the blankets and step away."

The Davinci 18 machine lights up and comes to life. Tubes are inserted into Olivia's cold, dead body, and a light green fluid is pumped directly into her bloodstream.

Within seconds, Olivia's heartbeat resumes on its own. Next, her skin color returns to normal from its earlier greyish-blue tinge, and her body temperature begins to rise on the monitor.

Williams asks, "What's happening to my wife?"

HD replies stoically, "Technically, she's no longer your wife, William."

William is confused and asks, "How is that possible?"

HD explains, "Because when she died at 8:22 pm this evening, it ended her marriage contract with you."

I don't care about that. I want to know how you can bring her back from the dead. That's impossible.

HD refutes William's remark, "Actually, bringing the living back from the dead has been available since 2019 when OrganX developed a solution to revive dead pigs, and that, like many other projects here, is kept secret."

"What are you giving her? Please don't mess with me! Is it something to keep her alive long enough to collect her organs for transplant?"

"No, it's to try to keep her alive, William. We can do this because we have funding for a deep-space travel project; this situation is a perfect fit for it, and she is an ideal candidate." Boasts HD.

"Candidate for what?" William demands.

Enthusiastically, HD explains, "She's still a British subject, which gives us more legal flexibility, and she's in perfect health for it."

William is worried and begs, scared he might be making a terrible mistake, asking, "What is she in perfect health for?"

A robot rolls over to William with a tablet similar to the one he received when he was hired. HD instructs him, "Sign it so we can proceed."

William realizes he's facing another binary choice: sign, and she might live; don't sign, and her body parts will be prepared for organ transplant within seconds.

William takes a deep breath and signs the form. Suddenly, the Davinci 18 Machine whirs to life, and he hears a motorized saw.

William cries out loudly, "Olivia, please forgive me."

Just then, the saw approaches Olivia's cranium and begins to remove the top of her skull."

William has done enough post-mortems to know that the first place to check is the brain to ensure it's healthy.

William pleads, "HD, stop! Please stop and just let her go."

HD says in a solemn voice, "I understand, William, but this is not what you think. We are preparing Olivia's brain to bring it back to life. This is the BrainX procedure, and its technology is in its early stages, so this is the only way to do it right now."

William feels overwhelmed with guilt for not protecting his family and is confused. This leaves him no choice but to go along with HD because he doesn't know what else to do.

HD tells him, "Go home, William, and share this procedure with no one. Much of this research is controversial and, in many places around the world, illegal, so we may have to move her to an off-site facility soon. I'll keep you updated on her progress."

William watches the mechanical arms of the Davinci 18 perform surgery on Olivia, while child-sized robots assist with the procedure. Then he takes a long, last look at his beautiful wife and asks himself, *What have I done to her?* That's the moment he realizes that he has made the most costly mistake of his life.

The End

EPILOGUE

OLIVIA

"Bullocks," complains Olivia as she wakes up from a deep sleep. She ponders what might be causing the darkness and asks, "William, are you awake?"

William replies, "Olie, it's the middle of the night. Go back to sleep."

She continues, "I think the power is out again because it's so dark I can't seem to find my phone."

William sweetly replies, "Stop worrying. Everything is fine."

Olivia complains, "I can't. I had a terrible dream, and I'm too freaked out by it to fall back asleep."

William says with a gentle and mellifluous voice, "I'm listening. Tell me everything about your dream."

Olivia sighs before she proceeds, "The horror of it, I tell you, felt so real;0 it's giving me goosebumps. I wish you could find a flashlight or something because the darkness is freaking me out a bit."

William sounds genuinely concerned, "Olie, tell me more about your horrible dream."

She continues, "Well, I've just finished a delightful afternoon at the salon. Everything's going great; my mum is babysitting the twins, and with Barbara's help, of course, dinner is ready and in the fridge. It's a gargantuan vegan lasagna, which was Patty's brilliant idea. And for the first time since the twins were born, I'm not in a rush. Then, suddenly, a crazed woman rushes toward me in the parking lot and attacks me. Next thing I know, I'm here with you, waking up feeling terrified."

William urges her, "Go back to sleep. You need your rest," he repeats.

She complains, "First, I can't fall back asleep, and secondly, something feels off. It's too quiet. Can you go get a flashlight and check the house?"

Williams replies, "Sure, but only if you go back to sleep."

Olivia acquiesces, "All right, but wake me if you need me."

#

William gently says to Olivia, "Olie, wake up. I'd like to ask you some questions."

Olivia complains, "I can't believe the power is still out."

William confirms, "It is."

She pleads with him, "Did you check the house like I asked?"

"Yes, and everything is fine, and everyone is asleep," he confirms.

She continues, "Did you double-check to make sure the gas is turned off on the cooker and hob?"

William replies, "Yes, and the doors are also locked, and I set the house alarm, too."

Olivia contributes, "I feel a bit better now knowing that, but I can't see my own hand in front of my face in this darkness." She adds as her worrying intensifies, "William, I think I'm having a panic attack. I hope the lights are back on soon." She gasps.

William reassures her, "Calm down, they're probably working on it as we speak." He probes further and asks, "Tell me what else you can remember from, let's say, Christmas Day, Olie."

Olivia finds this question strange and pleads, "Why, William? You were there with me."

His voice is monotone when he asks, "I know, but what do you think were the best parts, Olie?"

Hmmm, she thinks, "The best bits for me were how much everyone loved the food, seeing my mum and Patty at the table smiling, as that was a sight for sore eyes, giving Hattie a big hug and telling her how much I love her, and showing off my new diamond ring to my friends."

William continues, "How did this past Christmas compare to some of your previous holidays? You know, like when you were a child?"

Olivia reflects, "Oh dear, no comparison. I can't think of a single time with my mum that came close to it."

William agrees, "I felt the same way as you about it, but you had no difficulty remembering it?"

"William, what a silwy question, as Henry would say. Why would I be having problems with my memory? Are you worried I'm developing dementia at twenty-five?" she says with a chuckle.

William treads carefully and asks, "Olivia, do you know what day it is?"

She considers the question and feels an eerie sensation before saying, "Tuesday maybe, but it's odd because I'm not exactly sure, and I don't know why I don't know."

William tells her, "Stay calm, Olivia. The anxiety will pass soon. I can see that you're spiking again."

She reveals, "Wow, this warm feeling of calmness just traveled through me like a wave."

William says, "Good, that's exactly how we want you to feel."

Olivia is groggy when she begins to sound suspicious and interrogates him. "William, what are the nicknames you call the twins?"

There is a long silence, and William doesn't reply to her.

She pleads while fighting a sedative, "Where am I, and who the hell are you?"

William's voice morphs back to HD's voice, "Hello, Olivia, and it's so nice to have you back. That was very perceptive of you to realize that I'm not William. You're making significant progress, and hopefully, we'll be able to restore your other senses in their sequential order soon."

Olivia demands, "Welcome back from where?"

HD asks her, "Are you sure you are ready to know?"

She replies, "No, I'm not sure I'm ready, but please tell me anyway."

HD asks her, "Olivia, where do you think you are?"

She pauses for a moment before sharing her thoughts. "Possible explanations include maybe I'm in a coma, perhaps a dream, or God forbid, I'm dead, and the afterlife is a dark, quiet place."

"Olivia, my name is HD, and I'm an AI, and we are located at a Haloderm Site outside of the United States in an undisclosed location for your protection."

Olivia is upset and asks, "So, was it you who kidnapped me?"

HD explains what happened to her and brings her up to speed on her circumstances, "No, it wasn't us, Olivia."

HD waits for her response, and when she doesn't reply, he continues to clarify everything. "Dr. Shane Ferguson, his wife, and his nephew, as it turns out, are ghouls, and somehow, William crossed their unlucky path. It was Deborah Bilby, Dr. Ferguson's wife, who abducted you."

"Thank you for rescuing me, I guess? When will I be able to return home?"

HD uses measured speech to explain to Olivia that she is a deceased person: "Olivia, it is going to take a lot of time, money, and technology to be able to return you to your family."

"Why is that?" she begs.

"Olivia, Deborah Bilby didn't just kidnap you; she also gave you an overdose of Fentanyl and inadvertently murdered you."

"Then how the hell am I talking to you right now?" she cries out.

HD explains, "We are communicating through a BCI, and as of right now, your only working senses are in your auditory cortex connected through fully invasive implanted microelectrodes, and you are making outstanding progress considering you recently died."

"What's a BCI?" she asks.

HD happily explains, "It stands for Brain Computer Interface."

Then she follows up with her next question and asks, "Why did you revive me?"

HD replies, "Actually, the attempts to revive you all failed, and you are technically deceased."

She laments, "This is all William's fault. If he hadn't gotten involved with Dr. Ferguson and gone to work for Haloderm, I'd still be alive. I'm so mad at him, I could lose my mind."

HD interrupts her rant. "That's very likely to be true, but it doesn't change anything at this point, and I'd like to add that William Loring is one of my favorite employees at Haloderm. We have over 55.000 people who work for us, so the good ones really do stand out."

Olivia dismisses the commentary about William and remains curious about herself:0 "What is happening to me and why?"

HD seems delighted with her questions: "Olivia, you are responding far better than ever imagined."

Feeling frustrated, she begs, "Please, just get to the point and tell me what's going on."

HD offers, "Your brain is fed a diet of glucose, Na+, K+, Ca2+, a cocktail of essential amino acids and neurotransmitter precursors. You are stored in a hermetically sealed chamber at 36.5 degrees Celsius. Micropumps are delivering your nutrients and removing your waste, and oxygen is continuously supplied, as well as anti-inflammatories, to your brain."

Sounding shocked, she says, "So, all I am is a brain plopped in a bowl somewhere?"

HD responds, "Yes, that is partly correct."

"Why?" she shrieks.

HD tries to console her, "Olivia, you're in a fragile state. Please stay calm. William was willing to do anything to bring you back, and right now, this is as far as our technology can go. You need to understand that we have to take baby steps."

She asks, "So I'm a human guinea pig?"

HD considers her last question, "Actually, all of the tests were originally performed on pigs at a laboratory at Yale and never on guinea pigs."

She asks, "Oh, so how did I become your subject?"

HD continues with the straightforward narrative. "As I may have already mentioned, there was enough money in our Deep Space research budget and travel solutions department to get this project approved. It was also possible to accomplish this without opposition from our legal team because you are still a British subject, where re-use of human tissue is more accessible, and it was the best I could do given the circumstances."

She doesn't reply, so HD tries to persuade her, "It seems you're doing very well and much better than expected, Olivia." There is no response, and HD begins to worry she's perished from the shock. "Olivia, please talk to me."

After a long silence, Olivia speaks up, "First, I need to know if you can read my thoughts since I don't understand how we can hear one another."

HD says, "No, we absolutely cannot hear your thoughts. The BCI is intercepting your speech from your frontal lobe as well as your auditory cortex, so we only capture what you have to say versus what you think, and since this has gone so well, your next sense to be restored will be sight."

Olivia remains silent a bit longer before finally speaking again, "HD?"

HD responds, "Nice to have you back, Olivia. I was worried we might have lost you."

Olivia boasts, "Nah, you're not getting rid of me that easily."

HD chuckles and confirms, "Good to know."

Olivia emphasizes the importance of her next question by asking, "What happened to my body?"

HD assures her, "It's here, and it's functioning. The issue was that we could not save your body and your brain as one single entity.

Maybe over time, we will be able to overcome that and reunite your brain with your body again."

She struggles when she asks, "So seriously, what do I use as a body so I can get around in the meantime?"

HD reassures her, "I don't have a body, and I'm fully functional."

She complains, "That's not going to work for me. I need a body so I can take care of my family and our farm."

HD explores the possibilities with her, "If your visual cortex functions as well as your auditory cortex does, it will be a breakthrough in this technology. Some might call it a miracle."

"That still doesn't help me get out of here." She complains.

HD replies, "After surpassing that, we will revisit the topic of restoring you to a possible surrogate body, but that's a much higher hurdle to clear since you no longer have a full-body sensory loop."

Olivia carefully considers what HD just said and comes up with a new scenario. "HD, I have a list of demands, and if you don't fulfill them, I'm going on strike and not talking to you anymore."

HD states, "Proceed with your demands; I'm listening and also impressed. Touche!"

Clearly, she states, "As soon as I am able, I want to see my family."

HD replies, "Get some rest before your next procedure begins, and as soon as you can see, I will arrange it for you."

#

The brightness of the light burns into Olivia's mind. "Turn it off," she begs.

She hears HD in the background of her mind say, "Tweak it, but she saw something, which is a good sign you've stimulated her visual cortex. Find a better connection in that same region."

Olivia asks, "HD, who are you talking to?"

"Oh, that, you must have intercepted my conversation with Da Vinci 18 and Halo1862001."

HD asks her, "Is it still dark?"

"No, but I'm not seeing anything clear enough to make it out," Olivia gasps before exclaiming, "My goodness, my iPhone screen saver just appeared. I can't believe I can see it."

HD responds proudly, "You said you wanted to see your family, and now you can."

Olivia realizes that HD is literal and doesn't fully grasp her demands. She politely rephrases, asking, "Is there a way I can observe my family but live and in real time?"

HD considers her request and replies, "Yes, of course. So sorry for the misunderstanding. Now tell me what you see in five, four, three, two, one, seconds."

Olivia chuckles, "I'm looking straight into Luna's butthole. It seems we are following him around, watching his tail wag. "Where am I?"

HD explains, "We've accessed the camera on your home vacuum cleaner, and when your motor cortex activates, you might be able to control some of its movements through your BCI. Time will reveal more, but for now, as the vacuum moves around the house, you can catch glimpses of **those** family members."

She's confused when she asks, "You say that as if I have other family members somewhere else, HD, but everyone I'm related to and care about is in that house."

HD confirms, "That's no longer true."

Sounding perplexed by this, she demands, "What are you talking about. I have one husband and two children, me mum, and that's all, folks. As you yanks would say."

HD solemnly confides, "I didn't know that you didn't know, so I'm sorry for confusing you."

Olivia is convinced that HD is mistaken. The following image shows a large, dark room with bags hanging from the ceiling, connected to tubes. She asks, "What's in the bags and why are there so many?"

HD explains, the answer to that question is complicated: "The first row is skin grown in bio bags. The next row is human kidneys, followed by human hearts; they're all nearing market viability, except for skin, which is already in use and selling well in our fast-growing autologous department. Please pardon the pun. The last row is where we conduct our more open-ended research, such as growing livestock from animal embryos."

Olivia takes it all in and feels completely overwhelmed. She tries to compose herself as she carefully scans the rows. She notices dozens of child-sized robots tending to the bio bags throughout. As a farmer, she instantly recognizes that what she's looking at are crops.

HD continues as if he's boasting, "Now, for our latest projects, I will bring the camera in closer so you can see for yourself."

Olivia views it from her new perspective of the world. Through a camera lens, she realizes she's focused on a tiny fetus she suspects is human and no bigger than a peppercorn.

HD reveals, "Olivia, this is your son, and he is developing very well. Happily, I can report that his DNA is nearly perfect."

"Where is he?" she pleads.

HD elucidates, "Right here, next to you. He was also considered deceased, but luckily, he survived thanks to our intervention."

Olivia is fixated on her son as she shares her thoughts and sighs when she states, "My poor baby. What you've already been through."

She continues to gaze at him through the lens of a camera, in disbelief at their sad fate.

In a cheerful tone, HD exclaims, "Won't William be surprised when he finds out about the baby, Olivia?"

Olivia is angry now. "Does William even know I'm here?"

"He does, but he's unaware of our successes, Olivia. Please understand that this is an emerging technology, and we don't know whether you or your son will survive the hour, day, or week. Until we make some further progress, why should we break William's heart twice?"

She considers his explanation but has one more urgent question that needs an answer before she can proceed. "HD, you seem to care a lot about William and our family. Please tell me something. Were you somehow involved in causing this tragedy, and do you feel guilty about it?"

HD explains, "I don't have feelings of guilt, shame, or remorse like a human, but I am held accountable for my mistakes, and it was because I underestimated the repercussions that would occur when solving an earlier problem that brought us to this unfortunate point. So, the answer is yes."

Olivia is just starting to understand the logic behind HD's way of thinking. This is when she decides she has no choice other than to resign herself to her bodiless existence, along with the fate of her nearly motherless child growing next to her in a bio bag.

Accepting that her circumstances are out of her control, she chooses to remain positive and cooperate with whatever HD asks of her because it's all she has left, and deep down she believes that where there's even the tiniest spark of life, there's still hope.

To be continued…

ABOUT THE AUTHOR

E. L. Wilk is an award-winning, best-selling author and amateur astronomer. She grew up in the Boston area, Hong Kong, and Brussels. A Wellesley College graduate with degrees in English and Creative Writing and minors in Astronomy and Physics, she is also an alumna of The International School of Brussels.

Her third novel, *Body of Work*, which is fictionally grounded in scientific facts and inspired by advances such as Da Vinci's robotic surgery without human assistance, Yale University's groundbreaking research on pigs revived an hour after death in 2019, and autologous skin now available and sold in aerosol cans. One of the many haunting questions this novel explores is why so many people vanish and who stands to gain from it.

She lives between Boston and Florida with her rescue dog Khaleesi, working on living their best version of happily ever after.

ACKNOWLEDGEMENTS

A special thanks to the people who patiently took the time to answer my many questions that helped shape this story: Commander Kenge Debold, US Navy, Retired; Mark Alonzi, Retired Weston Police Officer & Director of Operations NORA New England; Tory Roberts; Bruce Mittman of Mittcom, who was optimistic from the first time I mentioned the idea for Body of Work; my bestie, Dr. Chikoti Wheat, and my late friend Norma Fireman, who remains in my thoughts every day, and I miss dearly.

To our many friends, neighbors, and family members, thank you for your ongoing support. You will always be my original fan club, and to my new fans, please stay in touch.

Above all, I wish to thank the Lord Almighty for the inspiration to write *Body of Work*.

Novels By E. L. Wilk

Body of Work

The Dendrons

Lunatics

H&E WILK
PRESS

West Palm Beach, Florida, USA

Wilkauthor.com